Praise for

DANCE OF SHADOWS

"A wild dance that leaves you breathless, yet wanting more. I couldn't put it down." —Alex Flinn, *New York Times* bestselling author of *Beastly* and *Diva*

"Written so dynamically that the reader quickly becomes absorbed in the world of a highly competitive ballet academy combined with an occult element. . . . The author has cleverly combined both worlds so that this book has appeal for both teen boys and girls." —*VOYA*

"The novel swerves between thriller territory . . . , coming-of-age angst . . . , and customary dancer rivalries. . . . Black pulls off an enticingly eerie conclusion." —*Publishers Weekly*

"The mysteries and corruption hiding out in this dance academy unfold with the controlled grace of an arabesque." —*Justine* magazine

DANCE OF SHADOWS

YELENA BLACK

BLOOMSBURY

NEW YORK   LONDON   NEW DELHI   SYDNEY

First published in the United States of America in February 2013
by Bloomsbury Children's Books
Paperback edition published in June 2014
www.bloomsbury.com

Bloomsbury is a registered trademark of Bloomsbury Publishing Plc

For information about permission to reproduce selections from this book, write to
Permissions, Bloomsbury Children's Books, 1385 Broadway, New York, New York 10018
Bloomsbury books may be purchased for business or promotional use. For information on bulk
purchases please contact Macmillan Corporate and Premium Sales Department at
specialmarkets@macmillan.com

The Library of Congress has cataloged the hardcover edition as follows:
Black, Yelena.
Dance of shadows / by Yelena Black. — 1st U.S. ed.
p.   cm.
Summary: Fifteen-year-old Vanessa follows her sister Margaret to an elite Manhattan ballet
school, not only gaining admission but also earning the lead in a production of *The Firebird*,
while trying to uncover why and how Margaret and other lead dancers have disappeared.
ISBN 978-1-59990-940-0 (hardcover)
[1. Ballet—Fiction. 2. Occultism—Fiction. 3. Demonology—Fiction. 4. Schools—Fiction.
5. Missing persons—Fiction. 6. Sisters—Fiction. 7. New York (N.Y.)—Fiction.] I. Title.
PZ7.B5313Dan 2012   [Fic]—dc23   2012016675

ISBN 978-1-61963-185-4 (paperback)

Book design by Regina Flath
Typeset by Westchester Book Composition
Printed and bound in the U.S.A. by Thomson-Shore Inc., Dexter, Michigan
2 4 6 8 10 9 7 5 3 1

To Emily,
For hanging out at the vending machines with me
when we should have been learning how to do the splits

DANCE OF SHADOWS

PROLOGUE

In the harsh glare of the lights, Chloë's shadow stretched across the stage. Her toes pointed and taut, her arms fluttering like wings, she arched her neck and watched as her own silhouette seemed to move without her . . .

A drop of sweat slid down her chest and seeped into the thin fabric of her leotard. There was no music. The room beyond was dark and empty, yet she could feel her master's eyes on her. She tried not to tremble as she lifted her chin to meet his gaze. Slowly, she extended a long, slender leg into the air.

He rapped his staff on the floor. "Again."

Chloë wiped her temples. The floor was speckled with sweat and blood from hours of practice, but still she took her position. On the choreographer's count, the thirteen ballerinas around her began to flit in and out in cascades of white, their shoes pattering softly against the wood.

"One and two and three and four!"

And before she knew it, her feet were moving soundlessly across the stage. She dipped her head back, fanning her arms toward the light.

"Now rise!" he yelled as she thrust herself toward the circle of dancers, keeping in step. "Transcend your body! Your bones are hollow! Your feet are mere feathers!"

Chloë twirled, her back flexed into a crescent as the dancers flew past, their faces vacant, their feet moving so quickly they seemed to blur.

"Yes!" cried the choreographer, his smile wide and triumphant. "Yes!"

Chloë was dizzy and exhausted, her leotard damp with sweat, but she didn't care. The routine was finally coming together. Her legs wove around each other with effortless grace, and her body followed, smooth and slippery, like a strip of satin gliding over the stage.

Letting herself go, she cocked her head back in a flush of rapture. Her chest heaved, and hot, thick air filled her lungs.

The other dancers reached for her, their faces a pale swirl. Chloë bowed out of their reach, dipping low and letting her fingertips graze the wooden floor. It felt strangely hot. The thin smell of smoke coiled around her, tickling her nose, and the choreographer's voice grew distant and watery. The overhead lights seemed to flicker, casting eerie shadows against the walls.

A wave of heat rippled through her body. It was strange, unidentifiable—a hot presence spilling into her veins, making her head throb.

A string of whispers began to unravel in her mind, the voices too soft to understand. She jerked her head, trying to shake them off, but they melded into one another, foreign and indecipherable, growing louder, shriller.

Her eyes burned. The room swam with red. The ribbons of her pointe shoes tightened around her ankles. Without warning, her legs bent backward, as if boneless. Her arms cracked and swung over her head. Against her will, her chin jerked upward to face the overhead lights.

Mine, a voice said inside her head.

Chloë teetered, her legs trembling as she fought to maintain her balance. Using all her strength, she forced her lips to move. "No!" she screamed convulsively, and fell out of position.

The dancers stopped midstep, their faces empty and distorted. From somewhere in the darkness, the choreographer's voice cut through the room. "That, my dear, was a fatal misstep."

"What?" Chloë whispered. "How can—" But her words were consumed by a stifling breath of heat. It enveloped her, licking at her legs, and she twisted in pain as the presence took hold, her blood boiling as it pulsed through her fingers, her arms, her chest, until she was filled with an unbearable, burning ecstasy.

The colors around her sharpened until they were so bright they burned her eyes. Something screeched in her ears—a shrill, deafening cry that she suddenly recognized as her own voice.

She blazed into a brilliant, coruscating light, her body dissolving into ash.

CHAPTER ONE

With a swish, her mother opened the curtains, letting the afternoon sun stream into the room.

Vanessa shielded her eyes. "Mom, *please*."

"There's nothing wrong with a little sunshine." Mrs. Adler pursed her lips as she stood back to observe. "Besides, it kills the germs. Who knows how properly this place has been cleaned." She dug inside her purse and withdrew a small bottle of Purell, squeezing a dollop into her palm. "Bacteria, be gone!"

Vanessa couldn't help but laugh, and then she let her eyes wander.

It was a simple dorm room, sparsely furnished with two beds, two desks, and two dressers. The walls were painted a pale yellow. A long mirror nailed to the back of the closet door reflected the unpacked boxes that littered the floor. The other half of the room was already decorated in loud, bright colors: movie posters, patchwork pillows, shoes and clothes spilling from the closet, but Vanessa's roommate was nowhere to be found.

Outside the open door, the hallway was bustling with chatter—girls laughing and gossiping about their summers, parents arguing while they squeezed heavy trunks through the corridor, little sisters spinning like delirious ballerinas.

Vanessa had once been that little sister, though she could barely remember the last time dancing had made her smile. She blew a wisp of red hair from her face and glanced at her father, who gave her a sympathetic shrug.

"Something's missing." Her mother moved a small vase from one side of the nightstand to the other. "That's better," she said, though it looked the same to Vanessa.

Her father sighed, and when his wife wasn't watching, he rolled his eyes at Vanessa. She laughed.

"What's funny?" her mother asked sternly.

Vanessa bit her lip. "Just thinking about something from the past."

"The past is nothing," her mother said, a slight quiver in her voice. "Focus on the future." She ruffled the edge of the duvet and ran a hand across her forehead, as if trying to erase the fine lines of stress and worry that had formed there over the past few years. "Of course, being here doesn't help."

There was a knock on the door. A girl with an upbeat ponytail stood in the hall, holding a clipboard.

"Yes?" Vanessa's mother said.

"Hi. I'm looking for Vanessa Adler?"

Vanessa took a step toward the door, but her mother didn't budge.

"I'm her mother, Mrs. Adler. And you are?"

"Oh, I'm Kate, the resident adviser." The girl tried to peer into the room. "I wanted to welcome Vanessa to the New York Ballet Academy."

"Resident *adviser?* There's only one of you?"

"There are two of us, actually," Kate said cheerfully. Her eyes were bright and blue, her hair light brown with blond highlights. "I'm in charge of the freshman girls, and Ben is in charge of the boys."

Mrs. Adler frowned. "I think I misunderstood you. You're trying to tell me that *you* are the only person watching over the freshman girls?"

Vanessa winced, and Kate flashed her an understanding look before giving Mrs. Adler a reassuring smile. "I am. But I promise you—"

Mrs. Adler cut her off. "Do you realize that there are only twenty dancers Vanessa's age admitted each year to the New York Ballet Academy?"

"I do—" Kate said.

"And that fifteen is a very impressionable age?"

Vanessa felt her face grow hot.

"I know. I was fifteen not that long ago—" Kate began to say.

"That's exactly my point!" Mrs. Adler raised her hands in the air. "You're barely older than Vanessa. How can you always know

7

where she is and whom she's spending time with? That she's doing her schoolwork and practicing her dance routines, when there are dozens of distractions surrounding her? Manhattan preys on naive young girls."

The entire room seemed to take a breath, including Mrs. Adler, who clutched the side of the dresser, fanning her neck. For a moment, Vanessa wished that her father would step in and tell her mother that she was out of line—but that wasn't how things were with her parents. Her mother was the one who gave the instructions; her dad merely followed them.

"I'm sorry," her mother said, composing herself. "I'm just worried about her." She turned to Vanessa. "I understand the need to dance. Really, I do; I was the same way. But are you absolutely sure you want to be here? Because there are other things out there, an entire world—"

"Mom, I'll be fine. Stop worrying."

They had already had this conversation—many, many times. Her mother wanted her to stay home, to go to public school back in Massachusetts. But Vanessa wanted . . . well, it wasn't so much about what she wanted to do. It was about what she *needed* to do.

And that was to be here. At the New York Ballet Academy. The same school that Margaret had gone to.

It had taken months of fighting and persuading her mom to say yes once the acceptance letter had arrived. The fact that Vanessa had been offered a full-tuition scholarship hadn't hurt. "The most talented dancer we had audition," the admissions officer had said. "Must run in the family."

Eventually Mrs. Adler had succumbed to the pressure.

Vanessa gave Kate an apologetic shrug, hoping her mother's diatribe hadn't already destroyed her reputation. Being an outcast in a class with only ten boys and ten girls wasn't exactly the fresh start that she wanted. But to Vanessa's surprise, Kate gave her a wink and turned toward her mother.

"Manhattan *is* an exciting place," Kate said, a cacophony of honking cars in the street below emphasizing her point. "And while I can't promise to know what Vanessa is doing all of the time, I *can* say that we do everything in our power to make sure our students are safe and happy. There are curfews and lockdowns, and for the most part, everyone here is so busy that there's barely any time to experience the city at all."

Mrs. Adler seemed to relax. "Good."

"Great." Kate tucked her clipboard under one arm. "Well, I'll leave you to your unpacking. Vanessa, I'll see you during orientation, which is in the main studio at Juilliard, on the third floor, in two hours. If you have any other questions, I'll be floating around."

Mrs. Adler glanced at Vanessa, then stepped into the hall. "I do have a few more questions," she said to Kate, following her down the hallway.

Once they were out of earshot, Vanessa shook her head, letting her wild red hair flail about her face. "Well, that was insane."

Her father smiled and wiped the sweat from his forehead. He was a handsome man, with strong, startling features that Vanessa had inherited, along with his height and fiery hair, though his had ripened to a distinguished auburn. She wasn't a delicate flower like her mother or her sister, Margaret, and that was partially why she was such an astonishing dancer. No one expected her to be weightless, but when she leaped into a grand jeté, she seemed to float with an ethereal lightness, her feet tiptoeing across the stage as she transformed herself into a white swan, a sleeping princess, or a Sugar Plum Fairy, her shock of red hair flashing beneath the lights like electricity.

He rolled up his shirtsleeves and reached for one of the ballet slippers on her dresser, letting its ribbons slip through his fingers. It looked impossibly small in his palm. "Ness, you know if you aren't happy here, you can tell me."

A group of girls walked past the doorway, chatting and giggling. Vanessa bit her lip, wishing she wanted to be here as much they did. The New York Ballet Academy was the premier dance school in the country. She *should* want to be here, but her heart had never been in it, at least not until recently. It was her older sister, Margaret, who loved ballet, who counted steps in her sleep and dreamed of being onstage. Vanessa was just following in her footsteps.

Yet somehow, all through middle school, she had found herself spending more time practicing barre exercises than seeing her friends. A part of her wanted nothing more than to go to a public high school, eat a cheeseburger with her friends without feeling guilty, and date a guy who didn't own tights or spandex. There was a time when she thought that might be possible, but it had quickly slipped away after things fell apart with Margaret.

Vanessa sighed. "You know I can't leave." She glanced at the door. "I know it's hard for her, but she isn't the only one who lost somebody."

"She's scared for you. She doesn't like this place." Her father put the shoe back on the dresser with care.

"Don't worry, Dad. It's just a school," Vanessa said.

"I know that. But your mother, she believes . . . well, you know what she thinks. She'd rather you be anywhere else. I support your being here if you think that's what is best for you. But if things get too much for you to handle, you can always come home. Choose a different path."

Dad gave a lopsided smile and patted Vanessa on the shoulder. She understood what he was saying, but what other path was there? Her grandmother had been a principal ballerina, her mother had been a principal ballerina, and Margaret had been one of the most promising students the school had ever seen.

Until she'd disappeared three years ago.

Vanessa could still remember when they got the phone call. It was February, and snow was falling over Massachusetts, floating past their kitchen window while she and her parents ate dinner. Her sister had run away, the program adviser had told her mother. "She fell in with the wrong crowd," he'd added. "The pressures of ballet sometimes lead girls in the wrong direction, no matter how hard we try to prevent it."

Her parents dropped Vanessa off with her grandparents that night and drove to New York to search for Margaret. By day, they worked with the police; by night, they wandered the city, combing its darkest and most desolate corners. After a few weeks, her father returned to work, joining his wife on weekends.

Six months later, her parents gave up the search and moved back home to take care of their remaining daughter. Margaret's belongings were stored in the garage.

Vanessa wanted to believe that Margaret was still out there somewhere, laughing with friends, living a fantasy life as a normal teenager.

Then they got a final package in the mail from the New York Ballet Academy: Margaret's school ID, a leotard that still gave off her faint floral scent, and a battered pair of pointe shoes, all of which had been in her studio locker when they packed the rest of her things. Vanessa's mother cried when she opened the box and saw Margaret's initials scratched into the soles, an old pair that Margaret had kept because they'd been a gift from her teacher back in Massachusetts. "What if she's dead?" her mother whispered, uttering the thought that had been haunting all of them.

Vanessa sat down and rested her head on her mother's shoulder. "Maybe she just doesn't need these anymore." She refused to believe her sister was gone.

After that, while Vanessa and her father tried to resume their lives, her mother barely left her bed for an entire month. She stopped showering and dressing; she left her food untouched; she even refused to listen to classical music. That's when Vanessa knew it was bad.

So one dreary Friday, she slipped her ballet shoes out of the closet and tiptoed into the master bedroom, where her mother was curled, unmoving, beneath the sheets. And as the rain trickled down the windowpanes, Vanessa performed, letting all of the grief pour out of her until she could feel nothing but the raw thumping of her heart.

Slowly, her mother sat up.

Soon, she was driving Vanessa to ballet lessons the way she'd always done, until one day Vanessa announced she was applying to the New York Ballet Academy. Her mother was shocked. She loved watching Vanessa dance, but never thought Vanessa loved it enough to follow in Margaret's footsteps. They had closed that chapter of their lives, she'd said.

But Vanessa hadn't. With her father's help, she applied to the same school Margaret had disappeared from, because she was determined not only to dance but to find her sister. She had to be here—in this school, in this life that had once belonged to her mother and to Margaret.

Now her father pulled over a box and sat down next to Vanessa. "I'm serious," he said. "I know you're a talented dancer. I just want to make sure you're happy too."

"I *am* happy," Vanessa said. *Sort of,* she told herself. Happiness was always complicated.

"Who's happy?" her mother asked, startling them both as she slipped through the door, dabbing her eyes with a linen hankie. She was always doing that, sneaking up on people, an omnipresent force in Vanessa's life.

"I am," Vanessa said. "I'm happy to be here."

"Of course you are," her mother said sadly. "It's the most elite ballet school in the world." She forced a smile. "I just visited Margaret's old room." Her voice cracked, and Vanessa's father wrapped his arm around her shoulders. "Promise me you won't ever take any drugs. Not even aspirin. I don't care how much your feet hurt."

"You don't have to worry about that," Vanessa said. Other girls, she knew, used painkillers, but her feet were so numb and calloused that she could probably drive a nail through her toe and not feel it.

A short while later, after a final cleanup of empty boxes, her father gave her a long, tight hug. "Call me if you need anything. *Anything,*" he whispered. "Even if it's just to chat."

Caught off guard by the softness in her father's voice, Vanessa relaxed into his arms. This was it, she realized, breathing in the scent of his aftershave. Only now had it sunk in that she wasn't going home with them. Vanessa pressed her cheek against his lapel. "I will."

"All right," her mother said. "It's my turn." And before Vanessa knew what was happening, her mother pulled her to her chest and squeezed, burying her face in Vanessa's hair. "Oh, I'm going to miss you," her mother said, rocking slightly as she held her. "You're going to be wonderful. I just know you are."

Vanessa allowed her arms to slip around her mother's slender body. "Thanks, Mom."

And suddenly, as if she had realized what she was doing, her mother released her and stepped back, smoothing her skirt and wiping her eyes with a tissue. "We should be off," she said briskly.

Vanessa watched as her parents disappeared into the hallway. *Now what?* She picked up a small box resting by her bed.

Nestled inside were Margaret's pointe shoes, their ribbons coiled around the worn pink satin. Gently, she traced the rough lines of her sister's initials on the soles. Just as she tucked them into her closet, a girl burst through her door.

"Was that your mom? Crazy lady who busted into my room without knocking? Who kept talking about someone named Margaret?" She was tall and lean, with dark-brown skin, sharp green eyes, and a hint of a smile.

"I'm sorry," Vanessa apologized. "If it makes you feel any better, she's been doing that to me for years."

"Damn. And I thought *my* mom was bad."

Vanessa bit her lip. "She didn't touch any of your stuff, did she?"

The girl pulled back her thick hair with a clip. "No, she just stood there and, like, vibrated. For a minute I thought she was going to sit on my bed, but I told her what's what before she got the chance. I might've made her cry."

"No, that wasn't you," Vanessa said, shaking her head. "She cries a lot these days." She paused. "I'm Vanessa, by the way."

"Vanessa? So who's Margaret?"

"My older sister. She used to go here . . . but now she doesn't."

The girl's eyes twinkled. "I'm Steffie."

"*Great* story." Another girl popped her head in. "And I'm TJ," the new girl said with a grin. "Your roommate."

She had big doe eyes and freckles. A tangled nest of curly brown hair was pinned on top of her head, a few stray ringlets bouncing around her face. "It's short for Tammy Jessica, but I think that's too girly. TJ's better, don't you think?"

Vanessa nodded. "I guess so."

"Define 'better,'" said Steffie.

"Nice to meet you too." TJ sat on her bright-blue bedspread. For a dancer, she had a generous frame. "I'm reinventing myself now that I'm here. Like I said: TJ. The T can stand for, like, tough as nails. And the J for . . . jazz. Or whatever. But that's who I am now. Going forward."

Vanessa smiled. The idea of a new beginning certainly was nice. TJ's name matched her image: she wore no makeup, not even eyeliner. Her features seemed expressive enough already.

"I'm from the city," TJ said, as if there were only one. "The Upper East Side. I could have just lived at home, but I wanted to get away from my parents. They're lawyers. Prillar & Prillar, so that's what our house is like. Always talking, talking, talking." She rolled her eyes. "It's going to be nice to be away from that."

Vanessa had to hide her smile. Talking, talking, talking. "Prillar?" she said. "Like the Prillar who's on the board of directors of NYBA?"

Steffie turned her head. "You didn't tell me that, TJ."

TJ replied, "Why would I? That didn't have anything to do with me getting in."

"Of course not," said Steffie. "I didn't mean to imply—"

But TJ just laughed. "I know. So where are you from, Vanessa? No, wait. Let me guess. California. No, Vermont."

"Close," Vanessa said. "Massachusetts."

Catching Vanessa eyeing the pile of clothes by her bed, TJ said, "Don't worry. I'm not this messy all the time."

Vanessa laughed. "Neither am I."

"Enough about your messy clothes," Steffie said. "I can't believe we get to go to school in Manhattan. How cool is that?"

"The city that never sleeps," TJ said.

"Where the sidewalks are paved with gold!" Steffie said. "Or is that Hollywood?"

"Doesn't matter," Vanessa said. "The point is, we're lucky."

"First thing I'm doing tomorrow morning is going to Times Square," Steffie said, pushing TJ aside and flopping down on the bed beside her.

"Ugh," TJ said. "The first thing I'm doing tomorrow is *not* going to Times Square."

"What's wrong with Times Square?" Steffie asked.

"Nothing, if you're a tourist."

"Well, I'm a tourist. I didn't live here my whole life like some people with big hair."

All three of them looked out the window to where Lincoln Center glittered in the late afternoon light. The central plaza fountain sprayed jets of water high into the air, and on every side was a grand building that Vanessa already knew by heart: the one with the dramatic glass windows was the New York City Ballet; the high arched windows was the Metropolitan Opera House; and the yellow marble-walled building was Avery Fisher Hall, home to the New York Philharmonic. Their new school, New York Ballet Academy, was tucked just behind Avery Fisher Hall, next to the Juilliard School: two modest buildings that were now Vanessa's home. The setting sun cast a brassy sheen on everything they saw—from the fountain to the buildings on the plaza, from the wooden water towers that speckled the rooftops of the many apartment buildings to the glassy skyscrapers in the distance whose windows looked like molten gold.

"It's really beautiful," Steffie said, her snark gone for the moment. "Hard to believe this is home for the next four years. We're at, like, the center of the universe."

"We're *almost* at the center of the universe," TJ said. "There's a whole lot to New York City that we'll probably never get to see. Lincoln Center is a safe little bubble."

Not that safe, Vanessa thought, but to her new friends she said, "It feels unreal, doesn't it? Like tomorrow I'm going to wake up at home and realize it was all a dream."

"Just wait till classes," TJ said. She smiled and flashed a set of bright, white teeth. "It'll feel real when our feet are blistered and bleeding."

Instinctively, Vanessa flexed her toes inside her canvas sneakers. Unable to stop herself, she stared at Steffie's muscular thighs and TJ's straight back, and wondered if they were better dancers than she was. She wasn't used to being surrounded by so many serious dancers; at home, Vanessa had always been the best by far.

But her thoughts were interrupted when two others drifted in: a tiny girl named Elly, Steffie's roommate, who had wavy blond hair and was carrying a laptop under one arm, and an Asian boy who followed on her heels.

"We heard voices and thought we would stop in and say

hello," the boy said, "because we're both *wonderful* and so obviously you need to know who we are. I go by Blaine." He held out his hand to no one in particular, as though waiting for it to be kissed.

Steffie made a face and sat on the windowsill, crossing her long dark legs and scrutinizing the newcomers.

"But it's not his real name," Elly teased in a sweet, southern drawl. Everything about her was sugary and bite-sized: her yellow bob, her button nose, her pouty lips. Even her clothes were a lacy baby pink. She elbowed Blaine. "Go ahead. Tell them!"

Blaine shook his head and gave her a semiserious look. "Don't you dare."

TJ pushed her curly hair off her neck. "So what's your real name?"

Blaine swatted her question away. "I'll never tell."

"Why not?" TJ asked, looking from Blaine to Elly. "You already told her."

"That's because we're both from the South. She understands."

"Understands what?" Steffie asked.

"That people are weirder down there," Blaine said, as if it should have been obvious.

"And wider," TJ added.

Blaine shrugged. "It's true. But look, I'm half Japanese and half Mexican. How many people do y'all know who wash their margaritas down with a shot of sake?"

"What's sake?" TJ whispered to Vanessa.

"Not to mention that I'm a guy who likes to wear tights and slippers," Blaine continued, "and doesn't eat red meat. It's not easy growing up like that in Texas. Do you know how hard it is to find a decent salad down there?"

The room erupted in a chorus of giggles. "It's not that bad," Elly said, folding herself onto the bed next to TJ. "And the South *does* have one thing that the rest of the country doesn't."

"An excess of Mountain Dew?" TJ joked.

Elly smiled, her lips forming a pink crescent. "Southern gentlemen, preferably from Alabama."

Blaine rolled his eyes. "They're all farmers to me. Farmers with big fat hoes."

Vanessa let out a laugh. "I'd take collared shirts and chinos over coattails and bow ties any day," she said. "But I'm from Massachusetts. I like prep."

"See, that's what I'm talking about," Blaine said. "Or I could settle for a Russian dancer. They're so severe. I love it. I wouldn't even care if he spoke no English whatsoever. As long as he made sweet, sweet love to me while feeding me caviar, and then helped me play with my set of Matryoshka dolls." He paused. "Not that I have any Matryoshka dolls."

Vanessa and the girls continued staring at him. "Then how would you communicate?" Elly asked quizzically.

"Darling," Blaine said, leaning forward and batting his eyelashes. "The language of love requires no words. Haven't you seen *The Little Mermaid*?"

That made even Steffie laugh. "Enough about Russian men and little dolls and Disney movies. We're here to dance."

Elly opened her laptop, which had a pink case and an enormous heart on the lid, and showed them photos of famous dancers who had graduated from their school: Anastasia Petrova in her leading role in *Giselle*, Alexander Garrel as the sinewy Rat King from *The Nutcracker*, and Juliana Faraday as an ethereal Princess Aurora from *Sleeping Beauty*.

"Those are the ones who made it out," Blaine said. "What about the ones who didn't?"

Vanessa grew rigid. "What do you mean?"

Elly cut in. "I heard a girl broke her leg last year during a rehearsal. One of the guys dropped her mid-jump. An upperclassman told me he could hear her bone snap."

Vanessa cringed.

"Twenty are called," TJ intoned, "but few survive long enough to graduate."

"I'm *serious*," Blaine said. "There are all these students who get hurt."

"Not to mention the broken toes," Steffie chimed in. "I almost broke one of mine last year," she added, a thin silver anklet jingling as she rolled her foot.

"Or the broken hearts," Elly added, giving Blaine a coy look. He threw a pillow at her.

"Or the girls sent home because of weight problems or drugs," Vanessa added.

"When you guys dance, do you ever feel different?" Steffie said suddenly. "Like you're—"

"Delirious?" Vanessa said, startling herself.

"Um—no, I was actually going to say weightless," Steffie said.

"Delirious?" TJ said with an amused smile. "Like dizzy? Maybe you're not spotting right."

Vanessa laughed sheepishly. "Just kidding," she said, embarrassed.

It only happened once in a while—the strange, delirious feeling. When Vanessa danced so perfectly the music was like a part of her heartbeat, the world around her spun into oblivion, and she felt like she was losing herself. But maybe it was just dehydration. That's what her mother told her every time she tried to raise the subject. When Vanessa looked up, she realized Steffie was studying her. She felt herself blush, but Steffie only gave her an understanding smile, as if to say, *Whatever your secret is, it's safe with me.*

"Orientation!" Elly said suddenly. Outside, the hall was strangely quiet. She glanced at her watch. "Crap. We're already late!"

Chapter Two

It couldn't be.

The rest of the group ran ahead, toward Juilliard, where the orientation was being held. But Vanessa stood frozen in place on the curb, arrested by the sight of a frail girl with long chestnut hair.

She was waiting on the corner by a bus stop, her shoulders bare above a cotton sundress, reading a magazine. Her arms were dotted with dark, familiar freckles.

Vanessa's heart seemed to stop. Could it be?

Slowly, Vanessa approached, pushing through the people on the sidewalk until she was just inches away from the girl. She took a step closer, gazing at her sister's delicate skin.

"Margaret?"

Exhaust from the passing cars made the air thick. Vanessa's long red hair blew about her face.

The girl glanced over her shoulder, her face foreign and strange.

Vanessa went rigid. "Oh, I—I'm sorry," she said, and backed away. She felt a hand on her arm and, startled, she jumped.

"Are you okay?" Steffie asked.

Vanessa nodded.

"What were you doing?"

"I thought I saw someone I knew," Vanessa said, her gaze lingering on the girl's back. "But it's stupid, right? I mean, New York has millions of people. What are the chances of finding one person out of all of them?"

"I don't think it's stupid," Steffie said softly.

Vanessa stared at the flood of people on the sidewalk and the crowded mess of storefronts and brownstones and sky-scrapers that framed them. The windows that dotted the sides of the buildings looked minuscule from the ground, and it suddenly made Vanessa dizzy to think that a person lived behind each little square of glass, thousands of them just in this three-block radius. Her sister was here somewhere.

And that was why she had come to New York: she wanted to find Margaret.

"Come on," Steffie said. "We're late."

When they caught up with the others, they were standing in front of a wooden door, looking lost.

"I thought it was here," Elly said, glancing down the hall-way full of dance studios. "But the door is locked."

"Maybe they locked us out because we're late," Blaine said.

"Here, let me try," Vanessa said. Using all her weight, she gave the door a firm push. It swung open, and the five of them hurried inside.

They were in a large ballet studio. Mirrors lined the walls, reflecting the warm light and making the room seem endless. The entire student body was sitting on the floor, staring at them.

"How interesting," a woman said in a slight German accent, scrutinizing them. She was so short that Vanessa had barely noticed her. She was middle-aged, her body plain and squat, with thick legs and dull brown hair. "Your first day and your timing is already off."

"We're sorry," TJ blurted out. "We got lost."

The woman squinted at them. Her face was round and maternal like a country farmwife, her gaze stern, yet somehow still kind. "Let's just hope your dancing is a little more elegant than your entrance. We have space for you—right—up—here." She pointed at her feet.

Trying to avoid everyone's eyes, Vanessa led them up to the front of the room. Her RA, Kate, sat by the barre with a few girls, smiling sympathetically. Other students' eyes met hers as she wove between them—girls with braids coiled into buns, tortoiseshell headbands and barrettes nestled into their hair, their lean shoulders bare beneath tight tank tops; boys in black jeans, white undershirts, and cutoff sweats that allowed a glimpse of rock-hard biceps and firm abs.

None of them bothered to move to let Vanessa and her friends pass.

Just before she sat down, she noticed a group of older girls leaning against the mirrors in the corner of the room. They were beautiful—long and languid—as they whispered to each other. All thirteen of them had sunburns, as if they had just come back from the beach.

"As I was saying," the woman up front said, clearing her throat. "My name is Hilda, and I will be your assistant choreographer."

Vanessa squeezed in next to Steffie, who smelled faintly of vanilla. She had noticed the older girls, too, because she said, "Someone forgot the sunscreen."

Vanessa was about to smile when Hilda caught her eye.

"And now I'd like to introduce your choreographer, Josef."

A sinewy man with the compact figure of a dancer approached the front of the room. He looked young at first, but as he grew closer and his features came into focus, Vanessa realized he was probably in his late thirties.

Hilda moved aside and Josef smiled, baring a set of charmingly crooked teeth. He ran a hand through his hair, which was wavy and brown, streaked with gray. He wore tight black jeans and a white V-neck tee with a lick of chest hair sticking out the top. Even though he was neither tall nor particularly good-looking, his presence filled the entire studio.

"Well, here we are." He spoke with a slight French accent. "At the apex of the world. Welcome."

With his words, the room seemed to lighten. Vanessa glanced around her and saw the other students smiling.

"Every dancer dreams of attending the New York Ballet

Academy, and rightly so. We are a school of dreams. Here, you will learn how to transcend this world. You will transform yourselves into fairies, princes, swans both pale and dark, wicked queens, and demons from the underworld. You will float like a cloud and disappear into shadows. The audience will think it's a trick of the light, but all of you will know that you *are* the light. You *are* the music. You are nothing but movement."

The room was so still, Vanessa could hear him let out a breath.

"Speaking of movement, I must mention that a quarter of the freshman class doesn't make it through the first year. This may come as a surprise, as you have worked so hard to come here that you cannot even imagine the prospect of dropping out." He paused, his eyes darting around the room. "I suggest you leave your preconceptions of ballet behind and come to rehearsal soft and malleable, ready to be molded."

Everyone glanced from side to side, eyeing the other students as if trying to figure out who would leave first.

"But enough of that," Josef said, suddenly upbeat. "Every winter, we put on a main stage ballet. I'm proud to announce that this year we will be performing Stravinsky's *The Firebird*."

For the briefest moment, Josef's gaze fell on Vanessa. She thought she saw a hint of recognition in his eyes before he looked away. Had he known her sister?

"The ballet centers on Prince Ivan, who enters a magical realm called Kashchei, named after its ruler. There, the prince captures a Firebird, who offers to assist Ivan in exchange for its eventual freedom. When Ivan falls in love with one of the thirteen princesses, it is the Firebird who helps him defeat Kashchei and win his true love."

In the mirror on the wall, Vanessa thought she saw a flicker of something dark and foreign, but when she turned to look, everyone remained still.

"The curtains will open on December 13. It is only September now, so this may sound far away, but I assure you it's not. Casting will take place in one month. The main roles almost always go to the upperclassmen, so for our newcomers, don't be disappointed if you aren't chosen. Your time will come. In the meantime, I expect to see you here, on barre. Practice is everything.

"There has only ever been one student who dazzled us enough to catch our attention from the very start. She was a freshman when we cast her in a lead role, and a magnificent dancer. Ethereal." Josef closed his eyes, apparently conjuring her in his mind. "Unfortunately, she collapsed under the pressure and dropped out. Her dream was shattered." He scanned the room. "Do not let this happen to you."

Margaret. Vanessa glanced around the studio, but no one seemed to know who Josef was referring to. No one, that is, except for Steffie, who watched Vanessa with a curious expression.

Embarrassed, Vanessa hugged her knees, trying to will herself to react more discreetly, when once again she thought she caught Josef's eyes flitting over her. But it could have been her imagination.

"Hard work and patience pay off just as much as talent. Which reminds me—the role of Prince Ivan has already been cast." Josef scanned the crowd. "Zeppelin Gray, could you please stand up?"

Vanessa saw his reflection first, his eyes deep and smooth like dark metal. He was sitting with the girls in the corner of the room. As he stood, he seemed to unfold himself, his shoulders broadening, his spine lengthening, until he towered over the rest of the room. He was like no one Vanessa had ever seen. He was too tall to be a dancer, too rough, yet he moved with grace, his black hair lustrous beneath the warm lights.

Zeppelin, she thought, her eyes traveling up the contours of his arms, when suddenly their eyes met.

His gaze was startling, unnerving, and as he tilted his head his face seemed to change, his sharp edges melting. His sunburn gave off a brassy glow, making him look like a chiseled sculpture. Vanessa felt like she could stare at him for hours and still not see what lay beneath the surface. She faltered, her lips trembling, but she couldn't look away.

And then, without warning, he smiled.

"Gorgeous, right?" Steffie said. "You should close your mouth. And stop staring."

Vanessa could feel herself blushing as she pried her eyes away from the senior playing Prince Ivan and turned back to her dinner. They were sitting around a thick wooden table in the building next to their dormitory. A giant brass chandelier dangled over the center of the room, which was loud with the din of conversation and clinking plates and silverware.

Vanessa picked at her salad absentmindedly, wishing she had gotten croutons. The dining hall was the strangest she had ever seen, with a massive salad bar in the center and a few lonely carousels offering bread and pasta. The dessert bar featured fruit salad and a lumpy vat of chocolate pudding that Vanessa was certain the school made intentionally unappetizing.

Across from her, TJ was gesticulating with her fork, her curly hair bouncing as she talked about how lame and boring the orientation had been.

But Vanessa wasn't paying attention. Instead, she stole glances at Zeppelin. Or Zep, as everyone seemed to call him. He was sitting at the corner table with the group of sunburned upperclassmen she'd seen at orientation. They were all frighteningly skinny.

"Don't get too attached," Steffie warned. "I heard he's dating Anna."

Vanessa tried not to look disappointed. "Which one is she?"

Steffie said, "Hard to tell, right? All those girls are in a dieting club. Dress the same, eat the same things, probably barf the same. But the one on the end is the leader." A pretty girl with long blond hair and delicate, doll-like features was sitting next to Zep, her fingers tickling his wrist. "Anna Franko. She's the granddaughter of Mimi Franko."

"The ballerina from the fifties?" Vanessa asked. "Who did that unreal jeté in *Romeo and Juliet*?"

Steffie nodded. "That's Anna's grandmother."

Vanessa felt something inside her crumple. She could still remember staying up with her sister, watching Mimi Franko's performance over and over until they had memorized every movement. She was enchanting, magical, her leaps so high and her steps so smooth that she put Vanessa under a spell.

"And apparently Anna is no different," Steffie continued. "She's by far the best ballerina here. Or at least she is now that her best friend Chloë Martin dropped out of school. Together, people say they were just amazing, and supposedly Chloë was even better than Anna. If she hadn't dropped out, she would have been cast as the lead in *The Firebird*. Now that she's gone, everyone's sure that Anna will take her place."

As much as she didn't want to, Vanessa had to admit Anna looked the part. She watched as Anna leaned over and said something in Zep's ear. He smiled at her, and together they stood up, moving in rhythm, Anna's white flats clicking against the floor tiles until they disappeared through the double doors.

With a sigh, Vanessa leaned back in her chair and tried to pay attention to the conversation, but her mind kept drifting to Zep.

"Where is he from?" she suddenly said, unintentionally speaking her thoughts aloud.

"Paris, obviously," Elly said. "He used to be a famous dancer. Haven't you heard of him?"

Vanessa blinked. Maybe that was why they had already chosen him for the role of Prince Ivan. "What do you mean? He's so young."

Elly frowned, an unnatural look for her petite, feminine face. "He looks younger than he is."

"Oh," Vanessa said, trying not to look surprised. "So why is he here then?"

"I don't know." With dainty gestures, Elly speared three peas on her fork. "I guess whatever he did wasn't that bad," she said. "Or they wouldn't have let him come here."

Vanessa stopped chewing. "What did he do?"

Blaine gave Vanessa a confused look. "Weren't you listening? We were just talking about how he was involved in some sort of scandal, and they kicked him out of the Paris Opera Ballet."

"A scandal?"

"I don't know," Elly said with a shrug. "I think it had something to do with an accident with a girl."

"A ballet accident, or *that* kind of accident?" TJ asked, a wicked grin spreading across her face.

Elly gave her a sour look. "A ballet accident. Though he has been known to have lots of affairs."

Vanessa nearly choked on a cherry tomato. "What?" she said, coughing.

"I heard he has three kids, all with different women." TJ wiped her mouth with her napkin. "Apparently they're all living somewhere in Europe."

"Zep has three children?" Vanessa blurted out.

TJ grinned and nibbled on a coil of pasta; she was the only one of them brave enough to touch carbs. "Oh, sweetie. Did you think we were talking about Zep?"

Vanessa swallowed, realizing her mistake. "Josef," she murmured. "That's who you were talking about—"

But the sharp sound of a whistle interrupted her. Hilda approached the front of the room, her stout figure draped in a dowdy black frock. "Curfew!" she said loudly.

The room was filled with the clamor of chairs scraping the floor, dishes clattering, doors swinging open and shut with a swish.

Relieved that everyone's attention had been diverted, Vanessa gathered her things and followed her friends outside. But while the rest of them filed back to the dorms, Vanessa turned to Steffie. "Manhattan awaits."

"In all its noisy splendor," Steffie said. "Just one look."

Together they snuck off to steal a glance at the city.

"Josef was involved in a scandal?" Vanessa whispered as they darted across the street and into Lincoln Plaza.

"I guess so," Steffie said. "I'd never heard about it, either."

They found a space on the ledge of the fountain. People lounged about, chatting and sipping coffee under the glassy facades of the buildings. Night had fallen over New York, and the city pulsed with activity—cars speeding up Broadway, their headlights streaking through the dark; traffic signals changing in waves visible as far as the girls could see; lights flickering on in the windows of apartment buildings.

Vanessa and Steffie leaned back and looked at the rich dark sky above the plaza.

"There isn't a single star," Vanessa said. "It's like we've left the real world and entered this weird alternate universe."

"You're right," Steffie said, gazing at the sky. "But, baby, in this world, *we're* supposed to be the stars. Come on."

She got up and pulled Vanessa by the hand from the plaza to the street, then turned uptown. Strangers passed them on the sidewalk, rushing along so fast they didn't seem to look at anything around them.

"I kind of think New York is a lonely place," Steffie said.

"It's ironic, isn't it?" Vanessa murmured. "We're surrounded by noise, but when you listen you can't actually hear anything. It just blends together."

Steffie nodded. "I didn't want to come here at first. I mean, I've always wanted to come to the New York Ballet Academy, but when I got my acceptance letter, it felt like I didn't have a choice. Because who could turn down an offer like this?"

"I know what you mean," Vanessa said. "Everyone in my family has come here. My grandmother, my mother, my sister . . . like the choice was made for me a long time before the letter came in the mail." Vanessa averted her eyes as she spoke, knowing that wasn't exactly true. The choice *had* been made for her a long time ago, just not by her mother, who didn't want Vanessa there at all. No, it had been Margaret and her strange disappearance that made Vanessa feel like she had no choice.

They meandered back to the dormitory, tucked just behind the plaza next to the dining hall. It was an exquisite old building, with marble stairs worn down in the middle and varnished wooden floors. They flashed their IDs and went inside.

"I hope no one notices we're late," Vanessa said as they got off the elevator on their floor.

"I'm sure it'll be fine," Steffie said. "Do you think TJ and Elly are asleep yet?"

"I doubt it," Vanessa said.

As they stepped into the hallway, Vanessa was surprised at how dim the lighting was, giving the space an eerie, vacant feeling. The RAs were supposed to be patrolling for curfew, but strangely, no one was around. Every single door was closed. There were no sounds of any kids unpacking or chatting on the phone. It almost seemed like a prison. She touched her fingers to the walls, the cold plaster guiding her.

"Is this how it always is?"

"Maybe it's because of curfew," Steffie whispered back, but her voice was uneasy.

"Finally," Vanessa said, pushing open her door.

But when she stepped inside, she froze. The floor beneath her was squishy and wet.

Quickly, she reached for the light switch.

Steffie gasped, then covered her mouth. They were standing in a puddle of something thick and red. A long, terrible drip seemed to echo through the room.

Vanessa felt the color drain from her face as she turned to Steffie.

Slowly, they looked up to see two pairs of ballet shoes dangling from the light, dripping blood.

Before Vanessa could scream, a hand closed over her mouth.

CHAPTER THREE

The hand was large and smelled of aftershave. Vanessa squirmed, trying to free herself, but his grip was strong.

"Vanessa!" Steffie cried, kicking as a hand closed over her own mouth.

That was the last thing Vanessa saw: Steffie's eyes, wild and fierce above the hand, as the two girls were ripped from each other. Screams echoed up and down the hallway outside as a blindfold came down over Vanessa's eyes.

Thrust into darkness, Vanessa writhed until she ran out of energy.

"A feisty one," her captor said to someone behind them. His voice was gruff. Vanessa tried to speak, but her words were muffled by the hand over her mouth. She could taste the sweat on his palm. Holding her tight, he leaned over, his breath hot against her ear. "Stop fighting and no one will hurt you."

She grew still. The screams outside had stopped, and the dormitory was again unnaturally quiet. Vanessa could feel the boy's heartbeat at her back, the hair on his arms tickling her neck.

He loosened his grip. "Don't say a word."

Vanessa nodded, and to her surprise he uncovered her mouth. Gently, he uncurled her fingers and placed another slender hand in hers. It was soft yet firm, with long fingernails.

Steffie, Vanessa mouthed. As if in answer, Steffie squeezed her hand.

"Don't let go," the boy said.

Vanessa nodded again.

"Now walk."

They were marched out of the room, the door swinging shut behind them. More trembling hands joined theirs as they stumbled through the hallway and down a staircase, the wooden floorboards creaking beneath them. Vanessa heard an occasional nervous giggle or a whisper cut short. They groped around in the dark for what seemed like an hour, turning left, then right, tripping up the stairs until the boy finally told them to stop.

"Take off your blindfolds."

Vanessa slipped the cloth off her head and dropped it onto the waxed floor of the ballet studio they had been in just hours before for orientation.

Candles lined the perimeter of the room, the flames flickering endlessly in the mirrors. Just a few feet away, a pair of ballet shoes lay, splattered with blood.

Vanessa cringed at the sight of the tangled ribbons, now drenched in red. All she could think of was Margaret. Staring at the bloody slippers, her mind traveled to the darkest recesses of her imagination. What had *really* happened to her sister?

She forced herself to look away, seeing Steffie to her right, Elly to her left, followed by Blaine and a few other freshmen. At the far end of the studio, Vanessa could see TJ's wild hair, her blindfold pushed over it like a headband. They waited in silence, their shadows dancing across the wooden floor, until the door opened.

A train of people proceeded inside, their faces hidden behind beak-nosed Venetian masks, their expressions vacant, ghoulish. Vanessa tried to pick out her assailant, but the mirrors seemed to multiply them into oblivion.

One final person slipped into the room, and the door clicked shut. As she took her place in the line of upperclassmen, Vanessa caught a glimpse of a pair of white flats. Anna Franko.

Before she could tell Steffie, a boy stepped forward from the line. He was wearing a white mask with a twisted face, its features drooping as if they had melted. The flames of the candles around him stuttered with each footfall.

"You may have thought orientation was over," he said. It was the same boy who had restrained Vanessa. "But you were wrong."

He scanned the line of freshmen, lingering on Vanessa for a moment before looking away. *Is it Zep?* Vanessa wondered.

"Welcome to the *real* New York Ballet Academy," he continued. "As you'll soon discover, the dirty work gets done after hours. Starting tonight."

He looked shorter in the dark, his shoulders more hunched. And his hair—was it longer than she had realized? Vanessa stared at the black sockets of his mask and tried to see the metallic glimmer of his eyes, but they were vacant.

"Take off your shoes. All of you."

Everyone around Vanessa began slipping off their shoes, but Vanessa gave Steffie a dubious look.

Steffie shrugged. "Don't worry," she said, sniffing the red fluid caked on the sides of her shoes. "It's not blood. Smells like . . . ketchup."

One of the upperclassmen must have heard her, because a voice bellowed across the room, "You. Step forward."

Another boy emerged from the line of upperclassmen, wearing a charred-looking gray mask. He pointed at Steffie. "You will be the first to make your mark."

A hush fell over the room. The boy in the gray mask removed a thin scalpel from his pocket, the blade glinting in the candlelight. "Come forth."

Everyone turned to Steffie, but if she was scared, she didn't show it.

"Don't do it," Vanessa said under her breath, but Steffie had already kicked off her shoes.

Her chin raised in the air, Steffie strode forward. "What do you want me to do?"

The masked boy held out the scalpel. "Cut the ball of your foot until you bleed. Then make your mark by dragging your foot across the back of the stage." The boy moved aside and gestured to a row of unvarnished floorboards behind him.

Leaning forward, Vanessa could see a long line of dark-brown streaks—at least a hundred of them, laddering from center stage to the right edge.

"But that'll hurt!" someone blurted out. Vanessa recognized TJ's voice. "This is messed up. We won't be able to dance."

Other freshmen chimed in. "Auditions are in a month," a boy said. "This will ruin our chances—"

"Silence!"

It was the boy in the gray mask. "You will bleed for us," he commanded, and the room fell quiet. "Ballet requires the bond of sacrifice. Now take this and do it swiftly, or there *will* be consequences."

Without saying a word, Steffie took the scalpel. She raised her right foot to her knee as if practicing *en barre*, her silhouette long and arched. She glanced over at Vanessa and winked.

No, Vanessa mouthed, too late, as Steffie plunged the knife into her foot. One of the freshmen next to Vanessa gasped. Without flinching, Steffie pulled it out as quickly as it went in, a bead of blood on its tip.

The masked upperclassmen closed in around her; they chanted something too soft for Vanessa to hear as Steffie crossed to the space where the floor met the wall. There, she dragged her foot across the wooden boards until she'd left behind her own thin smudge.

She stepped back, and the boy in the white mask approached her. He held out a wad of gauze and a roll of tape. *Zep,* Vanessa thought, hoping he'd glance at her again. Instead, he leaned forward and spoke something in Steffie's ear. Vanessa felt a twinge of jealousy as she watched him kneel and take Steffie's wounded foot in his hands, his fingers gentle as he bandaged it.

Vanessa watched as Elly, Blaine, and five others performed

the ritual, the boy in the white mask wiping the blade with an alcohol-soaked cloth in between each cut. When they were through, the boy in the gray mask turned to her. "Come forth," he said in a raspy voice, and held out the scalpel.

Barefoot, Vanessa stepped toward him. The upperclassmen closed in around her, chanting, *You're not good enough. You're not worthy.* The words came out hot and muggy through their masks. *You will never be a dancer.*

They're right, Vanessa thought, searching their hollow faces. The candlelight bounced off the masks, making it look like they were smiling.

Vanessa gripped the knife. Now she would know how Margaret had once felt. Whispering her sister's name, Vanessa raised her toe to her knee in a graceful passé, and slashed the ball of her foot.

A flash of red. A quick, sharp pain. And then a lull as she walked across the room and placed her foot on the unvarnished floorboards but accidentally slid it over an old mark.

The chanting grew louder, louder, until the words pounded through Vanessa's head.

S'enfuir. Fuir pour sauver votre vie. Sauver votre âme.

"What?" Vanessa said, whipping around. But the voice wasn't coming from the upperclassmen.

It grew louder, the voice murmuring the deep, thick French words. Vanessa pressed her palms to her temples. Her long hair cascaded over her face. "Stop!" she screamed. "Stop!"

The boy in the gray mask pushed her foot away from the streaks on the floorboard and wiped up the blood that she had smeared over the old mark. "Come on, clumsy," he muttered.

Immediately, the voices stopped.

Vanessa paused, trying to understand what had just happened. Regaining her balance, she pointed the ball of her foot at a clean space on the wood and drew a shaky line.

Just as she turned to go back to her place, a boy called out to her. "Wait."

Vanessa froze as the boy in the white mask approached and knelt down beside her. Zep? She searched the dark holes of his eyes but couldn't see anything.

"Are you okay?" His fingers grazed the back of her thigh. "Lift."

Vanessa swallowed and nodded, her skin tightening beneath his touch as he took her foot in his palm and began to wrap it with gauze. He was so close that she could smell his aftershave. *Look at me again*, her mind begged while she watched his shoulders shift beneath his shirt.

As if he heard her, he tilted his head up. "Thank you," she said, so softly that she wasn't even sure he had heard her.

Taking her place in line, she turned to Steffie while the next boy was called forth. "What was the French they screamed?"

"What are you talking about?" Steffie said, raising an eyebrow. "No one was speaking French."

"Yes they were," Vanessa insisted. "They kept saying S—*S'enfoor?*"

"*S'enfuir?*" Steffie said in perfect French. Vanessa raised an eyebrow. "My mom speaks French," Steffie said. "Don't judge. What else did you hear?"

Vanessa thought for a moment. *"Fuir pour sa—sa—sauver votre vie. Sauver votre aim?"*

"Votre âme?" Steffie repeated.

When Vanessa nodded again, Steffie gave her a scrutinizing look. "Are you playing with me?"

Vanessa shook her head, confused. "No. I don't even speak French."

Steffie's eyes darted to the upperclassmen. They were huddled around another freshman, chanting. She lowered her voice. "I'm pretty sure that means: *Run away. Flee for your life. Save your soul.*"

Chapter Four

Someone wanted Vanessa to leave. Or at least that was Steffie's theory.

"But why?" Elly asked. "Classes haven't even started yet. No one knows you."

The four of them were sprawled out in Steffie and Elly's room, half of which was decorated in muted shades of tan and black, while the other half looked like a frosted cupcake, draped in ruffles and bows. Elly's comforter and pillows were pink, and she'd replaced the curtains that had come with the dorm room with pink ones from Bed Bath & Beyond. The only thing that wasn't pink was the carpet.

"I don't know," Vanessa said, picking up a shag pillow. "Maybe they think I'm somebody I'm not."

"Speaking of somebody I'm not, I feel like freakin'

Strawberry Shortcake in here," TJ said to Elly. "What's the matter with blue? Or yellow?"

Elly smiled. "Maybe a little pink will do you some good." She pointed to a row of pink nail polishes lined up on her dresser. "I could paint your nails?"

"Touch me with a pink brush and I'll drop a brick on your toes," TJ said fiercely.

"Ladies!" Steffie said, laughing. "There is no need for violence."

The window was open, letting the warm Saturday-morning breeze into the room. Vanessa let her thoughts drift. Her dreams had been haunted by the boy in the white mask, his raspy voice hot against her neck as he ran his hand down her ankle. His hollow face was the last thing she remembered before waking, damp with sweat.

"But no one else heard any French, right?" Steffie said, bringing the conversation back to the secret orientation.

TJ shook her head, her mess of brown curls going every which way. She was sitting on the carpet with Blaine, who was flipping through a stack of glossy magazines they had bought at a bodega after breakfast.

"Blaine? What do you think?" Steffie asked.

"I didn't hear any French." He flipped a page. "Only super-creepy chanting. It sorta reminded me of gym class back in Texas, right before everyone would throw dodge balls directly at my head."

"If no one else heard French," Steffie said, "then one of the upperclassmen specifically told Vanessa to leave."

"Not just to leave," Vanessa murmured. "To *flee*. To save my *soul*."

TJ rolled her eyes. "Way too dramatic, if you ask me. If I were going to threaten someone, I'd choose a better word than 'flee.' And I'd probably say it in English."

"I know," Vanessa said. "It feels old-timey."

"I like it," Elly said. "Flee. It feels romantic. Like something a man would say to a woman he wanted to elope with."

Blaine groaned, and TJ fluttered her eyes as if she were in a daydream. "Elly's just jealous that someone else is living out her freaky domination fantasy."

"I am not!" Elly said, clutching a frilly pillow to her chest. "And I don't have any fantasies except to meet a nice boy, go steady with him for twenty-eight to thirty months, and then get married. We'll move into a nice four-bedroom house, buy real hardwood furniture, and maybe I'll start an herb garden. That's it. No freaks involved. Or domination."

There was a long pause as everyone exchanged looks of disbelief.

"Go steady?" Blaine said.

Elly frowned. "But I wasn't trying to be funny—"

"Herb garden?" TJ chimed in, laughing. "It sounds like you want to marry my grandfather. He loves gardening and is too hard of hearing to care about the other stuff. Plus, he's a minister. He'd say 'flee' and 'save your soul' to you all you like."

"Really, though," Steffie said as their laughter died down. "Why you?" She cocked her head at Vanessa. "Can you think of a reason why any of the upperclassmen would say that to you?"

Vanessa arched her foot, feeling the bandage stretch. No one here knew her yet, but maybe some of the older kids knew about her sister. Margaret had been cast as the lead ballerina in *The Firebird* when she was only a freshman. That alone would have been memorable enough, even without the disappearance, the canceled performance, and the long, fruitless search for her. And even though Vanessa, with her wild red hair and her rosy skin, didn't resemble Margaret at first glance, they did have the same round, hazel eyes. The same heart-shaped lips.

Flee, the voice had said. Which was exactly what Margaret had done.

But it seemed unlikely that anyone would have recognized her as Margaret's sister.

Vanessa felt Steffie watching her. She was the only one in the room who knew that Vanessa even had a sister, and that was only because she was living in Margaret's old room. The one they were sitting in now.

Vanessa glanced around at her new friends. "I used to have an older sister named Margaret," she said softly. Keeping her eyes trained on the floor, she told them everything, starting with that fateful phone call and ending with her applying to NYBA. "My mother thinks she's dead. She's still grieving. But I don't think so," Vanessa said. "I think she's out there somewhere."

A somber silence hung in the room when she finished, her friends frozen in shock.

"I agree," TJ finally said, giving Vanessa a hopeful smile.

"New York is a huge city, with tons of kids. She's probably out there having the time of her life."

Vanessa forced a laugh. "Yeah, well, if I end up running into her in a nightclub, I'm going to be pissed."

"Nightclub?" Blaine said, perking up. "You know, I wouldn't mind doing some reconnaissance work . . . if you want help." He gave her a coy wink, making her smile, and then continued, his voice sincere. "Seriously, though. If you need anything, I'm here."

"Me too," said TJ. "Just let me know when you need someone to lead the charge. Especially if it involves nightclubs," she said. "I'm tight with practically all of the bouncers."

"Yeah right," Steffie said with a laugh, and then added, "Me three."

"Me four," said Elly.

Vanessa felt herself blush. "Thanks. But do you think that's why the voices told me to flee? Did it have something to do with Margaret?"

Steffie shook her head. "I don't think anyone would joke about your sister. I bet it was just a prank."

"It was probably just some horny senior guy trying to check you out," said Blaine.

"Seeing red," TJ teased, gazing at Vanessa's fiery hair.

"Seeing red? They *were* red," Blaine said, looking up. "Didn't you see them in the dining hall?"

"Only the girls," Steffie said. "And Zep."

Blaine closed his eyes in a dreamy reverie. "I heard they all went on vacation to the Caribbean. Can you imagine that, being surrounded by ballerinas, Zep, and a horde of bare-chested bar boys serving us bottomless margaritas and huge mounds of exotic fruit?"

TJ laughed so loud that she snorted.

Blaine continued. "What I would do to see Zep with his shirt off . . ."

The girls laughed.

Elly covered her face in embarrassment. "So was it a boy's voice?"

Vanessa thought back to the previous night, which had already begun to feel like a strange, swirling dream. "Maybe. The thing is, it didn't sound like it was coming from anyone. It was piercing, like a voice had entered my head."

Elly frowned. "It had to come from someone. Voices don't just pop into your head, unless you're crazy."

They *were* all still strangers to each other, Vanessa thought. She could be crazy. Any of them could be.

On the first day of classes, the heat broke in a deluge of biblical proportions. Water sloshed down the streets, and black umbrellas bloomed along the sidewalks, making Manhattan even more anonymous.

Vanessa and Steffie darted down the sidewalk with their bags, rain dotting their T-shirts as they ran to the studios for morning rehearsal.

Wiping the water from her cheeks, Vanessa gave the door a firm push. The entire school was assembled in front of the mirrors, giving Vanessa the uncanny feeling that orientation was happening all over again.

"Déjà vu," Steffie whispered to her as they took a spot near the front.

For a moment, Vanessa could believe that orientation had never happened. The blond floors were spotless, and the soaked ballet slippers were gone. The only proof that the night had been real was the faded dark marks streaked across the unvarnished floorboards by the wall.

In the mirror, Vanessa could see the group of upperclassmen lounging in the corner, their sunburns faded, like masks being slowly peeled off. In the back, behind a group of boys, she thought she saw Zep's dark hair just as a voice said, "Time to get to work!"

A hush fell over the studio.

Josef strode to the front of the room, wearing black jeans and a fitted gray shirt, his footsteps reverberating through the studio like a communal heartbeat.

Josef clapped his hands together. "Take a look around. This is the last time you will be in the same studio together. Today, some of you will be coming with me to work on *The Firebird*." He lowered his head. "You know who you are."

A confused chorus of voices rose over the dancers. "What?" TJ said, sounding outraged. "Are the roles already cast?"

Josef raised his hand for silence. "While we have a number of seniors in mind already for *Firebird* roles, the final decision will not be made for another month. The rest of you will be working with Hilda, who will handle your morning classes."

On cue, Hilda stepped out from somewhere behind him, so commonplace in her frumpy brown skirt and turtleneck that Vanessa hadn't even noticed her.

"All of the freshmen to the—" she began to say, but Josef cut her off.

"Oh, and if you would like to observe the afternoon rehearsal, you are welcome to come under one condition. That you do not speak *at all*." He held up a finger. "Dance must be pure to be fully realized. *Bon*, now Hilda."

He gestured to her, and Hilda pressed her lips together in a smile, watching Josef make his way to the door, followed by a small group of upperclassmen. Arching her neck, Vanessa tried to catch a glimpse of Zep.

Instead, she spotted Anna Franko's long golden hair. A large hand was resting on the small of her back. Was it the same hand that had closed over her mouth in her dorm room, that had blindfolded her, that had bandaged her foot so gently?

Hilda turned to the rest of the students. "Gather your things and follow me. We're going upstairs."

Vanessa stood with everyone else, her eyes traveling up Zep's arm to his shoulder, his neck, the stubble on his jaw. His face was obscured by the other dancers around him, and she imagined that he was still wearing that white hollow mask as he pressed her to him in her room.

Her hair was still damp from running in the rain, the long red locks matted to her neck. Pushing it away, Vanessa turned to pick up her bag. Suddenly she could smell his aftershave. Its sharp scent tickled her nose. Confused, she looked toward the door, but Zep was already gone.

"Do you smell that?" she asked Steffie.

But when she spun around, Steffie was gone too, and Vanessa found herself inches away from a boy. Startled, she leaped back.

"Smell what?" he asked.

He was almost as tall as Zep, though fairer, with a clear gaze and a mess of sandy hair. Unlike most of the other guys in the room, he was actually wearing normal clothes: a pair of chinos and a loose blue polo. Preppy, Vanessa thought with approval, making a mental note that none of his clothing consisted of: a) tight denim, b) spandex, c) nylon, or d) a white undershirt the same size as her tank top. He would have been cute if not for his eyes, which were a cold blue as he studied her.

And then the faint smell of aftershave floated through the air again. To her surprise, it seemed to be coming from the boy in front of her. "You?"

"Excuse me?" he said.

Vanessa took a step back. "I—I'm sorry," she stammered. "I thought you were—"

"A friend?" he said, raising an eyebrow.

Vanessa looked away, suddenly uncomfortable.

"You dropped this," he said, holding out a small makeup bag.

"Thanks," she said, taking the bag and pushing her hair behind one ear. She was about to leave when he spoke.

"Is your name Vanessa?" he said.

She froze. "How did you know?"

"I recognize you." He seemed to be looking through her, as if when he saw her face, all he saw was someone else.

"Margaret," Vanessa whispered.

The boy nodded.

"Who are you?" Her eyes darted around her to make sure no one else was listening, but everyone had already left the studio.

"Justin," he said. "We were the same year. She used to talk about her sister, Vanessa."

"She did?" Vanessa said. If Margaret were still here, she would have been a senior.

"She was an amazing dancer, and so pretty," Justin said, eyeing Vanessa as if he were talking about her, not her sister. "But also pretty vacant. Always scared of failure."

Vanessa flinched. "Vacant?"

But Justin didn't seem to realize that he was insulting Margaret. "Toward the end she couldn't be bothered to talk to regular people. She kept warning us that she was writing everything down in her journal, but nobody ever found it."

Journal? If her sister had ever written one, it would have come home with all of her belongings.

Justin shook his head. "I think the journal was all in her mind. Though she kept saying everything would come out in the end somehow."

"What would come out?" Vanessa searched his face, as if the answer to what happened to Margaret were hidden beneath his heavy brow.

Justin threw his bag over his shoulder. "I don't know."

"But you must have an idea. It sounds like you were close to her, at least for a short amount of time."

"Look, I hate to be the one to break it to you, but your sister wasn't . . . all there. There was a point when nothing she said made any sense."

His words stung. "Right," she said tersely. "Well, it was nice meeting you."

Justin walked outside, falling in step with a girl who was about his height and heavyset—a rare sight for ballet school— with wide hips and bushy chestnut hair. She leaned in to hear Justin's whisper, nodded slightly, then glanced at Vanessa over her shoulder.

Vanessa glared at her. She had seen the girl before; she was hard to forget in a school where most of the students were half her size. She was always hanging around another boy who looked just like her.

Vanessa looked away. When she looked up again, Justin and the girl were gone.

"Nicola. She's one of the Fratelli twins," said Steffie as they filed through bright hallways on their way to a class with Hilda. "Her brother is Nicholas."

"She can't be a dancer," said Vanessa, trying to imagine the large girl in a jeté. "She's so . . . big."

Steffie pressed her books to her chest. "Apparently, they're supposed to be pretty good, even though the witless call them the 'Fat-elli' twins."

"That's so not funny," Vanessa said.

"And yet," Steffie said, "it sticks."

Her thoughts returned to her sister. Had she really gone crazy? If something terrible had happened at school, why didn't she just tell someone? Why hide it away in her diary? Could Justin have been right, and Margaret had run away—not because she *wanted* to be lost, but because she already was?

"Vanessa?" Steffie said, breaking into her reverie. "What are you thinking about?"

"Nothing," Vanessa said, and followed her to the studio at the end of the hall. The room was blond and polished, with wall-to-wall mirrors that made it look far larger than it actually was. Most of the freshman and sophomore class was already assembled by the barre, wearing the school uniform for dance class: black leotards and pink tights for the girls, white shirts and black tights for the boys. Vanessa was about to join them when she spotted Justin by himself, warming up.

She must have been staring, because suddenly his eyes met hers. Quickly, she looked away and lined up next to Steffie, TJ, and Blaine.

Hilda paced at the front of the studio, favoring her left leg—she had a slight limp. On her command, the students went through the basics, so familiar to Vanessa that her legs moved almost reflexively.

"Tendu!"

"Dégagé!"

"Grand battement!"

"Plié!"

Hilda observed the students, the arrhythmic sound of her limp punctuating their steps.

Vanessa could see the back of Justin's head bobbing up and down ahead of her, his sandy hair matted to his neck with sweat. His form was pretty good, she thought. So why was he in the underclassmen rehearsal if he was a senior? Maybe he hadn't been the same year as Margaret. Maybe he'd made everything up.

By late afternoon the rain had slowed, and the sky was a rolling gray. Steffie caught up with Vanessa as she walked toward the exit. "That was intense," she said, pulling on an oversized sweatshirt.

"Yeah," Vanessa replied. "I guess Hilda isn't as timid as she seems."

"I meant *you*. You were staring straight ahead the entire time."

"Oh," Vanessa said. "I was just . . . lost in my thoughts, I guess."

"Must have been a pretty gripping daydream," Steffie said. "Are you going to observe the class with Josef?"

Vanessa opened her mouth to answer when Justin pushed past them, brushing Vanessa's arm.

"Pardon." His eyes met Vanessa's for a moment before he lowered his head and ran up the stairs, two at a time. She had to admit—he would have been handsome if it weren't for the arrogant expression that seemed permanently embedded on his face.

Steffie grabbed Vanessa's elbow. "What was that about? He looked like he wanted to kill you. Or throw you against a wall and make out with you." She paused. "Or both."

"Justin. He said he knew my sister. That they were the same year," Vanessa said.

"So why is he in our morning class?" Steffie asked.

"I don't know," Vanessa murmured. "I thought maybe he was lying about being a senior, but now I think Justin might have been the boy in the white mask."

"No way," Steffie said. "The boy in the white mask was nice. This guy—*Justin*—seems like a prick."

"I recognize his aftershave. It's the same."

"It's probably a brand that everyone has," Steffie said. "Eau de . . . handsome-yet-questionably-gay-teenage-male-dancer. Come on, we're going to be late."

The dance floor was still empty when they slipped into the rehearsal studio. It was so quiet that it took a second look for Vanessa to realize that the rows of chairs in the back of the room were already filled with students.

"Remember," Steffie whispered. "No speaking. Josef's rules."

Vanessa scanned the crowd until she spotted TJ. She was nibbling on a packet of Junior Mints and whispering something to Blaine and Elly, her face flushed with excitement. When she saw Vanessa and Steffie, she waved, and the girls squeezed through the throng and wedged themselves in next to them.

Noiselessly, the twelve senior girls in Josef's class filed out onto the floor. Taking their positions, they raised their chins to the light and held steady. Zep, the only boy onstage, stood in the center, his arms outstretched. Vanessa held her breath, transfixed.

"One and two and three and four."

Josef paced in front of them holding a long stick, which he tapped on the wooden floor to keep the beat.

Zep's shadow trembled as he curled his arms inward. He glided across the floor, the light shifting over the contours of his body like the sun rising and falling over an extraordinary landscape. Why couldn't she look away? Something about his dark, steady gaze demanded her attention.

The other dancers arched their backs and braided themselves around him, slowly at first, then faster, like a flock of birds flying in formation. Josef had stopped counting and was now gesticulating wildly, swooping to the left, then low to the right, the dancers following, as if manipulated by his hands.

Vanessa leaned forward. Zep's face shifted in and out of the shadows while he danced alone, without a partner, the role of the Firebird still not cast. Vanessa tried to imagine what it would feel like to lean into his sinewy arms, to feel his hands grip her waist and lift her like a feather into the air; but the only face she could imagine onstage was Margaret's.

A scream interrupted her thoughts.

One of the dancers stumbled midstep, and the others froze. The entire audience turned in Vanessa's direction. Could it possibly have come from her? she wondered, her heart pounding.

And then she heard a gasp.

"I'm sorry," Elly cried from a few feet over. Her face was as pink as her cardigan, which was covered in club soda.

In desperation she turned to see who had spilled it on her. Sitting just behind her was Justin. He gave her an apologetic look but didn't say anything.

Outraged, Josef threw his stick across the room. Vanessa cringed as it clattered against the wall.

"You," he shouted at Elly. "Stand up."

Trembling, she stood.

"What is your name?"

"Elly Pym," she whispered.

Josef began to pace. "What did I tell everyone earlier?" he said. "Tell me, Elly."

Elly's chest heaved.

"I said that you could observe the afternoon lesson, so long as," Josef said, not waiting for an answer, "you didn't speak. Didn't I tell you that?"

Elly gave him a quick nod. She looked like she was about to cry.

"So why did you speak?" he shouted, his face red with rage. "You interrupted the dance; one of your classmates almost fell. Do you know how much damage you could have done?"

"I didn't mean to—"

Josef cut her off. "Silence. A ballerina must learn how to control her body *and* mind."

Though by that logic, Vanessa thought, the dancers shouldn't be affected by someone speaking.

Elly nodded again, her eyes trained on her feet. Vanessa leaned over and squeezed her shoulder.

"As punishment, you will not be attending the Lincoln

Center performance this Friday, and you are forbidden to leave campus until I deem you ready. I'll expect you in my office later, where we can discuss your progress."

Elly looked horrified.

"Did you hear me?" Josef asked sharply.

Elly glanced up. "Yes."

Josef turned, his hands clenched in fists. *"En suite,"* he shouted to the dancers. "One more time from the top."

Vanessa watched him walk to the left of the stage, where he stood with his arms crossed, his face contorted into a scowl. He looked so different from the charmingly rebellious choreographer who had delivered their orientation speech that Vanessa could hardly believe she had found him even remotely charismatic. All she could see now was a bitter man, standing halfway in the shadows, as if the rumors of his mysterious past were still clinging to his shoulders.

That's when Vanessa realized that he still wanted to dance. He was older than the average dancer, though in good shape and not too old to perform. So why couldn't he? What could he have possibly done that was so bad he could never dance again?

CHAPTER FIVE

Mornings arrived with the snap of a leotard, the smooth slip of a pair of tights, and the *shhh!* of the faucet splashing warm water into the sink. A straw unwrapped, and a can of Diet Coke being opened with a hiss. Bobby pins spilled across the counter. The door creaking open and shut, then footsteps. Breakfast was a rushed affair; most chose to skip it.

The girls' dressing room near the dance studio was dusted in talcum powder. Girls flocked around the benches, bending and beating their ballet slippers. Stray ribbons lay curled on the floor like petals.

The morning sounds were like a familiar song as Vanessa made her way to the mirror. They'd been in school for a week; she was beginning to know everyone's faces, and most of their names too. A line of girls—Jessica, Isabelle, Tabitha—wearing pink tights and leg warmers stood in front of the sinks, pinching and powdering their faces.

"Excuse me," Vanessa said, and they parted, letting her squeeze between them.

She splashed her face with water, rubbed her cheeks, and stuck five bobby pins between her lips. She twisted her mane of long red hair until it was tight against her head and fastened it in place with pins. She tilted her head left, then right, to make sure it was secure. With damp fingers, she brushed back the wisps.

Her friends were sitting on one of the long wooden benches that lined the dressing room, breaking in their pointe shoes. Vanessa dropped her bag and sat down beside Steffie, whose black hair was pulled back into an impeccable knot.

"It sounds like it was just an accident," she was saying to Elly and TJ as she unrolled a package of gauze. "He was dating the prima ballerina in Paris, but they fought all the time. Apparently, he has a really bad temper."

Since her meeting with Josef, Elly had seemed pensive, distracted. She'd said that Josef had reprimanded her for her inability to control her reactions. If she wanted to make it as a dancer, he'd said, she would have to learn how to be silent, and in keeping with his warning, Elly refused to divulge any other details about their meeting.

After Josef's outburst at rehearsal, Vanessa and Steffie had gone back to the dormitory and looked him up online, trying to figure out what the scandal was that had forced him out of his company in Paris.

"It went down like this," Steffie continued. "During a

rehearsal the other dancers heard Josef and the principal ballerina arguing backstage. Then, in the middle of a dance, the
ballerina leaped into an écarté, only instead of completing
the lift, Josef dropped her."

Vanessa shuddered, imagining the ballerina diving into the
air where Josef's arms were supposed to catch her. But instead,
she slips through his grasp and drops to the hardwood floor
with a loud crack. The scene had been haunting her ever since
she and Steffie had read about it.

TJ's eyes widened and Elly gasped, covering her mouth
with her hand.

"She broke an ankle and was out for the rest of the season.
She claimed Josef dropped her on purpose. He denied it, but
the company still forced him out. Intentional or not, no one
wants a lead dancer who drops girls onstage."

"What happened to the ballerina?" Elly asked.

"She recovered and started dancing again, but slowly went
insane. Really paranoid, like everyone was out to get her. She
eventually quit and disappeared."

A somber silence followed.

Steffie tied her ribbons around her ankle in a tight knot. "It
could have been just an accident," she said. "In Cincinnati,
there were lots of girls who tried to sabotage me for no reason
other than that they were haters. That's one of the reasons I
wanted to come here."

"But he dropped her," Elly said. "And you saw him at that
first rehearsal. What he said to me. He's . . . evil."

Steffie put a hand on her hip. "To be honest, you did *scream* when he specifically told us not to talk. I'm not siding with the guy, I'm just saying that we don't know what happened."

Elly shrank back, and TJ rolled her eyes. Steffie threw the rest of her stuff in her bag and turned to Vanessa. "Everyone's saying Josef might observe us today," she said. "And he might even be scouting for roles in *The Firebird*."

"Oh?" Vanessa said, trying to sound excited. Emptying her bag, she took out a pair of new pointe shoes, the satin still pink and clean, and began bending them.

"Do you think any of us will get cast?" TJ said. "I mean, obviously not in a lead role, but maybe something better than just corps?"

Elly sat sullenly by the wall. "Probably not me," she said softly. "I blew it already."

"Just dance well," Vanessa said. "Nothing else matters."

Elly nodded, though Vanessa could tell she wasn't convinced.

"I wonder if all of the roles will be taken by seniors," Steffie said. "Did you see the way they danced in Josef's rehearsal? I could barely see their feet, they moved so quickly. I wonder how much Red Bull they drink before class."

TJ stood in front of the mirror, examining her body in profile. She pinched her side and sucked in, puckering her big lips for show. Vanessa laughed.

"That's better," TJ said with a smile, though her eyes lingered on the tiny pouch on her belly. "I bet Anna Franko will be cast as the Firebird," she said, pinning loose wisps of hair to her head, and then anchoring the whole curly mess with hairspray.

Steffie coughed and swatted the misty cloud away with her hand.

"It only makes sense," TJ continued. "I heard she's one of the best dancers at school. And it can't hurt that she's dating Zep."

"I wouldn't be so sure," Vanessa said, stuffing the toe boxes of her shoes with lamb's wool. "If Josef were going to cast Anna as the Firebird, he would already have done it, like he did with Zep. So there's still a chance."

Steffie gave Vanessa a quizzical look. "How is it that you're so calm?"

Vanessa bit her lip. "What do you mean?"

"You show up twenty minutes after everyone else, with barely any time to get ready, and you're still totally cool. I mean, class starts in, like, ten minutes, and even though I just told you that Josef might be visiting, you've barely even broken in your shoes. Aren't you nervous at all?"

Vanessa shrugged. "I'm just going to do my best, and see how it goes."

Steffie let out an incredulous laugh. "I don't get you, but I envy you."

"You shouldn't," Vanessa said under her breath, but no one seemed to hear her. She gently peeled away the corner of the bandage on her foot. The cut beneath was red and scabbed. Wincing, Vanessa dabbed on a bit of ointment, replaced the gauze, and gently slipped her foot into her pointe shoe.

"I heard that a girl named Chloë was supposed to dance the role of the Firebird," TJ said.

"Why isn't she now?" Vanessa asked.

TJ began tying her ribbons. "She went missing over the summer. Just before school started."

Vanessa's back went rigid. "Like, she ran away?"

"I'm not sure," TJ said. "I'm sorry, Vanessa. I forgot—"

"It's okay. It happened. You don't have to pretend like it didn't." Vanessa stared at her pointe shoe, imagining her sister's initials scrawled into the soles. "Margaret was supposed to play the Firebird, too."

"Everyone says it's a really hard role," Steffie murmured. "They probably just felt too much pressure."

Vanessa nodded, yet she couldn't help but wonder. Was it a coincidence that two girls cast as the lead in *The Firebird* went missing? Maybe there was something strange about the *Firebird* ballet; maybe it was cursed. But as soon as the thought entered her head, she shook it off. *The Firebird* was renowned as a difficult dance. She dipped the toe of her right foot in the box of pale-brown rosin, rubbing it into the smooth sole of her shoe until it was rough enough to grip the waxed floor, then switching to the heel, and finally to her left foot. Steffie, Elly, and TJ did the same, barely speaking until a whistle blew from outside the studio, signaling the start of class.

Hilda was standing at the front of the studio when they filed out of the dressing room, her lips held in a tight frown. "Please line up in front of the mirror."

Vanessa filed in behind Elly and TJ, who both looked nervous as they took their places. Across the room, Blaine waved at her in the mirror. He gave Vanessa a wink and inched closer to the cute boy standing in front of him.

Hilda walked to the corner of the room and turned on the music, a long somber note on the cello. Pacing behind them, she began to dictate commands. "Fifth position. Grand plié. Now relevé!"

With the rest of the class, Vanessa lifted herself onto her toes, the bones of her feet stinging beneath her weight. But she held steady, her face not betraying so much as a wince while she waited for Hilda's direction.

The music wasn't anything she recognized. It was spare and dark, but the notes kept slowing down and then speeding up, collapsing in on themselves until Vanessa thought the sounds were going to burst into chaos. Hilda clapped her hand against her thigh, following its arrhythmic beat. Vanessa glanced at Steffie in the mirror and gave her a befuddled look. They had never been taught to dance to a tempo with no set time. Vanessa closed her eyes and listened to Hilda's tapping, trying to memorize the meter, but it didn't make any sense.

Nonetheless, on Hilda's word, Vanessa began to move, her feet arched and taut as she bent forward, extending her leg like the tail plumes of a bird.

"Now left!" Hilda said. "And hold. Now up, and lift."

Vanessa followed her commands, trying not to think about the strange beat, to feel it in her limbs. Gently, she lifted her right leg. She swept her arms over her head, then out to her sides and held them there until the next command, the arrhythmic beat batting her body around like a wooden doll.

"Good," Hilda murmured as she walked past Vanessa. "Very good."

Vanessa opened her eyes to see TJ in front of her, stepping completely out of the meter.

Hilda walked up behind her and put a hand on her shoulder. "First listen," she said, and tapped the rhythm onto TJ's collarbone. "Now try." But it was no use. TJ's limbs didn't seem to want to stay in place.

She wasn't the only one having problems. Vanessa could hear Steffie breathing heavily behind her. Up ahead, Elly struggled to keep in time, her legs a half beat too slow. The only other person who seemed to get it was Blaine, who had inched so close to the boy in front of him that he could touch the back of his tawny head.

"And now it switches," Hilda said. The music changed tempo again. "Imagine the seeds of a dandelion blowing away in the wind. We are trying to capture the pattern of chaos. One-two, and three and four, five-six, and one . . ."

Vanessa pressed her lids shut, trying to imagine herself as the long stalk of a flower standing in a breezy field.

And suddenly, it made sense.

Her body bent and arched and flexed and curved, her arms pushed this way and that, as if she had lost herself and become the flower.

And then a strange feeling took hold of her.

Her steps became quicker, her limbs seemed to move without her. She glanced at her reflection in the mirror, but it was too blurred to see. The beat of Hilda's clapping seemed to echo her own pulse, and time around her started to thin.

Faster, faster she twirled, her toes curling in their boxes as she spotted. The room began to warp, the floor melting away. Vanessa's classmates faded into a dizzying wisp of colors. Hilda's clapping sounded distant, watery. Her voice slurred.

Margaret, Vanessa thought. *Margaret*.

Hilda's loud clap brought her back to reality. She slowed to a stop and bowed her head, waiting for her eyes to refocus.

"You looked great," Steffie said while the other girls wandered away for a water break. "No one else could finish that turn, but you kept going like you were weightless."

"Just luck," Vanessa said, holding on to the barre to steady herself.

"Okay, that's enough." Steffie lowered her voice. "You're an amazing dancer, Vanessa. Like, *amazing* doesn't even do it justice. Your dancing kicks amazing's ass. When someone compliments you, all you have to do is say thank you. Okay?"

Vanessa gave her a sheepish smile and thought of her mother, who always told her to take a compliment when she was given one. Still, part of her *did* think it was just luck.

"If you don't want her accolades, then I'll take them," Blaine said, poking his head between them. "Those steps were *hard*." He wiped the sweat from his brow, reminding Vanessa that he had been the only other dancer who finished the exercise. "I know how you feel though," he said softly to Vanessa. "Like you're a fraud. Like every time you land a jump or finish a complicated step it's because some outside force helped you do it—not your talent."

Vanessa froze. It was as if Blaine could read her thoughts.

He let his gaze drift to his reflection in the mirror, studying it with a critical eye. "I thought it would go away if I became the best dancer at school. And when that didn't work, I thought it might go away when I got into NYBA, and now I keep hoping that if I just prove myself to Josef and Hilda and get cast in one of the productions, then I'll really feel like I deserve it." Blaine hung his head. "The better you are, the more pressure everyone puts on you to keep being good. And once you're at the top, the fall to the bottom is a lot longer and more painful."

Vanessa nodded but said nothing. She hadn't seen Blaine so sincere, so vulnerable before.

"You're lucky though," he said, filling in the quiet. "You could still be chosen for the Firebird."

Vanessa rolled her eyes. "Yeah, right."

"Unless I'm cast first," he teased.

Vanessa laughed. "You'd make a stunning Firebird," she said.

"Don't you have something to say to me?" Steffie coughed dramatically, reminding Vanessa that she had praised her dancing.

Vanessa took a breath. "Thank you for your compliment."

"See?" Steffie said. "That wasn't so hard." And together they walked to the water fountain on the far side of the room.

Vanessa took a drink, then said, "Have you ever felt things change when you dance?"

Steffie squinted at her. "What do you mean?"

Vanessa glanced around to make sure no one could hear them. "Sometimes when I get all of my steps right, things around me start to blur. Sounds get muddled and colors look like they're melting away. It's like time starts to slow down."

Steffie gave her a hard look. "That's never happened to me."

"Never?" Vanessa asked.

Steffie shook her head. "And this happens every time you dance?"

"Only when I get the steps down perfectly."

"I don't know—" Steffie began to say, but was interrupted by a cough.

Startled, Vanessa looked up to find Hilda right behind them, curiosity illuminating her small eyes. How long had she been there?

"Do you have something you'd like to share with us?" Hilda asked.

"What? Oh, um—no," Vanessa stammered.

"Why don't you share with us a hundred pliés at the barre then," Hilda said, a sour expression on her face, "so you won't waste your breath talking nonsense in class."

Startled at the harshness of the punishment, Vanessa exchanged a glance with Steffie as she walked to the barre and began her pliés, feeling the smooth wood beneath her fingertips, the sweat beading on her neck, the floor pushing back against her toes until her muscles burned. Hilda had brought her back to reality with her irrational punishment, and even though it hurt, Vanessa was relieved to feel the ground beneath her feet again.

CHAPTER SIX

The overhead lights blinked.

"It's time," Steffie said, smoothing her black silk dress.

Vanessa gazed over the balcony at the glass chandelier hanging above the orchestra section while they squeezed through the aisles to their seats. Josef had led them through Lincoln Center, past the Vivian Beaumont Theater and the Metropolitan Opera House, around the magnificent fountain, and into the New York City Ballet—where, if they were lucky, some of them would get to dance one day. The mezzanine inside the theater was crowded with luxury: high heels, expensive perfume, suits and pleats and tasseled leather shoes, carved combs, white mustaches, a shock of red lipstick, and the flash of lace stockings beneath the flounce of a skirt.

"I can't believe we're actually here," Blaine said, fingering the lapel of his suit coat. It was incredibly tight on him, its navy-blue color accented with a bright-pink tie.

"Did you get that in the kids' department at JCPenney?" TJ teased.

"Hey, Ms. Acorn Squash. Don't hate on me because I'm skinny," Blaine snapped, and buttoned his coat.

TJ—whose pleated orange dress *did* make her resemble a fall vegetable—blushed.

"This week lasted forever." Blaine sighed dramatically. "Plus, I haven't even found a boyfriend yet."

"A boyfriend?" Vanessa repeated. She'd barely ever kissed a boy back home, let alone had an actual boyfriend. "It's only been a week."

"I know!" Blaine exclaimed. "I thought it would only take a day. Maybe two." He gave her a wink.

"I honestly thought I was going to die after three toe lessons in a row," TJ added.

"I know," Steffie said, her long chain earrings dangling down to her shoulders like icicles. "It's like learning to dance all over again."

"Or realizing you never learned to dance," TJ interjected. "I suck."

"You don't suck," Vanessa said. "You got in here, didn't you?"

TJ suddenly looked sheepish. "Yeah, I guess," she said, reminding Vanessa of the way her roommate had reacted when she'd revealed that her parents were on the board of trustees. At first it made TJ seem sort of lucky, but now Vanessa wondered if being connected wasn't more of a burden. If TJ felt like she didn't truly earn her spot at NYBA.

"If Elly were here, she'd say that everyone has something they're truly great at," Steffie added. "You just have to find that thing."

The four of them fell quiet, feeling Elly's absence. For a few days, Elly had grown more and more withdrawn, and it showed in her dancing too. She'd been making elementary mistakes, and Hilda and Josef were noticing.

"What's she doing tonight?" TJ asked, brushing back her curls.

"She said she was going to stay in and read," Vanessa murmured, and glanced down at her playbill for the opening night of the New York City Ballet production of Tchaikovsky's *Sleeping Beauty*. "She seemed so sad when she told me. She really wanted to come."

"Speaking of sad," said Blaine, breaking the mood, "I went on a date with Andreas. That angular blond guy in our class? You know, the one who's friends with those two scrawny brunettes from Brooklyn?"

TJ gave him a sympathetic look. "Didn't go well?"

Blaine looked forlorn. "He has this bizarre obsession with Wagner. After dinner, he made me listen to the entirety of *Die Walküre* on his surround-sound speakers, and let me tell you— there's only so much horn this southern boy can take in one night, and that about filled my quota for the *year*."

TJ grimaced, but Vanessa and Steffie only laughed at the image of Blaine enduring Wagner at full volume.

"Watch your dress," he added as Vanessa climbed the stairs. "You have to kick and then take a step," he said, flourishing an imaginary gown. "That way you won't stomp on that lovely lace hem." He paused. "Don't ask me how I know that."

"Thanks," Vanessa said, tossing her hair over her shoulder.

Vanessa scanned the rows, looking for their seats, when she felt someone watching her.

A dissonant chord floated up from the orchestra pit as the musicians tuned their instruments. It mounted until it silenced the audience.

Slowly, Vanessa's gaze wandered to the opposite aisle, where Zep stood, his face sharp as forged metal. He was wearing a sleek black suit and a tie, his broad chest rising and falling as if it were going to burst through the fabric. His hair was slicked back, giving him a dapper look that was incredibly appealing— like a young Fred Astaire, only way hotter, just as he's about to whisk Ginger Rogers onto the dance floor. Zep was beautiful, that much was undeniable, and hearing Blaine talk about going on a date made her wonder what it would be like to sit down with Zep for a fancy dinner in a romantically lit restaurant and get to know each other properly.

Vanessa blinked and studied him again. One hand was hidden in a pocket; the other held a playbill. Anna Franko clutched his elbow, but his eyes were locked on Vanessa.

She felt him studying her face, her neck, her collarbone. She flushed, but she couldn't look away. The distance between them seemed to collapse, and it no longer mattered that they had never met, or that Anna Franko was standing beside him, her eyes narrowing as she gazed from Zep to Vanessa. It already felt like they were intimate, that they had known, maybe even loved, each other in some previous life.

Vanessa shuddered as the screech of the orchestra peaked and then came to an abrupt stop. Zep gave her the beginning of a smile.

In a moment of panic, Vanessa lowered her eyes and turned to follow Steffie, who was making her way into the row. She was being ridiculous. Zep didn't love her. He had a girlfriend.

They found their seats toward the middle, next to a group of girls from their toe class. The red plush seats were soft against Vanessa's thighs through the thin fabric of her dress.

"It's really awful Elly couldn't come," TJ said, gazing at the general splendor of the audience. She pointed to a man wearing a tuxedo, who was escorting a woman in a silk gown. "Everyone here is just her type."

"Maybe Josef will let her come next time," Vanessa said, smoothing out her dress.

"Excuse me," a deep voice said.

The people at the end of her row stood for Zep and Anna, who were pushing toward her. Vanessa looked straight ahead and swallowed, watching in the periphery as they took their seats on the other side of Steffie, just two seats away from Vanessa.

The lights dimmed. A lone violin quivered. The audience applauded as the conductor reached the podium. Out of the corner of her eye, Vanessa caught Zep stealing a glance at her. She smiled to herself just as the curtain rose.

The dancers swept across the stage in a flurry of toile, satin, and ribbons, moving more swiftly and lightly than any earthly beings. Vanessa didn't know how long it lasted, only that it was too short. There was something truly remarkable about the ballet. Even though Vanessa wasn't sure she wanted to be a ballerina, watching a troupe of dancers tell a story with such emotion and elegance, with exquisite music in the background, moved her deeply.

When Vanessa was dancing, she wasn't thinking about her missing sister or her overbearing mother. She could dance things she couldn't find the words to say. Feel emotion she didn't know how to show in everyday life. She could defeat the villain, seduce the prince, enchant the nymphs of the forest, find her true love, and live happily forever after, just like that.

Gazing at the dancers onstage, Vanessa wondered if they ever felt that ballet was a release from the real world. Vanessa thought about what Justin had said—how her sister said she was keeping a journal, how she didn't fit in. Maybe there wasn't anything sinister about Margaret's disappearance. Maybe she had simply . . . escaped.

When the last act ended and the music stopped, she felt as if she had been woken from a dream. The dancers gazed out at the audience and bowed, bridging the gap between their world and Vanessa's. The curtain fell, the applause slowed, and Vanessa sat back in her seat with a sigh.

Around her, as everyone began to filter toward the exits, Vanessa and her classmates stayed put. But when TJ raved about the ballerina's grand jeté in the final act, Blaine brushed her off. "Please," he said. "Any of us could do it ten times better. Didn't you see all of the mistakes she made?"

Steffie nodded in agreement, and though Vanessa had to admit she'd noticed some blunders too, she didn't mind. It was still lovely. While they bickered, Vanessa overheard Anna arguing with Zep in a low, furious voice. She leaned on her armrest, trying to make out what they were saying, but before she could catch anything, Anna stood up. Shooting Vanessa a livid look, she stormed down the aisle and through the doors.

"Is it just me, or does it seem like all the upperclassmen already hate you?" Steffie asked.

"Not *all* of them," Vanessa said, motioning to Zep.

Steffie's eyes lit up. "You're kidding," she said, lowering her voice.

Before Vanessa could respond, Josef strode up the stairs and stood against the balcony railing. Unlike everyone else, who had dressed up for the occasion, he was wearing a pair of dark jeans, a black V-neck shirt, and a wool scarf, which Vanessa guessed was the extent of his formal attire. As he approached, he yanked off his scarf, his face drawn into a scowl.

"I trust you all enjoyed the show," he said, sounding almost angry. "But not too much, for in just four years, many of you will be competing with those same dancers for their roles." He gestured over the balcony. "I hope you were paying attention."

The mood grew solemn as they stared at the theater—its marble columns and vaulted ceilings seeming all the more magnificent without an audience. The drawn curtains and abandoned music stands in the orchestra pit sent a chill down

Vanessa's skin as she realized she could be looking into her future: The musicians would tune their instruments, the curtains would pull back, and the spotlight would find Vanessa alone on the stage. And as the music started, a male dancer would appear in the wings . . . That had always been Margaret's dream, not hers, but perhaps all of this could belong to her too.

"*Bon*," Josef said, interrupting her reverie. "Let's head backstage."

They followed Josef downstairs, through a narrow white corridor that led to the dressing rooms. The hallway was bustling with people—stagehands balancing tall stacks of costumes, assistants carrying food and water, and dancers, their faces thick with makeup.

They all seemed to know Josef. He whispered something in one girl's ear, and she waved everyone to the back, where a group was gathered around the male lead and the principal ballerina.

"Dmitri," Josef said to the male dancer with a little bow. "Beautiful work."

Dmitri gave him a stiff nod. "The dancers were a beat off in the closing scene," he said in a Russian accent. "But I think I pulled it together."

"The prince of the show, as always," Josef said. His smile faded when he turned to the ballerina. "And Helen."

She gazed at him nervously, but instead of congratulating her, Josef turned his cheek. "You've shown us how important it is to keep learning," he said, his voice cold.

Steffie nudged Vanessa. "Oh snap," Blaine said under his

breath. TJ let out a muffled laugh, eyes gleaming at the drama.

Josef betrayed the slightest hint of irritation, but quickly smiled as if nothing had happened. *"Et voilà, Helen le magnifique,"* he said, with a bite of sarcasm. "And a graduate of the New York Ballet Academy, no less. How long ago was it, just two years?" Josef gave her a level gaze, as if challenging her, but her eyes were trained on the ground. "Well," Josef said, clasping his hands together, "as was probably obvious to everyone in the audience, Helen had a rough night."

Helen's eyes met Vanessa's by chance, and she seemed startled, as if Vanessa looked familiar. Suddenly she turned and stormed down the hall, slamming her dressing-room door behind her.

An uneasy silence ensued. Three girls started whispering near the back, and a few older boys chuckled. Even Zep looked uncomfortable as he stood near Josef, his face half-obscured by the shadows.

Josef turned to the group of students. *"Bon,* who has questions for Dmitri?"

Blaine raised his hand. "Who was your idol growing up?"

Dmitri scoffed. "I didn't need one," he said. "I was my own idol."

A sophomore girl wearing a puffy feather dress raised her hand. "Who is your favorite dance partner?" she asked.

Dmitri rolled his eyes. "I prefer to dance alone. Less complications."

"How do you keep that great shape?" Blaine blurted out.

Unable to control herself, TJ snorted, making half the room break up in laughter.

"I don't know what you mean. I have always been this shape," Dmitri said.

As the questioning went on, Vanessa noticed a few students leaving. Steffie nodded, shot a glance at TJ and Blaine, and together they ducked behind the crowd and snuck down the hall.

Unsure whether Josef would follow them, they ran down a stairwell to the practice room that Josef said they would eventually use to rehearse for *The Firebird*. To their relief, the metal door was unlocked, and Steffie pushed it open and flipped on the lights, illuminating the room in a wan yellow.

It was larger than any practice room they'd ever seen, with a circle of blackened varnish on the center of the floor. Vanessa traced the edge with her shoe, pulling back when she realized it was leaving an ashy residue.

"Look," Steffie said, her voice echoing.

Vanessa spotted her by the far wall. It was entirely black, save for a series of odd white silhouettes.

"They painted shapes of people on the wall," Steffie said.

Vanessa approached, skimming her fingers across the surface. She raised her hand to her face. Her fingers were covered in black ash.

"They didn't paint them on," she said, gazing up at the white silhouettes. "Those shapes are the only places where the paint didn't scorch. The rest of the wall was burned black."

Suddenly TJ and Blaine were beside her, touching the silhouettes.

"You're right," Steffie said, sniffing the ash on her fingertip, and recoiling at the smell. "It's totally scorched." She looked to Vanessa. "But how? A fire this big would have burned the entire building down."

Vanessa wandered to the center of the room and knelt by the black smudge on the floor. It was ash, the same as that on the wall. But if the fire had started in the center of the room, why were the rest of the floor and the other walls clean?

Standing, she pressed her fingers together, feeling the grit on her skin. "I don't know," she murmured.

But before she could say more, a loud pop echoed and the lights shut off, engulfing the room in darkness.

Chapter Seven

The darkness seemed to shift around her. Or was it her imagination? She couldn't see the silhouettes on the walls anymore, yet she could feel them around her as if they were real people, holding their breath. Vanessa backed away, one step, then another, until a hand brushed against her lips. Unable to help herself, she screamed.

To her surprise, the shadows screamed back.

"Get off me!" Blaine shrieked, swatting her away.

Relieved to hear his voice, Vanessa said, "It's just me." She heard TJ chuckle uneasily behind him.

"What happened?" Vanessa murmured, almost to herself.

"The light switch doesn't work," Steffie said from somewhere off to the right. "Maybe it blew a fuse."

"Maybe it's fate, telling us we're never going to be in the spotlight," TJ said.

"Or maybe someone was watching us," Vanessa whispered.

"Let's get out of here," Blaine said, still shaken.

Across the room, Steffie opened a door, and a thin seam of light widened into a broad pane across the floor. The shadows around it seemed unnaturally still, as if the walls were holding their secrets.

"Come on!" Blaine said. TJ and Steffie emptied out into the hall, glancing up the stairs to make sure no one had caught them sneaking around.

As Vanessa hurried toward them, the door swung shut behind her with a click.

"The fuses didn't blow," Vanessa said, gazing up at the dim lights that lined the stairwell.

"You're right," Steffie replied. "That is kind of weird."

"Do you think anyone followed us?" Blaine said.

"I don't know, but they definitely *heard* you," TJ said with a smirk, but Blaine didn't laugh.

"Oh, come on," TJ prodded. "So what—now you're scared of a dark room and a few creepy stage sets?"

"But there isn't supposed to be a set down there," Steffie said. "It's just a rehearsal room. The real dance is performed on the stage. And anyway, who turned out the lights?"

"So what do you think made those burns on the wall?" Vanessa asked quietly.

Steffie fingered one of her earrings absentmindedly. "I don't know. An accidental fire?"

"How could it even have started? It's a big, empty rehearsal room," TJ said, adjusting the strap of her high-heeled sandal as she climbed the stairs. "And besides, say a fire did somehow start there and was miraculously contained in that room. Don't you think we would have heard about it?"

"Maybe they're trying to cover it up," Steffie said, stopping in front of the door leading to the main theater.

"Maybe it was only a stage set," Blaine said as Vanessa gripped the railing, remembering how the shadows had seemed to shift around her.

"Yeah," she said, and followed Steffie through the door.

They were in the back of the darkened theater. The main stage stood before them, shrouded by the heavy red curtain. A dim beam of light shone out from the projection-booth window in the back, frosting the crimson velvet of the seats in the orchestra section.

Vanessa stared up at the billowing curtain, trying to imagine what it would feel like to stand behind it, when she saw something that made her stop. She reached out and touched Steffie's shoulder.

"Look." She nodded toward the stage. "There's someone there."

Blaine bumped into an empty seat. "Ow!" he cried, but cut it short when Steffie put a finger to her lips.

By the grainy light from the projection window, they could see a girl, standing in the center of the stage in front of the curtain. Her back was turned to them, and all they could see was the outline of her hair, which was wrapped in a tight bun.

Blaine motioned that they should leave, but Vanessa shook her head and approached the stage. She could see the girl's airy tutu, the same one she had worn as she leaped across the stage just an hour earlier. In the dim light, she could just make out the pale skin of her back, punctuated by the thin straps of her leotard, and her shoulders, hunched and trembling. As the girl turned around, Vanessa realized it was Helen, the principal ballerina.

Her eyes were red, and her face was streaked with makeup. Vanessa froze, waiting for Helen to say something. But she didn't seem to see her.

"Hello?" Vanessa said, her voice cutting through the silence.

The ballerina said nothing.

Vanessa took a step closer, Steffie following on her heels. "Excuse me? Are you okay?" She waited until she heard Helen whisper something.

"What?" Vanessa said gently and inched forward. "Is everything all right?"

But as she got closer, Vanessa realized the girl wasn't speaking to her all. Her eyes were sad and glassy, and her lips were quivering as she let out an unintelligible mutter.

"What's she saying?" Steffie whispered, her voice unsteady.

"I don't know," Vanessa murmured. "I don't think she even sees us."

Vanessa glanced back at Blaine and TJ, who gave her urgent looks and mouthed that they wanted to leave. She took another step forward as a voice boomed through the theater.

"What are you doing?"

The ballerina turned, and Vanessa and Steffie followed her gaze to stage left, where Dmitri, the male dancer they'd met earlier, emerged from behind the curtain, the shadows accentuating the contours of his muscles.

"She is not to be disturbed," he said to Vanessa and Steffie. "She is awaiting her punishment for misstepping in tonight's performance. It is not the first time she has had to be punished. There are those who are losing patience with her . . ."

"Punishment?" Vanessa said, but Dmitri cut her off.

"You're not supposed to be here," he said, his eyes dark as he came closer. Vanessa watched as Helen's back went rigid. "The theater isn't open to the public after hours."

"We're students at NYBA," Steffie said. "We came with Josef to see the show and got lost."

Dmitri frowned. "You know where the exit is, so why don't you run along?" He moved across the stage and touched the ballerina's wrist. She flinched and looked away, still weeping.

Steffie grabbed Vanessa's elbow. "Let's go," she said, and pulled her up the aisle toward the exit. Just before they made it out the door, Vanessa glanced over her shoulder, only to see another silhouette emerge from the wings—a man. He walked across the stage like a dancer, and he had a lean physique that reminded her of . . . Josef? But there was no time to tell.

Following Blaine and TJ, they burst through the lobby and out into the thick night air of Lincoln Center. People turned as they ran across the plaza and past the fountain, which was illuminated by lights, the water falling like broken glass.

"What was that about?" Blaine said as they reached the dormitory.

"I have no idea," Steffie said. "Something about punishing the principal ballerina."

"What kind of punishment?" TJ said, trying to catch her breath as they tore upstairs. Her curly hair fell out of its clips and bounced around her face.

Vanessa stopped and smoothed out her dress when they reached their floor, the warmly lit hallway humming with music and chatter. Composing themselves, they headed down the hall to TJ and Vanessa's room, past open doors with girls brushing their hair and filing their nails while they laughed and gossiped. Elly was nowhere to be seen, though Vanessa didn't blame her, considering everyone was talking about the ballet. She meant to knock and see how she was doing, but when they passed her and Steffie's room, the door was shut and the crack beneath it dark. Maybe she was already asleep.

"Helen was really upset," Vanessa said quietly.

"Everyone says she's pretty delicate. Emotionally," Blaine added. "She did miss that beat in the second act. If that had been me, I would have been crying too."

"She missed a couple of beats," Vanessa said. "I didn't think they were huge mistakes."

"Seriously?" Steffie said. "She almost fell over in the middle of a leap. It was impossible to miss." She narrowed her eyes at Vanessa. "Or maybe you were busy watching someone else."

Blaine frowned. "Who?" He looked at TJ, but she was just as confused. "What's she talking about?"

"I have no idea," Vanessa said, lying.

"Okay," Steffie said. "But admit it, I'm right. You were watching him."

"No," Vanessa said. "I was watching the stage."

"You were *facing* the stage," Steffie said with a smile. "But you were thinking about him."

Him, Vanessa thought. She didn't even want to let herself say his name.

And then suddenly, someone said it for her.

"Zep!"

He couldn't be here, on her floor. Could he? Vanessa ran a hand through her hair and turned to see TJ standing in front of their door, holding a piece of paper.

"It's from Zep," she said, looking perplexed. She stared at Vanessa. "And it's—it's for you."

They all gathered around Vanessa, leaning over her shoulder as she read.

> *Vanessa,*
>> *You looked radiant tonight. Nice to see you shine in*
>> *every way.*
>
>> *—Zep*

Vanessa's cheeks flushed as she walked into the room, the others trailing in after her. She imagined Zep coming to her room, knocking on her door, and when he heard no response, reaching into his pocket and scrawling these words. Words he would have told her in person, had she only come home sooner.

"Let me see that," Blaine said, grabbing the note and holding it up to the light. "Is this real?"

"It was tucked into our door," TJ said, as if she still couldn't believe it.

Blaine's mouth dropped. "Zeppelin Gray came to your room?" His voice was so loud that a group of girls outside in the hall stopped talking. Blaine cocked his head toward them. "Yeah," he said to the girls, hissing like a cat. "You heard me correctly. Now mind your own beeswax."

The girls immediately ran away, out of sight.

Vanessa put a hand to her forehead. "Geez, Blaine. You don't have to broadcast it to the world. I mean, what if it was a mistake?"

"A mistake?" His cheeks flushed. Blaine loosened his tie. "It says your name on it and Zep's, together on the same piece of paper!" He fanned himself with the note. "If I didn't like you so much, I'd hate you."

TJ hit him on the shoulder. "What about Anna Franko?" She turned to Vanessa. "Does she know about this?"

Vanessa swallowed. "I don't know."

"Judging from the way she stormed off after the ballet," Steffie said, "I'd say yes."

"But it's just a note," Vanessa said. "And all he did at the ballet was give me a look. It's not like anything happened. I've never even spoken to him." She bit her lip, trying to convince herself, but no one was buying it.

"Yet," Steffie interjected.

"Girl, you better watch yourself," Blaine said.

TJ rolled her eyes. "Oh, please. Anna is so slight I could eat her for breakfast. And I barely even eat breakfast. Just focus on dance. They're all going to hate you anyway, so what's the point in worrying about it. Right?"

"Right," Vanessa said slowly. TJ was right. She hadn't come here to make friends. Having Steffie and TJ and Elly and Blaine was a major bonus, of course. But if she was honest with herself, there was only one reason she'd come to this school in the first place: to find her sister.

She repeated that to herself—*it doesn't matter if Anna hates me, if anybody hates me*—after Steffie and Blaine left. Their floor was a mess, strewn with TJ's books and clothes and accessories. TJ tripped over a small box, then cursed and kicked it aside. Vanessa laughed and changed into a tank top, while TJ combed her hair and hummed a violin concerto.

They both crawled into their beds, but just before TJ reached to turn out the lights, they heard a knock on the door.

Vanessa sat up, her mind spinning. Zep. Could he have come back?

She stood up and was about to answer the door, when TJ whispered, "Your shorts!"

Vanessa looked down. "Thank you!" She was grateful to be spared the mortification of Zep seeing her in tiny boy shorts that were covered in pink cats. After throwing on a pair of leggings and running a hand through her hair, she turned the knob.

But when she opened the door, Steffie was standing there, still in her dress, her eyes wide and confused and . . . *scared*.

She didn't say anything for a moment, as if she were trying to find the right words.

"Steffie? Is everything okay?" Vanessa asked. She could feel TJ's gaze behind her in the dark.

Steffie gave her a blank look. "Elly is gone."

Chapter Eight

Vanessa had never liked going into Steffie and Elly's room.

Sure, she had sat on Elly's frilly cushions, reading magazines or hanging out, but every time she did, she had to push away the memory of Margaret. So when Steffie led Vanessa and TJ back to her room, Vanessa found herself hovering in the hall, not wanting to step inside.

The paint was chipped where the door met the wall, and suddenly Vanessa was overwhelmed with the urge to peel all the layers of paint away, as if her sister's secrets might be hidden underneath.

But all of that faded away when she heard TJ, her voice so soft she almost didn't recognize it. "You *have* to see this," TJ said.

Vanessa looked up to see a sliver of bare wall and Elly's bed stripped down to the mattress. It was dull blue in color, with a big ugly tag sticking out of the bottom—so different from Elly's pink pillows and ruffled comforter. And for a moment, it no longer mattered that the room had belonged to her sister, because now Elly was gone too. Shaking herself back to reality, Vanessa stepped through the door.

TJ and Steffie were standing in the middle of the room. Steffie's side was cluttered with clothes and jewelry and makeup, photographs and prints of dancers decorating her walls. Elly's was empty. Traces of tape were still stuck to the wall where her ballet posters had hung. Dust bunnies gathered under her bed, where her pink satin shoes had been neatly arranged. The only thing left behind was a single bobby pin, tangled with a few pale strands of Elly's hair. Vanessa bent down and picked it up.

"At first, I thought someone had broken into our room and stolen our stuff," Steffie said. "But then I realized that none of *my* things were missing."

"Do you think she left?" TJ said. "Like, moved out?"

"Without telling us?" Steffie said. "Why would she do that? She at least would have waited until we got back. Or left a good-bye note if it was so urgent."

"But what could have been so urgent?" Vanessa asked.

Steffie leaned on Elly's empty desk, staring at the bare shelves, which still had three glittery heart stickers stuck to the side.

"A death in the family?" TJ said. "Who knows?"

"*Someone* has to know," Vanessa said. "Elly couldn't have just moved out of her dorm room without telling anyone."

"Kate," Steffie blurted out. And without another word they slipped into the hall, the door clicking shut behind them.

The resident adviser's room was at the end of the hall. A bulletin board hung on the door, peppered with maps of New York, class schedules, and activity forms. Vanessa knocked.

Kate was on the phone when she answered the door. Behind her, the room glowed with warm, yellow light. Music blared from her computer. A mug of tea sat beside it.

"Hi, guys," she said, covering the mouthpiece of her phone. "What's up?"

"What happened to Elly?" TJ and Vanessa said at the same time.

"What do you mean?" Kate said, looking confused.

"You mean you don't know either?" Vanessa said, a flutter of nausea tickling her stomach. Beside her, she could hear TJ's breath quicken.

"Oh no," TJ whispered.

"Know what?" Kate said, lowering the phone.

Steffie swallowed. "Elly and all of her things are gone."

Vanessa blinked, remembering the last conversation she'd had with Elly. She was going to stay in and read, she'd said, her voice stilted as if she'd meant to say something else. Had Elly actually meant to say good-bye? A sickening feeling of regret passed through Vanessa, and suddenly she was back at her kitchen table at home, smelling her father's apple pie that had burned to a crisp after the call had come in. She had relived the scene hundreds of times, but now it wasn't just a memory. It was real. Only now, it was Elly.

Vanessa woke up just before dawn. The clock read six o'clock, hours before morning rehearsal. She rolled over, stretching, and tried to recall the strange dream she'd had. Something about Zep, a note, a weeping ballerina. Across the room, TJ's brown ringlets spilled across her pillow. Vanessa watched her shift in her sleep, and all the events from the night before came tumbling back.

When Kate had seen the state of Steffie and Elly's room, she'd just stood there, staring for what felt like hours. Finally she'd said, "I—I have to talk to someone about this. Josef."

"We'll come with you—" Vanessa had started to say, but Kate cut her off.

"No. It's late; you guys should get some sleep. I'll talk to Josef and tell you everything I know when I get back."

After Kate left, the others called Elly's cell phone, but she didn't pick up, so they left her a voice mail. TJ took it the hardest. Ever the lawyers' child, she was certain something terrible, something *criminal*, had happened to Elly, and it took Steffie and Vanessa the better part of the night to calm her down.

Standing up, Vanessa threw on a cardigan and tiptoed down the hall to Steffie's room. Just as she raised her fist to knock, the door swung open.

"Vanessa!" Steffie said, startled. She was holding her dance bag and a bottle of water. Dark circles hung under her eyes.

"You're awake," said Vanessa.

"I couldn't sleep with that empty bed across from me," Steffie said.

"Have you heard anything?" Vanessa asked.

Steffie shook her head. "I knocked on Kate's door again, but she didn't have any news. She said she called Hilda, Josef, a bunch of staff from school—to find someone who had Elly's parents' phone number. Apparently Kate only had Elly's cell on file. She finally reached one of the secretaries, who met her in the office. But just before Kate called, Hilda arrived and took over. Kate said Hilda assured her she would get in touch as soon as she figured out what was going on. And I tried calling Elly again, but got her voice mail. Have you?"

"No."

Not sure what to say next, they stood there in silence, both wondering where Elly had gone.

"Where are you going?" Vanessa asked.

"To the studio. I thought it might help take my mind off things. You want to come?"

"Sure."

The studio was dark when they arrived. They flipped on the lights, their reflections flitting across the waxed floors as they put on their slippers, and, without speaking, walked to the barre. Vanessa lifted her arm in the air and began to warm up in tandem with Steffie. Sweat beaded on her upper lip, and she thought of Zep, of the note he had left her and the way it made her insides flutter. She extended and lowered her leg, once, twice, three times, until her muscles burned and her breath grew short and everything melted away except for the barre, the mirrors, the waxed wooden floors beneath her feet.

When the rest of the freshmen poured into the studio for Saturday morning rehearsal, filling the room with pink and black nylon and the bright hum of chatter, Vanessa and Steffie sat in the corner, sipping water and watching the door, as if waiting for Elly to burst in. Instead, Blaine and TJ entered the room. From the look on Blaine's face, it was clear TJ had filled him in.

"Where were you this morning?" TJ asked, flushed. "For a minute, I thought you had disappeared too."

Vanessa shrugged. "Sorry. I couldn't sleep, so we came to practice."

TJ let out an exasperated sigh and began to stretch. "As if either of you need practice."

"Have you guys heard anything—" Blaine started to say when the door opened.

Josef strutted inside, cleanly shaven, his dark hair combed back. He clapped loudly, the room going silent as he walked to the center of the floor. Vanessa almost didn't notice Hilda, who had shuffled in behind him and was hovering by the door, her plain brown frock blending in with the wall.

Everyone gathered around Josef as he began to speak. "I told you in the beginning that some of you wouldn't make it through the academic year." He paused dramatically. "Many of you didn't believe me."

Everyone in the room seemed to be holding their breath.

"But this morning, I come to you not with warnings, but

with sobering news. One of your classmates, Elinor Pym, has decided to leave our community. She found the pressure and physical rigors too difficult to endure, and opted to explore other endeavors," Josef said. "And perhaps it's for the better."

"What?" Vanessa whispered to Steffie. "After a week? Did she ever tell you that she was stressed out?"

Steffie frowned. "Never."

"Me neither," Vanessa said, while Josef explained that some students weren't emotionally strong enough to withstand the daily stress that ballet dancers endure. But it didn't make sense. Even though Elly had been distant in the past few days, Vanessa had never thought she was planning on dropping out. Sure, she had made a few blunders in the studio, but so had everyone else. She was a strong dancer, always trying to be better, and she was passionate about dance. So why had she left?

"This probably won't be the only casualty of the year. NYBA is not a joke. Many of you won't last long enough to see the leaves change in Central Park." He clapped his hands together. "Let this be a warning to all of you."

People began to whisper, thinking his speech was over, when he said, "Oh, and one more thing. Vanessa Adler."

Vanessa went rigid. Slowly, she raised her hand.

"Ah, there you are," Josef said. "I'd like to see you in my office after classes are over."

All heads turned in her direction, and she heard a few girls muttering in the corner. Not saying a word, she nodded. While everyone else stood and made their way to the barre,

Vanessa sat for a moment, watching Josef disappear through the door.

"Why does he want to see you?" Blaine asked as they lined up.

Before Vanessa could reply, TJ cut in. "If she knew what he wanted to tell her, he wouldn't have called her in the first place, dummy."

"Maybe it's because of last night in the theater," Steffie said. "Maybe he saw us sneaking around, and you—you're the most noticeable."

Instinctively, Vanessa glanced in the mirror at her bright-red hair, now wound into a tight bun. Steffie had to be right. Why else would Josef want to talk to her? As Hilda began to call out exercises, the heads in front of Vanessa dipped and bobbed in rhythm, the same as every morning, except this time Elly wasn't with them.

The rest of the day slipped away. Vanessa kept scanning the passing students for Zep's metallic eyes, but with no luck. Even on Saturday, the halls were bustling with students. After their afternoon class, Vanessa, Steffie, and TJ caught up with Blaine, who was talking to a tall, athletic boy named Garrett. Blaine giggled as he introduced them, even though nothing was funny, then giggled again when Garrett told him in a deep, confused voice that he'd see him tomorrow.

"Is that your mating call?" TJ teased.

"Hey, at least I'm not padding up for the winter," he said, poking TJ's barely visible love handle.

"Back off," TJ said, a little more irritable than normal. "Don't you know not to tease a girl about her weight?"

"Hey," Steffie interrupted. "Have you guys heard from Elly?"

Blaine and TJ went silent.

"I think we should talk to Kate," Steffie said. "Maybe she has more information."

"I hope so," Blaine said. "Because what Josef said made zero sense."

As they made their way to the dormitory, Vanessa slowed her pace. "Guys, I can't go," she said.

Steffie put a hand on her hip. "Why?"

"Josef, remember?" Vanessa replied. Before she could say anything more, Vanessa's cell phone vibrated in her pocket. She took it out, hoping it was Elly, only to see her mother's name blinking on the screen. Her friends looked at her expectantly, but Vanessa only shook her head.

She shrugged and backed away, when in the distance, she caught a flash of lustrous eyes. Vanessa froze, and her heart began to race. Zep. He was a few yards away, his head just visible through the crowd of students.

She lowered her hand, letting her cell phone go to voice mail as she walked toward him. *Hi Zep!* she said to herself, practicing, and then shook her head. *I got your note*, she whispered in a sexy tone, but that just sounded silly.

She took a breath and reminded herself to act natural. But just as she stepped toward him, Anna materialized, her hand reaching for Zep's. She could see Zep talking to Anna, his face almost guilty. Anna's pink lips were pursed in anger. She slid her hand from Zep's and gesticulated wildly, and to Vanessa's dismay, Zep grabbed her hand and held it. *I'm sorry*, his lips said.

Unable to watch anymore, Vanessa spun around and wove through the crowd, taking the long route to Josef's office so she wouldn't have to see them. What was Zep playing at, leaving her a note and telling her she looked beautiful when he was clearly still seeing Anna?

Her phone began vibrating again, and this time, she picked up.

"Vanessa?" At her mother's shrill voice, Vanessa pulled the phone away from her ear. "Is that you? Why did it take you so long to answer?" Not sure what to say, Vanessa just stood there.

"Vanessa, are you there?" her mother's tinny voice echoed through the cell phone. "Why don't you say something?"

Vanessa swallowed, trying to appear calm, like someone who hadn't just seen the boy she liked hold another girl's hand. Like someone who wasn't about to go see the head choreographer to be expelled from the most prestigious ballet school in America. *Expelled*, she thought, her throat suddenly dry. *Was that even possible?*

"Vanessa!" her mother screeched.

"Yes, I'm here, Mom," she said. "I had a bad connection."

But her mother barely listened. "I've been calling and calling, but you never pick up. What's going on? Is everything all right?"

"Stop worrying. Everything's fine. I'm sorry I haven't called you back, I've just been busy. They announced which ballet we'll be performing and it's *The Firebird*."

"*The Firebird?*" her mother said. "The same one Margaret was supposed to be in?" Before Vanessa could answer, her mother continued. "You haven't been cast yet, have you?"

"No, not yet . . ." Vanessa lowered her voice.

This seemed to cheer her mother up. "Well, maybe it's for the better," she said. "You need to focus on your schoolwork. How's that going, by the way?"

"It's fine."

"You sound upset," her mother said. "You know you can come home at any time. Whenever you're ready. If you don't get cast, we can always enroll you in the public school here. The teachers are wonderful. I ran into one of them in the grocery store the other day, and she started telling me about their freshman curriculum—"

"Mom, I'm fine here. Things are going great."

"What did you say? It sounds like you're walking down stairs."

"I said things are going great. I'm—I'm going to the studio. To practice my exercises," Vanessa lied.

"Exercises? Maybe you should take a break. Go to the library."

"Okay, Mom, I'll keep that in mind," she said. After saying good-bye, she hung up. Vanessa stared at her cell phone. Still no response from Elly. Quickly, she dialed her number and listened as it rang, once, twice, three times. Then the sweet sound of Elly's southern drawl, saying that she wasn't available to take her call.

"Elly, it's me, Vanessa. I just wanted to make sure you're okay. You don't have to explain or anything. I just want to know you're all right." Vanessa hesitated, as if waiting for Elly to cut in. When she didn't, she hung up.

Josef's office was tucked into the first floor of the main hall. The dark wooden door was cracked open when she arrived, a dim light emanating from within. Catching a glimpse of a messy desk covered with papers, she knocked. "Josef?" she said, her voice wobbly. When no one answered, she pushed open the door.

The office was unnaturally still. A thick haze hung in the air, and the pungent smell of smoke tickled her nose. The shades were drawn, barring all light except what came from an old lamp, which flickered in the corner as if its bulb were about to burn out.

Vanessa took a step inside, still holding her cell phone.

The walls were covered with black-and-white photographs of Josef as a young dancer and autographed posters from famous ballerinas. She saw a wooden filing cabinet whose top drawer was ajar, revealing a row of files. Student files, she thought. For the briefest moment she considered searching for hers, but then came to her senses. Josef could walk in at any moment. The top of the cabinet was lined with trophies covered in a layer of dust. She studied them, until she noticed a gate leading to a darkened room lined with books. A library, she thought, and out of curiosity, tried the latch. It was locked. She turned to face the desk, behind which stood a tall pendulum clock, when she realized that the smoky smell had gotten stronger.

On Josef's desk, several odd-looking blocks of rosin were stacked beside a sketchbook and a metronome. They looked almost like the rosin Vanessa rubbed on her pointe shoes, except these were darker, almost amber in color, and translucent. Vanessa glanced over her shoulder to make sure no one was looking, then picked up one of the blocks. It was heavier than she expected, and sticky to the touch. Pinching it with two fingers, she held it up and sniffed it.

Her nose was overwhelmed with the smoky stench of burning sap. Thrusting it away, Vanessa felt the twinge of a sneeze. She crinkled her nose and closed her eyes, willing it to pass.

"Please do not play with my things."

Vanessa's heart nearly stopped.

Josef stood before her, his face contorted with the anger she'd seen once before—when Elly interrupted the rehearsal.

She dropped the rosin onto the desk and backed away. "I didn't mean to touch anything. I don't know what was I thinking. I'm really sorry."

Josef's face softened. "It's fine." He walked to the other side of the desk. "Please. Sit." He motioned to a chair across from his.

He waited until Vanessa had settled in before he sat down. A proper gentleman, her mother would have said.

"Vanessa," he said, leaning back in his chair, which creaked beneath him. "Vanessa. What are we to do with you?"

"What—what do you mean?"

"I knew your sister, you know. Margaret."

Vanessa gripped the arms of her chair. Even though she knew that Josef had to have worked with Margaret, the mention of her name made it suddenly real. She could almost imagine Margaret sitting in the exact seat she was in now, her legs primly crossed, her eyes nervously darting to the swinging clock pendulum.

"She was a beautiful—no, marvelous—dancer. So fragile. It seemed a miracle that such a delicate creature could stir the air the way she did."

Vanessa said nothing, even though she knew exactly what Josef was talking about. All she could think of was her sister, the way her slender ankles seemed like they were going to break every time she leaped. But somehow they never did.

"That's what ballet is supposed to do," Josef said, as if reading her thoughts. "To make the impossible seem possible. Your sister was almost there. She almost made us believe . . ." He let his voice trail off. "Ah, but of course you know this."

Vanessa blinked, her eyes suddenly watery with memories.

"You must be wondering why I called you here?"

Vanessa gave him a slight nod.

"I've been watching you."

Vanessa felt her heart drop. So he had seen her in the theater.

"Your form is perfect, you clearly have practiced all of your steps, yet when you perform them, it's as if they're natural, unchoreographed, flowing out of you like breath. Even your barre exercises look like art."

Vanessa's lips parted in disbelief. Did she just hear what she thought she'd heard?

"The legs," he said, motioning to her muscular thighs. "The

wild look in your eyes. The hair. You dance like you're a feral animal." He shook his head. "You're nothing like your sister, but you could be better. I think—" He held up his finger. "I think you could be tremendous. Frightening, but tremendous."

His dark eyes rested on her, waiting for her response, but all Vanessa managed was a hoarse, "What?"

Josef laughed. "You do not think so?"

"No—I—it's just that I thought you were going to expel me."

Josef raised his eyebrows with amusement. "Expel you?" He let out a chuckle. "See? Margaret never would have said this to me. You *are* fierce." He stood, looming over her. "But you are fierce in the wrong way. You have a passion for life, but not for dance. Don't deny it, I can see it in your face. You don't love it like the others do."

Embarrassed, Vanessa stared at her lap. How could he see all that?

"The Firebird would have been Margaret's role, had she stayed on at NYBA. I know I told the class that most of the roles would go to upperclassmen, but I'm still looking for a lead ballerina."

Vanessa's heart skipped a beat. Unaccountably, her thoughts flashed to Zep, his angular face, his tall, muscular form.

"Your dancing is impressive for your age, but even your perfect form cannot hide your lack of passion. In that regard, you have a long way to go before you fill your sister's shoes. It is almost as if you don't care."

Vanessa sank back in her chair, all of the hope dissipating from her chest.

"But if you do, somehow, find a way to transcend yourself in the coming weeks, and let the dance fill you with the kind of passion a leading ballerina must harness within her, I would be happy to consider you for a role in the ballet."

A role in *The Firebird*? Considering she came to Josef's office preparing to be expelled?

"Thank you, Josef," she said, beaming. "I—I just have a lot of things on my mind. But I can let them go; I know I can."

"You don't have to let them go," said Josef. "You just have to use them. For us, life and dance are not separate. Dance your life."

"Right," Vanessa said. "I'll do my best."

"Good," he said as she backed out into the hall. "I look forward to seeing it."

After the door clicked shut behind her, Vanessa ran down the hall, no longer able to contain her excitement, and let out a loud "Yes!"

"Shh!" a secretary scolded as she walked by, carrying a stack of files. But Vanessa didn't care. She ran up the stairs, trying to imagine the look on her friends' faces when she told them what had happened.

But halfway to the dormitory, she slowed to a stop. Something was missing. She checked her bag, and her wallet and ID were there. That's when she realized.

Her cell phone. She had been holding it when she entered Josef's office. She'd probably left it on the desk when she picked up the amber rosin. She made her way back downstairs and was about to knock on his door when she heard muffled voices. Inching closer, she pressed her ear against the door.

"And what of Vanessa?" a woman said. Vanessa recognized Hilda's voice.

"She isn't perfect," Josef said. "But she has real potential."

"Her steps are a little hasty," Hilda said. "It makes me wonder if her heart is in it, or if she is just rushing through the motions."

"After my talk with her today, I think things will be different," Josef said.

Hilda grunted. "You always say that."

"Vanessa is different. I can feel it. She has a fire in her."

"That's just her hair," Hilda said with a laugh.

"No, it's something more. There have been so many who have not lived up to their potential. Like Helen. Such a disappointment. I just hope Vanessa won't turn out like her sister," Josef said, his voice suddenly bitter. Startled, Vanessa gasped and went rigid. Josef had spit the words out as if he detested Margaret.

"Wait," Hilda said. "I heard something."

From inside, a chair creaked.

Vanessa's cell phone would have to wait. The sound of Hilda's limping gait grew closer. Soundlessly, Vanessa slipped around the corner into a shadowed alcove by the janitor's closet, where she could just see as Hilda threw the door open, looking left, then right. Vanessa pressed herself against the wall and held her breath. Across the way, a group of students ambled past, shouting and laughing. Hilda gave them a grumpy look before retreating back into Josef's office, the door shutting behind her.

CHAPTER NINE

As September ripened into October, the trees that lined Broadway burst into a fiery red, forming a brilliant canopy over the sidewalk. Vanessa and Steffie walked below them in the crisp autumn breeze, each sipping an iced tea. Last month when Elly disappeared, the leaves had still been green.

Vanessa still couldn't understand why Elly had left so suddenly without saying good-bye. Why hadn't she told them how she'd been feeling? Vanessa had called and texted her dozens of times, leaving her voice mails until the box was full. She'd e-mailed and messaged her on Facebook—they all had—with no response.

"Sometimes I wonder if we were even really friends," Vanessa said. "Maybe we never knew the real Elly."

"Don't say that," said Steffie. "Of course we knew her."

"Then why didn't she trust us enough to confide in us?" Vanessa said, remembering how she'd felt when Margaret had disappeared.

"I think she's just in a bad place right now. I mean, she hasn't even updated her Facebook page since she left. Can you imagine quitting dance? It would be like starting over again."

Vanessa took a sip from her tea, unsatisfied. Steffie's words made sense, but they still didn't explain Elly's disappearance.

"Look at this," Steffie said, catching an orange leaf and spinning it by its stem. "Even the trees are starting to remind me of *The Firebird* and how I'm not going to be cast. It's like the entire city is trying to stress me out."

"I know what you mean," Vanessa said, balancing on the curb, her eyes drifting across the crowd. "I keep having these warped dreams that Josef casts me, but just before I'm supposed to perform on opening night, I turn into a pigeon." She didn't mention her other dreams of Zep, slipping another note in her door, telling her to meet him at the studio, where he would take her in his arms and then . . . Because the reality was that it had been over two weeks, and Zep still hadn't spoken to her. She'd expected him to at least say hello, but every time she saw him in the halls he'd been with Anna, who clung to his arm as they laughed. It was as if Zep had never written the note to Vanessa in the first place.

Steffie choked on her tea, laughing. "A pigeon?"

"It's not funny," Vanessa insisted. "I know it's crazy, but I can't stop thinking about what I heard Josef say to Hilda."

After Vanessa had narrowly escaped discovery outside Josef's office, she left her cell phone there and ran directly to Steffie's room, where she told her everything. The next day before class, Hilda called Vanessa over and handed back her cell phone without a word, her face impenetrable.

"What is Josef hiding?" Vanessa continued. "He seems to know something about Margaret's disappearance. Maybe he knows something about Elly's too. You have to admit they're similar." She knew Steffie had to be tired of the conversation, but she couldn't help it.

Steffie raised an eyebrow. "You want my honest opinion?"

Vanessa nodded.

"I think you're reading too much into it."

Vanessa chewed on her straw, not wanting to admit that Steffie had a point.

"Then what do *you* think Josef was talking about?" Steffie pressed. "That he was involved in Margaret's running away? That she disappointed him and he whisked her away, and he did the same thing to Elly?"

Vanessa had considered all of those things, late at night, tossing around in her bed while TJ snored. But now that Steffie had spoken them out loud, they seemed absurd.

Suddenly a horn honked. Vanessa gasped as Steffie pulled her back onto the sidewalk just before a taxi would have hit her. The driver slammed on the brakes, cursing out the window.

"What is the matter with you?" Steffie said, loosening her grip on Vanessa's shirt. "You have to stop obsessing about Josef and take a look around you."

Vanessa took a deep breath. "You're right."

Steffie went on. "Plus, in all the conversations we've had about this, you've never even mentioned the most exciting thing Josef said."

Vanessa frowned, not sure what Steffie was talking about.

"That he thinks you have potential as a dancer?" Steffie said. "That if you practice a lot you might even get cast in *The Firebird*?"

"Right," Vanessa said. "But that doesn't make any sense either. There are tons of girls here who are just as good as I am, if not better. So what does Josef see in me?"

"Maybe he just thinks you're good!" Steffie said, exasperated. She threw her hands up. "Maybe when he said you had potential, he actually meant it!"

"Who thinks you have potential?" Blaine said, popping up behind Steffie. He was wearing a tight T-shirt and black pants and clutching a notebook with his name written across it in bubble letters.

Steffie ignored him. "Why does everything have to mean something? Why can't you just take him at his word?"

Blaine scurried behind them. "What are you guys talking about?" he asked. "Take who at his word?"

"Josef," Vanessa said as they pushed through the glass doors and headed inside. "And fine," she continued, looking at Steffie. "Maybe you're right."

Before the start of her last class, Vanessa was still turning Josef's words around in her head when she felt a hand on her shoulder.

She turned, thinking it was Steffie or TJ, only to see Zep looming above her. Startled, she jumped back, dropping her books.

"I—I'm sorry," she said, her face growing red as she bent down to pick them up. Then she felt Zep beside her, his strong arms brushing against hers as he gathered her things.

"No, I'm sorry," he said, his voice deep and sonorous. "I shouldn't have surprised you like that." He clutched her books while students shuffled down the hall around them. "I've wanted to talk to you for weeks now, but I've been so busy with dance and class and . . ."

Anna, Vanessa whispered in her head, completing his sentence.

"Breaking up with my girlfriend." He lowered his eyes.

"Oh," she said, taken aback. "I—I didn't know."

"Now you do," he said, his face vulnerable. He was about to continue when the bell rang, signaling the start of class.

Vanessa glanced over her shoulder at her teacher. "I have to go," she said. "But thank you for the note. And for helping me with my books."

A smile spread across his face as he handed Vanessa her things. "If you really wanted to thank me you could do me a favor."

His hand brushed against hers, making her chest flutter. "That all depends on what it is."

"Meet me Friday night at the fountain," Zep said, his gaze traveling over her body, making her want to melt. Was Zep asking her out on a date?

Vanessa hugged her books to her chest like armor and gave him the beginning of a smile. "And then what?"

"That I can't tell you. You'll just have to take the risk."

"Sounds like a two-part favor to me."

Zep laughed. "Consider me indebted to you then. Eight o'clock?"

Vanessa nodded.

"Until Friday," he said, his eyes soft.

"Friday," she whispered.

Vanessa was still reeling when she slipped through the classroom door and collapsed in the seat next to Blaine and Steffie, who were arguing about which Balanchine ballet was the best while their teacher wrote on the board.

Vanessa was about to tell them about her encounter with Zep when TJ burst through the door and took the empty seat beside them.

"Did you see it yet?" she said.

Steffie and Blaine stopped talking. "See what?" Steffie asked.

"Elly's message."

"Really?" Vanessa asked.

"Where?" Blaine chimed in.

TJ pulled out her phone to display the open e-mail. It was sent to all of them as a group.

Hi, guys,

I'm sorry for not writing to you sooner. I was overwhelmed and homesick, and I knew it would be easier to leave without saying good-bye. I'm trying to

live a normal life now, which means leaving dance and
NYBA behind. If you could help me do this by not
contacting me and reminding me of all I've given up,
I would really appreciate it.

Sincerely,
Elly

None of them spoke as they read and reread her message. It was strange, cryptic; it sounded like her, but then it didn't.

"She must really be freaking out," Blaine said, his voice uncharacteristically somber. "I knew how upset she was after Josef reprimanded her, but I didn't realize it was this bad."

"Why didn't she tell us?" TJ said, leaning on her desk. "We could have helped her."

"Maybe it just wasn't right for her here," Steffie said pensively. "Josef did say that lots of people drop out every year."

"But she was *good*," Vanessa said, thinking of Margaret. "She wanted to be a dancer so badly."

"So do lots of people," Steffie said. "And yet, we're the ones who are still here." Even though Vanessa knew that what Steffie was saying made sense, something about Elly's note didn't seem right.

Their English teacher turned and held up a hand to silence everyone. Mrs. Jasper was an elegant woman, with a long face and wavy, ash-gray hair that reminded Vanessa of a horse's mane.

"Myth and meaning," she said in an aristocratic tone. "Together, they form the backbone of every story, every drama, every character who has ever flitted across the stage and enchanted us with a flounce of a skirt or a beautifully turned leg." She stood behind her desk, gazing out at the class over her sloping nose. "After all, story and character are nothing but parts of myth. No?"

She continued lecturing about the history of mythology and how it gave birth to theater and drama, until the door opened.

Justin stepped inside, his scarf loose around his neck, a pencil stuck behind one ear. He wasn't carrying a bag or books. The Fratelli twins shuffled in behind him, their domineering figures filling the doorway.

He gave Mrs. Jasper a nonchalant gaze, barely acknowledging his tardiness. "We were meeting with Hilda," he said, and handed her a note.

Mrs. Jasper skimmed it, gave him a stern nod, and turned back to the board. Justin peered around the room, searching for a seat, until his cool blue eyes rested on Vanessa.

Quickly, she lowered her gaze. Everything about Justin bothered her, from his windblown hair to the cocky way he strutted into the room, like he was better than everyone else. He had none of Zep's mysterious charm. As if he knew she was thinking about him, he sat down directly behind her, the Fratelli twins on either side of him like bodyguards.

Vanessa shifted in her seat.

"Nice notebook," he said over her shoulder.

Vanessa turned, only to find herself so close to Justin that she breathed the scent of his skin, which smelled fresh, like the sun rising over the ocean. Vanessa felt herself blush and looked away, trying to ignore the sliver of skin peeking from the collar of his shirt. She didn't like it, she reminded herself. She didn't like him.

"At least I have a notebook," she said, and she turned to a blank page as Justin stretched his legs beneath her chair. She scowled and scooted her chair forward. "Why are you even here? Aren't you a senior?"

"In maturity, yes. In grade, no."

"What do you mean? You're supposed to be in the same year as my sister."

"I took a leave of absence. Kind of like she did."

At that, Vanessa turned back to him. "She didn't take a leave of absence. She ran away—"

"I know, I know. I'm kidding."

Vanessa looked at him with scorn. "That's my missing sister you're making jokes about, not some random girl."

The smile on Justin's face faded. "I'm sorry."

Vanessa faced the board. Justin leaned forward and said, "Please accept my apology."

She focused on the board, ignoring him.

Justin persisted. "If you have to know, I was injured during my freshman year, around the same time your sister ran away. I went to a party, drank too much, and somehow fell and broke my ankle."

Vanessa rolled her eyes. "Typical."

Justin paused. "I left school and spent the last three years in physical therapy. In the meantime, I was homeschooled. I begged the school to take me back. Thankfully, they did, but they would only accept a few of my homeschooling courses for graduation credit. So in some classes, I had to start over. Which is why I'm here. With you."

There was something about the way he said "with you," his voice gentle and yearning, and for a moment, she turned, allowing her eyes to meet his. They were a deep, watery blue; they seemed to plead with her. *Listen to what I'm trying to tell you*, they begged. *See me*. Vanessa's grip on her pen loosened, and she grabbed it just before it fell to the floor. Why should she sympathize with him?

She felt him watching her for the rest of class.

"For your first major assignment," Mrs. Jasper said, just before the bell rang, "each of you will write a report on a mythological story, researching its origins, its meanings, and its echoes in other mythologies." She glanced at the clock. "We have five minutes of class left. Do any of you have an idea of what you might write about?"

She waited for volunteers, but no one raised a hand.

"Anyone?" she probed.

Vanessa stared at the doodles she had drawn in the margins of her notebook. A pair of ballet slippers. Her sister's name. A bird flying out a window into the open sky. *Gone*.

Without realizing what she was doing, she raised her hand.

Mrs. Jasper smiled. "Yes, Vanessa. What are you thinking of writing about?"

"*The Firebird*," she said.

"What a wonderful idea," Mrs. Jasper said, clasping her hands together. "I'm sure we'd all love to learn more about this year's production. Perhaps when you're finished, you might consider presenting to the class too?"

"Sure," Vanessa said.

Behind her, Justin let out an obnoxious laugh. "You do realize that reading up on myths isn't going to make you a better dancer," he said under his breath.

Vanessa glared at him just as the bell rang. "And is peering over my shoulder every chance you get going to make *you* a better dancer?"

Justin stood up, towering over Vanessa, while everyone around them gathered their things and filed into the hallway. "No. See, that's the difference between you and me. I'm not trying to be a better dancer."

"You just told me that you spent three years in physical therapy, and then begged Josef and Hilda to take you back. And now you're telling me that you're *not* trying to be a better dancer?"

"I'm a complicated person," Justin said with a glint in his eye. "Full of paradoxes."

Vanessa let out a laugh. "Complicated? Oh, that's right. Because you're a sensitive recovering dancer *and* an insensitive jerk who's too cool to come to class on time. Or button your shirt or cut your hair." Her words came out sharper than she'd meant them to, and for the briefest moment, she thought she saw him flinch.

"That's quite a magnifying glass you put me under," he said quietly. "I just hope you use it on everyone else you encounter here too."

Vanessa paused, not sure what he meant. "Are you making fun of me?"

His face was calm, impenetrable. "No."

"So why are you here, if you're not trying to be a better dancer?"

"You seem to think you know a lot about me already," Justin said, backing toward the door. "So why don't you figure it out?"

Vanessa pushed Justin's words out of her head as she slid her iPad onto her lap to compose an e-mail to Elly. She stared at the blinking cursor, trying to figure out what to say. Finally, she typed out a brief note.

> *I know you don't want to hear from us, but I just*
> *wanted to tell you that I'm glad you're okay. If you*
> *ever want to talk, just let me know. I'm here.*
>
> *Love, Vanessa*

She tried to dismiss Justin from her thoughts in her afternoon dance class, but it was impossible to do so when every time she bent into a plié, she saw his head bobbing in front of her, far above all the other freshmen, and every time she extended her arms into an écarté, she saw his heavy eyes studying her in the mirror.

"And one-two-three, one-two-three," Hilda said, walking down the line of dancers, using a slender stick to prod their legs, their backs, their arms into position. "And lift!" she said. "And hold!"

Vanessa extended her leg behind her. Up ahead, she could

see Hilda snapping her stick against TJ's thigh. "Too much shaking!" Hilda said. "You're supposed to make it look easy, not hard."

Hilda marched on past Blaine, who was trying not to let the pain show on his face as he held the position, his form perfect. It was easy to forget how strong a dancer he was when they were outside the studio, as he would do anything to mask how much effort he put into dancing. He never talked about practicing after hours or about how much time he spent going over his steps, though Vanessa knew that he had to be working just as hard as she was.

"Higher," Hilda barked at one of the girls. "Suck in your belly. Point your toe. Try, for once, to look weightless!"

When she finally made it to Vanessa, she stopped. "Good," she said, her gaze following the turn of Vanessa's leg. "Now one-two-three, one-two-three. Fouetté."

Vanessa spun on the barre, spotting, the room around her blurring until all she could see were Hilda's beady eyes watching her intently.

"Good," Hilda said. "And again."

Vanessa followed her orders, feeling her weight on her toes as she spun. Wisps of hair clung to her temples as she bowed her body away from the barre, arching her neck into a dramatic dip.

In the mirror, she could see Justin sneering at her while Hilda stepped away to observe Steffie. Hilda grunted with distaste.

"Too stiff," she remarked to Garret, Blaine's lab partner. "Too artificial."

Finally, she snapped her stick against the barre. "Stop! Everyone stop. You're all dancing like stale strudels."

Vanessa suppressed her urge to laugh when she saw that Hilda wasn't trying to be funny.

Hilda narrowed her eyes. "Except one. I want you all to watch Vanessa, and see how a dancer can will her limbs into submission."

Vanessa bit her lip, trying to hide the beginning of a smile, when she heard a groan from a girl in the corner of the room.

In the mirror, she could see TJ sigh. Even Steffie had stepped away from the barre and was wiping the sweat from her forehead, looking slightly impatient. The only one who didn't seem upset was Blaine. He didn't reciprocate when TJ rolled her eyes at him. Instead, he caught his breath and studied Vanessa, waiting to see how her form could help inform his.

"Now fourth position," Hilda said to Vanessa.

Taking a breath, Vanessa looked straight ahead, trying to avoid the bored stares of her classmates, and began to dance.

"Don't get me wrong—I love you, and I know you don't want to be a teacher's pet, but your technique is perfect," TJ said between sips on her water bottle as they walked up the steps to their dormitory. Her black leotard was spotted with sweat. "It's the rest of us who need help. So why isn't Broomhilda giving us any attention?"

"I know," Steffie said, pulling on a sweatshirt. "It's like she didn't even want to help us get better. She was just looking for an excuse to go back to you."

Vanessa slung her bag over the opposite shoulder and

pushed her hair behind one ear. She didn't know what to say. On the one hand, she couldn't help but feel giddy that Hilda thought she was the best, and a small part of Vanessa liked to think she deserved the praise. But on the other hand, she didn't want people to think she was sucking up. "What do you want me to do?" Vanessa said, looking to Blaine for help. "I'm not asking for it. I'm just dancing."

"Don't worry, girl, I'm on your side," Blaine said, his face still flushed. "I never would have figured out that last combination of steps without watching you first. It's all about that twist in the heel." He turned to TJ and Steffie. "Maybe if you girls weren't rolling your eyes so much, you'd learn something from Vanessa too."

"We know, we know," TJ said. "Maybe you could just mess up a little once in a while? Give the rest of us a chance."

Vanessa stared at the grimy dorm hallway carpeting. "I guess I could . . ."

"I'm joking!" TJ said, poking her. "It's Hilda we're pissed at."

"They're obviously considering Vanessa for a role in *The Firebird*," Blaine said to them. "Why else would they watch her so closely?"

"What?" Steffie shouted. "No way."

"Ugh, I take it back," TJ chimed in. "I do hate you."

Vanessa raised an eyebrow, feeling strangely guilty. "Um, thanks, guys."

"I just mean that it's impossible. We're freshmen. We're way too young to be cast," said TJ.

"Speak for yourself," Blaine said. "I'm going to make sure I get cast as something better than corps, even if it means going down to Josef's office and doing his laundry."

"I'd do that and more," TJ said, raising a seductive eyebrow.

Steffie grinned and dug around in her bag. "Oh, Vanessa. I meant to give you this."

She held up a creased piece of paper. On the top, words were typed: CAST LIST.

The color drained from Blaine's face. "That is not what I think it is." He grabbed it from Steffie. "How did you get your hands on the cast list? I thought it wasn't going to be posted till next week."

"I didn't," Steffie said, grabbing it back. "It's an old list, from when they did *The Firebird* three years ago. And it's for Vanessa."

Vanessa grew stiff.

"But it was never staged," Steffie said softly, looking directly at Vanessa. "The lead dancer dropped out of school without giving any notice. Even though they had an understudy, Josef canceled the entire production in a rage. I heard some of the upperclassmen talking about it. It sounds like he really went off the rails."

"How did you find the cast list?" Vanessa said.

"I'm doing a project for my journalism class, and I came across it. But I think it might help you for . . ." Steffie paused. "For your report on *The Firebird*. Maybe it's worth talking to some of the older dancers?"

Vanessa took the paper from her and scanned the roster:

Adler, Margaret...................................*The Firebird*

She touched her finger to her sister's name, but when she lifted it, her sweat had smudged the ink across the page. Vanessa let out a quiet gasp. The name *Margaret* was blurred, the letters barely visible. All that was left was *Adler,* as if the fates had already erased her sister, leaving an empty space just big enough for Vanessa to fill.

CHAPTER TEN

Vanessa rolled on a pair of stockings, squeezing her shoulders as she slipped on a dress, zipping it all the way up. Quickly, she ran a comb through her hair, taming it with a barrette. Her cheeks were flushed. She smoothed on a bit of makeup, a lick of gloss on her lips—*smack*—and she was ready. She inspected herself in the mirror, and, smoothing her hair one last time, she glanced at the clock.

A minute past eight. She was late.

Grabbing her purse, she ran out the door.

A part of her didn't believe he would actually show up, that she had made the entire date up in her head or that somehow it would slip away from her, the same way his note had. But when she reached the fountain in the middle of Lincoln Center Plaza, there he was, his silhouette as real as the shimmering water that fell behind him in droplets, his lean frame packaged in a sleek black suit like a gift. He had his back turned to Vanessa, his hands resting casually in his pockets.

"Zep," she said, and reached up to touch his shoulder.

He turned, the light catching his face with a glow of warmth. "Vanessa," he said, taking her in. "You look . . ." His eyes fell over her as he searched for the right word. "Unearthly."

She smiled, thankful for the darkness, that he couldn't see her blush. She pushed a lock of hair away from her face. "Me?" she said with a laugh. "No. I'm just a normal girl who came to New York to become a ballerina."

Zep laughed. "So that means you won't mind having just a regular, low-key Friday night in New York with me?"

Vanessa smiled and shook her head, then she felt someone staring at her across the plaza. Justin.

"Good," Zep said, and turned toward Broadway.

But Vanessa didn't follow. Justin stood beneath the lights, his gaze steady and almost melancholy, as if seeing her with Zep had frozen him in place.

Zep gave her a questioning look. "Is everything okay?"

Vanessa felt a rush of guilt as Justin turned his back and walked away. But why? She didn't owe him anything. She looked up at Zep and smiled. "So where are we going?"

"Oh," Zep said with a mischievous glint in his eye. "Just somewhere normal."

He led Vanessa across the street, down the stairs, and into the subway, where they squeezed onto a crowded train. Music and chatter filled the car, along with lipstick, high heels, big earrings, backpacks, and high-top sneakers. People pushed in behind them, pressing Vanessa to Zep's chest.

The car shuddered to a start, and suddenly Vanessa felt alive. She gripped the pole as they sped downtown, the wheels screeching against the rails, making everyone in the car sway back and forth in a slow, choreographed dance. The doors chimed open, and three men with guitars and sombreros boarded and began to croon in Spanish, their music slowing as the train threw everyone around a bend. Vanessa toppled into Zep, who caught her just before she fell, his hand firm around her waist as if they were paired in a duet.

"Are you all right?" he asked, his lips so close she could almost taste his words.

Vanessa was about to nod when a jolt from the train pulled them apart, pushing her into one of the guitar players. "Sorry!" she said. Zep closed his hand over hers on the pole, holding her steady until the train around her seemed to blur and the last vestiges of Justin slipped from her mind.

They got off in the West Village, where the winding, narrow streets were lined with restaurants and bars and food trucks, the sidewalks crammed with people. Everyone seemed happy.

"This is *nothing* like Lincoln Center," Vanessa said.

"I know. There are as many different New Yorks as there are neighborhoods," Zep said, and took her hand. "Come on!"

The warmth of his fingers closing around hers made her legs go weak. She willed them to move as he pulled her through the maze of streets. After the fourth turn she gave up keeping track of where they were going. He finally slowed when they reached a charming street that branched off from the main avenue, its quiet sidewalks dotted with streetlamps.

"This is it," he said, leading her to a tiny pizzeria with a line of people out the door. "It's the best in New York."

Surprised, Vanessa gazed up at the neon sign and then through the windows at the red counters, the stacks of napkins, the shakers of oregano and red pepper, the men in aprons working dough in the air and manning the oven, sweat beading on their temples.

Zep looked at her nervously. "What do you think?"

The smell of tomatoes and cheese and rising dough wafted outside, making Vanessa swoon. "It's perfect."

They sat on a stoop by the corner and ate pizza, watching the city move past them. The subway vibrated beneath their feet; the cabs screeched as the traffic lights turned red. People rushed to cross the street, only to rush back when the light changed amid the sound of car horns. "Shut up!" someone yelled from a window, making Zep and Vanessa laugh. Beside them, queues of people waited outside the bars and restaurants, music spilling into the night every time the door opened.

"I think I like New York," Vanessa said.

Zep cast a satisfied eye over the crowded streets. "Me too."

He turned to Vanessa, taking her in as if he were seeing her for the first time, and a smile spread across his face.

Vanessa blushed. "What?"

"You know, most girls wouldn't be okay with this. Sitting

on a dirty stoop with me in the West Village and eating a greasy slice of pizza from a paper plate. You're different than all the other girls I've taken out."

Vanessa shrank back at the mention of other girls. In her mind, Zep's past was composed of a never-ending succession of tall, waifish beauties. In comparison, she was this inexperienced freshman who had barely even kissed a boy. What did he see in her?

Zep must have realized how she felt. "I'm sorry," he said, sounding nervous. "That was a compliment. What I meant to say is that I've never met a girl who I could sit with on a stoop and still enjoy myself as much as if we had gone to a show and an expensive restaurant. It sounds absurd, but I never feel comfortable at those places. I'm always waiting for them to escort me out."

Vanessa let out a soft laugh. "I know what you mean."

Zep touched her hand. "You're real," he said, pushing a lock of hair from her face.

Vanessa melted beneath his touch. She gazed up at him. "Are you?"

Zep clutched his chest as if her words had stabbed him. "Of course I am. How can I prove it to you?"

Vanessa bit her lip, pretending to be deep in thought. "You could get something caught in your teeth. Or say something embarrassing."

"I can do those things," he said, the smile fading from his face. "But first, I have a very serious question to ask you."

Vanessa swallowed. "Okay."

Zep leaned toward her, his face so grave it made her worry. Then, in a low voice, he said, "Do you have any soda left? Because I'm all out."

Vanessa laughed and handed him her cup.

"Thanks," he said with a grin, and sipping from one straw, they shared her drink, no longer staring out at the city, but blending into it until they were just another couple sitting on a stoop, enjoying a warm autumn night. Afterward, Zep took her down the street to a cozy patisserie with hammered-tin ceilings and a long glass counter filled with trays of colorful cookies and petit fours. Cakes and meringues stood on tall platters by the register, where an old woman was arranging mugs and teacups. She smiled as Vanessa leaned down and peered at the cakes in awe.

Zep bent down next to her, amused. "Does anything look good?"

"There are so many choices," she said. "I can't decide."

He glanced from Vanessa to the cakes beyond the glass. "I think I know exactly what you want."

"Oh really?" she said with a daring look. "And what would that be?"

Zep searched her face, as if trying to read her thoughts. "Do you trust me?"

Vanessa hesitated. "I think so."

"Good," he said, and stood up. "Why don't you grab us a table? I'll be there in a minute."

"Okay," she said with a skeptical smile. She watched him from afar as he leaned over the counter, talking to the woman behind the register until she nodded and disappeared into the kitchen.

Zep ordered a café au lait for himself and a mulled cider for Vanessa, carrying them to a corner table where they shared a slice of almond cream cake, with frosting so delicate it melted away just as it touched Vanessa's tongue.

"I thought you'd like it."

"How did you . . . ?"

"I've had my eye on you for a while." He touched a strand of her long hair, letting his hand drop down to the pale freckles on her shoulder. "It's hard not to notice you. You aren't like the other girls here. Or anywhere, for that matter."

Vanessa gave him the beginning of a smile. "That's not true," she said, shying away. "There are a lot of girls like me."

Zep smiled. "See, that alone makes you different. Not everyone would say that."

Vanessa knew a lot of girls who would say that—Steffie, TJ, Elly—but she didn't mention it. Instead, she inched her fingers closer to his until their thumbs were touching. "What about you?" she asked. "I don't know anything about you."

Zep raised an eyebrow. "What do you want to know?"

"Anything," Vanessa said, pulling her hair over one shoulder. "Where are you from?"

"A small town in Minnesota," he said. "All snow and ice and factories. That was my childhood. Long, bleak winters and hard work."

"What do you mean?"

"I grew up with my mom and my three younger sisters. My

mom was a nurse, always working the late shifts, so we rarely saw her. All I remember of my dad are his hands—big and rough and chapped from the wind. He worked at a factory, I think, but he left when my sisters and I were really young."

Vanessa listened, licking her spoon, as he told her about growing up, how there was never any food. Once their heat got turned off in the dead of the winter, and their pipes froze. He had to drag his sisters a mile down the road to their neighbor's house so they wouldn't freeze in the night.

"That's what it was like, more or less. Even as a kid, I worked a part-time job after school at the local diner, cleaning floors and washing dishes. It was the worst job ever," he said with a laugh. "You really don't want to know what turns up in public bathrooms. But late one night, when all the customers had left, I turned on the radio and accidentally flipped to a classical station. The music blasted through the place, filling the air with Tchaikovsky, and suddenly everything changed and I felt the life seep back into me. My work passed by so quickly that I turned it on the next night, too, and then the next. The music became the only way I could get through the day. I remember looking out the window, the snow blowing across the ground in swirls, and thinking that it looked like an elaborate dance."

Something inside Vanessa's chest swelled as she listened to him. He told her about how he had started dancing at the gym by himself, how the kids at school had ostracized him. "They'd call me 'Billy Elliot' and kick my ass, but I didn't care. I asked around until I found a woman who was holding ballet classes in her basement. It was all girls except for me, and I think my sisters were mortified, but I had no other choice. Dancing was the only way I could be happy, the only chance I'd have to be successful and eventually support my family. There was nothing for me in that small town. So when I discovered the New York Ballet Academy, I knew I was going. I had to. There was no other option."

Vanessa leaned closer. She had never met anyone who loved dancing as much as Zep. Even Margaret hadn't talked about ballet the way he did. It was as if it held answers for him, that ballet wasn't just something he did, but it was the way he moved, the way he understood the world. *Beauty,* Vanessa thought, listening to the sound of his voice until the café slowly emptied and they wandered out into the street.

"Do you ever get . . . nervous, though?" Vanessa asked.

Zep glanced at her strangely. "What do you mean?"

"Like you're not good enough, no matter how hard you try. Like you'll never be . . . enough." Vanessa wasn't sure where exactly that question came from, but there it was. She couldn't take it back now.

Zep paused for a moment, his face still. Then he touched her cheek. "You *are* enough, Vanessa. More than enough."

Vanessa felt herself blush. She couldn't remember how long it had been since she hadn't thought about her family and Margaret, about Elly and ballet and Josef and *The Firebird.* But walking with Zep beneath the streetlights, Vanessa didn't feel like a ballerina or a sister or a daughter or a friend. She just felt like a girl walking with a boy in the West Village, hoping that by the time they got home, he would kiss her.

Zep hailed a cab, but just as it pulled over something caught her eye. A girl with a blond bob stepped out of a restaurant, her back turned. She wore a pale-pink dress, Elly's color. Vanessa froze.

Zep held the cab door open for her, but she didn't step inside. "Is that—?" she said to Zep, just as the girl turned.

Vanessa's heart sank when she took in the face that was older and far more jaded than Elly's. She watched the girl bum a cigarette from a man, leaning on a mailbox while she took a drag.

"From the back, she looked just like Elly," Vanessa explained, embarrassed, while she climbed into the cab.

"I know," Zep said, trying to make her feel better, though it didn't help. There were probably thousands of girls in the city who looked like Elly from behind.

"You were friends. You miss her," Zep said gently. "I would feel the same way too. It's a shame what happened to her."

Something about his tone made Vanessa pause. "What do you mean?" Vanessa said. "What happened to her?"

"I don't know," he said. "Just that she disappeared so suddenly. It's like she fell off the face of the earth."

"Disappeared," Vanessa repeated thoughtfully. "It is like that, isn't it?"

The mood had become somber by the time the cab pulled up at Lincoln Center. Seeing it, suspended in the sky, Vanessa suddenly felt guilty for not thinking about Margaret all evening. And even though she hadn't planned on telling Zep anything about Margaret, she somehow felt that she could trust him.

"Did you know my sister?"

"Margaret," Zep said, as if he'd been waiting for Vanessa to feel comfortable enough to bring her up. "She was a beautiful dancer."

Vanessa stared at her feet, unable to look Zep in the eye while she told him about the day they got the phone call. The months of searching, of the police calling, telling her parents they had no news. Zep listened intently.

"Did you think she was crazy?" Vanessa asked him, thinking about what Justin had told her.

"I barely knew her," Zep said. "I thought she was talented and passionate about dance. She seemed fragile, but who isn't before a big performance?"

Vanessa nodded, somehow relieved. She didn't want to think that her sister was crazy. "Elly's disappearance reminds me of hers. Do you think that's insane?"

"No," Zep said. "They both dropped out suddenly, and they were both close to you."

Vanessa bit her lip. She wanted to tell him that it wasn't just the circumstances that seemed so similar. It was something more intangible, a bad feeling she got every time she looked at Elly's empty half of the room. But she said nothing. And while they walked back toward the dormitory, Zep took her hand. "Wait," he said, and pulled her to the fountain.

"The truth is," he said softly, "I don't want to go home."

Vanessa felt something inside her catch. "I don't either," she whispered. "But I'm already late for curfew—"

"I know," he said, putting a finger to her lips. "Just one

more moment." He pulled her toward him, his hand pressing into the small of her back. Her hair blew about her cheeks as he leaned closer, his breath grazing her lips. But before he kissed her, Vanessa hesitated.

"What about Anna? Is she still your girlfriend?"

"Girlfriend?" His breath tickled her lips. "I don't have one—at least not now. Though I do have my eye on someone if she'll have me."

A gust of wind blew water from the fountain across the plaza, sprinkling them with cool droplets, and they both broke out laughing. When the wind died down, Zep wiped her cheek with his thumb.

"Vanessa?" said a gruff voice. It belonged to a woman.

Vanessa's smile faded. She turned to see Hilda's squat frame standing by the entrance of the David Koch Theater, squinting into the darkness.

"We have to go!" Vanessa said. Zep grabbed her hand, and together they ran through the buildings and back to the dormitory.

CHAPTER ELEVEN

The weekend passed by in a slow ache. Vanessa went to breakfast with her friends and meandered up Broadway with them, until they finally settled down to study in a coffee shop a few blocks from school. Vanessa's mind was far away, though, feeling the weight of Zep's hand in hers, her cheek still cool from the sprinkle of water that the wind had blown between them, her lips still waiting for his kiss.

TJ interrupted her reverie. "And you want an iced tea, right? One sugar or two?"

"Actually," Vanessa said, "I'll have a mulled cider today."

A hushed giggle passed over the table.

"I know where you are," Blaine said with a wink. He pushed up the sleeves of his sweatshirt and leaned forward. "Lost in a dream. A sexy dream."

Vanessa felt her chest grow hot. "No," she protested. "I'm here, really. I just—"

"Suddenly like mulled cider," Steffie teased.

"We don't blame you," TJ said. "Hell, if I could go on a date with Z—"

"Shh!" Vanessa said. She had told them about the date but sworn them to secrecy. She didn't want to think about what everyone at school would say if word got out.

"With you know who," TJ continued. "I'd be checked out of reality so quickly you'd forget what my voice sounded like."

Blaine raised an eyebrow. "You? Stop talking? Impossible."

Steffie and Vanessa laughed. TJ rolled her eyes and retreated to the counter to order their drinks.

The four of them sat around the table studying in the afternoon sunshine, the buttery aroma of mulled cider filling Vanessa with memories: a lick of almond frosting, a hand buried in her hair, a tickle of breath on her neck.

To keep her mind off Zep, Vanessa spent the rest of the weekend in the NYBA library, reading about Igor Stravinsky for her *Firebird* report and relishing the quiet. It was there, sitting on a windowsill overlooking Manhattan's Upper West Side, that she read about the strange phenomenon that had occurred in Paris during the original opening night of Stravinsky's ballet *The Rite of Spring*.

According to historical accounts, when the orchestra started to play the opening notes, the audience began to shift in their seats. The sounds were odd, unfamiliar, the chords dissonant and unnatural. As the dancers contorted their bodies to the strange music, people covered their ears or looked away, unable to watch. Someone booed. Someone else shouted at the dancers. People were standing and yelling, throwing playbills at the stage. A group of women in the front row fell into a strange fit of hysterics.

Vanessa shivered, staring at a drawing of the riot, the faces of the people in the aisles sending goose bumps up her skin. They looked wild, possessed, like something had taken hold of them and wouldn't let go.

"That's dark stuff," a voice said over her shoulder.

Vanessa sat up with a jolt, knocking a stack of books off the windowsill. Trying to compose herself, she stood, only to see the tawny mess of Justin's hair as he bent over her books, now scattered across the floor.

Vanessa blew a wisp of hair out of her face. "Do you make it a habit of sneaking up on people, or are you just trying to sabotage my dancing by giving me a heart attack?"

Justin looked up at her, a mischievous grin spreading across his face. "What, did I scare you?"

"No," she said, glancing over his shoulder. "Speaking of scaring, where are your bodyguards? I didn't see them with you when you were spying on Zep and me in the plaza. Don't you travel everywhere with them?"

But just as she spoke she heard heavy footsteps, and Nicola and Nicholas Fratelli slipped out from the narrow passage between the bookshelves. They glanced at Vanessa, their faces solemn, and sat down to read just a few tables over from her.

Vanessa shrank back, embarrassed.

"Them?" Justin said. "We're just friends. And as for the other night, I wasn't spying on you. I was on my way to a date."

"A date?" Vanessa asked, surprised by how anxious the idea made her. "With whom?"

"Now who's spying?" Justin said, still grinning.

"I—I'm not, I was just wondering. But never mind."

Justin shrugged. "Just a girl," he said. His blue eyes lingered on Vanessa's. He lowered his voice. "No one special."

Vanessa broke his gaze. "I, um, I should go."

Ignoring her words, Justin opened one of her books. "*Russian Composers and Their Muses,*" he said, reading the title. He picked up another one. "*Dance Macabre and the Ballerina.*" He chuckled. "Doing a little *Firebird* research, are we?"

"Yes," Vanessa said, grabbing the book from him.

"You know that—"

"It won't make me a better dancer," Vanessa said curtly. "You told me that before."

Justin leaned against the windowsill, the muscles on his arms flexing beneath his shirt. Catching herself, Vanessa quickly looked away.

"I was going to say that if you want to know what Josef's favorite ballet is about, you should probably ask the people who have danced in it before." Justin picked up Vanessa's pencil case and looked like he was about to open it.

"Don't go through my things," she said, grabbing the case and stuffing it back in her bag. "I already tried that," she said, producing the three-year-old cast list from her binder. "I can't find contact information for anyone on the list. I even found cast lists from earlier *Firebird* productions here—it looks like the school has *tried* to put it on almost twelve times now over the past two decades—but I can't even find listings for those dancers. It's like after they left NYBA, they just vanished."

"You can't find them because the old players aren't around anymore," Justin said.

"What do you mean? What happened to them?"

Justin fanned the pages of one of her books. "Who knows?"

Vanessa slammed her palm down on the book cover, tired of the way he was fiddling with her things. "They disappeared?"

Justin shook his head. "You, of all people, should know that when people disappear, it's usually because they don't want to be found. So call it whatever you want. They graduated and faded into obscurity, or—"

Vanessa glanced at her watch, and Justin's voice trailed off. Suddenly he stood up, his back rigid. A dark look passed over his face.

Vanessa followed his gaze to the far end of the reading room, where Zep's broad shoulders filled the doorway. The warm light seemed to bend around him as he ran his hands through his hair and scanned the room, looking for a place to sit. He was about to head for the east corner when his eyes rested on Vanessa.

She felt her heart skip as their gaze met.

"Dropped out of sight," Justin said, finishing his sentence. "Which is exactly what I'm going to do now." He gave Vanessa a disappointed look, but she was barely paying attention to him. Justin gathered his things and nodded to the Fratelli twins, who closed their books and stood up. "Remember what I said in class about putting me under a magnifying glass," Justin murmured, but before Vanessa had a chance to process what he'd meant, he and the twins were gone.

Zeppelin Gray was a beautiful paradox: his body rough yet smooth; his movements heavy but weightless; his eyes so deep and lustrous that they seemed to contain an entire universe. He walked toward Vanessa, his muscles shifting, sharp and lean, as if carved out of metal.

Tearing her gaze away, she glanced at one of her books and pretended to read. He couldn't be coming this way, could he? A looming shadow answered her question. Willing herself to stop blushing, Vanessa looked up.

"Vanessa," Zep said, his voice deep and buttery. "What are you doing here?"

"Oh, Zep, hi," she said, trying to sound unfazed. "I'm just reading."

"I would have thought you would be out with your friends," Zep said, placing his hand inches from hers on the windowsill.

"Why would you think that?"

"You just seem like the kind of girl who's always busy. I'm glad I found you alone."

Had he been looking for her? She felt her heart swell.

Zep lowered his voice. "Is that revealing too much?"

"A little," she teased. "If I had known you were looking for me, I would have made myself easier to find."

Zep gave her a daring smile. "What did you think I've been doing all weekend?"

"Leading a life of mystery and intrigue, I suppose," Vanessa said. She had no idea what Zep did in his free time. "Whisking girls away to beautiful cafés where you win their hearts by ordering them the perfect dessert."

"No," Zep said with a laugh. "I only do that with you." He stepped closer. "But does that mean that I won your heart?"

"You seem to know me better than I know myself. Why don't you tell me?"

"If only I could," he said.

"So now that you have me alone, what do you want to do with me?"

A glimmer of surprise flickered over Zep's face. He inched closer until his fingers were barely touching hers. Leaning in, he traced his finger along the spine of her book.

"What I was thinking of isn't exactly right for the library."

Vanessa trembled as he slammed the book shut and stood up.

"Let's get out of here," he said, and held out his hand.

Vanessa couldn't remember what happened next, only the feeling of Zep's hand around hers as they slipped through campus and into an empty studio. She laughed as Zep ran a finger down her arm and then closed the door behind them, turning on only the far lights so most of the studio was still dark.

Vanessa dropped her bag on the floor and twirled into a delirious pirouette before she sat down. As she pulled her pointe shoes out of her bag, Zep came up behind her.

"May I?" he said softly.

Vanessa swallowed, then nodded.

Gently, Zep took her leg in his hand. He slid off one sandal, then the other. Her slippers looked delicate and small beneath his hands, the ribbons tangling around his fingers. He lifted her right foot and slipped the shoe on, his grip soft as he wrapped the ribbons up her ankles.

"Too tight?" he said, tying them in a knot.

Vanessa shook her head, unable to speak.

When he was finished, he put on his own shoes and held out his hand. Vanessa's long hair was tied in a loose braid, and Zep grazed a wisp of it with his fingers. "The Firebird," he whispered.

"I don't know all the steps," Vanessa said.

"That's okay," he said, his voice gentle. "Just follow my lead."

Suddenly, she was in his arms, his broad hands firm against her waist. Their feet wove together, sliding across the floor as if it were natural, as if it weren't a dance at all, but a long, tender caress. The smell of his skin, his sweat, surrounded her as she leaped across the studio, fanning her arms as she spun. She began to lose herself; she couldn't stop it. The mirrors seemed to warp as time slowed, bending everything in the room except Zep, who reached out and caught her just before she collapsed.

"Vanessa." He pulled her close to him.

She blinked, the room returning to her. "Zep." She could feel his chest expanding and contracting against her thin dress.

Zep ran his fingers across her cheek. "You're breathtaking."

Vanessa shivered.

Zep lifted her chin. "You're alive, angry, passionate. You're not dancing, you're living. I can see it in your eyes."

Vanessa stared at her reflection in his eyes. "Really?" she replied.

Instead of answering, Zep pulled her toward him and ran

his hand up her spine. Something inside her grew faint as he pressed her body against his. Vanessa closed her eyes. His strong hands tightened around her waist, pulling her closer, when the door cracked open. A ray of light shone across the floor, followed by a shadow of a boy. Justin.

She could feel Zep grow rigid beneath her fingers. And then, to her surprise, he moved away from her. Only an inch, but it was just enough space for the light to shine across her face, revealing her to Justin. As if Zep wanted Justin to see her.

Justin tilted his head as the realization of what he had inter-rupted spread across his face. Vanessa watched as his expression softened into sadness, as if she had somehow let him down. And for reasons she couldn't explain, she suddenly felt guilty.

Even though she hated Justin, even though everything about him made her want to scream, she wanted to call out to him. To explain to him why she was here with Zep and what they were doing. But she didn't.

For a moment, Justin stood there, watching them. And then, without a word, he left. Vanessa lowered her eyes as the door slammed shut behind him, repeating itself in every mirror on the wall.

CHAPTER TWELVE

Vanessa didn't tell anyone. How could she when *she* wasn't even sure it had been real? Zep wasn't her boyfriend, and she had to admit to herself that in many ways, he was still very much a stranger.

She didn't know what he did or where he was when he wasn't with her. She didn't even have a way to get in touch with him other than Facebook. Besides, the mystery was part of his appeal. Zep was the epitome of movement—a flash of him here, another flash there, and then he was gone, leaving Vanessa with nothing but the memory of his body moving with hers. And she wanted more.

She went through the rest of the week in a daze, listening to her teachers lecture in class, but all she could hear was Zep's breath as he danced. She sat with her friends in the library, but only stared at her book. She couldn't stop thinking about the way her body had felt in Zep's arms. Even now, she couldn't help but glance at the bookshelves where Zep had stood just days before, the wood dark as if his shadow were lingering there.

"Are you okay?" Steffie asked, putting down her highlighter.

"Yeah," Vanessa said. "What makes you think I'm not?"

"Because you haven't turned the page in twenty minutes. And you barely said anything at breakfast. What's going on with you?"

Vanessa hesitated. Had Zep really pressed her to his body, his hand sliding down her back? She could almost feel it, and yet now, in the daylight, it seemed unreal. After Justin had left, the room deflated, and all the electricity that had just passed between Zep and Vanessa seemed to fizzle out. Though neither said a word about it, they both knew they couldn't finish their dance, not then. So instead, Zep picked up Vanessa's things, his hand grazing hers but not holding it as he walked her outside. That's when Vanessa realized how delicate it all was. She worried that if she tried to say what had happened out loud, it would just vanish into thin air.

She glanced across the table. TJ had earplugs in and was busy taking notes from her history book, and Blaine was reading, bobbing to music from his headphones.

Steffie tapped her fingers on the table. "So . . . ?"

Vanessa lowered her voice. "Sunday in the library, I ran into Zep."

Blaine slipped off one headphone. "What's going on?"

"Oh, nothing," Vanessa said quickly, giving Steffie a look that said *shh!* The last thing she wanted to do was to share her secret with Blaine. "I'm just a little out of it today." And she spent the rest of the afternoon buried in her book.

When they returned, the dormitory was unnaturally quiet. Even the common room was deserted.

"I don't like this," Blaine said as they peered around the corner of the kitchen, which was also empty. "It feels like orientation night all over again."

"Look," TJ said. She pointed out the window at two girls from their floor, who were running across the plaza as if they were late.

"Why are they in such a rush?" Steffie said. "Classes are over."

A few moments later, a boy named Paul from their dance class also ran across the plaza. He yelled something unintelligible to Jenny, an upperclassman, who was reading by the fountain. Immediately, she shut her book, stuffed it into her bag, and followed him. Vanessa watched them disappear through the glass doors of the studio building.

"What is going on?" she asked.

Blaine slung his bag over his shoulder. "I don't know, but I'm going to find out."

They ran outside and through the doors, into the foyer of the studio building. As they approached, they heard the hum of voices. The entryway was flooded with students, all gathered around a bulletin board.

Vanessa peered over the heads, trying to see what everyone was staring at.

"It's the cast list," a girl named Sandy said. "They posted it a day early."

"What?" Vanessa said. She saw Blaine already pushing his way through the crowd, TJ's thick curls bouncing behind him. Beyond them, Vanessa could just make out the small piece of paper pinned to the board, dozens of fingers tracing the list, looking for their names.

"This is so unfair!" an older girl shouted suddenly. Vanessa recognized her as one of Anna Franko's friends, Laura.

A hush fell over the room as Laura tore the list off the bulletin board, crumpled it, and threw it against the wall.

The crowd parted as she turned, her face pinched with anger. Spotting Vanessa, standing by the edge of the crowd, she said, "I hope you're happy," and stormed off.

The room went quiet. "Happy about what?" Steffie asked.

Vanessa stared at the swinging door, confused. "I have no idea."

A sophomore near the front of the room reached for the cast list. She smoothed it out and pinned it up again.

The students gathered around again, scanning the list for their names. "It's all upperclassmen," a boy said with a groan.

Vanessa's shoulders slumped. Some small part of her had hoped she would be cast. After all, hadn't Josef told her she had potential? Hadn't Zep said she was breathtaking?

Vanessa ran a hand through her hair and backed out of the crowd.

"Hey, where are you going?" Steffie said. "Don't you want to see?"

Vanessa shook her head. She was about to turn back to the dormitory when a girl from her floor glared at her before stalking away.

"What?" Vanessa said, but the girl didn't turn around. Next, two girls from her history class saw her and started whispering. Vanessa frowned, trying to ignore them, when a hand closed over her wrist, and TJ pulled her through the crowd.

"What are you doing?" Vanessa said, trying to wriggle out of her grasp.

"Just look," TJ said, and pointed to the cast list.

There, on the top, was Zeppelin Gray, cast as the male lead, Prince Ivan. Beside it was Vanessa Adler. The Firebird.

It had to be a mistake. A typo. Maybe Vanessa was supposed to have been cast as one of the thirteen princesses, but surely not the Firebird. That's what everyone was whispering in the halls, in the dressing rooms, in the dining hall and dormitory. And now that her initial fizzy feeling of elation had faded, Vanessa had to admit that she didn't blame them; she could barely believe it either.

"Seriously though," TJ said later that evening. "How did you do it?"

They were in her dorm room, Blaine leaning against

TJ's bedpost and Steffie sitting in Vanessa's chair, her long legs propped up on the desk. Vanessa folded herself onto the bed.

"You know you're not going to be in rehearsal with us anymore," Steffie said. "You're going to be with the princesses now."

"Wait, really?" Vanessa said. It hadn't even occurred to her that she would be separated from her friends.

Steffie gave her a sympathetic look. "I think so," she said. "Just you and Zep and Anna and all of her princess friends in the studio. Like one big happy family."

Anna. A lump formed in Vanessa's throat as she thought about the prospect of being stuck with those girls.

Blaine's eyes grew wide, and he turned and said to TJ, "I wonder if she'll get along with Anna."

"Highly unlikely," TJ said to him. "I bet Anna is mortified. To have a freshman steal her role right out from under her, and then to be cast as the thirteenth princess instead?"

Vanessa watched them, incredulous. "Hey, I didn't steal her role—"

"Always a bridesmaid, never a bride," Blaine said.

"Stop it!" Vanessa said.

Finally Blaine turned to her. "Stop what?"

"You're already gossiping about me! You're treating me like I'm a stranger or something. Like I'm one of the princesses."

"Yeah, well you are now, honey," Blaine said. "So you'd better get used to the idea. Believe me, there's a lot more where this came from."

Vanessa leaned back against the wall and sighed. "It's not like I'm disappearing. I'll still be in class with you."

Blaine lowered his voice as he turned to TJ. "That's what she thinks."

"You do realize I can hear you," Vanessa said.

Blaine rolled his eyes melodramatically, making TJ laugh. "She's just stressed out from the pressure," he said. "We shouldn't take it personally."

Before Vanessa could continue, she felt her phone vibrate. Slipping it out of her pocket, she turned away from her friends and answered.

Her mother practically exploded at the good news. Vanessa had to hold the phone five inches away from her ear while she shrieked. Across the room, her friends exchanged a muffled laugh as they stood and gathered their things.

"Are you guys going to dinner?" Vanessa asked, getting off the phone.

TJ shook her head. "I have to cram for my Spanish test."

"And I have to see the physical therapist for my knee," Steffie said.

Blaine gave her an apologetic look. "I have a date. With Tad from our English class." He gave them a mischievous look. "That Mississippi drawl of his is like eating banana cream pie on the porch with a warm, humid breeze."

Vanessa let out a laugh and rolled her eyes, trying to hide her dread of walking into the dining hall on her own. Before she went inside, she sat on the ledge by the doors and dialed Elly's phone number one more time. Elly had never replied to Vanessa's e-mail, and though Vanessa should have taken the hint, part of her just didn't believe Elly really wanted to be left alone.

Vanessa imagined what she would say if Elly picked up. There was so much she wanted to tell her. She missed her, they all did. But the phone rang until an automated voice answered, telling her that Elly's mailbox was full.

The dining hall was loud with clanking plates and forks, the occasional crash of someone dropping a tray. Vanessa glanced around, trying to spot a friendly face, but the girls from her hall were packed into a tiny table by the windows, and other than them, she didn't know anyone. Trying to hide the panic bubbling inside her, she walked through the room, looking for an empty seat.

Through the din, Vanessa imagined she heard people talking about her: *Vanessa. Firebird. Freshman.* She lowered her head and made for a secluded table at the far end of the room, when she felt someone watching her.

Anna Franko was sitting at a table full of senior girls, most of whom had been cast as the other twelve princesses. Vanessa bit her lip as she saw Anna stand up, her pale hair tied into a ponytail, her pretty face pinched with anger. One of her friends touched her arm and whispered something in her ear, which seemed to calm her down. She gave Vanessa one last furious look and stormed out of the dining hall.

There was a lull in the room when the door slammed.

"How did she do it?" she overheard a girl named Azalea say. Vanessa recognized her from dance class. She was hunched over a salad with a group of girls from Vanessa's floor.

"I heard she met with Josef in his office," a blond girl said. "Privately."

"And did what?" another one whispered.

The blonde popped a cherry tomato between her teeth. "Isn't it obvious?" she said.

Vanessa found an empty seat in the corner of the room, next to a table of bookish upperclassmen who were arguing about the third act of *Hamlet*. She recognized her RA, Kate, among them. Taking a cue from them, Vanessa set her tray down and promptly opened a book, hoping that if she hid her face, everyone might forget that she existed. But it didn't work. Halfway through her salad, she heard a tray clatter against the table.

"I thought that was you," Justin said, flicking the end of her hair with his fork.

Vanessa leaned away from him and tossed her hair over her shoulder. "Please don't touch me."

He held up his hands in surrender. "Okay, okay. You're a landed woman now. I get it." He sat down. "Prized property," he added.

"Excuse me?"

Justin twirled spaghetti around his fork. "You know what I'm talking about. Sunday night. With Zeppelin." He pronounced Zep's name slowly, dragging out the syllables.

Vanessa put down her book. "I'm not anyone's property," she said. "And who said you could sit here?"

Justin took a sip of water. "I didn't realize this table was anyone's property either." He relaxed his shoulders. "So what do you know about Zep?"

"I don't see how that's any of your business. Why do you hate him so much, anyway? Because you're jealous that he has the lead role and you weren't even cast?"

"As a matter of fact, I was cast," Justin said. "As his understudy. Which is exactly what I wanted."

Vanessa tried to hide her surprise. Zep and Justin, the only boys she was drawn to, for better or for worse, were now cast in the same role.

Justin lowered his voice. "And I never said I hated Zep. Let's just say I'm interested in him."

"In Zep?" Vanessa said, backing away. Without warning, Justin took her wrist in his hand and raised it off the table. Her muscles tightened beneath his palm.

He pointed to the shadow their hands had formed. "In this," he said.

Vanessa stared at the table, confused. "In what?"

"His shadow," Justin said. "His dark side."

Wriggling out of his grip, Vanessa pulled back. "What—" she started to say, when a voice cut over her.

"Leave her alone," Zep said. He looked down at Vanessa, his eyes lustrous, wild. "She's got enough on her shoulders."

Justin's chair scratched the floor as he stood up. "You would know, wouldn't you?" he said cryptically.

Confused, Vanessa looked between the two boys. "What is he talking about?" she asked Zep, but he ignored her.

"And you wouldn't," Zep said, taking a step toward Justin until their chests were almost touching. "Because you're not half the dancer I am."

Justin studied Zep with cool eyes. "I pride myself in that," he responded. Vanessa could almost detect the sound of pity in his voice. "I would never want to be the kind of dancer you are."

"Which is what?" Zep said. "Or are you not man enough to say it to my face?"

"Maybe I'm not," Justin said, stepping back. "Why don't you tell her?"

"Tell me what?" Vanessa said. "What is he talking about?"

"I have no idea," Zep murmured.

Justin laughed in disbelief. "Exactly what I expected," he said to Zep. "Be careful, Vanessa," he added, giving her a steady look, and stalked off.

When Vanessa stood up, she realized the entire dining hall was silent. All heads were facing her. She saw the table of girls from her class whispering by the window. Suddenly she felt her stomach swirl, like she was going to throw up.

"Let them stare," Zep said in her ear, and held out his hand.

With the beginning of a smile, she slipped her hand in his, and together they walked through the center of the room and out into the crisp October evening.

Bars of buttery light stretched across the stones in front of the opera house. It was all happening, Vanessa thought as they walked across the plaza. She was here with Zep, holding his hand, and everyone knew. A part of her was still waiting for the curtain to roll down, to wake up in her old life without Zep or the Firebird, because all this—the tall glass buildings, the clear night sky, and the distant lights that shone down on them like stars—seemed like a fantasy. Vanessa stopped. "Zep, wait. Can I ask you a question?"

"Of course."

People meandered past them, stopping by the fountain to take photographs. Vanessa lowered her voice. "Did you talk to Josef about me? I mean, did you tell him to . . ."

Zep inched toward her, a lock of hair falling over his forehead. "You're worried that the only reason you got the role was because I convinced Josef to give it to you."

A cool breeze tickled the back of Vanessa's neck. She crossed her arms and nodded.

"I was planning on meeting with him tomorrow after rehearsal."

Vanessa paused. "So you haven't met with him yet?"

Zep shook his head. "No."

"So he chose me on his own?"

Zep took her by the waist and pulled her closer, his wool sweater soft against her face as he enveloped her in his arms. "Yes. Do I have to spell it out for you? You're an amazing dancer. You should have more confidence in yourself."

"It's just that the other girls—"

"Who cares about the other girls?" Zep said. "I don't."

Vanessa's insides seemed to melt beneath his touch.

"Come on," he whispered, lowering his hand. "Let's get out of here."

They ran through the evening into the empty studio where they had danced before. This time, Zep left all the lights off, keeping them in darkness, save for the dim beam that shone through the window in the door. Her toe shoes on, Vanessa walked to the center of the floor and closed her eyes until she felt Zep behind her. Gently, he lifted the hem of her sweater, pulling it over her head and tossing it on the floor. He ran his hands up the sides of her camisole and down her bare arms.

Without speaking, she extended her leg high into the air. Zep lifted her from the floor as if she were weightless. She landed on one foot, her body shivering as they tried it again and again, practicing until it was perfect. Vanessa laughed as Zep lifted her over his head and lowered her into his arms.

"See?" he said as he bent over her. "It's not that hard. All you needed was to feel your way through the dark."

Vanessa raised her hand to his cheek, which was obscured in shadows. "Like this?" she said, and ran her other hand up his neck and into his hair.

Zep let out a soft moan and gripped her waist. "We keep getting interrupted," he breathed, his lips grazing hers.

Vanessa felt something inside her shudder. This was a real kiss, from a boy she actually liked, and now that she was standing here with Zep in the dark, she didn't know what to do. Was it like dancing?

Zep slid his hand up her side, arching her back. Gently, he ran his thumb over her trembling lip. She closed her eyes, feeling the weight of his body, the taste of sweat lingering on her tongue as she let him envelop her in a warm and salty kiss.

When Vanessa got back to her room, she closed the door and slid down the wall into a smiling heap. She could still smell him on her clothes, feel his weight against her ribs. Zep had given her his thick sweater to wear, the dark wool still warm from his body. Leaning into it, she breathed in his earthy scent.

TJ was still at the library, so Vanessa had the room to herself. As she slipped off Zep's sweater and tucked it between her pillows, she noticed a small box beneath her bed.

Vanessa never remembered seeing it before, though it had clearly been there for a while, judging from the amount of dust clinging to it. It must belong to TJ, Vanessa thought, and accidentally got kicked under her bed. But when she turned it over, she saw her name on it.

Confused, she opened it. Inside was a thin piece of rosin, the same kind Vanessa had seen in Josef's office, except this one was wrapped in a piece of paper. She held it up to her nose, recoiling from its smoky smell. Holding it away from her face, she slipped off the square of paper and unfolded it.

> *Just heard the craziest convo between J and H. Come by my room as soon as you get back, and I'll show you what this does. Don't tell anyone. Hurry.*
>
> *—Elly*

Her handwriting was messy, as if she had written it in a rush. Vanessa reread the note, confused. Elly had been gone for almost a month. Did that mean that she had written this before she dropped out of school? And why had she written an actual note instead of just texting or e-mailing? The only reason Vanessa could think of was that she didn't want anyone to find this except for herself and TJ. But why?

She glanced down at the slice of rosin, sticky in her hand, and turned it over, examining its dark-amber hue. Had Elly taken it from Josef's office the night they all went to the ballet, and then slipped it into Vanessa's room before she disappeared? The box was small enough that Vanessa could have overlooked it, especially since TJ's side of the room was more than a little messy. What did she mean by "what this does"? And were "J and H" Josef and Hilda?

Placing the rosin on a napkin by her bed, Vanessa wiped her hands on a towel and picked up her cell phone. She punched in Elly's number, but just as it had before, the call went straight to voice mail. Vanessa listened to the automated message, the voice stiff and lifeless, as it told her one more time that Elly's mailbox was full.

CHAPTER THIRTEEN

Steffie paced around her room, holding Elly's note. The block of rosin sat on her desk. Vanessa and Steffie had spent the last hour rubbing the rosin on paper, on their skin, on their ballet shoes; they dunked it in water, pressed it between their palms, even cut off a corner and heated it in the kitchen microwave until it melted. The resulting smell was so unbearable that it was all they could do to scrape the bubbling syrup into the trash and evacuate to Steffie's room.

"Taste it," Steffie said. Behind her, the Manhattan night drifted through the open window, the lights from the high rises dotting the sky like stars.

"No way. You taste it. She was your roommate."

"But she left the rosin in your room," Steffie said. "Which means she specifically wanted *you* to see it."

Steffie had a point. Why would Elly have slipped it under Vanessa's door when she could have just shown it to Steffie? Was there something about the rosin that made Elly think of Vanessa? She gazed at the amber block, its smoky smell drifting through the room.

"Let's both do it together," Vanessa said finally.

"Fine."

Both girls approached the desk and pinched off a bit of rosin from the top. It was gummy, like congealed maple syrup.

"One . . . two . . ." Vanessa lifted it to her lips. "Three."

The moment the rosin touched her tongue, Vanessa felt her face tighten into a grimace. She lunged for a tissue on Steffie's nightstand and spat it out. Steffie did the same.

"Well, that definitely wasn't what Elly was talking about," Steffie said, passing Vanessa a bottle of water. "What now? I wonder why Josef has it in his office. Maybe it's some special rosin that he only gives to the best dancers. What do you think?"

Vanessa stared at Elly's bare mattress, the rosin's warm, bitter taste still lingering in her mouth. Standing in her sister's old room, talking about the note, the rosin, and Elly's strange absence, pulled Vanessa back to sixth grade, eating dinner in the kitchen while a stranger on the phone told her mother that Margaret had disappeared.

"Zep kissed me," Vanessa said suddenly, the words coming out before she realized what she was saying.

"What?" Steffie said. "When? Where? How?"

"Tonight," Vanessa murmured, trying to remember the way he smelled when he leaned over and pressed his lips to hers. "In the studio."

Steffie grew still, her eyes wide with awe, before a smile spread across her face. "I can't believe it took you this long to tell me."

Vanessa coiled her hair around her finger. "Me neither."

"Okay, so spill it," Steffie said, sitting on the bed. "Tell me everything."

And just like that, Margaret, Elly, and the mysterious rosin all seemed to vanish.

You can't ignore the past. That much Vanessa gleaned from history class early the next morning. Outside, the sky was overcast, the same gray hue as the stone buildings that loomed on the horizon. The autumn mornings were growing darker and cooler. Vanessa yawned and stared at the board, distracted by the girls whispering in the back of the room. Were they talking about her?

"Shh!" TJ said. She glared at the girls over her shoulder before turning to Vanessa and giving her a wink.

Thanks, Vanessa mouthed, just as Mr. Harbor put down his chalk.

"Now I want you to break into groups and come up with three examples of events going on today that might also have been experienced in Ancient Rome. Whatever you don't finish, you'll take home and do for next Monday."

The room filled with shuffling chairs and the low chatter of voices. Blaine, TJ, and Steffie pulled their chairs around Vanessa. She opened her book to the section on the Roman Empire and was about to speak when Steffie pushed the book aside.

"We'll do the assignment later," she said, and took out her iPad. She lowered her voice. "Remember during orientation, when Josef said that at least a quarter of every class quits before the end of the first year?"

TJ leaned back in her chair. "Remember?" she said with a laugh. "Those words have been haunting me for weeks!"

Steffie bit her lip. "Well, there's more." She gazed around, her eyes somber. "Elly's only the latest. They don't just drop out. A lot of them disappear entirely."

Vanessa felt her throat tighten.

"What do you mean, disappear?" Blaine asked.

"Like they are never heard from again," Steffie said. "At best, they're shrugged off as runaways or drug addicts, and at worst—well, you'll see.

"I was doing research in my journalism class this morning when I started coming across articles about runaway ballerinas," Steffie continued. "So I downloaded all these articles about missing students."

She slid over her iPad.

Vanessa had barely read the first headline when she felt a wave of dread. BALLERINA MISSING. She looked at the photograph of a young girl, the caption stating her name, age, and the last place she was seen. With TJ and Blaine huddled over her shoulder, she began to read about missing dancers—girls who had simply vanished, their photographs printed beside the article with the caption: *MISSING. If you have any information regarding this person, please contact the NYPD.*

The oldest article dated back twenty years, and the most

recent was published in August, with the headline HIGHS AND LOWS OF THE NEW YORK BALLET ACADEMY. It was a full-length feature about NYBA and its history of girls dropping out. Most of it was familiar, the high pressure put on girls from choreographers and even parents, the physical stress and medical risks of rehearsals and dancing *en pointe*.

"She just picked up and left," a former NYBA student said of one girl who, like many of the others, had been cast in a lead role. "She left a note saying she couldn't take it anymore. I thought she was going home, but I guess she wanted to start over."

Vanessa was surprised to see Anna Franko's name before the next quote. "I heard she was living with a boyfriend in Queens," Anna said of the most recent disappearance, Chloë, who had dropped out just before school began. "She cried a lot toward the end. But it was probably for the better. She wasn't happy here." When asked if she had talked to Chloë since she'd dropped out, Anna dodged the answer. "I don't want to talk about that," she'd said.

"Anna?" Vanessa whispered. Something about her last answer wasn't right. Even though all of the disappearances were explained—just like her sister's—none of them really made sense.

"It's a cover-up," Vanessa said, just as their teacher bent over their desks.

"And how is everything going over here?" he asked. Steffie quickly slid her notebook over her iPad.

"We just started compiling a list," Blaine said, holding up a piece of paper scrawled with illegible notes.

Mr. Harbor squinted at them, trying to make out the words. "Very good," he said, and moved on to the next group.

"A cover-up?" TJ said once he was gone. "What do you mean?"

"Doesn't it seem a little strange that so many girls went missing without ever being heard from again?"

"But didn't you read the quotes?" TJ said. "None of their friends thought anything sketchy was going on."

"But none of their friends ever heard from them again either. Dropping out and going home is one thing, but disappearing completely? That's not normal."

"The police don't seem to think so," Blaine chimed in.

"The police don't know everything," Vanessa began to say, but Steffie cut her off.

"I did a little research of my own, and found out that a lot of these girls were supposed to play the Firebird."

"What?" said Vanessa. The articles didn't mention that.

"I know," Steffie said. "I guess the school never divulged it to the police. But I went through all the old cast lists, and it's true."

"Justin knows," Vanessa whispered. She thought of that afternoon in the library, when Justin had told her about all the old cast members who had disappeared. She had brushed him off, but he'd been right.

"I don't understand," said Blaine. "How come we never heard about this?"

"Because the school is probably trying to keep it quiet," Steffie said. "I mean, if you'd had so many leading ballerinas drop out over one ballet, the hardest one, would you announce it to everyone?"

"My parents . . . ," said TJ. "They never mentioned anything like this to me. I doubt they even know." She paused. "But then what about Elly? She disappeared like these girls. But she wasn't cast as the lead . . ."

"Elly has nothing to do with this," Steffie said firmly. "She's fine. She said she dropped out. And she's at home. If she had disappeared, her parents would be here looking for her."

"But what if her parents don't know she's gone?" TJ said, unable to control the tremble in her voice. "What if the school never told them because they're covering something up? Her e-mail didn't sound like her. Something's wrong."

Steffie and Blaine exchanged a worried look. Vanessa had to agree that what TJ was saying did sound extreme, but TJ seemed so shaken that Vanessa didn't want to upset her further—so she said nothing. She was so lost in her thoughts that when the next article came up, she wasn't prepared.

At first she didn't understand what she was seeing. That long, familiar chestnut hair. Those soft hazel eyes staring back at the camera; the delicate lips pursed in a smile. Vanessa touched her finger to the screen. Even in the gritty newspaper photograph, she looked rosy, full of life. And then she read the caption.

MISSING: MARGARET ADLER, BALLERINA

A silence fell over the group as they stared at the smiling girl on the screen, her face a thinner, more delicate version of Vanessa's.

A memory flashed before her eyes: years ago, back in Massachusetts, when she and Margaret were kids.

"I'm coming for you!" her older sister had yelled. It was the middle of the summer, and their father had set up a sprinkler in their backyard to cool them off. They'd used the hose to fill a few leftover balloons from a birthday party, and now they were having a water fight. "Watch out, Vanessa!"

Vanessa had ducked as Margaret tossed a balloon in the air. It missed her and smashed against the back of their house. Vanessa giggled and ran, her toes slipping through the wet grass. She passed the garage, and then everything was a blur. Suddenly there were two arms holding hers, stopping her from falling.

She looked up.

There was Margaret, her hair soaking wet, tiny beads of water running down her face. "Ness, you've gotta watch where you're going." Margaret pointed to the street outside their house, where cars were passing by. Vanessa had almost run out into the middle of the road without looking.

"I'm sorry, Margaret," she had said.

"Don't worry." Margaret gave her a kiss on the forehead. "I'll always protect you."

Turning away from her sister's face, Vanessa pushed the iPad across the desk. "I—I don't want to read anymore."

"Hey," Blaine said gently. "Are you okay?"

Vanessa gave him a quick nod but couldn't look at him directly.

"Oh, honey, don't do that," Blaine said, and pressed his

hand to her brow. "If you want to frown like that in the privacy of your own room, fine, but I can't sit here and watch you ruin that pretty skin with wrinkles."

TJ swatted his arm. "Leave her alone."

"I'm serious," Blaine said. "We're not going to look like this forever. We have to start planning for the future."

TJ rolled her eyes. "Do you want to talk about it?" she said to Vanessa.

Vanessa bit her lip. "There's nothing to say. Everything I know is probably in that article."

But Blaine didn't relent. "Are you sure you don't want to talk? Like really, really sure?"

"Yeah," she said, glancing up at him. "I'm fine. It was a long time ago."

Blaine let out a melodramatic sigh. "Fine," he said. "But I hope you realize that if you were anyone else, I would nag you until you told me. You know how much I hate suspense."

Despite herself, Vanessa let out a laugh.

"Seriously though," Blaine said, his voice earnest. "You know you can talk to us."

"You're not exactly who I'd go to with my deepest, darkest secret," TJ said to Blaine. "No offense."

Blaine was silent for a moment. "I know I have a brash—and beautiful—exterior. But I can be serious too. Mostly it's just easier to make fun of yourself before other people have the chance."

TJ pursed her lips and reached out to squeeze Blaine's shoulder. "I get it."

Vanessa felt surprised by how close she felt to her new friends. "I was just cast as the Firebird too," she said softly. "Maybe it's my turn next."

"Your turn for what?" Steffie said. "Maybe all these ballerinas disappeared because they were stressed out. Maybe they ran away, or just dropped out without telling anyone. It doesn't necessarily have to be sinister."

"But what if it is?" Vanessa said. "You have to admit this is a bit too coincidental. Lead girls disappear—lost without a trace. There is a pattern here, one that seems to have started twenty years ago, and that means someone or something is behind it. Right?" She looked around at her friends. "Otherwise, why would it center around girls performing *The Firebird*?"

"Maybe it's a particularly difficult dance," TJ said.

Vanessa shook her head. "Enough to drive someone to drop out? I don't think so."

"But then what caused it?" TJ pressed. "Steffie said most of the girls who disappeared were cast as the lead in *The Firebird*, not all. Like Elly. She wasn't cast in any production. There's no rhyme or reason."

Blaine gave a brief smile. "One never needs a reason to rhyme." The girls stared at him. "What?" he said. "It's true."

Vanessa ignored him, leaning her chin on her palm. A part of her had never really believed that her sister had just run away. Margaret had been too happy at NYBA. And she was a good sister—if she had left school to start a new life, she would have told Vanessa. No, something else had happened to Margaret and the other girls. But what could explain all of the disappearances?

"Justin," Vanessa suddenly blurted out. The other three turned to her.

"Justin killed them?" Blaine said, a little too loudly. As a few of their classmates turned around, he lowered his voice. "How do you know? I always thought he had a rage problem!"

Vanessa shook her head. "No, I meant maybe Justin would have more information. After all, he did know that cast members were disappearing."

"Can you remember if he's ever said anything else?" Steffie asked.

Vanessa thought back to all of her exchanges with Justin, her mind drifting to the one conversation that she couldn't shake from her memory. "He said Margaret kept a journal. She never showed it to anyone, but she told people that if anything happened to her, all would be revealed in her entries. He thought she was crazy, that it was all in her head, but maybe . . . ?"

"Justin said that?" Blaine asked. "I'm surprised he paid attention to anything she said."

"I think he liked her," Vanessa murmured, thinking back.

"So she rejected him," Steffie said. "And he concluded that she was insane."

"Yeah," Vanessa said, remembering how he had mentioned that she had stopped talking to him. "Though he didn't seem bitter exactly. More sad. I mean, he couldn't have thought she was that crazy or he wouldn't have repeated what she'd said."

"*If anything happened to her?*" TJ repeated. "So she knew something was up."

"I guess so," Vanessa said. "But everyone thought she was crazy."

Steffie leaned on the desk, deep in thought. "Sounds like an insurance policy in case anything happened to her."

"What did it say?" TJ asked. "The diary."

"I've never seen it. They shipped all of Margaret's things back home after she disappeared. When my mom finally opened the boxes, I was there. I would have remembered a diary," Vanessa said. "There wasn't one."

"Do you think she was lying about keeping one?" Blaine asked.

"No way," Steffie said, answering for Vanessa. "If she thought someone was out to get her, she wouldn't have left it in plain sight for anyone to find. She would have hidden it."

"But where?" Blaine asked.

"If I were her," Steffie said, "there's only one place I would hide it." She paused. "In her room. And by her room, I mean my room."

At the sound of the bell, they raced back to the dormitory. Steffie's side of the room was cluttered with clothes and papers, but Elly's side was as bare as the day she'd left.

The slice of rosin was still on the desk from the night before. Vanessa wrapped Elly's note around it and tucked it into her bag. Then she got on her hands and knees and, with the others, began to search. They looked everywhere—under the bed, behind the dresser, the underside of the drawers and the closet shelves; Vanessa checked the floorboards to see if any of them were loose. They emptied all of Steffie's furniture, throwing her things in a pile in the center of the room. TJ even reached inside the radiator, emerging with a tangle of dust and spiderwebs.

Blaine collapsed on Steffie's stripped mattress. "Nothing."

Vanessa blew a strand of hair away from her face. "I guess it's hard to believe that it would still be here after all these years." She glanced out the window, where nothing but a thin screen separated the tiny room from the sprawling city. Was her sister out there somewhere? Was Elly?

Steffie bent down and picked up one of her old pointe shoes. It was worn and tattered, the pink satin discolored with use. "But if the diary isn't here, and it's not at your house, then where is it?"

Chapter Fourteen

Monday morning, and the clock on the nightstand blinked five twenty-nine.

Thwarted by a deluge of homework, Vanessa and her friends had spent the last week in the library, which was so crowded with students studying for midterms that they could barely say a word without practically the entire school hearing it.

Vanessa had stared at the arched entryway, waiting for Zep to walk through it, but he never did. Instead, her eyes fell on Justin, who was hunched over his books, scrawling quick notes with a pencil, the Fratelli twins on either side of him like bodyguards. With them around, there had been no way for Vanessa to approach Justin. And even if he knew something about her sister, did she really want to talk to him?

The only time she had been able to steal with Zep had been

during the previous week of preliminary rehearsals for *The Firebird* while they were becoming familiar with the score and learning their steps. They couldn't talk; rehearsals were silent unless Josef spoke; though just being close to Zep was enough. She barely noticed the other girls glaring at her, or Justin following their movements like a shadow.

In those early days, Zep caught up with her after rehearsal, his chest damp with sweat, and together, they'd walk out of the studio and down Broadway, Zep's warm hand grasping hers as if they were still dancing. They sat close to each other at dinner, squeezed into a tiny table until their knees knocked against each other. They laughed and chatted; Vanessa told him about how worried she was about living up to the expectations of her role, about how difficult the steps were and how she had so much to learn. Zep assured her that her technique was perfect; she just had to practice more. He touched her hand, sending a shiver of warmth up her arm and making her forget herself, if just for a moment.

She should have been brimming with happiness, yet something about each date was strange. It wasn't just that they were exhausted, parting ways at the end of the night quicker than she would have liked. It was the sense that he was holding back on her. She was always the one divulging her feelings, and he the one who comforted her, but whenever she asked about him and how he spent the rest of his time, he dodged her questions. He was really busy, practicing and working with Josef. On what, she didn't know. Only that it had to do with his technique and getting him into a good corps next year.

She wanted to press him but held back. Maybe because he was a senior and she a freshman, because he was Zeppelin Gray and she was just Vanessa, the redhead who somehow won Zep's heart, though no one, including herself, could understand why. Even his texts were brief, and though they seemed sweet on the surface, they felt somehow impersonal.

You were beautiful at dinner tonight.

Loved dancing with you this morning.

Vanessa couldn't pinpoint exactly what about them disappointed her. They were walking through the steps, saying all the right things. But to her it didn't feel like a relationship; it felt like a rehearsal.

Then, as the week progressed, the little time they had together began to vanish. Vanessa noticed that Josef seemed more impatient with Zep, barking at him for reasons Vanessa couldn't quite grasp. And that wasn't the only thing that seemed off. Once, through the window in the door, Vanessa thought she saw the Fratelli twins glaring at Zep, but when she blinked, they were gone. She was seeing things, she concluded. Yet every day when they were through, Josef would pull Zep away to his office—to discuss his part, Vanessa guessed—and she retreated to the library, burying herself in her books. But all she could think of was Zep, and when she would see him again. Was he her boyfriend? Was it real? Or was he somehow slipping away from her?

TJ turned over but did not wake as Vanessa slipped out of bed. She muttered in her sleep—nothing but gibberish, though her tone was pained. She hadn't been sleeping well lately, and had been short-tempered, especially when the subject of Elly came up. She didn't understand why no one else was as worried as she was. Vanessa made sure not to wake her.

Outside, the streets of New York were quiet, save for the soft *swoosh* of cars rushing down Broadway. She dressed and tied her hair in a loose ponytail. She slung her dance bag over her shoulder and slipped into the hallway.

She had planned to go to the dance studio downstairs, to stretch out and warm up for the first real rehearsal, when they would dance, rather than walk through, their parts. But when she reached the lobby, she hesitated. Through the glass panes on the door she saw a group of teenagers walking down the sidewalk past Lincoln Center, carrying skateboards and backpacks. Vanessa watched one of them buy a donut from a street vendor. Her bag slid down her shoulder. She realized she didn't know what it felt like to take a leisurely walk with friends and not talk about ballet or rehearsal, to eat a donut and not feel guilty afterward, to have afternoons free to do whatever she wanted. She *could* go, she realized. The lobby was deserted. No one would see her leave.

She glanced down the hall toward the studios, understanding for the first time how her sister must have felt when she decided to run away. All she had to do was push open the door, and she could leave everything—the *Firebird* cast, the catty upperclassmen, the mysterious disappearances, Justin and his two sidekicks, even Zep and his aching absence—behind.

She took one step forward, and then another.

And then her phone rang.

As Vanessa fished her cell out of her bag, a janitor appeared from around a corner, carrying a mop and pail. She must have stared at him, because he gave her a curious look as she answered the phone.

"Mom?"

"Oh, Vanessa, I'm so glad you picked up." Her mother sounded breathless.

Vanessa went rigid. "Why?" she said, glancing at the clock over the foyer entrance. "It's six in the morning. Is everything okay?"

"No, I don't know what came over me. My throat went dry, I began to sweat—which as you know, I never do—"

"What happened? Do you need to go to the hospital?"

"No, nothing like that. I'm just so glad you picked up. You never pick up anymore. It worries me."

Vanessa let out a sigh of relief. "I'm sorry, Mom. I'm just so busy with *The Firebird* and all."

"I was just thinking about that and how proud your sister would be. And how proud I am. I know I haven't been as supportive as you'd like, but I just don't want you to literally follow in her footsteps."

"What do you mean?"

"Your sister was so young when she was cast as the lead, and she—I guess she was too young, and she couldn't take the pressure. And now you're the lead, and I—I just don't want to lose you too."

Vanessa glanced out the doors at Lincoln Center, a pang of guilt passing through her. "Don't worry, Mom." She picked up her bag. "I would never run away. I'm actually on my way to the studio now."

Vanessa watched the janitor mop a circle of the floor by the stairwell. He caught her eye when she finished speaking, as if he knew what she had been considering. She broke his gaze and began walking down the hall to the practice studio.

She could hear her mother breathing on the other end. "Okay, honey, I believe you. Really I do."

"Hey, Mom. Did Margaret ever tell you about a diary she was keeping?"

"Not that I know of," said her mother. "Did you say you were going to the studio? Isn't it awfully early for that? I don't want you to hurt yourself or spend all of your free time practicing."

Vanessa was ready with a response, but when she heard her mother's words, she went quiet.

"And what about your dizziness? Is that getting worse?"

Vanessa glared at the phone. "You're making a big deal out of nothing," she said. "It only happens when everything goes right, so I don't see why you think it's such an issue." But the truth was, Vanessa had been disappointed when she realized that none of her new friends seemed to suffer from the same problem.

"I'm just trying to help you," her mother said. "You know you can come home at any time. We can set up your room the way it was before you left. It will be just like old times."

Vanessa bit her lip. She couldn't leave now. What about her friends? And Zep? For once, she finally felt like she was getting somewhere, slowly collecting all of the odd pieces of information surrounding Margaret's disappearance. If she left now, she would never know how they fit together. "I can't, Mom. But I'll be home in December. It's not that far away."

Her mother sighed. "I understand, honey. Just thought I'd try." She paused. "I miss you."

The pain in her voice made Vanessa's heart feel heavy. "I miss you too," she said, and it was true.

The girls' dressing room downstairs was dark when Vanessa ran inside, slamming the door shut behind her, suddenly furious with her mother for mentioning her dizziness. The fluorescent lights buzzed in the silence. She threw her bag down in the corner and fiddled with her locker. For some reason it wasn't opening, and, without thinking, she kicked it hard. It popped open, spilling out all her clothes and supplies.

She let out a cry and collapsed on the floor, rubbing her foot, which was already sore and blistered from daily classes and rehearsal. Gingerly, she slipped off her shoe. Her toes were taped with bandages, the skin around them cracked and bruised. She flexed her foot and winced. A pair of scissors lay among her things on the floor. The metal was cool against her skin as she cut the tape and began to peel it off.

She could still hear her mother's voice clearly as she ripped off the first bandage. *We can set up your room the way it was before you left.*

She ripped off the next bandage. *It will be just like old times.*

Her toes were caked with scabs, swollen, and stiff. Using a

cotton ball and ointment from her bag, she dabbed her feet with hydrogen peroxide. A sharp, searing pain shot up her leg. She closed her eyes. If she were honest with herself, she would have admitted that in an odd way, she liked how it felt. She pressed her lips together, bearing it.

Vanessa practiced alone, blasting Stravinsky through her headphones, until the *Firebird* rehearsal began. Every time her mother's voice cut through the music, she turned the volume up and pounded harder. A flutter of the flute and she inched across the floor, spreading her arms by her sides. A horn, sudden and abrupt, and Vanessa flung her body, the music tugging her forward and back. Then an eerie whisper, like fog crawling through the forest, and she lofted herself onto her toes. The ribbons bit into her ankles, but she closed her eyes and began to spin until the floor felt hot beneath her feet, and the music grew slower, stranger.

She grew dizzy.

The mirrors bent and warped, distorting the room. Her limbs seemed to buckle beneath her, and, unable to support herself any longer, she set her heel to the floor and came to an abrupt halt, her body wavering as she regained her sense of balance. It wasn't an issue, she told herself. But a part of her wondered if this time her mother might be right.

After she finished her early morning practice, Vanessa sat in the corner of the studio, stretching, her leotard damp with sweat. When the rest of the troupe filed in—the girls who would play the thirteen princesses—she wiped off her forehead and checked her makeup, hoping none of the other dancers would realize that she'd already been practicing for hours. They were all seniors, most from the group who'd been rehearsing with Josef since the first week of school.

Even up close, they looked so similar that Vanessa had a hard time remembering who was who. Three Laurens, another two Lauras. Laurel. Lara. Tara. Tiffany. Leigh. Two Jessicas. Was that right? It didn't matter, because none of them even graced her with a look, let alone a hello.

Finally Anna Franko strutted through the door, the thirteenth princess, her skin a pearly white, her blond hair tied into a perfect little knot.

She was laughing at something one of the girls was saying, her slender throat arching as she tilted her head back. As she passed, her eyes flitted to Vanessa. The mere sight of Vanessa's flushed face seemed to startle her. The smile faded from Anna's strawberry lips, and suddenly Vanessa felt incredibly small.

She slipped off her headphones. "Hi," she said timidly, gazing up at Anna's beautiful face.

But Anna said nothing. She merely walked by, leading the other girls to the opposite side of the room, where they resumed their chatter as if Vanessa weren't there. Vanessa just sat there, a lump in her stomach, realizing that it didn't matter how well she danced; she would never be one of them.

The girls laughed, Anna's voice high above the rest. Her eyes narrowed as they met Vanessa's, taunting her.

Vanessa broke her gaze and began to stuff her things into her bag, trying to pretend she was too busy to notice the other girls, waiting for Zep to stride through the door, but the only boy who entered the room was Justin. He gave her a nod before throwing his bag down by the barre. She leaned back against the mirror, deflated.

When the clock struck nine, the doors burst open and Josef sauntered across the room in a gray T-shirt and tight pants, holding a long staff. Zep strode in behind him. Vanessa studied him, trying to catch his eye, but he didn't seem to see her.

"*D'accord*," Josef said, his eyes brightening as he gazed out at the dancers. "Welcome to the first *real* rehearsal for *Firebird*. No more listening to the score or memorizing steps. It's time to get to work, to dance. I trust you are all prepared. I have personally hand-picked each of you for your talent, dedication, and perseverance." His eyes rested on Vanessa. "Every one of you has something that transcends the ordinary."

He took a step toward Vanessa and spoke softly. "There is a *je ne sais quoi* in each of you, as if you had reached out and touched me, and suddenly your *coeur* was beating with mine."

The room was silent. Vanessa felt herself blush, feeling Josef's eyes lingering on her.

"A quick reminder about our schedule: In the morning rehearsals, we will work on various dances from the *Firebird* suite. But in the afternoons, we will work on one dance in particular, called *La Danse du Feu*, or the Dance of Fire. In addition to your academic classes, of course."

The French rolled off his tongue in a hot breath, as if he were speaking the name of his lover. *La Danse du Feu*, Vanessa repeated in her head, but she couldn't remember any dance in the *Firebird* with that name.

She raised her hand. "What is the fire dance?" she asked Josef. "I've been watching the *Firebird* since I was a child, and I've never seen it."

Josef smiled. "I'm glad you asked," he said, giving her a slight bow. "*La Danse du Feu* was once part of the original ballet, but it was quickly removed because it was too difficult. Ballerinas were falling, injuring themselves. They complained about the rhythm and how it did not match the rest of the dance. So the early choreographers struck it from the ballet, and it has rarely been performed since."

A murmur passed over the room. Josef held up a finger for silence. "It is a dance like no other. When I first saw it performed, I thought the life would leave me."

Taking slow steps, he began pacing. "I believe that you can perform this dance. That *we* can, together. *Non*, it will not be easy, but nothing worthwhile is ever easy."

He stopped walking and gave the cast a level gaze. "We will start now, using this rehearsal to practice the fire dance, as the afternoon rehearsal will not take place today. I will be observing the student body to choose the understudies for the Firebird and the thirteen princesses. Starting tomorrow morning, normal practice will resume, and we will get to work on the rest of the ballet."

Vanessa gazed around the room, wondering if the others

were as nervous as she was. But it wasn't just anxiety she felt; it was excitement. This was a chance for Vanessa to prove herself. From the corner of the room, she could feel Zep's eyes sweeping over her. She shivered but didn't dare meet his gaze, for fear that something inside her would melt.

"*Vous êtes prêt?*" Josef asked, and clasped his hands together. "*Bon.* Let's get to work."

He arranged them about the room, Vanessa and Zep in the middle, the thirteen girls around them. On the side of the room, Vanessa could feel Justin watching her. She looked away, checking her posture in the mirror until Josef began to clap an odd, erratic beat. He dictated directions. "No music," he said. "Just feel the beat deep within your body. Now, fourth position!

"One and two and three and four! And right leg back, and brace arms out!"

It started off easy, Vanessa's legs moving to Josef's commands as if they were natural, as if he didn't need to speak at all. Around her, the other ballerinas followed her pace, their steps simpler versions of Vanessa's.

She felt Zep's hands on her waist as they moved together, the steps becoming harder to follow, the thirteen other girls swooping around them. She shivered beneath his touch, his breath against her neck as he lifted her into a leap. Her body arched above him, coming to life. When she landed, she rolled her neck and lifted her leg into an arabesque. She could feel herself losing control, the room darkening as she extended her hand to Zep.

Shadows played across his face, warping it into something vacant and terrible. She gasped as he stepped toward her, his eyes black and hollow. She wobbled, about to fall.

"Steady," Josef warned somewhere in the distance.

Vanessa blinked and the world returned to normal. Zep was in front of her, his expression concerned.

Josef paced around them, still clapping the rhythm. "Now down," he said, and Vanessa allowed her foot to slide across the floor. "So stiff," he said, as if it pained him.

Heat flushed Vanessa's face. She wanted to please him; she wanted to perform, to look beautiful in front of him, but she couldn't get it right. She heard one of the other girls let out a bitter laugh. They were happy to see her fail. They wanted her to lose everything. And even more confusing, they all seemed to feel more comfortable with the strange dance than she was. They didn't fumble their steps or flinch at the change of rhythm.

It was as if they had practiced it before.

Vanessa faltered, barely catching herself, and suddenly Josef was right there next to her, so close his cool skin tickled her arm. With strong hands, he took hold of her thigh, grasping it as if they were lovers. And sliding down, he lifted her leg.

She winced as a sharp pain shot up her thigh, but quickly muffled it.

"Hold it," he said, his fingers pressing into her leg until she was sure they would leave bruises.

"Like this." His voice was a low growl, his breath hot against her ear; he pressed her knee down, the inside of her leg burning. Just when she thought she couldn't hold the position any longer, he let go, and she stumbled back.

"Now again," he said, tapping his staff on the floor.

Vanessa tried to follow his directions, but her mind was overwhelmed with claps and commands. Zep's eyes hardened as she fumbled, her body exhausted from her early morning practice.

"You're never going to fill your sister's shoes," Josef said into her ear while gripping her arm tightly in position. "You're inadequate to the role." He jerked her body into the proper form as if she were a marionette. "You're trying to destroy everything we've worked for.

"Straighten your leg," he snarled. "Arch your spine!" They continued for a few more beats until finally he stopped them with a grunt. "Enough!" he shouted. "Enough."

Zep fell back, clearly frustrated, avoiding Vanessa's eyes. She felt something inside her crumble as he walked away from her. But her attention quickly shifted back to Josef. "*Qu'est-ce que c'est?*" he demanded, his voice echoing through the studio. "Why can you not get it right? It is very simple. Just follow your steps perfectly. The rest will unfold before you."

She wiped the sweat from her forehead, trying to hold back her tears. "I'm sorry," she said. She could feel the rest of the dancers staring at her. "I just—I don't know this dance. I haven't practiced it yet."

On the periphery, she could see Zep take off his shoes and stuff them into his bag.

"So start learning," said Josef. "You're the only one who cannot keep up."

Vanessa's eyes flitted across the room. "I—I'm sorry," she said again, her glance resting on Zep. "I'll do better next time."

"Next time?" Josef roared. "Are you going to say that on the night of the performance? Is that how you're going to treat your audience? Your colleagues?"

"N-no," Vanessa said, biting her lip. Tears stung her eyes.

"And stop saying you're sorry," Josef said. "Because I am the one who is sorry. For choosing you."

Vanessa swallowed a sob as he turned away from her and walked to the center of the room. The other dancers were bending over their bags, pulling on their sweats and sipping water bottles. She gazed at them, searching for a friendly face, but none of them would look at her.

"I must add that starting tomorrow," Josef continued, addressing the entire ensemble, "we will have our afternoon rehearsals in the basement practice room in Lincoln Center, which shares the same dimensions as the main stage."

The burned room, Vanessa thought, rubbing her fingers together absently as if she could still feel the ashy walls.

"We will issue all of you passes, so you can practice on your own"—Josef's gaze turned to Vanessa—"if you wish."

Wiping her cheeks, Vanessa glanced around, hoping to find comfort from Zep, but sometime during Josef's speech he had left, and she didn't see him for the rest of the day. The only eyes she could feel on her were Justin's. She thought he was laughing at her, pleased with her utter failure of a rehearsal, but when she finally allowed her gaze to meet his, she was startled by his soft expression. He didn't mock her or laugh, or even look at her with pity. His eyes seemed sympathetic, as if he understood what she was going through.

"Of course she hates you," TJ said, later that afternoon. "You're the lead role. And you have Zep."

"Correction," Blaine said. "You *took* Zep from her."

"I didn't *take* him," Vanessa said, feeling worse. During rehearsal he hadn't spoken to her, and he'd left without saying good-bye.

"Why don't you try talking to them?" Steffie said. "They're probably nicer than you think. I mean, wouldn't you be a little put off if a freshman took the lead role?"

So that evening in the dining hall, when Steffie, TJ, and Blaine sat down at a table by the far window, Vanessa hesitated.

A loud laugh sounded through the room. Vanessa immediately recognized it as Anna's. She turned and saw her sweep of blond hair at a table in the center of the dining hall. The other twelve princesses sat around her. Even at dinner, they all looked the same—their clothes in shades of pink and heather gray, their hair hanging loose around their shoulders in casual waves. They were even eating matching salads—greens with olives, oranges, and cherry tomatoes.

Vanessa glanced over at her friends. Steffie had turned, still holding her tray, and was giving her a quizzical look. Vanessa shrugged, and without saying anything, she lifted her head high and walked over to the table of princesses.

Vanessa cleared her throat. "May I sit with you?" she said, trying to look friendly.

At first, no one seemed to hear her. They were busy listening to Anna. "I heard there have been a half-dozen disappearances in the past," Anna said. She leaned over the table and lowered her voice. "Every single time, the lead dancer went insane. Some even disappeared."

Vanessa was about to try to get their attention again, but when she heard Anna's words, she gripped her tray and froze.

"Every single lead dancer?" a girl asked.

"Not all, but most," Anna said softly. "Just like Chloë."

Laurel, a sultry brunette with big lips and a penchant for dark eyeliner, spoke up. "And not just crazy, but like mad as a hatter with mercury poisoning and off her rocker," she emphasized. "Maybe the annual production is cursed!"

"What?" Vanessa blurted out, forgetting she was listening in on their conversation.

The conversation halted, and Anna Franko looked up, surprised to see Vanessa. "What do you want?" she asked.

Vanessa swallowed, her tray suddenly heavy. The table went quiet. "I—I'm sorry," she said, her voice trembling. "I guess I'll just sit somewhere else then."

"Maybe you shouldn't be eating," Anna said with finality. "Maybe you should be practicing."

The other girls stared down at their plates, ignoring Vanessa as if she didn't exist. She searched the room, hoping to see

Zep stand up for her, but no luck. Maybe this was how it started, she realized, taking a weary step backward. She didn't want to go back to her friends and eat dinner and explain what had happened. Instead, she wanted to chuck her tray and run back to her darkened room until everyone forgot about her. Until she really did disappear.

CHAPTER FIFTEEN

Vanessa's shoes tapped softly against the stairs. One, two, three flights, the voices of the girls from dinner still echoing in her head. She walked down the corridor until she reached the door at the far end of the hall. To her surprise, it was identical to her own, the dark wood smooth and worn.

Vanessa touched the brass knob, imagining that the cool metal was Zep's hand, but recoiled when she heard an echo of voices down the hall. A group of seniors piled into the corridor, barely noticing her as they filtered into their rooms, laughing. To Vanessa's relief, none of them were from the table of princesses.

When their voices faded, Vanessa held up her fist, letting her shirt sleeve fall back until she could see a purpling bruise shaped like Josef's thumb on the inside of her arm. Taking a breath, she knocked.

Nothing. She listened for movement within. "Zep?" She stared at the grain of the wood, waiting for his deep voice. "Are you there?"

She took a step back and fished through her bag until she found her cell phone. Typing quickly, she wrote him a text.

I'm sorry I let you down.

She held her fingers over the keys, trying to decide if she should say anything more, when she heard Anna's voice floating up from the stairwell. She pressed send, and slipped into the darkness of the back stairwell, hoping that no one except Zep would know she had ever been there in the first place.

Vanessa waited for a response, but a day passed and she hadn't heard from Zep. He didn't come to her room or surprise her in the library. She'd seen him only briefly in the dining hall, his metallic eyes gazing at her through the crowd. They seemed to be apologizing, looking past her as if distracted, though before she could go to him, her friends surrounded her, chattering about class. She took out her cell phone only to see a text from him pop up.

Sorry I've been distant. So busy. It's not about you.

She read it again, confused. Why hadn't he just told her in person?

His absence was the most pronounced in rehearsal.

"I'm afraid Zeppelin is sick," Josef announced on the second day, and turned to Justin, who had been warming up on the barre. "I trust you know the steps for the prince?"

Sick? Vanessa's face fell. Why hadn't he told her?

Justin wiped the sweat from his brow. "By heart," he said, glancing at Vanessa.

"Act one, then," Josef said with a clap.

Vanessa took her position, trying to avoid Justin's eye, and on Josef's count, they began to dance. To Vanessa's dismay, Justin was actually good, his footwork bringing the prince to life before her eyes, as if, through some cruel twist of fate, he had always been meant to replace Zep.

After two days passed with no other sign of Zep, though, Vanessa began to worry. She stopped by his room every night to see if he was okay, and when he didn't answer, she texted him, asking how he was, but he never responded. Was he really sick, or was he just avoiding her? Maybe he was in the hospital.

Those were the thoughts that tormented her during morning rehearsal, when the entire cast filed into the studio except Zep.

At nine o'clock, Josef closed the door and clapped his hands. Justin was stretching by the barre with the other understudies. Realizing Zep wasn't going to show, he stood and was about to take the place of the prince for the third day in a row, when Josef raised a hand.

"Zeppelin will not be here again today, but instead of practicing the normal *Firebird* scenes, I would like to work on *La Danse du Feu*."

A few of the dancers groaned but then went quiet when Josef narrowed his eyes. "I know we normally only work on that in the afternoon rehearsals, but the scene needs far more practice than the others."

Vanessa's chest seemed to cave in on itself. Just the thought of working on the strange dance twice in one day exhausted her.

"Halfway through," Josef continued, "the prince fades off-stage and the finale focuses on Vanessa, the Firebird." He let his eyes rest on her. "And the thirteen princesses around her." He turned to Justin. "We will not be needing you today, as we will be focusing on the second half of the dance. If you could just observe, that would be *excellente*."

Justin froze, his face betraying a slight hint of embarrassment before he sat back down. He avoided Vanessa's gaze while Josef pointed Vanessa and the thirteen princesses into position. Vanessa kept one eye on the door as Josef began clapping. She had memorized the steps to the final scene by now, and her body moved automatically, landing each step perfectly. A smile spread across Josef's face. "Yes!" he shouted. "Yes!"

When the dance was finished, she lowered her leg to the floor and let her body fall out of character. Josef began clapping. "Spectacular," he said, his eyes traveling over Vanessa's body, now damp with sweat. "Just spectacular."

Anna rolled her eyes and walked behind him toward the corner of the room. "Luck," she whispered as she passed Vanessa. The other twelve princesses followed her.

Too startled to think of a retort, all Vanessa could do was stand there stupidly in the center of the studio.

"Don't worry about her," Josef whispered in her ear.

Vanessa jumped, not expecting him to be standing so close to her.

He followed her gaze as Anna slipped out the door. "If you can do what you did just now in our afternoon rehearsal," he said, "no one will be able to stop you."

Vanessa should have been happy, but she wasn't. The only person she'd wanted to see hadn't been there. Where was he? Why hadn't he shown up? She wandered toward the door when someone called her name.

"Vanessa," Justin said, beckoning her to the wall. "I wanted to tell you—"

But Vanessa didn't have the energy. "I can't, Justin. Not now," she said before he could continue, and pushed past him into the hallway.

Her thoughts absorbed her for the rest of the afternoon, so by the time she met up with Steffie and TJ in the dining hall, it took her a moment to register what they were saying.

"Have you heard from Elly?" TJ balanced her tray by the salad bar, spooning a bit of lettuce onto her plate. "She still hasn't responded to any of my messages."

"Elly," Vanessa murmured. She had actually been planning on sending her a letter, but had yet to write anything down.

"It's like she's a different person," TJ said. "The Elly I knew would never have acted like this. She never would have just left us behind and asked us not to talk to her. It makes me want to go to her house and shake her. I just don't get it."

"I know what you mean," Vanessa said. Her mind drifted to

Zep, who also seemed to have two personalities—one that Vanessa understood and one that was completely foreign and unpredictable. "You think you know someone, and then they just change. They stop showing up or telling you where they're going, and you have no way of knowing why."

"Exactly!" TJ said.

Vanessa's words had come out more passionately than she had intended, and Steffie paused, confused. "Did I miss something here?"

"She's upset because her boyfriend hasn't been showing up for rehearsals," Justin said from behind them.

Vanessa turned around, only to be met with a smug smile. "He's not my boyfriend. And you're just the understudy."

"That doesn't mean that I don't know what's going on in there," Justin said.

"Oh, because it's such a secret," Vanessa said, her tone sarcastic.

Justin gave her a level look. "Maybe it is."

Vanessa waited for him to laugh, but he didn't. "I don't know what you're talking about," she said finally. She cocked her head at Steffie and TJ, and together they went to the register and swiped their IDs.

As they found a table and sat down, Justin stood near them, holding out his tray. Vanessa couldn't help but look at the clean lines of the muscles on his arms as he pushed his hair from his face, his T-shirt lifting at the bottom, betraying a sliver of smooth skin. Quickly, she looked away. He leaned forward. "Exactly. That's how secrets work."

The basement studio was always exactly the same—wide and mirrorless, the walls scarred with burns and caked in thick black ash. Vanessa wanted to ask someone what it was from, but the other dancers still barely looked at her. Stenciled into the ash were the white shapes of ballerinas, the only spots where the original paint was still preserved. They lined the room like an accordion of paper cutouts, except each dancer was in a different pose.

That afternoon she was so distracted by them that she almost didn't notice the boy standing by the edge of the room, his broad shoulders bent as he put on his shoes.

"Zep?"

He stood up, looming over her. She could see her silhouette in the reflection of his eyes. He looked almost guilty as he parted his lips to say something, but before he could speak, Josef's voice sounded through the room. "Let us commence!"

The afternoon practices were small, intimate, with just the primary cast. On occasion, Josef asked Justin to show up, since he was the primary understudy, but more often than not, it was just Vanessa, the princesses, and Zep. Vanessa's understudy was Anna Franko, who he sometimes asked to observe Vanessa, just in case. Now everyone in the room crowded around Zep, asking if he was all right before shuffling into position. Vanessa stood back, waiting. She had wanted to see him for days, but now that he was here, he didn't look like he had been sick. He looked healthy.

"Vanessa." Zep held out his hand to her cheek, but she flinched.

"Are you okay?" she asked. "Why didn't you tell me you were sick? I tried knocking on your door but you never answered."

"I was at the infirmary," Zep said.

"Oh," Vanessa said, feeling suddenly guilty. Here she had been imagining all of these awful things when really, he'd been sick. "Why didn't you tell me? I was so worried."

"I wasn't myself," Zep said, confused. "It wasn't about you."

It wasn't about you. His words, so similiar to his earlier text, made her wince as if she had been slapped. Something about the way he looked made her want to disappear, to run out into the crisp New York afternoon and not stop until she was so far away from NYBA that she wouldn't be able to find her way back if she tried.

She looked away, not wanting to see the pity in Zep's eyes, but when she glanced in the mirror, she was only met with Justin's reflection. Caught in the act, he tried to pretend like he hadn't been listening, but Vanessa could tell from the uncomfortable look on his face that he'd heard it all.

Vanessa let out an exasperated laugh. She couldn't get away. Everywhere she turned, Justin or Anna or the rest of the princesses were looking at her, waiting for her to misstep.

"Positions!" Josef said, eyeing Vanessa and Zep.

Vanessa took her place at the center of the floor, just inches from the ashy scar. Zep stood behind her, so close she could feel his breath on her shoulder.

"I'm sorry I didn't tell you."

Before she could respond, Josef raised his hand. "One and two and three and now—"

Following Josef's commands, Vanessa arched her head up to the lights, raising her arm.

"I should have been more thoughtful. I was just so tired that I could barely open my door," Zep said, his hand tickling the small of her back.

The dancing princesses circled them in a strange and erratic rhythm. All the while, Josef counted out the beat, which changed meter so capriciously that Vanessa could hardly keep up. She slid her leg outward on Josef's command, and leaned back into Zep's arms.

"Your door? But I thought you were in the infirmary?" Vanessa whispered, confused.

Zep's eyes seemed dull as he stared down at her.

"I was. Until last night, I mean. They sent me back after dinner."

"Now lift," Josef said to Vanessa. "Slowly, as if you're a coil of smoke."

Zep had been in his room?

"Higher!" Josef said. "And release, two-three, one-two-three."

Vanessa struggled to keep up with Josef's counting. She knew the steps, but today it was as if the beat were at odds with her body, trying to shake her from completing the dance. Still, she pressed on, Zep gliding smoothly beside her.

"Did you hear me knock on the door?" she breathed when he lowered himself over her.

He hesitated, his hair dangling over her forehead. "No."

Vanessa let her body sink backward into a languid dip.

"Yes!" Josef said. "Beautiful! You are nothing. You are a wisp of smoke curling into oblivion!"

For a moment, it felt true.

"What about my text from the other day? Did you get it?"

Zep gave her a guilty look. "Yes. I'm sorry I didn't respond. I should have tried to get in touch with you earlier," he said. "I was just really distracted."

Vanessa felt his hand slide up her leg as she extended it into an arabesque.

"Too stiff!" Josef said. "Too slow! The rhythm is changing. You must change with it."

Vanessa's body grew tight. "Distracted? By what? I thought you said you were sick."

She waited for Zep to answer, but he only looked surprised to have been caught in a lie.

Horrified, she pushed away from Zep. She was off the beat, but she couldn't help it. Her eyes stung and her face felt hot, so hot that it might burn up.

"Keep in line!" Josef shouted, circling her. "Control your body! Straighten your legs. Count with me. One-two, one-two, two-three-four, two-three-four . . ."

Vanessa resumed her position, but the rhythm kept confusing her legs, making them go faster, then incredibly slowly, in a switch so abrupt that it felt as if her body were being thrown about the room by a blustery wind. *The dance doesn't want to be performed,* she thought. It wanted to be unconquered.

"Non!" Josef said, shaking his head. "Stop thinking and let your body take over!"

Her muscles burned. She wanted to please Josef, but it was useless. She lifted herself up and balanced *en pointe*, her weight pressing down through her bones until her legs trembled and her feet ached. She could feel Zep behind her, could smell the sweet fragrance of his sweat.

"I'm sorry," he said. "I didn't mean to hurt you. I want to make it right."

She closed her eyes, feeling his fingers graze her back, and went rigid.

"Non!" Josef's voice was so loud that it halted everything in the room. *"Non, non, non."*

He strode toward Vanessa, who stepped out of position, her feet throbbing in pain. Without warning, he rapped his staff against the back of her thighs, shocking them into position. "Straight!" he shouted, and pressed his hand to her back, pushing it erect. *"Comme ça,"* he said coldly, and positioned her arms above her head.

She must have cringed, because he seemed to see the fear in her eyes and released her, his expression softening.

"Something is bothering you," Josef said, studying her face.

Unable to help herself, Vanessa gazed up at the figures on the wall.

"You are distracted by the decorations? They are for another performance. Don't worry about them."

Vanessa shook her head.

"Then tell me," Josef demanded.

She looked up at Josef. "Why do you think I can perform this dance when no one else could?" Even her sister ran away before she had to perform it, she wanted to say, but didn't.

Josef stepped back, surprised. "Is that what you are worried about?" He laughed. "Vanessa, I chose you to be the Firebird because I've never seen anyone dance like you do." He walked around her, his eyes traveling over her legs, her arms, her neck, as if she were a statue carved out of marble. "I gaze at you," he said, his voice so intimate it made Vanessa tremble, "and the rest of the world melts away."

With a swift motion, he pulled her close to him. "Let me show you."

He placed his hand on her ribs and guided her across the room, away from Zep. Her skin quivered, his body warm and hard against her back. "Shh," he told her. "Not so stiff."

She swallowed and tried to make her body relax.

"You are trying to count the beat. To memorize it," he said. "But that won't work. Let the time push you forward. Let it weigh you down, feel its tedious thumping in your chest." With that, he let go of her arms and watched as she danced, the color filling her cheeks until she felt the heat pulse through her veins. *Alive*, she thought. *I am alive.*

Josef paused, studying her. "Beautiful," he murmured. "Should we try again, then?"

Vanessa gave him a timid smile. Maybe Josef was right. Maybe she could do it.

"*Bon*," he said, and turned to the rest of the dancers. "From the beginning."

Raising her head high, she walked toward Zep, who put his hand on her waist. "Let's start over," he whispered. And then the dance began again.

Another week passed, and while Vanessa improved, she was not able to duplicate her one early success with *La Danse du Feu*. Josef would shout, and all of his kind words melted away, his compliments replaced by counting, always counting, the rhythm fighting her, trying to get her to quit. Day after day, she barely managed to finish the steps, her feet stumbling over Zep's in a confused jumble, her legs still tender from the day before. The princesses sneered, their own steps simpler versions of hers.

Josef lashed at out at Zep, too, his narrow eyes scouring Vanessa and him while he made them repeat their steps over and over. Every so often, he would lurch in and correct the angle of Vanessa's leg, the position of her waist beneath Zep's hands, the crest of her neck. Vanessa was so involved in her own dancing that she never noticed the mistakes Zep had made. Was it her fault? Were her errors making Zep stumble too?

All she knew was that Josef was deeply dissatisfied, and not just with her. That much was clear at the end of every rehearsal, when he called Zep to stay late and practice. Every night, Zep threw a towel over his shoulder and gazed back at her, his shirt damp with sweat, his eyes exhausted and vulnerable. *Stay with me*, they seemed to say, but Vanessa couldn't. Why was Josef so upset with Zep, and why hadn't he asked her to rehearse after hours too?

The regular *Firebird* rehearsals were going fine; it was the afternoon sessions—when they practiced the strange dance—that she struggled with. She wanted to talk to Zep, but every afternoon Josef called him over as the dancers were filing out, before Vanessa could even say good-bye. Finally, on Friday afternoon, she worked up the courage to ask him out. "Would you want to get dinner with me tonight?" she whispered in the middle of the dance.

Zep gripped her waist. "I would love that."

Vanessa smiled to herself, and they finished the sequence in silence.

At the end of rehearsal, Vanessa gathered her things and waited for Zep by the door. But before he approached, Josef's voice rang out over the studio. "Zeppelin. Wait for me in my office. We have work to do."

Vanessa felt something inside her collapse. Zep's gaze met hers in what seemed like an apology, as Josef came up behind her and swept her into the hall. "I want to talk to you about your practice schedule," he said, pulling her into the shadows.

Vanessa tried not to wince as he grasped the inside of her arm, where a collection of yellowing bruises still lingered. "Okay," she said, gripping her bag.

"The performance is upon us soon, and I want to make sure you're taking it as seriously as the rest of us."

Vanessa frowned. "Of course I am."

Josef examined her, looking concerned. "Yes, but you are not getting better. Are you practicing after classes?"

Vanessa shifted her weight. "Well, sort of."

Josef's face hardened. "That is not enough. If you want to be a professional ballerina, you must act like one. By Monday, if you haven't improved, I will be forced to make changes."

Vanessa felt the color leave her face. Before she could respond, the door opened and the rest of the dancers spilled out into the hallway. Josef backed into the crowd and gave her a solemn look.

"I'll do better," she called after him, and then turned back to the studio to look for Zep. But to her dismay, he was already gone.

Lincoln Center Plaza was lonely when she stepped outside, the chilly night air biting into her cardigan. Across the plaza, she could hear Anna and the other princesses, their laughter echoing off the tall buildings. Without thinking, she turned and headed toward Broadway.

The night air blew in a brittle swirl, stirring the leaves on the sidewalk around Vanessa's ankles. She didn't know where she was going, only that she needed to be alone, if only for a moment. Across the street, the long glass panes of Lincoln Center glowed a buttery yellow. She saw silhouettes against the glass—two people kissing, a mother and child licking ice-cream cones, an elderly couple sitting on the edge of the fountain, holding hands. The traffic light turned red. Vanessa waited beneath a streetlamp and watched the figures move as if part of a gentle, meandering dance.

And then, out of the corner of her eye, something else moved. Vanessa glanced over her shoulder, but there was no one else around, only a tall stone building swallowed by darkness. Ignoring it, she turned back to the street when she saw it again—something shifting in the night. This time she was sure it was real. She pretended to check her bag and glanced behind her, only to see a shadow detach itself from the building.

The figure came up quickly, its looming shape stalking directly toward her. It looked like a man, but she couldn't tell, and she didn't want to find out.

She didn't wait for the light to change; after making sure no cars were coming, she hurried across the street. For a moment she thought she was wrong, that no one was actually following her, that it was just the darkness acting upon her imagination. She stopped at the edge of the plaza, catching her breath, when she heard a car horn. Then footsteps.

A second later and she wouldn't have seen him. The shadow that had terrified her was Justin, passing beneath a streetlamp, the Fratelli twins on his heels. Vanessa tucked herself into a crevice on the side of a building and waited.

They walked toward her, stopping just feet away from her hiding spot. Why were they following her? As if sensing her thoughts, Justin turned. His face was furrowed in a scowl, his lids heavy and dark, as he and the twins moved away.

Vanessa pressed herself closer to the wall and held her breath. She glanced across Lincoln Center Plaza, hoping that if he did find her, someone would hear her scream. But all the people seemed to have left. The sidewalk was, for the moment, deserted.

Not sure why she was so frightened, she ran along the

border of Lincoln Center, staying close to the buildings, until she reached the glass doors of the New York City Ballet. A security guard stood inside. Taking one last look over her shoulder, she flashed him her pass.

"Has anyone else come in tonight?" she asked.

"No, ma'am," he said.

Vanessa let out a breath, relieved that Justin and the twins didn't seem to know where she was heading.

The guard asked, "Is everything all right, miss?"

She met his gaze. His kind, droopy eyes seemed safe, and for a moment, she wanted to tell him. But what? That three of her classmates had followed her? She didn't even know why she'd hidden from Justin and the twins, or why the look on Justin's face had frightened her so much.

"Miss?"

"I'm fine," she said, trying to sound normal. Her hands were trembling, and she stuffed them into her pockets.

"How late are you here?" she asked.

"All night." He paused. "Are you sure everything is okay?"

Vanessa nodded.

The guard tipped his hat and waved her through.

The basement studio was dark and still, almost peaceful. It was hard to believe that it was the same room she had rehearsed in, morning and afternoon, every day this week.

Vanessa dragged her hand over the figures on the wall, feeling the smooth paint where their faces would be and trying to imagine their expressions. For a second the wall felt warm, as if she were touching not paint, but the cheek of a flesh-and-blood girl. But as quickly as it came, the feeling vanished. Vanessa recoiled, frightened. What was happening to her?

Soon she found herself just inches away from the burned circle in the center of the floor. It was fainter than it had been before *Firebird* rehearsals started. She slipped on her pointe shoes and traced the black mark with her toe. Vanessa knew the circle had to be nothing more than a place marker for the dancers, but as she bent down to touch it, it felt like real ash, as if there had actually been a fire here.

But no, that was impossible, Vanessa decided, and shook off the thought.

She unbuttoned her cardigan and tossed it aside. Standing next to the mark, she arranged herself in fourth position and tried to remember the odd rhythm of Josef's clapping. But all she could hear was his voice, barking in her ear, the other girls gossiping, and Zep's breathing, loud and frustrated, when she stumbled. She could almost smell the coffee on Josef's breath as he circled her, raising her leg, straightening her spine, adjusting the angle of her arm. She could see the disappointment on Zep's face when he turned away from her, leaving class without even saying good-bye.

Pressing her hands to her ears, Vanessa stepped back. Slowly, she opened her eyes, almost comforted by the white figures on the wall, watching over her.

Vanessa's gaze rested on one that looked particularly

similar to her sister. The narrow crest of her nose, the thin, upward line of her neck, as if she were raising her face to the sun.

"You're the one who's supposed to be here," Vanessa said to her, exasperated. "So why aren't you?"

But the white figure said nothing; she just remained straight and still, balancing on one toe.

Copying the figure's pose, Vanessa lofted herself upward, extending her chin toward the ceiling. Her shadow stretched across the wooden floor, an exact replica of the white dancer on the wall. Vanessa turned to the next girl, whose leg was arched into an *attitude en pointe*. Moving slowly, Vanessa copied her too, and when her shadow mimicked the second figure on the wall, she realized she knew these poses. They were the steps to *La Danse du Feu*. When there was a gap, she filled it in from memory, remembering the changing meter.

Soon she was dancing. She didn't have to look at the figures or think about the rhythm. She didn't have to think at all. Instead, she let her body go, allowing her legs to move through the air as if each step were fated, inevitable.

She glanced at the floor, at her shadow as she leaped across the room. Slowly, her surroundings faded away. The lights above her seemed to grow dim, the floor swaying beneath her feet, threatening to make her collapse once again.

But this time Vanessa didn't fall. She caught herself just in time, and spread her arms wide, balancing on one delicate toe.

Breathless, she twirled her arms, turning in a fouetté, when something caught her attention.

The white figures on the walls around her had brightened, their outlines bursting with light, like thin seams. Dizzy and disoriented, Vanessa blinked. Still, she kept dancing as they began to move, detaching themselves from the wall, following her. They were transparent, glowing, as if written in hazy light.

Startled, Vanessa stopped, and the figures dissipated like a handful of settling dust.

She stood impossibly still, gazing at the air around her. Were they real? Or was she seeing things? She wiped her forehead and blew a wisp of hair out of her face. The room was empty, the figures frozen on the wall.

Placing her legs back in position, she lifted an arm above her head and started the dance where she had left off. Again the figures peeled themselves from the walls and circled her, copying her motions. This time, they were brighter, clearer, their hazy outlines hardening into arms, legs, fingers. Vanessa could see their eyes, their noses, their brows, their lips—all iridescent, yet clearly formed.

Enraptured, Vanessa watched them, their limbs moving in tandem with hers like a reflection. She studied their faces, trying to figure out who they were and why they were mimicking her, when she realized that their newly defined expressions were all the same.

Vanessa lifted herself into a pirouette, her gaze traveling from one figure to the next. Each of their lips were parted, as if in surprise, their eyes open wide with terror.

The dance was almost over. Unable to stop, Vanessa moved faster, twirling in a heat of ecstasy until the figures began to fade away from her, blurring back into the wall, all except one. The slender girl with a narrow nose like Margaret's glowed so brightly that Vanessa could barely look at her. All she could see was the outline of the girl's legs, moving in pace with her own, the radiant trail that the girl's arms left, her fingertips almost touching Vanessa's.

She was so close that Vanessa could feel the heat emanating from the girl's body. Or was it her own? She couldn't tell anymore. The floor beneath her felt hot, but Vanessa couldn't stop now. She was almost there, almost done. Her chest heaved.

The air grew hot, thick. Vanessa gasped. Her head began to spin, and her legs felt weak, until, unable to catch herself, Vanessa stumbled out of step. The figure beside her froze, her face twisted with terror. Vanessa watched, horrified, as the girl jerked left, then right, her body bending like rays of light refracting off a mirror. The glare engulfed the ceiling. Vanessa covered her face. The last thing she saw was the outline of the girl's lips, pursed open as her figure ripped into a blinding curse of light, the rays streaming from her mouth like a scream.

Chapter Sixteen

Vanessa couldn't remember what happened next.

Only that the door burst open, and suddenly she was swept up in two strong arms and carried outside, through the cool autumn night, across the plaza and into another building. Vanessa blinked, staring at the heavy, darkened chandeliers of the NYBA dining hall. Someone laid her gently on a table, and she saw a broad back disappearing into the shadows by the kitchen. Who was it? And what had happened to her? She had a vague recollection of dancing, of shapes and outlines of light.

A light was turned on in the distance. She lifted her head and tried to call out, but her mouth was as dry as cotton, her back stiff and sore, her hair matted to the base of her neck with sweat.

She heard footsteps returning, and someone placed a mug

next to her cheek, the smell of warm chamomile tea shaking her alert. She looked up to see a pair of kind, familiar eyes.

"Zep?"

He brushed the hair away from her face, and placed a wet cloth on her forehead. "Vanessa." His deep voice soothed her.

"What? You? How?" Vanessa fumbled, overwhelmed.

"You collapsed in the practice room." His dark hair fell over his forehead as he bent over her, removing her toe shoes. He gave her a curious look. "What happened?"

Vanessa curled her toes under his touch. Had Zep actually found her and carried her here? It was so surreal that she couldn't believe it. Just hours before, he'd left the studio without saying a word to her. Why had he come to the basement dance studio? Had he followed her there to apologize? Suddenly, she saw a flash of light in her mind, and the memories came tumbling back.

"They came to life," she said, thinking of the white figures. "The dancers on the walls. I was dancing when they started to glow, then they peeled themselves off the walls and copied me. And—"

Vanessa closed her eyes and thought of the girl who had stayed with her, the girl who looked like Margaret. Thinking of the terror in her eyes, Vanessa shivered.

She opened her eyes. "I need to go back. I need to find out who those girls were."

Zep put his hand on hers. "Can't that wait?" he asked, his face concerned. "I think you need to rest."

Vanessa shook her head. "I never finished the dance, which

is probably why . . ." She paused, trying to find the right words to describe what she had seen. "Why she burst into a ray of light. She was following me for a reason. I need to know."

"A girl? Bursting into a ray of light?" Zep said. He clearly didn't believe her.

"I saw her," Vanessa insisted. "It was real."

"I don't doubt that you saw something, but maybe it was just a trick of the light. You've been working so hard these past few weeks. You were exhausted, maybe dehydrated."

Vanessa swallowed, her mouth still dry. She had to admit that he was right, but she also knew what she had seen, and it was real.

"All I'm asking is that you wait. If you want to be the best dancer you can be, you have to know when to let yourself rest. Whatever it was that you saw will probably still be there tomorrow."

Vanessa felt herself blush as he curled his fingers around hers. "Right," she said softly, her heart melting as he played with the thin strap of her leotard. The soft light from the kitchen revealed the stubble on his cheek, the bridge of his nose, the arch of his eyebrow, the hollow of this throat. All so perfect.

He handed her the cup of tea. "Drink this. It'll make you feel better."

She sat up and sipped, letting the liquid warm her. "How did you find me?"

Zep hesitated, then gave her an embarrassed smile. "This may sound strange," he said, his fingers tracing the inside of her forearm, "but after I got out of my meeting with Josef, I came looking for you. I saw you heading there, and followed. I'm sorry we haven't had a chance to talk all week. It's Josef. He barely leaves me alone."

His gaze was so intent that Vanessa found herself unable to meet it.

"Why are you so distant?"

"It's this dance." He glanced up at the ceiling. "This whole place. I'm under so much pressure. You have no idea."

"It's hard for me too—"

But Zep cut her off. "No, you don't understand," he said softly.

His words hurt her, but she resisted the urge to pull away. "So help me understand."

Zep shook his head and looked up at her. "I—I can't."

"Why?" Vanessa said. "If you're worried about me thinking less of you, or telling someone your secrets, you don't have to. If anything, I'm the one with the past."

Zep waited for her to continue, but she didn't know what else to say. Should she tell him about seeing Margaret's figure in the basement practice room, about her suspicions that something stranger was going on than girls just dropping out? Or would he think she was crazy?

"It doesn't matter," she finally said. "The reality is that I'm here now, just like you. Right?" She looked at Zep, hoping he would open up to her, but he remained silent. "I feel like we never get a chance to see each other," Vanessa said. "Josef keeps pulling you aside after class . . . and then you just vanish. Are you trying to avoid me?"

"Is that what you think?" Zep grazed his hand down the side of her cheek, his touch making something come alive within her. "Of course I'm not trying to avoid you."

"Then why does it feel like you don't want to see me?"

Zep touched a strand of her hair, letting it fall from his fingers. "It's not you. I'm just preoccupied . . ." He let his voice trail off. "Remember when I asked you if you trusted me?"

Vanessa nodded.

"Do you trust me now?"

"Yes."

"Then trust me on this. It's my problem and no one else's."

"Does it have anything to do with what Justin said in the library? Something about the kind of dancer you were, and how you should tell me yourself?"

"Justin?" Zep said. "I can't remember what he was talking about that day, but I'm sure it was something he invented. He loves to hear the sound of his own voice."

"That's true," Vanessa said with a laugh.

Zep traced shapes on her palm. "Still, I think you should stay away from him."

"Why?"

Zep hesitated. "He likes you."

Vanessa laughed. "Justin? He doesn't like me. We're practically enemies."

But Zep didn't smile. "Haven't you noticed the way he looks at you? I don't want anyone making eyes at my girl."

"Making eyes at your girl?" Vanessa teased, but really she could barely believe it. Zep nodded, closing his hand around hers, and they sat like that, whispering to each other into the early morning hours, until her eyelids grew heavy and she fell asleep on his shoulder.

When she woke, he was carrying her up the stairs to her dorm room, cradling her head against his chest.

"Vanessa," he said when they reached her door. He set her down, guiding her toward him.

"Zep," she said, savoring the taste of his name. "Zep."

His lips were soft and warm when they touched hers. She fell into him, feeling him bury his hands in her hair, lingering as if he didn't want to let go. "I wish I didn't have to say good-bye." He ran his hand down her back.

Vanessa wanted to collapse in his arms, to let him scoop her up and carry her off. But instead she pulled away. "So don't," she said, smiling. "Just say good night."

Inside her room, a giddy smile spread across Vanessa's face. It was real. Zep was real. They were real. She hadn't been sure for so long. Ever since they started rehearsing the dance—that strange, arrhythmic dance that she couldn't get right—that was when Zep had started pulling away from her. Now she wanted to burst with the news, to yell it out the window and tell all her friends and the girls in the lunchroom that it was true. Zep was her boyfriend. But it was too late to do that, and TJ was asleep, her legs tangled in the sheets. A mess of her brown curls spilled out over the pillowcase beside her history book. Her reading light was still on above her desk. Vanessa flipped it off.

On her own bed was a note written on a scrap of notebook paper:

WHERE HAVE YOU BEEN? WE MISS YOU.
xoxo TJ (and Steffie and Blaine)
P.S. Wake me up when you get back so we can chat.

Vanessa smiled when she read it and was about to tiptoe over to TJ's bed when she saw her cell phone vibrating on her desk, where she'd left it before rehearsal. Picking it up, she saw she had one voice mail.

"Hi, honey, it's Mom." Her mother's voice, lyric but shrill, made Vanessa cringe, and she held the phone a little farther from her ear.

"And Dad," her father chimed in.

"I hope you're off with friends, enjoying yourself. Just wanted to let you know that we bought tickets for the opening night of *The Firebird*," her mother said.

"And they weren't cheap!" her father added, joking.

Vanessa could practically see her mother's eyes roll as she shooed her father away. "Anyway, we just wanted to make sure everything was going well. We can't wait to see you dance *The Firebird*. We're just so proud of you, Vanessa." She hesitated on her name as if she were about to say something else. *Margaret.*

Her father shouted something in the background. It sounded like "I love you," but it was drowned out by her mother's voice, telling her to take care of herself and eat right. Vanessa let out a breath, half relieved she had missed the call. Just as she deleted the message, there was a soft knock on the door.

Zep? Vanessa mouthed, staring at the shadow of two feet beneath the door. Quickly, she scooped her dirty clothes beneath her comforter, ruffled her hair, and ran to the door, but when she opened it, she pulled back with a start.

"Vanessa?"

The smile faded from her face as she took in Justin's sandy hair, his pressed shirt collar, and his muddy sneakers. He ran a hand down his hair, as if to comb it.

"Justin? What are you doing here?"

He swallowed, looking nervous. "I just wanted to see if you're all right."

"Why wouldn't I be?" Vanessa said, scrutinizing him. In the dim light of the hallway, she realized what was different about him. He looked cleaner, crisper, as if he had been shampooed, starched, and ironed.

"I don't know. You just seem stressed out recently. In rehearsal. Especially the afternoon sessions. If it's Josef, you shouldn't worry about him. He yells at everyone."

"How would you know that?" Vanessa said quickly.

Justin lowered his eyes, and suddenly Vanessa felt guilty. "People talk," he said with a shrug. "And the girls—they're just jealous," he said quickly, though Vanessa knew he was lying. "No one believes them. Anyway, I just wanted to make sure everything was okay."

"You did?" Vanessa said, narrowing her eyes. Had Justin actually come to her room late at night to see if she was okay?

It seemed out of character. She glanced over his shoulder and down the hall. It was empty.

"What are you looking at?" he said.

"You left your henchmen behind."

Justin gave her a quizzical look. "I don't know what you mean."

"The Fratelli twins. They were with you tonight, weren't they?"

A wave of panic passed over Justin's face, but he quickly shook it off. "We're friends," he said carefully. "Nicholas and Nicola are with me a lot."

"You don't have to lie," Vanessa said, lowering her voice. "I saw you."

"What are you talking about?"

"Tonight. You were all running down Broadway." Vanessa paused. "Were you following me?"

Justin looked away, fidgeting. "Yes," he finally admitted, meeting her eye.

"Why?"

"It doesn't matter."

"Of course it does," Vanessa said. "Why didn't you just tell me you were there tonight? And why bring the twins, who have barely ever said two words to me?" She watched him run a hand through his hair again. "What do you want from me?"

"Zeppelin Gray follows you. And you don't think that's creepy."

"Zep is just looking out for me—" Vanessa began to say, when Justin cut her off.

"So am I."

But Vanessa held up a hand to silence him. "Wait, how did you know that Zep follows me? And why would I need protecting from him?"

"You don't know what he's really like," Justin said.

Vanessa put a hand on her hip. "Oh, and you do?"

"I have some ideas. I've known him much longer than you have."

"I thought you dropped out for three years."

"I did," Justin said. "But I saw enough freshman year to know what he was about, and I really don't think you should be hanging out with him."

Vanessa leaned on the door frame. "Is that what this is all about? You're jealous of me and Zep?"

"No, it's nothing like that," Justin insisted.

"Right," Vanessa said. "So you just decided to follow me all evening, then come to my room late at night and knock on my door to make nasty comments about Zep? I mean, do you really expect me to believe—"

"I know."

"It all makes sense now," Vanessa said, almost to herself, realizing that maybe Zep was right. "Why I always bump into you, why you're constantly rude to me—"

"Can you just get over your ego for one minute and listen to me?" Justin said, a little too loudly.

Vanessa went quiet.

"I know you want to think that everyone at NYBA wants to date you, but it's not true."

Enraged, Vanessa opened her mouth to speak, but Justin held up a finger and continued.

"Remember in the library when I told you that all the previous lead ballerinas in *The Firebird* had disappeared? It doesn't stop there. NYBA has a history of girls going insane before they vanish. Girls start to lose their minds, then they disappear. Girls like Elly, your sister."

"Elly didn't disappear. She dropped out. Same with my sister," Vanessa said.

"That's how it always starts."

"How do you know?" Vanessa said. "Why couldn't they have just dropped out?"

"Because that's not what happens here."

A shudder ran up Vanessa's arms as she thought of the newspaper articles, of the girls who'd disappeared and were never found. Their faces were seared into her head now, no matter how much she wanted to forget them.

"You know what I'm talking about," Justin said, studying her. "It's about something . . . sinister."

"Sinister?" Vanessa said in disbelief. It was a word she reserved for sorcerers and serial killers. "But the police said they were runaways," she began, trying to convince him as much as herself.

"Yes, but what do *you* say?" Justin said. "Your sister disappeared. Did that make sense to you? If she turned up dead in the river, would you accept that?"

His words made her stomach tighten. "My sister isn't dead," she said. "And don't you ever try to convince me that she is." She took a step back into the safety of her room.

Realizing that he had crossed a line, Justin's face softened. "Exactly my point."

Vanessa was about to close the door in his face, but he held it open. "What now?" she asked.

"What about Elly?" Justin persisted. "She didn't seem like the type to disappear either. Isn't that a little strange?"

"Elly wrote us an e-mail telling us she was fine."

"What did it say?"

"That she was at home and didn't want us to contact her." But Vanessa knew the e-mail hadn't sounded like Elly. For a moment, she considered telling Justin about the strange note wrapped around the block of rosin, but she thought better of it. No, Elly was the only person who could give her answers. She had to talk to her.

"You think it out of character," Justin said, reading her thoughts.

"What I think is none of your business," she said.

She got ready to shut the door, when Justin spoke. "What if it was?"

Slowly, she looked up and met his gaze, challenging him. "If you want to know what I think, ask me, instead of prowling around at night, trying to squeeze your way into other people's secrets." She took a step back into her room. "And if you want so badly to compete with Zep, you should spend less time doing research and more time dancing."

"I told you before that I wasn't trying to be a better dancer," Justin said calmly. "I have personal reasons for wanting to be here. And Zep—well, I already told you how I feel about him.

If you don't want to listen to me, then fine. You can work it out for yourself."

She glared at his smug face, wishing she could crumple it like a piece of paper. "What exactly does Zep have to do with this?" she asked.

"Nothing yet. But he has the lead role in the production. And you're—"

"The Firebird," Vanessa said impatiently. "I know what you're thinking. That I'm going to disappear and a few weeks later my picture is going to show up in the newspaper as another missing girl."

Justin went quiet. "I just wanted to make sure you were okay," he said, his voice surprisingly gentle.

"Well, I'm fine," Vanessa said. "And I can take care of myself. Good night."

She closed the door, a sigh of relief passing through her when the knob clicked shut. Vanessa waited until she heard the sound of Justin's footsteps disappearing down the hall and then crawled into bed.

Just before she pulled up the covers, TJ sat up. "What was that?" she whispered, her voice groggy from sleep.

"I'll tell you in the morning," Vanessa said, but TJ rubbed her eyes. Her frizzy hair stood on end.

"No, I'm awake," she said, and turned on her bedside light. "I heard a boy's voice."

"Justin," Vanessa said, sitting up, and after glancing at the door to make sure no one was listening, she told TJ about the exchange.

"Justin thinks something happened to Elly too?" TJ said, now fully awake. "What does he know? Maybe he has information that we don't?"

"Information from whom?" Vanessa said, shaking her head. "I think it was all hot air. He wouldn't say anything specific, only that he had suspicions."

"I knew it," TJ said, pushing a wisp of hair from her face. "I mean, I don't know exactly what, but if Justin thinks something strange is going on, and so do you, then it's possible, right?" She stood up and began pacing around the room. "Maybe I'll write her another e-mail. Or Facebook message. No—a letter," TJ muttered to herself. "I'll send it to her parents' house. That way if she doesn't get it, at least they will." And then, as if remembering that Vanessa was there, she turned. "Wait, where were you?"

"With Zep," Vanessa said quietly, watching TJ's face light up. And unable to resist the urge, she spilled everything. The voices, Zep, and the kiss. They talked for another hour about love and boys, about Zep and how he always seemed to show up at the strangest moments, about Justin sneaking around following them both, and Elly, her absence still as strong as the day she disappeared. Just like Vanessa's sister.

Margaret? Vanessa thought, settling under the covers. *What happened to you?*

CHAPTER SEVENTEEN

"What if he's right?" Vanessa said over breakfast the following Saturday.

It had been over a week since Justin had shown up at her dorm room, yet his words still haunted her, despite the fact that she had been working on the final dance with Zep almost every evening.

They met after dinner and walked hand in hand through Lincoln Center Plaza to the basement practice room, laughing and dancing until their bodies were damp with sweat. And every evening he walked her back to her room and kissed her in the dim hallway, leaving her with a dizzying smile before slipping back into the shadows like an apparition. She still didn't know what he did in his spare time, and he rarely picked up his cell phone or responded to her texts. No, he was clearly the one in control.

Maybe that was why Vanessa couldn't get Justin's warning out of her head. Like the final dance of the Firebird, Zep was elusive, undefined, even though he was her boyfriend.

"If a guy called you 'his girl,' does that mean that you're his girlfriend?" Vanessa asked. The dining hall was bustling with the sound of dishes and silverware, students talking, eating, rushing away to class.

TJ's eyes brightened. "Is this hypothetical guy Zep?" Her hair was frizzy and unkempt, in stark comparison to Blaine, who was impeccably dressed in a dark jeans and a tight polo, his hair slick with gel.

"Maybe," Vanessa murmured, picking at her oatmeal.

"I don't know," Steffie said, playing with one of her earrings. "It's kind of vague."

"Typical New York guy," TJ said, shaking her head. "They never want to commit."

Vanessa looked at Blaine, but he only bit his lip. "If he meant you were his girlfriend, he could have just said that," he said. "You know?"

Vanessa nodded, deflated. "What if all those girls didn't just drop out because of stress?" she said. "I mean, it's always girls that disappear. And most of the time it's the lead ballerina. We're supposed to be the best, the ones who can handle all the pressure. It really doesn't make sense that so many of us can't take it."

"What exactly do you think is happening?" Steffie said. "That someone is killing or kidnapping all the lead ballerinas? Or forcing them to go drop out? Why would anyone do that?"

Vanessa pressed her spoon to her lips, thinking. "I don't know."

"I think Justin just likes you," TJ said. "And he's looking for an excuse to talk to you."

"Which is probably why he hates Zep," Blaine added with a grin.

Vanessa collapsed back in her chair, unsure of what she thought. She didn't know why she was clinging to Justin's words. Maybe it was because he seemed to know something about Margaret's disappearance, and in order to believe him she had to at least consider his doubts about Zep. Or maybe she still didn't understand why Zep had chosen her over Anna.

"Sometimes I wonder if Zep really likes me, or if I'm just some passing thing for him."

TJ groaned in disbelief.

"He spends all his time with you, rehearsing for *The Firebird*. We never see you anymore," Blaine said. "Honestly, I don't know how you're not on fire with happiness right now. If Zep just bumped into me in the hall, I would probably pee myself with excitement."

Steffie rolled her eyes while the rest of them laughed. "Which is exactly why you're going to be a virgin for the rest of your life."

"Ha-ha," he said sarcastically. "Seriously though"—Blaine lowered his voice—"if I had someone like Zep chasing me, I wouldn't be taking him for granted. Do you know how hard it is to find someone who can reciprocate your feelings?"

The sincerity of his words startled her into silence.

"Unless, of course, you have the good looks that I have," he said with a smirk.

Vanessa shook her head and laughed, then she caught a glimpse of Steffie's watch. "It's already nine?" she said. She slung her bag over her shoulder and picked up her tray. "I have to go. I'm late for rehearsal."

"But it's Saturday," Steffie said. "And we only just sat down."

Vanessa gave her an apologetic look. Her friends didn't understand how hard rehearsal was, or why each moment of extra practice with Zep was precious. "Save me a seat at dinner," Vanessa said. "Okay?"

Steffie nodded, looking skeptical. "Don't work too hard," she said. "It's supposed to be fun, remember?"

But her words were lost as Vanessa wove through the tables toward the door. Just before she stepped outside, she felt Justin's eyes on her. His gaze was steady, penetrating, as if to say *be careful*.

"You have to focus," Zep said later that night.

His voice reverberated through the basement rehearsal room. Night had fallen hours ago, and the bright overhead lights made everything seem all the more confused. Not that Vanessa had had a chance to go outside. She'd been alone in the studio with him since the afternoon rehearsal had ended.

"I can't," Vanessa murmured.

"You're trying to remember your steps *and* my steps, and count your beat *and* my beat," Zep said, leaning on the wall.

"But it's impossible to dance like that." Behind him, the white figures stenciled into the ash stayed frozen in place. Suddenly she realized how absurd it was that she was standing here, in front of a boy everyone else in school would die to be alone with, and instead of listening to him, she was waiting for the paint on the wall to peel off and start dancing. She really was losing her mind.

"Vanessa?" Zep said. "Are you okay?"

"I—I'm sorry," she said. "My mind is just . . ." Her eyes settled on Zep, on the stubble that dotted his cheeks, on the metallic, rolling color of his eyes, which seemed to brighten as he rested his gaze on Vanessa. "Well, it doesn't matter. I'm here now."

"Good," Zep said. "Shall we try again?"

Vanessa nodded, and he took her hand and pulled her in front of him once more. Standing behind her, his chest pressed against her back, he put a hand on her waist. "Now do what I do," he said, and he began to move with her in the irregular, unsteady beat of Josef's dance.

"Let go of your thoughts. Let go of what you can see. Don't pay attention to me. Just feel the rhythm, and let your body move the way it wants to."

Vanessa let out a laugh. How could she not pay attention to him, when his muscular body was pressing against hers, with nothing between them but their leotards?

Zep frowned. "What's funny?"

Vanessa shook her head. "Nothing," she said. "You just make it sound so easy."

"It will be easy," he said gently, lifting her chin. "When you decide it is."

What did he mean? No matter how many times Vanessa practiced the dance, she couldn't finish it perfectly. Either she made it halfway through before stepping out of rhythm, or, on the rare occasion when she made it almost to the end, the room began to shift and spin.

"I know how you feel," Zep said. "When I first practiced this dance with Josef, I thought it was frustrating, irregular, and useless. But after I mastered it, I understood."

"Understood what?" Vanessa whispered.

"That it isn't a dance. It's a love affair, with rhythms and steps that are so complex, so painful, that it feels like you will never overcome them. But like love, once you master it, it will stay with you forever," he said. "You will be the master of every dance."

"The master?" Vanessa's voice cracked.

"Don't think about it. *Feel* it." He ran his hand down her arm until it was extended outward into her starting pose. And then on his count, they began.

"Love." He pressed his leg against hers until her toe slid across the floor. "You need me. You want me. You've always wanted me. But you can't have me."

Vanessa listened to his words, feeling them pulse through her veins. She arched her back in a painful plea.

"Fate is against us," he whispered. "Still, you offer yourself to me. You seduce me."

Her arms fluttered before her, and slowly, she arched her body into an arabesque, giving herself to him.

"I try to resist you, but I cannot."

Vanessa felt herself grow weak as she leaned into him, letting his hands roam up her body as if they weren't dancing at all, but merging into one. She closed her eyes and breathed in the scent of his sweat.

"But our love is violent. It cannot last. I cast you off." Suddenly the rhythm changed, and Zep thrust her away. Spotting him, she spun across the floor.

"You don't understand. You beg me. You ask me why I can't love you."

Vanessa threw herself down before him. For the first time, the dance seemed to make sense, and slowly, she lost herself to it. The steps were strange; there was no getting away from that. But with Zep guiding her, Vanessa began to feel it.

Her body jerked left, then right, in a tortured romance, the moves becoming natural, ingrained in her muscles until they were written to memory, and she didn't notice when Zep fell away from her. Nor did she notice when she began to pick up the pace, dancing by herself.

As she moved across the wooden floor, she began to feel warm, then hot, sweat beading on her back until her leotard was matted to her skin. She realized it wasn't just heat, it was desire. But desire for what? She spotted once, twice, the room spinning. The lights above were mesmerizing; the waxed floor unbelievably glossy, the mirror so sharp it seemed almost transparent. She kept dancing, her breaths long and deep, until her eyes rested on Zep.

He had stopped dancing entirely and was standing across

the room, gazing at her in awe. "You are beautiful," he murmured. "So incredibly beautiful."

All she could see of him was his dark, wavy hair, his swirling eyes, the contours of his neck as he watched her. She felt
something open within her.

Something inside her started to boil, blossoming beneath
her skin. Losing herself, she glided across the boards toward
him. His hair was soft and thick beneath her fingers as she
grabbed the back of his neck and pulled it toward her, pressing
her mouth to his. Vanessa pulled him closer, her fingers tight
around his body, until gently, he broke out of her grip.

She took a step back. "Why can't you love me?" Vanessa
said, repeating his words, her voice low and not her own.

Zep backed away, his eyes searching hers for understanding. He almost looked sad, as if he wanted to tell her something but couldn't. "Love," he said, just as he had when they
were dancing. "You need me. You want me. You've always
wanted me. But you can't have me." His shoulders collapsed, as
if it pained him to say the words. "And I want you. But fate is
against us."

Vanessa could do nothing but stand there, her breath growing thin, her vision swirled and possessed, as all the color
seemed to fade from the room. Until suddenly, the spell broke,
and the scuffs in the polished wood floor materialized as everything returned to normal. Vanessa let out a gasp as something
left her and her muscles finally relaxed. She stumbled back like
a marionette with its strings cut.

"I—I don't know what got into me."

Zep's face softened. "Great dancing can open you up and invite in all sorts of things . . . hidden, forbidden, dangerous consequences."

"What do you mean?" Vanessa said.

He stepped closer. "You know that feeling you get when you dance, like the world we exist in is thinning and disappearing?"

It took a moment for Vanessa to process what Zep had said. "Do you feel it too?"

"No," Zep said. "I'm not that talented. But *you* are."

His gaze was so intent that she had to look away. "I don't think that's talent," she said. "I always fall when that happens."

"Remember what I said? That's because you haven't mastered it yet."

"Mastered what?"

"The dance. What you can do. It's magic." His voice was so steady that Vanessa couldn't tell if he was joking.

She let out a nervous laugh. "Magic. Right."

Zep didn't say anything. He strode toward her, and with a force Vanessa had never felt before, Zep took her by the waist and pulled her into a wet, violent kiss.

And even though it was exactly what she thought she'd wanted—for Zep to kiss her like this, to desire her, to choose her—he didn't feel like the Zep who had stared at her over the velvety seats of the Lincoln Center ballet, the Zep who'd run through the night with her until they were breathless. This Zep felt different, like a stranger.

"I try to resist you but I can't." He touched his forehead to hers.

Vanessa closed her eyes, feeling his damp skin against hers and wishing she could believe he was hers. *But our love is violent,* his voice repeated in her mind. *It cannot last. I cast you off. You don't understand. You beg me. You ask me why I can't love you.*

"Why can't you love me?" she asked, her lips grazing his.

She felt him stop breathing for a moment, and in his hesitation, she knew. She didn't need to wait for him to speak, for his body had already betrayed him. She didn't know why, but she knew she couldn't have him.

She backed away, searching his eyes for an answer.

"Vanessa, wait," he said, reaching for her, but she pulled back.

"Why?" she said. "I don't understand."

"Can't we take it slowly?" he said gently. "This is new to me too." He stepped toward her, but Vanessa turned away, not wanting him to see the tears in her eyes. Without saying anything more, she grabbed her things and ran out the door, his voice lost as she burst into the hall and out into the comfort and anonymity of the night.

CHAPTER EIGHTEEN

The light shone around Vanessa, casting her shadow across the room. Sweat trickled down her neck. Her leg trembled as she held it behind her for four, five, six counts. On the periphery, she could see Zep frozen in position, his eyes willing her to hold it longer, straighter. She forced herself to look away.

She had been practicing the same sequence for a week, and every time she had fumbled. She told her friends about the problem when they were hanging out in her dorm room, but they didn't understand. "All dance is rooted in some kind of emotion," Steffie had said. "If you can't feel it, it's probably because you haven't experienced that emotion yet. You know?"

"Are you saying I lack life experience?"

Steffie shrugged. "I'm just saying that it's hard to dance about love or grief if you haven't gone through those things."

"It's more than that, though," Vanessa had said. "It's like an emotion that isn't from this world."

Steffie had raised a skeptical eyebrow, and Vanessa turned to Blaine and TJ, who were sitting on the bed doing algebra.

"Don't ask me," TJ said, looking up from her notebook. "I don't even know why I'm here. I can barely keep up with barre work."

Blaine told her she should take a break and get a long massage. Maybe indulge in some retail therapy.

"Why don't you talk to Zep?" TJ said finally. "He's your dance partner, right?"

Vanessa nodded. "I do. If it weren't for his help, I probably wouldn't have made it this far." Though they never spoke of that tense night in the studio, the words remained between them, like a magnetic force pulling them together, pushing them apart.

Every day in rehearsal, their bodies spoke the words neither of them could bring themselves to say aloud. Strangely, it was helping; Vanessa started to feel each step deep within her body until they were as natural as falling in love, teetering with yearning, jumping back in anger. The dance felt so intimate that she went warm with shame every time she caught the eye of one of the princesses, reminding her that the entire cast was watching her conversation with Zep. Did they all know what had happened? Could they read it from his body like she could?

Every day Vanessa expected to hear Anna and the other princesses gossiping about the tension between Zep and Vanessa, but to her surprise, they didn't seem to notice. In fact, no one did, with the exception of two people.

The first, to Vanessa's dismay, was Justin. In the morning full-cast rehearsals, when Justin wasn't working on the steps of the prince, he sat in the corner with his arms crossed, watching Vanessa and Zep.

The second was Josef. He watched their first afternoon rehearsal of the week in complete silence, his eyes following them across the floor. He looked almost nervous as Zep backed away, leaving Vanessa alone for the finale. And, miraculously, she swept into her last pose without stumbling or confusing her steps. It wasn't perfect, but it was getting there. When it was over, she stood, frozen in place, her chest heaving.

The only sound was the clicking of Josef's shoes against the waxed wood. He squinted at Vanessa, trying to figure out what had changed. His gaze shifted to Zep, giving him the same close scrutiny, and he rubbed his chin. *"C'est incroyable,"* he murmured, barely audible, then looked up at Vanessa. "Better," he said. "Much better."

He clapped, signaling the end of rehearsal, and Vanessa quickly threw her shoes into her bag and slung it over her shoulder, only to see Josef with his hand on Zep's back, speaking in low, impatient tones, ushering him into the hallway. Zep glanced over his shoulder just before the doors closed, his eyes meeting Vanessa's. *I'm sorry,* they seemed to be saying, *please trust me.*

But sorry for what, exactly, Vanessa didn't know, and never got the chance to ask. Every day now it was the same—Josef whisking Zep away before she could even say good-bye. If anything, as Vanessa improved, Josef seemed more impatient with Zep. But why? Zep danced his role perfectly every time. She wanted to ask him what Josef was making him work on after hours, but she barely caught sight of him outside of rehearsal until Halloween.

The floor was strewn with white powder. It dotted Steffie's dresser, her armchair, her desk; it was streaked across the wood boards at the foot of Elly's naked bed, and dusted over the rug. Vanessa wove around the furniture to join Steffie, who stood in front of the mirror, dabbing her cheeks with a makeup brush. Her long legs were swathed in white tights, and her face was unrecognizably pale.

Beside her, TJ and Blaine were slowly erasing themselves, covering their necks and arms and shoulders with white paint. TJ's brown curls were dusted like a baroque wig, and Blaine was applying black lipstick. They moved over when they saw Vanessa approaching, her skin as white as her leotard, as if she were nothing but bones. Even her red hair was dusted white.

Steffie put down her eyeliner and blinked, letting powder sprinkle off her eyelashes. "You look like—"

"Margaret," Vanessa whispered. With her own vivid coloring erased, her reflection in the mirror looked thin and delicate, just like her sister's. The result was a cruel coincidence, since, like her three friends, Vanessa was dressing up as a dead dancer from the Danse Macabre. She quickly pushed the thought out of her mind. It was Halloween, after all.

"Hurry up!" Blaine said. "We're going to be late!" After

finishing the last touches of black-and-white makeup, they hurried out the door.

It was a Halloween tradition for the students at NYBA to dress up as a famous character in dance history and run through Central Park, using the winding paths as their stage. It was a chance to perform a more primitive dance, the kind that existed before auditoriums and overhead lights, before velvet seats and playbills, when dance was nothing more than people moving to the sounds of nature.

The October air was a blustery mix of warm breeze and frigid chill. November was around the corner, and with it snow, winter, and the December performance of *The Firebird*. The moon hung large and yellow, like a gaping eye. Around it, the sky was dark, empty, starless.

"Is it just me, or does it feel darker tonight?" Steffie said to Vanessa as they walked to join the rest of their classmates, all in costume, waiting by the fountain.

"I know what you mean," Vanessa said, gazing up at the sky. "It's like the universe knows that it's Halloween."

Their classmates were dressed in ethereal tutus and green nymph costumes, nutcrackers and swans and sword-wielding rats, their faces shrouded with hoods and face paint. They talked in whispers, as if the voices weren't their own but had drifted in from some distant, past land.

As Vanessa approached, she noticed a tall figure in a long black cloak and a mask. He was standing toward the front of the group, holding a scythe. *Death*, she thought.

When he saw her, he stepped forward and bowed, his long

robes gathering on the ground. Vanessa leaned closer, standing on her toes to try to peer behind the dark slits of his mask. But it was no use. "My Firebird," Death said in a deep, guttural tone. *Zep?* she wondered.

Before she could speak, he reached into his robes and produced a rose, the color of bone. Vanessa took it with fingers so white they seemed to mimic its delicate petals.

"Thank you," she said, sure the figure behind the mask was Zep. Who else would call her his Firebird and bring her a flower? But instead of staying with her, Death only bowed again and then swept away to the front of the pack, leading them all down Broadway and into Central Park.

Streetlamps lined the winding path, their flickering lights illuminating the wet leaves matted to the ground like a rust-colored carpet, soft beneath Vanessa's feet. Suddenly they were running soundlessly through the park, contorting their bodies in imitation of the trees. They wove in and out of the underbrush, surprising passersby. Vanessa's long white hair trailed behind her as she ran, holding Steffie's hand. She arched her neck, trying to find Death, but all she could see was the tip of his hood. If it was Zep, why wasn't he with her?

"Hey." She tugged Steffie's arm. "Let's go up to the front."

"Okay," Steffie said, laughing, and together they squeezed through the crowd.

Vanessa followed the bobbing head of Death until there were only a handful of people between them, so close she could almost reach out and touch his billowing robes. When Steffie leaned over to talk to a swan on their right, Vanessa let go of her hand and inched toward Death.

Then she froze, tripping up the people behind her.

"Hey," someone said. "What's the deal?"

But Vanessa didn't move.

On either side of Death's billowing robes were a handful of princesses, dressed in pale tutus, their slender waists looking as if they might snap. They giggled and leaned into him, their unspoken language screaming: *take me!* Vanessa's eyes rested on the princess directly to his left, a coil of blond hair pinned artfully to her head like a yellow rose. Anna. She strode next to him with the ease of an old lover, sauntering while his hand rested on the small of her back.

Vanessa shrank back, suddenly light-headed. Above her, the branches tangled together like skeletons, bending and twisting in the breeze. She heard someone calling her name, and in the distance she saw Steffie, but Vanessa didn't answer. She had already disappeared, or at least it felt like it. People flowed around her, barely noticing her shivering in the middle of the path. They laughed and shouted and filled in the space between her and Death until all that was left was his black hood melting into the starless sky.

Steffie found her standing in the same place, her arms crossed over her chest as the wind swept her hair about her face.

"Vanessa?" Steffie asked, breathless. "What happened?"

Vanessa hung her head. "Zep," was all she could manage.

Gently, Steffie touched Vanessa's elbow. "Hey," she said. "You're in luck."

"Is that what this is?" Vanessa said miserably. "Because it doesn't feel like it."

Steffie let out a laugh. "No, I mean you're lucky it's Halloween."

Vanessa watched the crowd of students drifting down the path. "Why's that?"

"Because tonight you get to stop being yourself. For the next three hours, you don't have to be Vanessa. You can be anyone you want."

"Says who?"

"Says me. Come on," Steffie coaxed, grabbing her arm. "Let's shed ourselves for one night, pretend our problems don't exist." She lowered her voice. "Let's disappear."

Once again, Vanessa found herself running down the path with Steffie, following the mass of dancers until they arrived back on campus, where Blaine and TJ greeted them with a scream. Linking arms, they merged into the crowd, inside and up the stairs to one of the larger practice studios.

A pulsing red light reflected off the mirrored walls. Cobwebs and streamers dangled from the ceiling, transforming the room into an eerie otherworld. Drinks and tubs of ice were lined up on tables by the barre, and music blared from a speaker on the far side of the room, mingling with the sound of feet thumping against the floor. Dancing.

Vanessa and her friends meandered through the tangle of arms and legs and faces, none of whom she recognized. They were all disguised in thick, bright makeup, masking their expressions. The sweet smell of peach schnapps and bourbon floated through the room.

"Where are we going?" TJ shouted from behind her. Blaine had already broken off and was grinding with a boy dressed as the devil. Vanessa peered over the crowd, still looking for Death despite herself. In the center of the room, a scythe cut through the air, but before she could follow, he had disappeared onto the dance floor, hidden from her among the flashing lights and undulating limbs.

"What happened to TJ?" Vanessa asked, suddenly realizing she'd lost her roommate too.

"She's over there," Steffie said, nodding to the far side of the room where TJ's nest of hair curled above the crowd. "Talking to a minotaur."

"I wonder who it is," Vanessa said.

Steffie took a sip from her drink. "Who cares?" she said with a grin. "It's better sometimes when you don't know."

Vanessa was about to laugh when she heard TJ shout.

Beside the minotaur stood a fairy. She wore a pink costume and a wig of pale blond hair, just like Elly's. "How dare you dress up as her," TJ cried. "Do you know what happened to her? Are you the one who did it?"

The fairy backed away, frightened, and her date, the minotaur, stepped forward. "Hey, why don't we all just calm down."

"Calm down?" TJ shouted. "Your girlfriend is dressed up as a missing person." A hush fell over the crowd around them.

"Look, I don't know what you're talking about—" the minotaur began to say, but TJ cut him off.

"Tell her to take off that stupid wig," she yelled, throwing her cup aside. Red spiked punch splattered across the floor, staining the outfits of the girls around her, who started to yell back at her.

"I'm tired of this! Why doesn't anyone care about Elly? Why isn't anyone listening?"

Vanessa and Steffie ran and grabbed TJ from the crowd. "Come on," they said. "We're listening. Let's just go outside."

Across the room, Vanessa spotted Hilda, her beady eyes set on TJ with an intensity Vanessa had never seen before.

"I'm fine," TJ said once they were away from the crowd, her breath sour. "Really." She stepped back and gazed at Vanessa. "You know, all white like that, you remind me of those shapes on the walls in that basement practice studio."

Vanessa grew still. Since the night they'd first come to life, the figures on the wall hadn't moved. Had she just imagined them? She remembered how real they looked, the way they'd peeled themselves off the wall, their frightened expressions as they danced around her. The outline of the girl who looked strikingly similar to Margaret, just before she burst into light.

Before Vanessa could respond, TJ sank to the floor in an exhausted heap. "I'm sorry, guys," she said, holding her head. "I shouldn't have done that."

"Don't worry," Steffie said. "By tomorrow, no one will remember." She turned to Vanessa, who was searching the crowd for a pair of metallic eyes.

"You're still bummed about Zep," Steffie said.

"No," Vanessa said. When Steffie gave her a look, she corrected herself. "Okay, fine. I am. But I can't help it. He's just— it's all so baffling . . ."

Steffie waited for her to continue, but Vanessa didn't know what else to say.

That's when she saw it: a door opening at the far end of the hall. A sweep of a robe around the corner, followed by voices. Vanessa put a finger to her lips. "I'll be right back," she said, and crept through the shadows toward the figure of Death.

When she finally found him, he was outside, his long mask still frozen in the same expression. Except now he was talking to the thirteenth princess. Anna.

Vanessa waited in the darkness behind a column, unseen. Her body went rigid as Death leaned toward Anna, whispering something she couldn't hear. He handed her a small bouquet of white roses, which looked exactly the same as the one he had given Vanessa earlier that evening. Anna took them, breathing in their aroma.

Vanessa stepped back, her heart racing. It felt like someone was twisting her insides as she watched them together, but she couldn't look away. Slowly, Death put his hand on Anna's arm.

Anna immediately pulled back, looking like she was about to strike him. "You keep trying to do that," she said, her voice wavering. "Stop it."

Was she crying? Vanessa couldn't tell. All she could see was the white lace covering her shoulders as she hunched over the bouquet of roses.

Death moved toward Anna. "It's okay that Zep's attentions have turned elsewhere." His voice was muffled by the mask, but a wave of relief passed through Vanessa. It wasn't Zep after all, but Justin.

"Get over your broken heart and get the hell out of here," Justin was saying.

"I can't leave," Anna said. "I'm not strong enough."

Justin motioned to Lincoln Center, his robes swaying in the wind. "You're not alone up there onstage—there are all those dancers who have gone before."

But Anna only shook her head. With a sob, she clutched the bouquet of flowers to her chest and ran through the courtyard, petals scattering after her.

Justin growled in frustration. It was a cold sound, one Vanessa recognized from the way he sometimes talked to her. Suddenly she felt angry. Her legs moved without conscious thought until she found herself standing before him.

"What did you just tell Anna? You're trying to turn everyone against Zep." The words tumbled out of Vanessa's mouth before she realized what she was saying. "What is your problem? Why are you so hateful?"

Justin seemed taken aback by her presence. "You don't understand what you're talking about," he said.

Ignoring his comment, Vanessa persisted. "I know why you follow me around. You're jealous of him."

Justin let out a laugh. "I'm not jealous of anyone," he said. "And I know all about you and what happens when you dance—the way you lose yourself. You're not the only one to experience that, you know."

Vanessa was about to interrupt him when she realized what Justin had just said. Who could have told him?

Justin studied her. "See, I know things about you too," he said. "People are talking about it, people like Josef. It's dangerous. That's why you got the part, not because of—"

"Shut up!" Vanessa shouted.

Justin stopped talking in midsentence, to Vanessa's surprise. "The only dangerous things here are the lies that come out of your mouth." And with that, she turned and ran after Anna.

She made it across the plaza just in time to see Anna's blond hair disappearing into the Lincoln Center ballet building. Vanessa watched her through the glass as she crept through the lobby, flashing her pass at the security guard. She was heading to the basement practice room.

Vanessa was about to follow her when she saw something moving behind her, reflected in the glass. She spun around, but the plaza was empty.

"Justin?" she said. "I know you're following me."

Beneath a pillar, the shadows shifted, but no one emerged. Still, she could feel someone watching her.

Vanessa stepped toward the shadow, but then stopped. If it was Justin, why did she care? Turning back to the doors, she flashed her pass at the security guard and hurried into the warmth of the lobby.

Walking nervously past the box office window, she stole down the stairs to the practice studio. All was dark save for a glimmer of light shining through the cracked door. Vanessa slipped off her shoes and inched soundlessly forward until she could see the pink of Anna's tights. She was standing in the middle of the floor, over the scorched circle in the center. Around her, the walls were still burned black, the white figures still frozen on the wall.

Anna was bent over, her back to Vanessa. Willing the floor not to creak, Vanessa leaned in, trying to see what she was doing.

Anna lowered the bouquet of roses onto the floor, the white

petals already beginning to wilt. Why had Justin given them to her, Vanessa wondered. Anna brushed tears from her cheek and touched her fingers to the burned scar in the wood. She stifled a sob as she stood up, her makeup streaked with tears.

Vanessa ducked back into the shadows as the door opened and Anna stepped into the hallway, her outline barely visible in the darkness. She was so close that Vanessa could smell the floral shampoo she used on her hair. Vanessa held her breath and waited until she'd gone, until all that was left of Anna was the floral scent, dissipating into nothing.

CHAPTER NINETEEN

In Vanessa's mind, the last two months had unfolded like a ballet.

In the first act, the ballerina meets her prince, a handsome gentleman with eyes the color of metal. Against all odds, they fall in love.

Then, in act two, tragedy strikes. They're separated by evil forces, plotting to keep them apart. And then her prince begins to act strange, unpredictable. A weeping maiden runs off with a bouquet, roses white as bone. She places it in the center of a stage, atop a black spot of ash from a long-ago flame.

In the third act, everything would come back together. The the ballerina would be reunited with her prince, the ballerina's sister would return from her long journey into the underworld, and all would end in happiness. Or . . . everything could fall apart. It all depended on what kind of ballet it was—a romance or a tragedy.

After Vanessa watched Anna run from the basement studio, she peered out into the hallway, listening for the sound of Anna returning, but all was quiet. Slowly, she crept into the studio. The lights shone down on the bouquet of white roses. She gently lifted the petals, searching for a card—anything that might give her a clue as to who they were for—but there was nothing.

She left the flowers in the center of the studio and crept outside as Steffie and TJ appeared in front of the building, two white wraiths against the marble.

"TJ?" Vanessa asked, recognizing her wild curls. "Steffie? What are you doing here?"

"I saw you run in there after Anna," Steffie said.

"And I followed Steffie," TJ added. "Anna just left."

"Did she see you?" Vanessa said, trying to hide the panic in her voice.

"Hey, give me some credit," TJ said, balancing on the marble ledge that lined the walkway. "I can be discreet, too, you know."

Vanessa let out a sigh. "Sorry," she said. "I know."

"So Anna was crying because she still loves Zep?" Steffie said, removing her eyeliner with a damp cloth.

They had retreated to Vanessa and TJ's room, and Vanessa had told them everything.

"I guess so," Vanessa said, fidgeting with her towel, which was streaked with face paint. "But then who were the flowers for?"

"Maybe . . ." TJ gazed at Vanessa in the mirror. "Maybe they were for Zep. Maybe they—"

"I thought about that," Vanessa said quietly. "But why would she leave him flowers that Justin gave her? And why on that spot? You should have seen the way she was crying. It was like she was visiting a grave, like she was in mourning."

"Why don't you just ask Zep?" Steffie asked as she wiped white makeup from her face with a washcloth. "If anyone can tell you what's going on with Anna, it's him."

"Because I haven't seen him since rehearsal the other day," Vanessa admitted, embarrassed.

"Why don't you just call him?" Steffie said.

"I—I will," Vanessa said, not wanting to tell them he never picked up. TJ caught her eye in the mirror, her gaze sympathetic, but Vanessa looked away.

"Sounds like he's hard to pin down," Steffie said.

"Oh no," Vanessa said. "It's not that. He just—" But she didn't know how to finish.

"If I were you," Steffie said, her lips still black in places, her brown skin emerging from the white makeup, "I'd be careful. My mom always says to watch out for guys with secrets. And Zep definitely has plenty of those."

Vanessa went rigid. "What do you mean?"

Steffie wiped her lips with a washcloth and inspected herself in the mirror. "But the big question," she pressed, ignoring Vanessa, "is why was Justin trying to convince Anna to leave?"

"Because Justin is a jerk!" Vanessa said loudly. "He's jealous of Zep. He's probably trying to date Anna now that she's all vulnerable. He kept rubbing her back, trying to comfort her. Maybe that's why he gave her the bouquet of flowers."

"Maybe," TJ said. "Justin could like her. But don't you think it's all a little suspicious?" TJ sat on her bed, coiling a lock of hair around her finger. "What if Justin is right that there's something strange going on at this school? Something feels wrong."

"All I'm sure of for now is that none of this has anything to do with Zep," Vanessa said hotly. "This is about Anna and Justin."

Steffie rolled her eyes. "So, you'd rather think that some sort of evil conspiracy is happening at this school than consider the possibility that Zep might not be loyal to you?"

Her words stung, but Vanessa shook them off. "Until I hear differently from him," she said, "that is exactly what I'll believe." She sounded tough and sure of Zep, but that was only because of how very scared she was that Steffie was right.

November began with rain and continued overcast and drizzly for the next three days. Vanessa ran through it on Monday afternoon to the *Firebird* rehearsal, holding a newspaper over her head like a proper New Yorker. She shook the water from her hair, still half expecting to see the bouquet of flowers on the floor of the basement practice room. But when she arrived, all she saw was a flock of girls in leotards and tights, stretching and warming up, paying no heed to the burned black spot, which lay in the midst of it all like a dark eye.

Vanessa dropped her bag in the corner of the room, searching for Zep, but he was nowhere to be seen. In fact, she hadn't seen him since the last rehearsal, the Friday before Halloween, three days ago. She began lacing up her pointe shoes, trying not to look over her shoulder every time the door opened.

Just as the clock struck four, Hilda lumbered into the room. She wore a clear rain bonnet over her frizzy hair, and her shoes squeaked against the wood floor. Directly behind her stood Justin. *What is he doing here?* Vanessa wondered. The morning rehearsals were for the entire company, including the understudies, but the afternoon sessions were usually only for the primary *Firebird* company—the thirteen princesses, Vanessa, and Zep. Justin must have sensed her thoughts, because the sides of his mouth turned up into a smirk, as if to remind her that he knew something she didn't. To her surprise, he sat down just feet away from her, and without further acknowledging her, he began to stretch.

"So who did you have to threaten to get into afternoon rehearsals this week?" Vanessa said to him, surprised at how cruel her words sounded.

Justin glanced over at her. "Oh, Vanessa. Hi," he said, giving her a smug smile that made her insides boil. "Alas, no threats were required this time."

"What do you mean?" Vanessa said, narrowing her eyes. "Understudies haven't been coming to the afternoon sessions."

"I don't see how that's any of your business."

"Of course it's my business," Vanessa said. "I'm the lead dancer."

"And from what I hear, you should probably focus on that, because the word on the street is that you still need a bit of work."

Vanessa felt her face grow hot with rage. "As if you know what it's like to dance a lead role," she snarled. "You've barely left the practice barre since school started."

"That's not good news for you, then," Justin said cryptically, and stood up.

"What's that supposed to mean?"

"You'll see."

"See what?" Vanessa asked, but before he could respond, Hilda clapped her hands.

"Good afternoon, everyone," she said. "I hope you're all well rested, because we have a lot of work ahead of us. Josef will not be with us this afternoon, which means I will be leading the *Firebird* rehearsal."

She cleared her throat. "Zeppelin Gray also will not be joining us today, and Justin will be dancing his role. We will start with the first duet in act one."

A murmur arose among the dancers. Justin gave them a cold nod, his eyes lingering on Vanessa. She had to dance with him? To touch him? To trust him to steady her, lift her, catch her?

"Vanessa?" Hilda said sharply. "Are you ready?"

It was only then that Vanessa realized everyone else was in position. Justin stood at stage left. The overhead lights shone down on him, casting a shadow until his eyes looked dark and vacant, impossible to read. Leaning toward her, he extended a long, muscular arm.

"Yes," Vanessa said softly, and took her place by his side.

They waited in silence for the music to start. She thought she heard him say something under his breath, but before she could turn to him the trembling sound of a lone violin pierced the air, and they began.

Justin's hand was surprisingly warm as he took her fingers in his, sliding gently down her arm, firm against her waist when he lifted her into a leap. She closed her eyes, imagining he was Zep. And when she opened them, all she could see was his hair, his rolling shoulders, his muscular legs moving in time with hers. Vanessa could feel the heat emanating off him; she could smell his sweat mixed with his aftershave, filling the air with a sweet, yet bitter, aroma.

It all happened so easily that it felt natural, fated, as if they were meant to dance together. Vanessa arched her back, her foot sliding across the wood boards, and let out a breath of relief, feeling her heart beat to the rhythm of the music, when she felt someone bump into her.

She caught herself just before she fell, noting a misstep in Justin's footwork. *It was just a mistake*, she thought. Justin was not nearly as accomplished a dancer as Zep. To his credit, he was probably doing his best.

Vanessa pressed on, slipping across the floor as she teased and taunted the pale princesses fluttering around her. She felt weightless, delicate, her feet soundless against the wood. But when she dipped beneath Justin's arms, he was a beat off again, and accidentally hit her cheek with his wrist.

"What was that?" she breathed as Justin leaned away from her. If he'd heard her, he didn't let on. At the edge of the practice room, she could feel Hilda watching her, curious. Vanessa forced a smile and continued.

She let the satin edge of her shoe slide down the floor, when she felt something heavy come down on her toe. Pain shot up her leg, and she cried out, pulling her foot away. Had Justin stepped on her? She gazed around the room, but no one else seemed to have noticed. She turned to him, expecting his gaze to be apologetic, but instead it was dark, defiant, his eyes flickering with amusement.

That's when she realized Justin had done it on purpose.

She thrust him away from her, enraged. He was trying to ruin her dance. Another pirouette, another blunder. Justin was an inch too close, his body forcing hers out of balance. She stumbled, falling off pointe.

"What are you doing?" she asked furiously.

He squeezed her waist a little harder than normal, pulling her toward him. For a moment, she thought she heard him whisper something, but she was moving too quickly to make out what he was saying.

"Stop trying to sabotage me," she hissed.

"Vanessa, it's not what you—"

But she didn't want to hear it.

"Don't speak to me." She lunged away from him, not caring that she was out of step. The music clashed with her movements, and the dancing princesses slowed, their faces confused.

Vanessa felt Justin's chest against her back as he braced for their lift. "Don't touch me!" she said, loudly enough for everyone to hear. And finally, Justin listened.

"Fine. Have it your way," he said, and let go.

Vanessa dropped to the ground, collapsing with a sharp thud. The princesses gasped.

"That's enough!" Hilda shouted. She shut off the music and stormed toward Vanessa.

Justin stepped toward her, holding a hand to help her up, but Vanessa only glared at him in disbelief.

"Vanessa, what are you doing?" Hilda said forcefully, her hands knotted into fists.

"It wasn't my fault," Vanessa said. She pointed to Justin, who backed away, holding his hands up as if he were innocent. "He dropped me."

"I don't want to hear it," Hilda said. "There is only one person who controls the dancer's body," she said, her eyes trained on Vanessa. "If you can't get that into your head, you might as well just do us a favor and leave now."

Vanessa opened her mouth to respond but then thought better of it.

"Well?" Hilda asked. She gestured to the door. "Do you want to leave or stay?"

"Stay," Vanessa said softly.

"Then why don't you two practice on your own instead of wasting our time."

Vanessa didn't look up while the rest of the company filtered out of the practice room, leaving her alone with Justin. When the door finally shut and the last ballerina was out of earshot, Vanessa stood up.

"What is your problem?" she said to Justin. "Are you purposely trying to make sure I lose this part?"

"Actually, yes," Justin said.

Vanessa shook her head in confusion and anger. "Why? I could have broken my leg. You could have ruined my career!"

"Don't be dramatic," Justin said. "I wouldn't have let you break a leg. And you're fine."

"I'm not fine. There's only a month until opening night, and I still haven't gotten my steps right."

"And whose fault is that?" Justin asked.

"Why are you even here?" Vanessa said. "Where's Zep? He never would have made those mistakes. When I dance with Zep, everything is perfect."

"Is it?" Justin rubbed his chin pensively. "Well, that must be the only perfect thing about Zep. You really should stay away from him. And while you're at it, ditch this part."

"What is it about Zep that gets to you so much?" Vanessa replied. "It isn't just that he's a better dancer . . . it's something more. He has everything you wish you had."

But Justin just laughed. "Zep? God, no."

"Then what is it?" she asked, guessing wildly. "You say things are so dangerous here, but I don't see *you* leaving. You're still here, trying to badmouth Zep so you can take his role—" She had more to say, but Justin interrupted.

"I'm not trying to take his role, I'm trying to help you," he began, but Vanessa wouldn't let him finish.

"You're lying," she said. "You think you're smarter than everyone else. But I know—"

"For once just listen to me!" Justin shouted, so loudly that his voice reverberated through the studio. "If you don't want to end up like your sister, you'll forget about Zeppelin Gray and this school and go home. Take your weird talents and get the hell out of this place before it's too late."

Vanessa heard the slap before she realized what she had done. Stunned, Justin put a hand to his face in disbelief.

Vanessa trembled with adrenaline. "You don't know anything about my sister," she said, trying to steady her voice.

Justin let his hand slide away from his face. "I know she got in over her head, and I don't want the same thing to happen to you. Look, you seem like a sweet kid—"

"Don't call me a kid," Vanessa said, backing away from him. Everything about Justin disgusted her, from the sweat stains on his leotard to the overgrown stubble on his cheek, where her red hand mark was now fading away. "And don't ever speak to me again. Not about Margaret, or about anything else."

Justin opened his mouth to speak but caught himself, as if he could read the loathing on her face. For a second, Vanessa sensed that he was waiting for her to come back to him, to trust him. But without looking back, she pulled on a sweater and left him standing on the dance floor.

She ran up Broadway, trying to convince herself it was the cool autumn air that was making her eyes tear. The sidewalk was bustling with men in suits and ties, women in high heels and panty hose, parents pushing strollers. In the midst of them was a girl with narrow shoulders, her brown hair pulled into a bun.

Margaret?

Vanessa darted toward her, only to crash directly into an older man wearing a hat. His briefcase dropped to the ground with a loud thump. A cab honked, just as the girl turned. She was a stranger.

"I'm so sorry," Vanessa mumbled, watching the girl cross the street. What was happening to her? She wanted to be alone, to find a quiet place where she could think.

The rush-hour traffic sped by with the familiar sounds of horns and screeching brakes, the strident melody of cab drivers cursing through the windows. Vanessa wove across the street, not sure where she was headed until she saw the knobby branches of Central Park reaching out above the buildings like hands, beckoning her.

The smell of rotting leaves and roasting chestnuts filled the air as Vanessa neared the park entrance. Just the sight of its long, winding paths and pastoral bridges calmed her down. She was about to step inside when she heard footsteps. They followed her toward the trees, far too close for comfort. She slowed, listening to the gritty sound on the path, as a hand closed around her wrist.

Vanessa gasped as cold fingers pressed into her skin. She

was about to scream when she noticed how delicate they were: pale and slender, with long, chipped nails that looked as if they had once been manicured. Above them, she saw a bony arm, clothed in a tattered pink sweater that needed to be washed, a pale neck wrapped in scarves. Her captor was the principal ballerina, the one who had danced the lead role in the performance they'd seen back in September. The one who'd been "punished" by the male lead, Dmitri, in the darkened theater after the performance.

"Helen?" Vanessa said.

In the dreary afternoon light, Helen's face was dull and sunken, as if all the color had drained out of her. Traces of old makeup were smudged beneath her eyes, and her hair hung about her shoulders, stringy and limp, as if it hadn't been washed in days.

"Are you all right?" Vanessa asked, glancing down at Helen's hand, still clutching her wrist.

Helen searched Vanessa's face, her eyes wide and desperate.

"What—what do you want?" Vanessa surveyed the sidewalk for passersby, in case she needed help.

"Tell no one you've seen me," Helen finally said. She pulled Vanessa closer to the benches that lined the sidewalk outside the park, scattering the pigeons. "I know you're a dancer like me." Her voice was hoarse, strained. "J-Josef boasted about your talent eclipsing mine."

"Look," Vanessa said. "I don't want to replace you. I'm just trying to dance and do my best." She tried to wiggle out of Helen's grasp, but the ballerina's grip was surprisingly tight.

"No," Helen said, her gaze so steady it was unnerving. "It's not just dancing, what you and I can do. When we dance, the world doesn't just *seem* to disappear, it really does. The right steps with the right dancer can wreak havoc."

Vanessa stopped trying to escape. "What are you talking about?" she said slowly, even though she knew exactly what Helen was referring to.

"He tried to use me," Helen said. "He tried to put me in, but I escaped. And now he's watching. He's looking for me."

"Put you in where?" Vanessa asked. "Who's looking for you?"

"The walls." Helen gazed around her as if the street and trees were walls themselves.

"You mean someone is trying to lock you up?" Vanessa said, trying to make sense of her, but Helen didn't answer.

"You must leave," Helen said. "Get out while you still can."

"What?" Vanessa asked, narrowing her eyes. She knew that Helen had graduated from NYBA just two years ago, which meant she might have known Margaret and some of the seniors. Anna. Zep. And Justin. "Did he put you up to this?"

"Who?"

"Justin."

Helen's eyes went blank. "Who is Justin?"

Vanessa didn't know how to answer. Just as Helen opened her mouth again, a cab pulled up to the curb in front of them. She went rigid, watching the man inside pay the driver.

"Helen?" Vanessa said, trying to get her attention.

"Did you bring someone?" Helen said, her voice fearful. "Did you have someone follow me?"

"What?" Vanessa said. "You were the one who followed me."

"Josef?" Helen said, and watched in horror as the cab door opened and a man stepped out. He was roughly the same build as Josef, with dark wavy hair and a tight black shirt.

"That isn't Josef," Vanessa said, but the remaining color drained from Helen's cheeks, and her hands began to tremble.

"No," she whispered. "No."

"Why are you so scared of Josef?"

The wind blew through the thin fabric of Helen's scarf. Beneath it, Vanessa could barely see the traces of a collection of small yellow bruises on Helen's collarbone, their small oval shapes pressed into her like fingerprints. Before Vanessa could say anything, Helen turned.

"Find the Lyric Elite," Helen said. "Trust no one else!" She ran across the street and away from the park, dodging cars and disappearing into the crowd.

CHAPTER TWENTY

Over the next week, Vanessa kept reliving her encounter with Helen. At first, Vanessa thought she was crazy. None of her friends had ever heard of anything called the Lyric Elite, and she couldn't find any information online.

But Vanessa kept coming back to the same details: the steadiness of Helen's voice when she said to find the Lyric Elite and trust no one else. And the blankness in her face when Vanessa had asked her if Justin had put her up to it. "Who is Justin?" she had replied, so sanely, so sincerely, that it had given Vanessa the chills.

Something about the way Helen spoke to her, in clear, deliberate words, made Vanessa wonder if she wasn't insane at all, but so frightened that it consumed her entirely.

As exhausted as she was from rehearsal, Vanessa couldn't

sleep. She tossed between the sheets, slipping out of her dreams and into the eerie darkness of her room, until she wasn't sure what was real. She saw Helen running wildly through traffic, her dingy pink sweater flapping around her frail body. But when Helen turned to look at her, Vanessa realized it was Margaret. "Leave while you still can," she said, before disappearing into the crowd.

Suddenly there was a knock on her door, and she was back in her dormitory, comforted by the sight of TJ sleeping soundly on the opposite side of the room. Vanessa couldn't remember rolling out of bed, only that the door was open, and Justin was standing before her, his sweat-stained shirt clinging to his chest.

"Ask me to come in," he said, stepping closer. He smelled of wet leaves and cold autumn nights, his eyes clear blue like the sky, as he pushed his hair back and blinked, his gaze roaming over Vanessa's body, as if he couldn't help himself.

Behind Vanessa, TJ snored softly. "I'm not alone," Vanessa whispered.

"Then we'll have to be quiet."

"What do you mean?" Vanessa asked, even though somehow she knew. She had always known.

Justin inched toward her, pushing her back into the darkness. TJ turned onto her side, still sleeping, her hair spilling over the pillow.

"Why are you here?"

Justin didn't answer; he only stepped closer, pressing Vanessa against her bed. His collared shirt was unbuttoned at the neck, revealing smooth skin punctuated by a lone freckle. Vanessa stared at it, inhaling the trace of his cologne.

"You know why I'm here," he said.

"What do you want?" Vanessa whispered, gripping the side of her bed.

Justin inched closer, his legs tangling with hers. His eyes wandered from her neck to her collarbone to the thin straps of her camisole. "You know what I want."

Gently, he ran his hand up her thigh. It was bare, cold in the night breeze. She trembled beneath his touch. She wanted to pull away, but for some reason she couldn't. Justin pressed his body against hers.

"You have to leave," he said, his lips against her neck, kissing her. "You have to leave." She felt his hands tangling in her camisole, pushing the strap off her shoulder, pressing into her skin until she couldn't help herself. Her body went limp in his arms, and she buried her hands in his hair and pulled him toward her, surprised by the intensity of her response.

Justin groaned. "You have to leave," he murmured. "You have to leave to be safe. But I don't want you to leave."

Vanessa breathed in his words, letting them course through her. She arched her neck as if dancing the part of the Firebird, but just as he bent her back, kissing her shoulders, her collarbone, her neck, she spotted a shadow in the doorway.

She gasped and sat up. Though he was shrouded in darkness, she knew who it was. "Zep," she whispered.

The light from the hallway illuminated slivers of his face as he gazed between her and Justin. His expression hardened.

Vanessa wanted to call out to him, to apologize and say she never meant it. That she loved him, not Justin. But for some reason, the words didn't come out.

Zep strode inside, his eyes burning. Justin stepped in front of Vanessa, challenging him. "Don't go," she wanted to say to him, but when she opened her mouth, no words came out.

There was a loud knock on the door. Vanessa sat up and opened her eyes. She was in bed, the sheets damp and tangled around her. Neither Justin nor Zep was anywhere to be seen. Confused, she glanced across the room at TJ, who was curled up with a pillow, snoring. Otherwise, the room was dark and quiet. Had she been dreaming? She could almost smell the sweat and wet leaves on Justin's shirt. But he wasn't there.

Vanessa swallowed, her mouth parched. She was about to take a sip of water when someone knocked again. A thin line of light shone out from beneath the door, interrupted by the shadow of two feet. Zep? She pulled on a sweatshirt and tip-toed over.

"Vanessa?" a boy said from the hallway. She jumped back, startled to hear Justin's voice. "I know you told me never to speak to you again, but please open the door. Just this once."

Vanessa hesitated, trying to understand why she was suddenly so nervous.

"Please," he repeated. "I promise, I'm not here to threaten or insult you."

She turned the knob and opened it just wide enough to see his face, damp with sweat and speckled with golden stubble. Now that he was standing before her, it was all too clear that she had been dreaming. But why would she have been dreaming of Justin and not Zep?

Afraid he would be able to read her thoughts, she averted her eyes. "What do you want?" she said, staring at his hands.

She half expected him to answer the way he had in her dream, but instead, he said, "I just wanted to apologize. I shouldn't have messed up your rehearsal. You could have been hurt, which is the opposite of what I want."

Vanessa frowned. The opposite?

"Anyway, I don't want to keep you up, and I don't expect you to say anything. I just wanted you to know that I'm sorry."

She wanted to ask him what he meant. About Helen and what he thought had happened to her. But as he stood there, his lips dangerously close to hers, she felt an unbearable urge to pull him inside and kiss him, long and hard until they were breathless and tangled beneath her sheets.

"Do you still think I should leave?" she asked.

Justin seemed surprised by her question. "Yes."

"Why?"

"That's the part I haven't figured out how to explain yet. All I can say is that there's a reason for what I did in rehearsal. I wasn't trying to hurt you."

Vanessa let out a nervous laugh. "What exactly were you trying to do, then?"

Justin's steady gaze seemed almost kind. "To save you." And before Vanessa could say anything more, he turned and stole down the hallway.

"Wait," she called out to him. "What do you mean?"

Justin paused, glancing back over his shoulder. "Good night, Vanessa," he said. And he was gone.

"What if he's right?" Vanessa said over lunch the next day. "What if something strange is going on here, and Helen knows about it too?"

"Or what if Helen's just crazy and scared of Josef because he roughed her up in practice, and Justin is a jealous prick?" Blaine said. "That sounds more likely to me."

"Blaine has a point," TJ said, spooning sugar into her tea.

Vanessa put down her fork. "I know, but it's weird, isn't it? That they both gave me the same advice, separately?"

"But neither of them told you why," Steffie said. "Isn't that a little suspicious?"

Vanessa sighed. "Justin said there was a reason he tried to sabotage my dancing. That he wanted to save me."

Steffie stopped eating. "Are you actually considering dropping out of school because Justin and a crazy ballerina told you to?"

"No," Vanessa said firmly. "But you should have seen the way she looked. She hadn't showered or washed her hair in weeks. Her clothes were disgusting. And her eyes. They were desperate."

"All the more reason *not* to listen to her," Blaine concluded. "Also? She sounds kinda like my mom."

"I wonder what happened to her," TJ murmured. She cocked her head at Blaine. "Helen. Not your mom."

"She probably just cracked under the pressure," Steffie said. "Remember when we saw her after the performance? She was practically in outer space."

"What about the punishment Dmitri mentioned?" Vanessa said.

Steffie shrugged. "Maybe she was going to have to do pliés or extra barre workouts. Josef and Hilda make us do that all the time when we mess up."

"Yeah, but I know what Vanessa is saying. Punishment?" TJ said, smoothing back her hair with her fingers. "It's a weird choice of words."

"Dmitri's from Russia," said Steffie. "His English isn't perfect. Plus, he's arrogant and brutish."

"And sexy," Blaine said.

"She found me by the park," Vanessa said, shoving him. "Maybe we can find her again. Even if she does turn out to be crazy, it can't hurt to ask her what happened. Right?"

Steffie looked skeptical. "Sure, let's ask the mad ballerina why she cracked."

"The thing is, I don't think she cracked," Vanessa said. "I think someone cracked her."

"What do you mean?" said TJ.

"I mean, yes, to an outside observer she would come off as crazy," said Vanessa. "But the way she talked? She knew what she was saying, she was just scared."

"Of what?" Blaine said quietly.

But no one had an answer for that.

The basement studio was empty when Vanessa arrived, a few minutes early. She threw her bag in the corner and flipped on the lights. She walked toward the familiar white figures on the walls, wondering what Justin had meant by saving her.

Where was Zep? It had been weeks since they'd really talked.

Tentatively, she touched one of the white figures, then another. They were warm beneath her fingers, as if the walls were burning. Vanessa recoiled, only to see the first figure she touched begin to brighten. Frightened, she backed away, when she heard a soft whisper, a lone girl's cry. *Vanessa.*

"What?" Vanessa said shakily. It sounded as if it had come from one of the figures.

Vanessa, another girl seemed to hiss. *Vanessa.*

"What do you want?" Vanessa said. "Who are you?"

The figures around her began to glow, their outlines brimming with light until they peeled themselves from the wall, their faces contorted with horror. *Chloë,* they hissed. *Margaret. Elizabeth. Katerina. Joy. Rebecca. Hannah. Josephine . . .*

"Margaret?" Vanessa said, her eyes darting wildly about the room, searching for her sister.

The calling, they whispered. *The summoning. Your soul for the taking.*

Vanessa turned, her hair whipping across her face.

We are you. You are we. We are you. You are we.

"What?" Vanessa choked out.

They burned brighter as they chanted. *We are you. You are we. We are you. You are we.* They glowed, their faces twisting with agony. Their surfaces began to bubble, and large blisters formed on their arms. And before Vanessa had time to shield her eyes, they burst into brilliant red flames, their voices mounting into a hellish, tortured shriek.

"What are you doing?" Hilda's voice boomed from the doorway.

Vanessa opened her eyes, only to find herself alone, cringing in the corner of the room. She lowered her hands from her ears and gazed at the figures on the wall. They were still and glossy with caked paint. There was no fire or smoke, no sign of burning. Had Vanessa imagined it?

"Did you hear anything?" Vanessa asked Hilda. "Just now?"

"Hear what?" Hilda asked, giving Vanessa a suspicious look. "What's wrong?"

"I—I don't feel well," Vanessa said. Her legs were wobbly as she stood up, steadying herself on the barre. "I think I have to lie down."

Across the room, Hilda's stout figure came in and out of focus. Behind her, the door opened and a pair of broad shoulders loomed behind her. Vanessa blinked.

"Zeppelin," Hilda said. "Perfect timing. Vanessa isn't feeling up to rehearsing today." She inspected Vanessa, her gaze piercing. Startled, Vanessa studied Hilda as if there was more to her than met the eye, but the woman's face quickly softened. "Please escort her back to her dormitory and make sure she gets some rest."

Zep let his bag drop off his shoulder and rushed to Vanessa, his face worried.

Vanessa should have been happy, but instead she was over-whelmed with guilt. "But what about Josef and rehearsal?" she asked. "We can't both leave—"

"I'll deal with Josef," Hilda said. "Don't you worry about him."

Zep held out his hand. "Hi," he said softly.

Behind him, the princesses filtered into the room, swinging their dance bags and laughing.

Vanessa stared down at Zep's hand. It was still there, wait-ing for her. He was here now. Without saying a word, she laced her fingers through his, and together they pushed past Anna and her friends and walked out into the bright autumn afternoon.

Neither of them spoke while they meandered around the stone walkway between Lincoln Center Plaza and Juilliard. Vanessa didn't look up at Zep once; instead, she studied her feet, which moved in tandem with his, as if they were still dancing.

"Where have you been?" she asked suddenly, just as he spoke. "With Josef."

Their words mingled together, and when Vanessa realized they had read each other's thoughts, she smiled.

"Here," he said. "Do you want to sit for a minute?"

Vanessa nodded and he led her to a sunny spot on the marble ledge, protected from the November wind by the glassy buildings of Lincoln Center to their left.

"Why do you spend every evening with Josef?"

Zep hesitated. "He's tutoring me," he said finally.

Tutoring? If that was the big secret, why hadn't he told her before?

"It's been difficult for me. I don't like to admit I'm having trouble with something. Especially with dance."

"So he's teaching you in private?" Vanessa said. "But aren't all your scenes with me?"

"No," he said slowly. "I *do* have two solos."

All that time for just two solos?

Zep added, "They're difficult. The way you're having trouble with the final scene? I'm going through the same thing."

Vanessa shook her head. "I still don't understand why you didn't just tell me before. It's nothing to be embarrassed about."

"You have enough to worry about," Zep said. "I thought you just assumed I was practicing."

"Right," Vanessa murmured. "I guess that does make sense. The entire ballet doesn't revolve around me."

"Don't worry," he said, laughing. "It does sort of revolve around you."

The sun felt warm against Vanessa's cheek. Zep squeezed her hand, which looked impossibly small in his palm. But even with Zep beside her, she couldn't get the hoarse, chanting voices of the white figures out of her head. *We are you, you are we, we are you, you are we.* Their faces, their voices, their screams as the fire engulfed them—it all seemed so real. Yet Hilda hadn't heard any of it. Was Vanessa losing her mind?

"Hey," Zep said, bringing her back to the present. "What's going on in there?" He traced his finger along her forehead, pushing the wisps of her hair away from her face.

Should she tell him? She wanted to but didn't know how. What if he thought she was crazy? She didn't want him to walk away from her.

Zep touched her cheek. "I'm here," he said. "And I'm not leaving."

Vanessa hesitated. "You won't think I'm losing it?"

"The only thing I'm worried about losing is you. And if I can help it, that won't ever happen."

Vanessa gave him the beginning of a smile, and then she told him everything: how Helen grabbed her and told her to leave school, to trust no one but this mysterious Lyric Elite; about the voices in the basement studio that spoke her name; the rumors about how the lead ballerinas at NYBA kept disappearing. "What if it's true?" she said. "What if I'm next?"

To her surprise, Zep didn't look worried at all. "Is that what's been bothering you?" he said, as if she had just told him she'd spilled a glass of milk.

Vanessa nodded, confused.

"And here I was thinking you had some sort of dance injury or fatal illness." Zep laughed. "I don't think you have anything to worry about," he said gently. "All that's happening to you is nerves. I mean first of all, Helen. She was two years ahead of me at NYBA, so I knew her a little bit, and all I can say is that she's *always* been on the edge. She used to cry during rehearsals when Josef yelled at her. And sometimes she would just zone out, not even answer if I talked to her. Believe me, you're nothing like her."

Zep continued, "It's true that a lot of girls do drop out, but that's only because ballerinas tend to be, well, delicate. That's partially why they're such wonderful dancers, but it also lends itself to . . . insecurity."

Vanessa bit her lip. She hated the stereotype, but she knew it was true.

"Have you heard any of the other legends about NYBA?"

Vanessa's eyes widened. "No."

Zep leaned back, squinting in the sun. "Well, there's the one about how Hilda is a witch, and she chooses one boy each year to ensnare with a love spell."

For the first time in days, Vanessa let out a real laugh. "You're making that up."

"I wish I were," Zep said, smiling. "I've actually heard people talking about it in the lunchroom. Another legend is that one of the old costume designers haunts the dressing rooms beneath the main stage. The rumor is that she strangled herself to death with a roll of ribbon. Oh, and don't forget Balanchine's scale. It's tucked away behind the main stage. If you step on it, you'll gain twenty pounds."

Vanessa couldn't help but laugh. "You're joking," she said. "That is the most absurd thing I've ever heard."

"I'm not," Zep said. "Do you want to go step on the scale then? Test the legend?"

"And risk gaining twenty pounds? I don't think so," she said with a smile.

"You would be just as lovely," he said, gazing at her.

Vanessa blushed.

"As for the voices you heard this morning," Zep said gently, "I think you're just overworked and stressed out about the performance. The things you heard the figures say—they almost sound like audience members heckling you."

Vanessa furrowed her brow. *We are you, you are we, we are you, you are we.* The chanting did sound like an angry audience, sort of.

"I really don't think you have anything to worry about," Zep said, grazing his fingers over the back of her hand, making her tremble. "You're the most incredible dancer I've ever worked with. If I've ever seemed frustrated, it's because I thought I wasn't going to be able to match your skills."

Vanessa searched his face. "Really?"

"Really."

Vanessa traced the lines in his palm with her finger. "There's one more thing."

"Okay."

"On Halloween, I saw Anna talking to Justin. She was crying. He told her to leave school, and then he gave her a bouquet of flowers. She ran to the basement studio and placed the bouquet on that ashy spot in the center. And then she left."

"How do you know all of that?"

"I—I followed her," Vanessa admitted. "Well, I was following Justin, because I thought he was you. Where were you that night?"

"I was with Josef, going over my steps. I wanted to be there. Josef pulled me away before I had a chance to tell you."

"So you're not seeing Anna?"

"Anna? No."

His hand on her cheek interrupted her thoughts. "You're the

only one I want," he said. "You know that, right?" He pulled her toward him, his hand tickling the back of her neck as he pressed his lips to hers. She kissed him back, her knees touching his, and for a moment, everything felt like it was going to be okay.

But when she got back to her dormitory, everyone else was at class and Vanessa was alone again. Her smile faded as she climbed the stairs to her room, trying to remember what Zep had said that made her stop worrying, but his voice kept drifting away from her.

Instead, she heard other voices, soft ones that grew louder, shriller. *Your soul for the taking, your soul for the taking, your soul for the taking. The summoning. The summoning.* Quickly, she ran into her room, slammed the door, and slid onto the rug, pressing her hands to her ears.

Without thinking, Vanessa picked up the phone and dialed the only number she knew she could count on. "Please pick up," Vanessa said. "Please."

"Hello?"

Vanessa had never been more relieved to hear her mother's voice. "Mom? It's me."

"Vanessa? You sound out of breath. Are you all right?"

Vanessa shook her head. "There's something really wrong at this place," she said. "I don't know how to explain it, but I know it's real. The walls, they're . . . there are girls in there."

"Vanessa, I can't understand what you're saying. Something about a wall?"

"Yes," Vanessa said. "I keep hearing them. I can't get them out of my head."

"What?" Her mother paused. "Vanessa, where are you?"

"I'm in my room."

"Aren't you supposed to be in rehearsal?"

"Yes, but I wasn't feeling well. They excused me from practice."

"Excused you from practice?" her mother said sharply. "Is anyone with you?"

"No. Everyone's at class. But I can't tell anyone. They'll think I'm crazy."

A long pause. "Okay, Vanessa, what I want you to do is to take a deep breath, hang up the phone, and go to bed."

Vanessa shook her head. "No. Then they'll come back." She heard papers rustling in the background.

"Vanessa, you need to rest. You're overworked and stressed out about your performance. Try and catch up on sleep. You'll feel better in a few hours."

"Stress? No, Mom, it's not like that. I really hear them. They're not made up—"

Her mother swallowed. "Hear what?"

"Voices. Girls in the wall. I saw them. They were burning."

She heard her mother exhale deeply. "Vanessa, please try to get some sleep. Promise me you will. This is all stemming from fatigue. I'm going to call your doctor."

Vanessa's breath caught in her throat. "What? I don't need a doctor. You told me to call you if anything was wrong, if—"

Vanessa stopped herself. If she went on, her mother would

probably come and pick her up from school. She would take any excuse to get Vanessa out of NYBA. But was that really what she wanted?

No. She had to stay.

"You're right, Mom." Vanessa changed the tone of her voice to something softer, less urgent. "I do need some sleep. I haven't had a break in weeks. I'm sure I'll feel better after a short nap."

"Exactly, honey," her mother replied. "Rest your head for a few hours. Take care of yourself. I'll call you tonight and see how you're feeling. Okay?"

Vanessa nodded. "Okay."

But after she hung up, Vanessa didn't go to bed. She stared at the phone, thrusting it back in her pocket. Now what? There was no one left to call. Except . . .

Vanessa searched through her contacts list until she found Elly's cell phone number. But she had tried that dozens of times with no luck. What she needed was Elly's home phone. But how? None of them had it.

Vanessa thought back to the morning after Elly left, when Steffie told her that their RA, Kate, had gone to the main office, where she had found Elly's home number. She was about to call, Steffie had said, when Hilda stopped her. *Kate might still have the number,* she realized, and ran down the hall.

Kate's door was decorated with autumn leaves cut out of construction paper and a sign counting down the days until the first performance of *The Firebird*. Vanessa knocked, but no one answered. She knocked again and tried the knob. To her surprise, it was unlocked. After glancing over her shoulder to make sure no one was watching, she opened the door and slipped inside.

Kate was organized. All Vanessa had to do was sift through the files on her desk until she found a school directory. She scanned the pages and found Elly's name. Beneath it was printed an address and cell phone number. Written into the margins next to it in Kate's loopy cursive was a second number, labeled *HOME*. Vanessa scrawled it on the back of her hand with a pen and ran to her room.

Seconds after she punched in the number, Elly's mother answered the phone. She had a warm southern drawl and sounded like she was in the kitchen. Vanessa heard dishes clinking together in the background.

"Hi, I was wondering if I could speak to Elly," Vanessa said.

"Elly?" her mother said with a laugh. "Well, honey, Elly's at dance school in New York and won't be home until Christmas."

Vanessa felt the color leave her face. "Dance school?"

"Of course. In fact, she sent me an e-mail only two days ago saying how much she's loving the city. Her cell phone is broken, so I wouldn't recommend calling her there, but I can give you her e-mail address."

Vanessa lowered the phone from her ear, her hands trembling. What was going on?

"Who is this again?" Elly's mother said, her voice now tinny and far away.

It can't be real, Vanessa thought, staring at the mouthpiece. A lump formed in her throat. Elly had to be home.

"Hello?" Elly's mom said. "Are you still there?"

Not knowing what to do, Vanessa hung up. She leaned against her bed, wishing that her mother had been right; that she could just crawl into bed and close her eyes, and when she woke up everything would be simple once more.

CHAPTER TWENTY-ONE

"What the—?" Steffie said, catching her books before they dropped.

Steffie was unlocking the door to her room when Vanessa burst down the hall, nearly bowling her over, deeply relieved to see Steffie's face—pinched frown and raised eyebrow included.

"What are you—"

Vanessa didn't let her finish. "Quick," she said. "Get inside."

They fell into the room, Steffie stumbling as her papers scattered across the floor. "What is up with you?" she asked as Vanessa locked the deadbolt behind them. "Aren't you supposed to be in rehearsal now?"

"I wasn't feeling well," Vanessa said, opening Steffie's laptop.

"That much is obvious." Steffie watched, hand on hip, as

Vanessa turned up the stereo until music blared from her speakers. "And what are you doing? Did I say you could touch my stuff?"

"No," Vanessa said. "But I don't want anyone to hear what I'm about to say."

"Which is?"

"I called Elly—"

"And her cell phone was off?" Steffie said, looking unimpressed. "I left a message the other day for her birthday."

"Her *home* phone."

Steffie furrowed her eyebrows. "What home phone?"

"I had to talk to her, so I broke into Kate's room and found the number."

"You what?" Steffie said with more force than Vanessa had expected. "Why? You could have gotten caught, kicked out of school—"

"Her mom answered," Vanessa said, interrupting. "Elly isn't there either."

That silenced Steffie.

"I asked for her, and her mom said she was at ballet school in New York. That she had just sent them an e-mail a couple of days ago."

Steffie shook her head, her eyes wandering to the other side of the room, where Elly's bed had been bare since she'd left school almost two months ago. "I don't understand. She wasn't there? And they didn't even know she had left? Don't they ever talk on the phone?"

Vanessa shook her head.

"Are you sure you had the right number?"

"Yes."

There was a long pause as Steffie lowered herself onto her bed. "So what does that mean?" she asked. "She e-mailed her parents, telling them she was at school, and e-mailed us in September, telling us she was home. Did she just run away somewhere and lie to all of us?"

"Maybe . . . ," Vanessa said, thinking of her sister. If Elly had run away, she wouldn't have been the first. Though something about Elly's disappearance sent shivers down her spine. Why had Elly left Vanessa that note with the block of rosin wrapped inside? The note had made it sound like Elly had *wanted* to talk to Vanessa. So why would she have run away without telling her friends?

"Unless," Vanessa said carefully, "she didn't run away."

Steffie narrowed her eyes. "And what? Something happened to her?"

Vanessa thought of her sister and the secret diary, the one they'd never found. Both her sister and Elly had vanished without any warning. Why? What was the connection?

The screams of the white figures from the practice room rang in her ears, together with Helen's words: *The right steps with the right dancer can wreak havoc. Get out while you still can.*

"There's one more thing that I haven't told you," Vanessa said.

Steffie's eyes were open, waiting. "Okay."

Vanessa told Steffie everything, about the basement practice room, the way the luminous figures peeled themselves from the walls and surrounded her, chanting, then screaming: *You are we, we are you, you are we, we are you.* And the names. *Elizabeth. Katerina. Joy. Rebecca. Hannah. Josephine. Chloë . . . Margaret.* She didn't stop, until her throat was dry from speaking and her hands were trembling from everything she had just said.

When she finished, Steffie was clutching the bedpost, her warm brown face pale. "Figures?"

"I know it's hard to believe," Vanessa said. "If I hadn't seen them, heard them, I wouldn't have believed it either. But they were there. It wasn't just in my head."

"Those names," Steffie said, shaking her head in disbelief. "Those were the exact names they said to you? You didn't make them up?"

"No," Vanessa replied, thinking of the way they hissed her sister's name. "Why?"

"Those are the names of the missing girls in the articles I showed you," Steffie said. She pulled her iPad out of her bag and turned it on. "The girls who disappeared. And not just some of them," she said. "All of them."

Together, they scrolled down the articles. Even though she had already seen them, Vanessa's stomach still contracted at the sight of the photographs. Steffie was right; nearly all of the missing girls, the ones who had been cast in a lead role, had been named by the white, luminous figures.

"I don't get it," Vanessa said. "Why would they whisper those names?"

"Maybe they're trying to warn you about something,"

Steffie said. "You are the lead dancer. Just like those girls were."

"But warn me about what?"

Steffie let out a nervous chuckle. "I can't believe we're talking about figures on a wall," she said.

"I know," Vanessa said. "But they were real. I saw them."

"I believe you," Steffie said quietly.

Vanessa met her gaze. "Sometimes I wonder if I'm just losing my mind. If the pressure is getting to me."

"Maybe it isn't just the pressure," Steffie said, lingering on the last article frozen on the iPad's screen. "All of these girls were cast in lead roles, and all of them disappeared. They couldn't all have cracked and run away."

"So . . . what?"

"We have to find out more. It's not like every girl who was ever cast as a lead here has disappeared. What was it about these particular girls?"

"I don't know," Vanessa said. She was trying to help, but all she could think of was Margaret.

"We have to figure out what they have in common," Steffie said.

Vanessa gazed at the article on the screen, which dated back almost a decade. She didn't know whom to trust. Something strange was going on, and in a small school where gossip traveled quickly, she didn't want word getting out that she was researching a line of missing girls. How long had Josef and Hilda been at NYBA? A while, she thought, though she couldn't ask either of them. Unless . . .

Vanessa sat up and turned to Steffie. "I have an idea. But you'll have to skip your next class."

Black leotard. Black leggings. Black cardigan. Vanessa pulled her hair back into a low bun, hoping that would make its red color less noticeable. "Ready?" she said to Steffie as she slipped on a pair of black flats. Also clad in black, her friend nodded. They had thirty minutes until classes let out.

Light streamed into the lobby of the building next door, where all of their classes were held. It was empty, silent, save for the water fountain humming by the stairway. Vanessa and Steffie moved soundlessly across the marble floor, knowing that everyone else was at class or rehearsal.

Josef's office was nestled into an alcove at the end of the hall. During her last trip to his office, the top drawer of his file cabinet had been slightly ajar, revealing files marked with students' names. Vanessa led Steffie toward the door, remembering that experience, when she'd overheard Josef and Hilda.

"Are you sure he's gone?" Steffie whispered as they crouched outside the door.

"Yes," Vanessa said. "Well, ninety-nine percent sure."

"What? Why?"

"He's supposed to be in afternoon rehearsal today, but Hilda was the only one there when I left."

Steffie opened her mouth to respond, but Vanessa cut her off.

"He probably got there late. Besides, we're here now, aren't we?"

"Yeah, but if he's here and we get caught, we could be expelled," Steffie hissed.

"So you'd rather wait around until someone else disappears?" Vanessa said.

Steffie hesitated, then shook her head. "Go ahead. Open it."

Gently, Vanessa gave the doorknob a slight turn. It was unlocked. She pushed it open, peering into the darkness. She glanced over her shoulder at Steffie, and like a pair of black cats, they snuck inside.

Josef's office was just as she remembered. The desk was scattered with papers, books, and a few blocks of the strange, sticky rosin. Glass-fronted shelves lined the walls, filled with trophies and medals. Just past them were the gates that led to Josef's private library. Steffie ran her hands down them, rattling them slightly to see if they were unlocked. No such luck.

"Over here," Vanessa whispered, and led her to the file cabinet behind Josef's desk. She flipped on the desk lamp, illuminating the room in a dim orange light, and opened the top drawer. They looked for every name that the white figures mentioned.

At first they couldn't find any, until Steffie thought to check the bottom drawer, which held all of the documents for former NYBA students. Some of the files were faded, the older ones so bent out of shape that it seemed a miracle they were still intact. But after searching, Vanessa and Steffie slowly picked out each of the missing girls named by the luminous figures. They were all here.

While Steffie flipped through the files, Vanessa pulled out

a single manila folder, labeled MARGARET ADLER. She was surprised at how thin it was. Somehow, she had expected it to be thicker, filled with information about her disappearance. Instead, it held only a few measly papers.

"There's nothing here," Vanessa murmured, half to Steffie, half to herself. She flipped to the next sheet, and the next, but it was all things she already knew or didn't care about. Margaret's school schedule, her grades, her dormitory assignment, some notes Hilda had jotted down about her form.

Vanessa squinted at the handwritten scrawl on the last sheet of paper. It was a record of Margaret's dancing, what her strengths and her weaknesses were. *All normal,* Vanessa thought, until she reached the bottom.

"It says here that right before she disappeared, my sister was cast as the lead in *La Danse du Feu.*" Vanessa looked up. "That's what Josef calls the extra dance from *The Firebird.*"

Steffie looked up from her files, her face flushed in the lamplight. "It says the same thing on this one." She held up Chloë's folder.

They went through the rest of the files for the girls who'd been named by the luminous figures on the wall. *Rebecca Harding. Hannah Gary. Josephine Front.* Each one had the same handwritten notation. "Lead in *La Danse du Feu.*" And each ended with the same signature. *Josef.*

"If it's just the final dance scene, then why would Josef have noted it as a separate performance?" Vanessa said. "If she were the lead in *The Firebird*, then obviously she'd be the lead in *La Danse du Feu*, right? So why bother putting it in the file?"

"I don't know," Steffie murmured. "But it looks like the *La Danse du Feu* was performed thirteen times in various productions, the first time being twenty years ago. He must add it to different ballets. It's not just performed in *The Firebird*. It's something . . . extra."

"Do you think—" Vanessa said, but stopped herself, her mind racing. "Do you think it's a coincidence?"

"There is one way to find out," Steffie said, closing the file. "We start looking deeper."

They searched through everything: his drawers; the books and papers on his desk, most of which were in French or Russian; current student files. Steffie's said nothing out of the ordinary; neither did Blaine's or TJ's. And to their surprise, neither did Elly's. It didn't mention anything about her dropping out. The notes just stopped in September, as if after that she had ceased to exist. Justin's folder said nothing in particular, either, though the Fratelli twins had a peculiar notation at the bottom. *Lyric Elite?* someone had scrawled.

Zep's folder was missing, and so was Vanessa's.

"Look at this." Steffie held up the oldest file for one of the missing girls. She pointed to the last page, where it said the girl had been cast as the lead in *La Danse du Feu*. Next to the notation, there was a tiny string of numbers.

"What is it?" Vanessa said.

"A Dewey Decimal number," Steffie said. "From the library."

They turned to the locked gate that led to Josef's private library. Inside, they could see dozens of dusty, ancient, leatherbound books. Without speaking, they stood up and began to search—rifling through Josef's shelves and drawers, beneath papers and sticky blocks of rosin. But they couldn't find the key to the gate anywhere.

"Maybe he keeps it with him," Vanessa said.

But Steffie wasn't ready to give up yet. "Why would he do that," she said, "if the only place he uses it is here?"

To keep out people like us, Vanessa thought, just as Steffie walked toward Josef's wall of trophies. In the center, on an open shelf, stood the largest trophy, in the shape of a bronzed pointe shoe. Steffie reached out and tipped it over, and a key fell onto the desktop.

The library gate unlocked soundlessly. There were candles in sconces mounted on the wall, but they didn't dare light them, lest the smell float outside and alert someone to their presence, so instead, they used the glow from their cell phones. Feeling their way through the dark, they wandered along the shelves, which were stacked with hundreds of old books on dance and choreography, on the history of drama and the anatomy of movement. Steffie stopped every so often, examining the numbers on the spines.

"This way," she whispered, and led Vanessa deeper inside.

Steffie crouched low, her body blending into the darkness. When she stood up, she was holding a heavy book bound with dark-red leather. She brushed off the cover, but there was no title.

Inside, its pages were brittle and yellowed, the edges smudged with oily fingerprints, as if they had been read dozens of times. "There's nothing here." Steffie flipped from page to page. Each one was blank: not a single word, picture, or drop of ink.

Just as they flipped to the last page, which was still infuri-atingly blank, a noise sounded from the other room. Vanessa held up her hand to silence Steffie, and together, they pocketed their cell phones and listened to the sound of the office door opening. Vanessa felt her heart pounding in her chest.

Josef? Steffie mouthed to her.

Vanessa didn't wait to find out. She grabbed the book and slipped it back into place. *This way,* she mouthed to Steffie, pulling her behind a low shelf in the back of the library.

Footsteps sounded in the other room. They were slow, soft, and heading directly toward the library.

She heard the gate open.

The footsteps stopped, and Vanessa closed her eyes, sud-denly realizing that they hadn't locked it. Josef would know that someone had been there. But there was nothing they could do but wait. Vanessa could feel Steffie's skin against hers, warm and moist with sweat, and smelling faintly of vanilla.

The footsteps continued into the library, sounding gritty against the dusty stone floor.

Vanessa held her breath as the person walked toward her, and then suddenly changed direction. In the faint lights, her eyes traveled up his leg, his waist, his collared shirt. They didn't look like they belonged to Josef. They were too young, too preppy, and the footsteps were too quiet, as if whoever it was knew he shouldn't be here either.

He scanned the shelves, moving quickly, until, to Vanessa's surprise, he turned down the row where she and Steffie had just been. There, he bent down, reading the spines.

She swallowed a gasp and grabbed Steffie's wrist. She looked at the ground, hoping he hadn't seen her. To her relief, Justin inched to the left, absorbed in studying the books in front of him.

Finally, he found what he was looking for. He pulled out the same crimson-bound volume Vanessa and Steffie had just put back. Vanessa arched her neck, trying to see what he was doing.

Justin didn't seem put off by the blank cover or spine. He opened it to the first pages, turning them delicately, as if they were dried leaves. Leaving the book open, he set it on a shelf. He reached into his pocket and took out a book of matches and a block of sticky rosin, wrapped in paper.

Slipping the amber rosin out of its casing, he rubbed it over his left hand, coating it in a thick, greasy layer.

And then, to Vanessa's horror, he struck a match and lit his entire hand on fire.

CHAPTER TWENTY-TWO

Justin held up his burning hand, and for a moment Vanessa thought he was going to set the book on fire too.

She was about to stop him from setting the whole place ablaze, when Steffie grabbed her arm and put a finger to her lips.

Justin must have heard something, because he turned to them, his face lit a fiery red from the flame. They both froze. He extended his burning hand forward, shining the light in their direction, before passing over them. Vanessa's shoulders slumped in relief as he turned back to the book.

They watched, barely breathing, while he took a voice recorder out of his pocket and turned it on. Illuminating the blank pages with the burning rosin, he began to read aloud. He spoke quickly, his voice too low for them to make out much.

"Must be thirteen dancers," he murmured, turning the page. "Plus one more. With the conjunction of the planets.

"The series of calendars." He squinted at the text. "Converging on the thirteenth of December, in the second decade of the second millennium."

He paused, then read the date again. "The thirteenth of December." He frowned.

Vanessa exchanged a baffled look with Steffie. That date—it wasn't just any day in December. It was one that everyone at NYBA knew, including Justin. The opening night of *The Firebird* performance. But why was it in an ancient book?

Justin glanced at the clock on the wall. It was almost five o'clock, which meant that Josef would be back any minute from rehearsal. Justin turned off the recorder. Slipping the book back onto the shelf, he waved his hand through the air in one brisk swish, extinguishing the flame. And just like that he was gone, leaving the girls in darkness.

When they heard his footsteps disappear through the office door, Vanessa and Steffie snuck out from behind the bookshelf and ran to the aisle with the blank book. A bitter smell hung in the air from the smoky rosin. Steffie grabbed the book and stuffed it in her bag, and they tiptoed out of the library, locking the gate behind them.

Vanessa did a quick sweep, making sure everything was in its right place—the key inside the brass trophy, the files tucked safely into the cabinet, the papers on Josef's desk artfully messy. She picked up a sticky block of rosin. It felt warm in her hand, like a piece of melting caramel.

Taking a stray piece of paper from under Josef's desk, she wrapped it up like a bar of soap and followed Steffie to the door. Making sure the lobby was clear, they slipped outside.

A class had just emerged from one of the studios. Vanessa and Steffie let the crowd swallow them up until they looked like any other students, sweaty from a long workout. "I have matches in my room," Steffie muttered. The chatter around them drowned out her voice.

"I'll meet you there," Vanessa muttered back. "I'm going to the dining hall first."

Steffie gave her an inquisitive look.

"The waffle machines," Vanessa said cryptically. A handful of fire extinguishers were stacked beneath the waffle makers. "If we burn down your room, they'll definitely be onto us."

"Good idea," Steffie said. Vanessa could see the outline of the book through her bag.

"See you then," Vanessa said.

"See you."

While the rest of the dancers walked through the double doors, their laughter fading into the November dusk, Vanessa snuck down the empty hall. But when she turned the corner, she bumped, headfirst, into someone.

"Watch where you're going," she said, when she felt a hand close around hers.

Justin pulled her toward him, pressing her against his chest. He squinted at the amber residue on her fingers, his dark eyes flickering as he understood. His nose flared slightly at the bitter scent of grease and smoke. Vanessa tried to wriggle out of his grip, but he was strong. That much she remembered from dancing with him.

With a swift movement, he pried the block of rosin from her hand.

"I thought I heard someone in there," Justin said. Like Vanessa and Steffie, he too was dressed entirely in black. "I'll admit, I'm relieved. I thought it was someone . . . else."

"Let me go," Vanessa said defiantly, glancing up at him over her shoulder.

"No," Justin whispered in her ear, his hair tickling her neck. "It's time to let you in on what's going on."

"I'm not going anywhere—" Vanessa began to shout, but Justin clamped a hand over her mouth, muffling her voice. Her eyes darted around the building, hoping someone would see her, but the hallways were empty and the studio doors were shut. She tried to will her body to stop shaking. How could she have been so stupid?

Justin tightened his grip on her mouth until she could taste the salt on his skin. "I'm sorry I can't be more gentle. But you're giving me no choice. I don't care if you don't trust me or don't want to believe me. This time, you're going to hear me out."

He pulled her down the hall and into a coat closet, shutting the door behind them. Once there, he removed his hand from her mouth.

"What are you doing?" Vanessa cried. "What do you want from me?"

A lone lightbulb hung in the middle of the room. Justin turned it on and stood in front of the door, blocking her way.

"Let me out!" she cried. "Let me out or I'll scream!"

But Justin ignored her protests. "Josef isn't training you to dance *The Firebird*. He's training you in a ritualistic dance. A dance of the occult."

Vanessa went quiet. "What?"

"*The Firebird* is just a foil. *La Danse du Feu* that you rehearse every afternoon? That's not an extra scene. It's a ritual dance that opens up a portal to another world. That's why it was never performed in the original productions, or any production since. Because it's more than just a finale. It's a final dance."

Vanessa let out a nervous laugh. "A portal?"

Justin's expression was steady, grave. "I know it's hard to believe, but it's true. I've been following Josef for a long time." He held up the rosin he had pried from Vanessa's fist. "Earlier this year I did exactly what you did. I hid in his office and watched him use this bizarre rosin to read an ancient book about ritualistic dance. Since then, I've been going back as much as I can. The books in his library are written in some sort of ancient invisible ink. The only way they can be read is through the light of a rosin torch. I don't know what the ink is or where it came from—no one does, and no one has been able to re-create it for centuries. Possibly it involves an extra-dimensional element."

Vanessa pressed her hand to her head, trying to understand everything Justin was telling her. Ancient books about occult dancing, mystic invisible ink protecting their secrets. *Thirteen dancers,* Justin had read into the recorder. *Plus one more. The conjunction of the planets. The thirteenth of December.* After Zep's role ended halfway through *La Danse du Feu*, there were thirteen ballerinas plus one more.

Vanessa.

It was true that Josef had been making them practice the strange dance far more frequently than the other scenes from *The Firebird*. She thought back to her encounter with Helen at the entrance to Central Park. *The right steps with the right dancer can wreak havoc,* Helen had warned. Could Justin be telling her the truth?

Vanessa opened her eyes, still skeptical. "So this book says that the dance opens up a portal to another world? That's why Josef is making us perform the supposedly missing dance from *The Firebird*?"

Justin relaxed, seemingly relieved that she was still listening. "Yes."

She shook her head in disbelief. "Why?"

"According to myth, if the dance is done correctly, with the right dancer, a spirit will pass through the portal."

"What do you mean? Like—like a ghost? Of someone who died?" Was that why the white figures had come to life when Vanessa danced? Why the figure who looked so strikingly similar to Margaret had approached her? Had Vanessa summoned it?

"No," Justin said. "Not a ghost. An evil spirit." He hesitated, lowering his head, his eyes dark. "A demon."

Vanessa went rigid. Could Justin really believe what he was telling her? "No," she said. "Demons aren't real. That's just—they're not."

"But ghosts are?" Justin said. "You don't have to believe me. Just look at the facts. There are a whole slew of choreographers who have dabbled with the occult over the years. Josef isn't the first person to attempt this, only the most recent. It's been tried, for the most part unsuccessfully, countless times throughout history. Josef is closer than anyone has come in a long time."

"Unsuccessfully? So isn't that just a dance, then? If nothing happens?"

"Not quite," Justin said. "I think you've gotten a taste of what it feels like at first."

Vanessa shook her head. "What do you mean?"

"When the right dancers achieve a sublime execution of the right dance, it thins the walls between worlds. It blurs reality. The walls start to spin. The ground tips until it's no longer level. Light bends in odd ways, and colors seem to dull. Time slows until this world isn't real anymore."

He paused, watching Vanessa's face. She thought of all those times when she had gotten the dance nearly perfect, remembered how her body felt when it moved in tandem with nature.

"I think you know what I'm talking about," Justin repeated softly.

Vanessa swallowed, unable to meet his eye. The closet suddenly felt incredibly intimate.

"When that happens with all of the dancers, an opening is formed between this world and the next. The ring of thirteen dancers acts as the perimeter of the portal. And the final dancer—the principal ballerina—becomes the demon's host. When it's called forth, it pulses through her limbs, inhabiting her body as she dances and devouring her soul. That's how it comes to this world."

Vanessa couldn't speak. Only one word rang in her head. *Margaret.*

She had been the principal ballerina, the Firebird, the same role as Vanessa. Did that mean that Margaret was the fourteenth dancer? Had she tried to summon a demon? Had her soul been devoured? Is that why she disappeared?

As if reading her thoughts, Justin stepped closer. "But legend has it that a demon has only been called forth four times in history, all centuries ago. None of those times were by Josef."

"How do you know?"

"According to lore, those four times, when the demons were released on the world, complete chaos ensued: massacres, plagues, widespread death and suffering. Reports of villages becoming possessed, of men losing their minds and destroying entire towns. None of that is happening now, is it?"

Vanessa shuddered at the cold edge in Justin's voice. "If it's so destructive, then why does Josef want to do it?"

"Because if it's done with the right dancer, the demon can be controlled. Can you imagine harnessing that kind of power? Instead of destroying things, you could . . . command people. Lead armies. All that crazy business."

"I don't understand," she said hesitantly. "What happens to the dancers if it's unsuccessful? If the demon doesn't pass through?"

"They become . . . stuck," Justin said. "In between worlds. Not here, not there."

The luminous white figures danced through Vanessa's mind, and suddenly she realized that she already knew the answer. The white figures on the wall, the burned spots, the ashes in the center of the room, directly on top of where the principal ballerina was supposed to finish. She remembered what Helen had said: someone was trying to put her in the walls. Then she remembered the figure that looked like Margaret, her bloodcurdling scream as she burst into flame. That was what had happened to her.

"So she's still alive?" Vanessa said. "Margaret?"

Justin bowed his head. "I don't know."

"You don't know?" Vanessa asked. "So where is she? What happened to her?"

"I don't know," Justin repeated. "All I know is that it wasn't successful." He looked suddenly somber. "None of Josef's attempts were."

Vanessa studied him. "Chloë," she suddenly realized. "This summer. The senior girls. The sunburns."

"Those burns weren't from the sun," Justin said. "And the date you heard me reading? That was just one out of a list of many others. They mark the dates when the portal is ripest for opening. The last one was in August, when Josef called a preseason rehearsal."

"So you're saying all those girls were there when it happened to Chloë?" Vanessa said. "And they're all choosing to take part in it again?"

"I'm not sure it's their choice. Josef might be forcing them into it. There are dark magics that can control minds."

"But how? Why? Chloë was their friend. Why wouldn't they tell someone? It doesn't make any sense." Vanessa eyed him suspiciously. "How are you so sure it hasn't worked any of those times? Maybe the dance worked with Chloë and my sister, and they're still alive somewhere."

"They might be alive," Justin said. "But their dances didn't succeed. Think about it. If Josef had already called forth a demon, then why would he be training you to perform another *Danse du Feu*?"

"Me," Vanessa repeated. She could almost feel the way her limbs grew taut, as if everything inside were bending and buckling. The way the ribbons seemed to tighten around her ankles. The way her chest heaved with heat, with passion, as if everything inside were coming to a boil. Could that have been . . . ?

"Yes," Justin said. "You. Josef chose you because you're the strongest dancer he—or anyone else—has seen in a long time. You aren't delicate like most ballerinas. He knows you have the strength to finish the dance, to call forth the demon, to let it inhabit you. That's why he's been training you so intensely. Why he gets so upset when you can't finish."

All Vanessa wanted to do was run, as far away from the school as possible. "But why?" she asked again. "Why does Josef want it so badly?"

"Because when demons are brought to this world, they serve the one who called them. There are only two people who fill that title. The first is the demon's master, the choreographer. When the demon is brought forth, it will be forced to pledge its allegiance to Josef. It will do whatever he asks, in exchange for its eventual freedom."

"And who is the second person?" Vanessa asked, not sure she wanted to know the answer.

"The dancer. She is the most powerful thing in the room."

"You pulled me in here to tell me that I'm doomed? That my sister is stuck in some in-between world, and Josef is training me to call forth a demon?" Vanessa pressed her hands to her temples, her head throbbing. "Even if you are telling the truth, you aren't trying to help me. You're trying to use me, just like everyone else."

"I'm not—" Justin started to say, but Vanessa cut him off.

"Why should I believe you or even listen to you after all of the things you've done to me?"

"It's true I was trying to mess you up in rehearsal the other day. I guess I hoped I could make Josef change his mind about you . . . I didn't want you to get hurt."

"Why didn't you just tell me?" Vanessa said.

A single bead of sweat slid down Justin's temple. "I didn't know if I could trust you. Your sister had been involved in *La Danse du Feu* before she disappeared, and then you show up and Josef is immediately enamored with you. You land the lead role as a freshman—*a freshman*—just like your sister. What if you were somehow . . . in on it?

"Josef is more powerful than you realize. If I'm right, then he's somehow been able to coerce a dozen dancers over the past two decades to help him call forth the demon. Every year or two he'll trick a lead ballerina into helping him, and when that fails and she disappears, he waits a while so as not to draw attention to himself, and then tries again. That includes your sister." He paused for emphasis. "And Anna Franko and the other girls? He somehow makes them do it, even though they watched their friend Chloë go up in flames. It's like their brains are fogged. Josef has ways of making people do things against their will."

Vanessa's heart raced at the mention of her sister. Had Margaret gone along with it and met the same fate as Chloë? What about Elly?

"That's why I followed you," Justin continued. "That's why I kept such a close watch on you."

It all made a sort of twisted sense, but something about the tone of Justin's voice made Vanessa want to scream. "I'm not a child," she said. "You think it's okay to follow people around the streets of New York at night? To show up at odd hours at their door and deliver cryptic messages? Do you have any idea how that made me feel? I thought I was losing my mind."

Her words took Justin by surprise, and he shrank back. "I—I'm sorry," he said. "I was only trying to help."

"What about the rumors you were spreading about Zep? The things you told Anna? You gave her a bouquet of flowers and told her to leave school. Were you trying to help then too?"

"Those flowers weren't for her," he said defensively. "They were for Chloë. I told her what I'd learned. And yes, what I told her that night was meant to help. Just like the things I told you about Zep."

"What do you know about Zep?" she said. "Why is he so dangerous?"

Justin hesitated. "Are you still seeing him?"

"Yes," Vanessa said, relieved that she could finally say it with certainty.

"And you think he's trustworthy?"

Vanessa narrowed her eyes. "Yes, I do trust Zep. He's never done anything to make me think I shouldn't. But you—you sneak around like a coward; you spread lies that you have no way of proving, and you think you're some sort of hero? For all I know, you could be the one responsible for my sister's disappearance. Maybe that's why you left school three years ago. You wanted to lie low until the scandal went away, until you could come back to NYBA without any suspicion."

Justin snorted. "You're not listening. Me, responsible for the disappearance of your sister?" He stepped toward her, leaving the door unguarded. "No. That was *Josef.*"

She didn't dare look back. She dashed past him, out of the closet and into the empty hallway. The cold air harsh against her lungs, Vanessa ran across the courtyard toward the dormitory, bounding up the stairs and bursting through Steffie's door without knocking for the second time that afternoon.

"Oh," Steffie said, clutching her chest. "Vanessa. It's you."

Vanessa locked the door behind her and collapsed on the bed.

"What took you so long?" Steffie said. "And where's the fire extinguisher?"

Once she had caught her breath, Vanessa told her everything. How Justin had trapped her. The ritual dance. The portal. The sacrificial host, the principal ballerina. The demon. And Josef, its master. Steffie listened quietly.

"I—I don't know what to believe," Vanessa stammered. "It makes sense, but then it doesn't. I mean, it's insane, right?"

Steffie hesitated, her lips pursed as if she didn't think it was insane at all. "Maybe we should see for ourselves," she said finally, and picked up the book from Josef's library. She opened it to the first page and set it on the bed. The paper was thick and yellowed, with no trace of any writing. The only visible marks were the oily smudges of fingerprints on the edge of the page.

"Rosin?" she said, holding out her hand.

Vanessa went stiff. She didn't have the rosin anymore. "Justin took it."

"What?" Steffie said. "Without it, we can't read anything. And we can't go back to Josef's office."

Vanessa stared at the blank pages of the book, trying to figure out a solution, when suddenly she stood up. "I'll be right back," she said, and ran to her room, picking up the piece of rosin Elly had left beneath her door, with the note still wrapped around it. Vanessa unfolded it.

Just heard the craziest convo between J and H. Come by my room as soon as you get back, and I'll show you what this does. Don't tell anyone. Hurry.

Vanessa gasped, finally understanding Elly's message.

"Elly knew," Vanessa said upon entering Steffie's room. She held up the note. "Remember this? After Elly screamed during that rehearsal, she was sent to Josef's office. And while she was there, she must have seen the exact same thing we just saw."

"Plus something strange between Josef and Hilda," Steffie added, rereading the note. And placing it carefully on her desk, she took the block from Vanessa's hand and dragged it across her hand until her palm was coated in a thick layer of rosin. "Now we'll know too." Steffie pointed to the votive dancing on her nightstand. "Candle, please."

Vanessa held it out while Steffie carefully dipped her hand into the flame. It immediately ignited, her entire palm bursting into a brilliant red blaze.

"Are you okay?" Vanessa said, jumping back, but Steffie only nodded.

"It doesn't hurt," she said. "It just feels hot," she added, gazing at her fingers. "Like bathwater that could be a few degrees cooler."

In the light of the flames, the book flickered to life. Ink leeched onto the page, forming lines, dots, patterns; letters swirling into each other; sketches materializing out of nowhere.

"It's beautiful," Steffie murmured in awe.

Vanessa studied the curling ink, watching as the words spread across the parchment. But something was wrong. She tilted her head, trying to read them, but she couldn't.

"It's all in Russian!" she said.

Steffie waved her hand slightly, casting shadows over the page, as if that would make a difference. But it was useless. "I didn't know Justin spoke Russian," Steffie said.

Neither did Vanessa. "Great," she said. "Do you know any-one else who can read this?"

But Steffie didn't respond. "Never mind that," she said, gazing up around her. "Look at the walls."

Vanessa followed her gaze. As the light from the burning rosin flickered off the walls, words began to form, in a cramped scrawl that Vanessa knew so well it could have been her own. Almost reflexively, Vanessa grabbed Steffie's arm and guided her burning hand upward, illuminating the ceiling, the walls, the doors. Words spilled out over them, jumbling together in corners, curling around the doorknobs.

"What is it?" Steffie whispered.

Vanessa shivered, feeling the warmth of the fire tickling her skin, as if it were her sister's breath, whispering in her ear. "Margaret's secret diary."

CHAPTER
TWENTY-THREE

They didn't know where to start reading, but to Vanessa's surprise, Margaret had anticipated that.

"There," Vanessa said, pointing Steffie's arm to a line above Steffie's bed. The text was cut off by a poster, which Vanessa quickly pulled off the wall.

> *There is no beginning. Or if there is, I don't know about it. Do I believe in black magic? In alternate worlds? In demons? I never used to, but now I can't help but think that I'm wrong, that I'm trapped here, that I'll never escape. I thought I knew what dance was, but I knew nothing.*
>
> *I know more now. All because of Josef. The necro-dancer who commands me.*

Josef is only the most recent. There were others before him; I read about them in books. Secret books. And if he fails, there will be others who come after him. And if I fail, he fails. I have bruises from him. They line the insides of my arms, my thighs, my hips, my ribs. At first it was from his rod, the one he uses to keep the beat. If I fell out of step, he would straighten me with it, and if I stepped out of line, he would push me back with it, and if I complained, he would silence me with it.

It wasn't my fault. I should have left earlier, but now I can't. Josef knows where we live. He knows he can have her if he wants her. She is a better dancer than I am. If I fail, Josef will get her to do it instead. I can't let that happen.

I've heard whispers about the Lyric Elite. Who are they? Why have they kept silent? Can they help? How do I find them?

It feels like Josef's here with me all the time. Like he's inside me, speaking to me, telling me what to think, where to step, when to breathe, and when to stop. He's working with someone else, too, like a dark shadow behind him, everywhere he goes. I don't know who. Today Josef brought me into his office. It was dark and smelled like burning wax. The rosin. He didn't know I knew what it was for. He didn't know that I snuck into his office and watched him.

He said, I heard the other students are worried about you. They say you're not well. That you wander the halls at night, whispering things about our meeting together. That you shout in your sleep and wake the other students. Is this true?

I don't know, I said.

He slammed his hand on the table.

You're lying, he said. You're going to destroy everything we've worked for.

I can't help it. I feel so weak. I want to go home. I need to rest.

That is impossible.

Why?

I made a promise.

To me?

To the Guest. I promised your hand in marriage.

Marriage? But I'm too young.

That matters not.

I don't want to get married.

It is a symbolic marriage. Like a marriage in a dance.

I don't understand.

You don't have to. Just follow your steps perfectly. The rest will unfold before you.

Vanessa gasped, lingering on Josef's words, the same ones he had said to her. She could almost hear him whispering them in her ear during rehearsal. Margaret's scrawl continued.

Who is the Guest?

The Guest of the dance. La Danse du Feu.

Someone from the audience?

Something like that.

Is he handsome?

Very handsome. But you can only have him if you dance perfectly. He will fill you. He will consummate all of your desires. He will free you from the trifles of this world.

I don't know what Josef means. He says it's like love, the way the Guest will consume me, will fill me with a fiery heat. But I've never been in love before. Does it hurt? Everything Josef does to me hurts, but I can't tell anyone.

The only people who understand are the dancers who've gone before me. They visit me late at night, when I'm by myself in the studio. They come to me like part of a dream. They're cloudy, luminous; they dance with me, hold me up when I'm too tired. They want me to help them, but I don't know how, or if I'm strong enough. I'm going to be like them soon. I can feel it.

And then who will help me? E.? Can I trust him?

The rosin on Steffie's hand burned out before they could read any more. And just as quickly as the slanted, maddening scrawl had appeared, it vanished, and the walls of Steffie's room returned to normal.

Vanessa stared at the white space above the bed, where her sister had written her name. Her diary had never been a book, boxed up to come home with the rest of Margaret's things. It was here all along, and nobody had realized it. *If I fail, Josef will get her to do it instead.* Margaret had known what was going on, but she had stayed at school to protect her sister. Vanessa's eyes darted across the chipped paint, Margaret's words echoing in her head.

"Justin wasn't making things up," Vanessa whispered. "Josef was training Margaret to call up a demon."

"Do you think it worked?" Steffie whispered.

Vanessa shivered. The crazed handwriting on the walls was her sister's; she recognized it, but then it wasn't. It seemed delirious, obsessive, paranoid. Words had been written over other words, spiraling through paragraphs, as if by the end, Margaret could no longer control her hands. "No. I think she failed."

"Then what happened to her?" Steffie asked. "And to all of the other girls? Where did they go? And Elly. She wasn't cast as a lead. What does she have to do with this?"

Vanessa grabbed Elly's note. "She didn't have anything to do with it at first, until she discovered what Josef was doing," she said, piecing everything together. "Elly knew about the rosin. She learned about it when she was sent to Josef's office. And then he . . . he . . ." A sickening feeling made Vanessa sway. She steadied herself on the bedpost, unable to finish her thought.

Vanessa stared at the empty walls, which seemed to mock Margaret's disappearance with their blankness. Somehow, her sister had managed to find and use the strange invisible ink Justin had told her about. Ink from another dimension. If Justin was right, then Margaret had far more secrets than Vanessa could even fathom. "And the girls from the walls . . . I don't know. All I'm certain of is that I'm next."

Steffie reached for the block of rosin, about to drag it across her hand again, when Vanessa stopped her.

"We could spend *days* reading the rest of her journal," Vanessa said. "We don't have time for that. Josef could already have noticed that someone took some rosin. We're not safe here. We have to get Blaine and TJ."

"Don't you think we should tell someone? Like a teacher?"

"Who can we trust? Josef is in on it; the others might be too."

"The police, then?" Steffie said.

"And say what? That our choreographer is training us to channel a demon from another dimension?"

Steffie went quiet.

"We can't take the chance," Vanessa said. "Get Blaine and TJ and bring them downstairs. I'll meet you there."

"Where are you going?" Steffie asked.

Vanessa hesitated. There was only one other person she wanted to see, and it didn't matter if she trusted him or not. "Upstairs."

Zep's door looked the same as always—plain, unadorned wood. Beneath it, a light was on. Suddenly nervous, Vanessa raised her right hand, which was still sticky from rosin, and knocked.

No one answered. She glanced over her shoulder, then knocked again. "Zep? Are you there?"

Something within thumped, like a shoe falling on the floor. Vanessa shifted her weight. Why wasn't he answering? In any other situation, she might have left, but she didn't have time to waste. She turned the knob and let the door swing open.

Zep was sitting on his bed, typing on a laptop. A stray wave of hair fell across his face. It took him a moment to notice Vanessa, but when he did, he sat up and ripped off his headphones. Tinny music sounded from the earpieces.

"Vanessa," he said, lowering his hands. He looked impossibly tall, as if he could never fit into the narrow dormitory bed. "You surprised me."

"Why didn't you answer when I knocked?" Vanessa asked.

"I was listening to music." His eyes glinted in the light as they darted to his headphones. "I didn't hear you."

His room had the same oak furniture as Vanessa's, yet something about the way it was arranged, austere and neat, gave it a musty feeling, as if Vanessa had just entered a mahogany library. Two dark leather boots had been kicked off near the bed.

"I was just thinking about you," he said with a smile.

Vanessa searched his face. Did he sound nervous? For a moment, Vanessa thought he did, but it might have been her imagination.

The smile faded from his face. "Is everything okay? You look upset."

She tried to find the right words, but she didn't know where to start.

"Vanessa?" he said, touching her arm, his hand warm and

rough. Slowly, he pulled her toward the window. "Talk to me. Tell me what's wrong."

She sat on the windowsill beside him. Outside, the sun was setting, bands of light filtering in through the window shades. "What I'm about to tell you is going to sound insane," she said. "But it's not. Just promise you'll hear me out."

Zep looked confused, but he nodded. "I promise."

Vanessa took a breath and told him everything, from the luminous figures on the walls and the chilling phone call with Elly's mother to Josef's private library, Justin and the burning rosin, and Margaret's secret diary. When she had finished, she couldn't look Zep in the eye. She half expected him to laugh at her. But to her surprise, he didn't.

Zep lowered his hand to his cheek, rubbing the stubble on his chin. His gaze was faraway, troubled. He didn't say anything for a long time.

"Do you believe me?" Vanessa said, trying to read his expression.

As if emerging from under a spell, he turned to her. "Of course I do," he said. His eyes met her gaze, and suddenly she was in his arms, his salty scent wrapping itself around her, making her feel safe. "Don't worry," he whispered into her hair. "We're together now. Everything's going to be okay. We'll figure this out."

Vanessa let herself collapse into his embrace, relieved. "What do we do?"

"I'm not sure yet," he said thoughtfully. "Justin told you all of this?"

"Not all of it. But some."

Zep gripped the edge of the windowsill, deep in thought. "I don't trust him."

"He read about this in a book in Josef's library. I saw it for myself, it exists."

"But did you read it yourself?" Zep said.

"No," Vanessa said softly. "It was in Russian."

"Exactly. He could have told you anything. Justin obviously reads Russian, and so does Josef. They could be working together."

"So you think he made up the whole thing?" she asked, trying to rearrange the pieces. "That my sister also made it up? What about all the girls who went missing?"

"No," Zep said, lowering his voice. "Only that Justin might have altered bits of it to make you trust him. It makes sense: Justin knows Russian, he says he doesn't want to be a better dancer, so he must have some other reason for wanting to be here. Maybe *he's* involved with Josef. I know he's been following you and Anna around, spreading rumors. Don't you think he's trying to figure out how much you know?"

"I—I'm not sure," Vanessa said.

"Did Justin tell you anything else? About the dance or what Josef is planning to do?"

"I think he told me everything he knew. The rest we learned from Margaret's diary."

"Justin doesn't know about that, does he?" Zep said, narrowing his eyes.

Vanessa shook her head as Zep let out a sigh of relief. "Good. Can you show it to me?"

Vanessa hesitated. "Do you think we have time? I mean, we

took some of the rosin from Josef's office. He might know by now that someone was there."

"It'll just take a minute. And I'll be with you, so don't worry about Josef. He'll have to get past me first," Zep said, squeezing her hand. "Let me just get my things together. I'll meet you down at Steffie's room in five."

Vanessa gave him a faint smile. "Okay," she said, and made for the hallway. As she closed the door behind her, she stole one last glance into his room.

Zep was standing by his bed, his back turned as he picked up his phone. Someone must have answered, because Zep said, "It's me." A long pause. "It's time. I'll need your help." Another pause. "We can't wait. The situation is delicate. It has to happen now, or we'll lose our chance."

Who was he talking to? But there was no time to think. As Zep hung up, he leaned back on the bed to put on his boots, so the top of the laptop was visible on the covers beside him.

When Vanessa saw it, she gasped.

Zep must have heard her, because he turned around. "Vanessa," he said. "You're still here?"

But she barely heard him. All of her attention was focused on the big pink heart sticker that adorned the lid of the laptop.

"That's just like Elly's laptop," she said, letting the door creak open as she studied its familiar design.

Zep followed her gaze to the computer. "What do you know," he said, smiling. "It *is* like Elly's laptop."

Vanessa gripped the door frame, her eyes wandering from

the pink heart to Zep. "It's kind of weird how similar they are." The heart was even ripped slightly on the left side, just like Elly's.

Zep laughed and stood up, inching toward her. "Okay, you caught me. It actually is Elly's laptop."

"What?" Vanessa said, her back going rigid.

Zep stepped closer. The soft grin lingering on his face confused Vanessa. Was he joking? "But the only reason I have it is because she doesn't need it anymore."

"What do you mean? Did Elly give it to you?" As the words left her mouth, Vanessa realized she already knew the answer. It was the answer she and her friends had been avoiding for two months. The answer that Vanessa still tried to deny, even after the phone call to Elly's mother.

She backed into the hall, her heart skipping in her chest.

Suddenly Zep was in front of her, his frame filling the narrow corridor. "You see, someone needed to write to her parents after I handed her over to Josef." He grabbed her wrist.

"No," she whispered.

His hand closed around her mouth.

She felt a sharp tug as he pulled her into the deserted stairwell, his body pressing against hers until their legs were tangled. She tried to scream, but her voice was muffled by his hand.

With deliberate steps, he walked her backward, their limbs moving together in a long, intimate dance. She half expected him to narrate their tragic love story again, to tell her how she wanted him but could never have him; about their violent love and how the dance wasn't over. Except now he said, "That crazy story you just told me? It's all true."

Slowly, he leaned down and whispered in her ear, his voice low, like the trembling notes that sound just before the curtain rises for the final act. "I know. Because I'm part of it."

CHAPTER TWENTY-FOUR

A single spotlight shone onto the basement practice studio, illuminating the scorched spot in the center of the floor. Beyond that, all was dark.

Vanessa could feel the muscles in Zep's chest shifting against her back; his arms tightening as he pushed her toward the spotlight, the door slamming behind them.

Were they alone? She blinked into the darkness, waiting for her eyes to adjust. She couldn't see anyone, but she could hear a strange gurgling sound from the corner of the room. The squeal of a sneaker dragged over the floor. Silence.

Zep loosened his grip. Twisting away, she tried to free herself from his arms, but to her surprise, just before he let her loose, he leaned toward her. "Vanessa, I'm sorry," he said, so quietly she wasn't sure if she had imagined it. "It was never about you. All I've ever wanted was to learn to dance so magnificently that the world stopped. Don't you understand?"

"No," Vanessa said.

"I tried to warn you that we could never be together," he said. "Fate is against us."

"It's not fate," she said firmly. "It's your decision."

"Just wait," he said. "You'll understand." He released her arm and nodded toward the spotlight. Vanessa spun around just as he stepped back, disappearing into the shadows. Her eyes darted around the room as shapes began to appear out of the darkness—a flash of pale skin, a glint of an eye, a white hand poised above a head.

At first Vanessa thought they were the white figures on the walls, but no. She listened, waiting, until she could hear the faint sound of breathing. They were people. Girls. The cast of *The Firebird* and *La Danse du Feu*. They moved as if they were sleepwalking.

She wanted to run to them, to shake them and tell them what was going on, but before she could, someone threw a pair of pointe shoes across the floor. They slid over the wood, their ribbons tangling before resting in the circle of light.

"Put them on," Josef's voice boomed out.

Vanessa stared at the creamy satin of the slippers, knowing they would fit because they belonged to her, an extra pair she kept in her locker in the girls' changing room. Still, she couldn't bring herself to move.

"Put them on," Josef repeated.

Vanessa thought she saw a shadow shift beside her. She

spun around, only to see another shadow out of the corner of her eye. She turned, and when she did, a dim light flipped on around the edge of the room.

The first thing she saw was the princesses, all thirteen of them, their faces powdered a milky white to match their leotards. Behind them, the white figures were still frozen onto the wall, one for each ballerina, as if the white figures were their shadows. The ballerinas stood in a circle around her, in position, their arms poised above them. Their lips were thin and red with lipstick, and their eyes were lowered. She recognized Anna among them, her blond hair swept back into a sleek chignon.

"Anna." Vanessa tried to catch her gaze, but she seemed frozen in place, her frail arms extended.

"She won't respond to you," Josef said, stepping forward. The light played across his face, his heavy brow casting shadows over his eyes until they looked hollow.

Josef held his hand up to one of the princesses, grazing his fingers over her shoulder. She didn't move. He pulled away and clasped his hands together. "None of them will. They're already mine."

Vanessa was about to turn to the door and run as fast as she could when she heard the gurgling sound again. She followed it behind the circle of ballerinas to the edge of the studio. A pile of what looked like clothes sat in the shadows. Vanessa leaned forward, squinting into the dark, when she saw it move.

Josef smiled as she walked over to investigate. She spotted a shoe, then an ankle swathed in black tights. Vanessa froze. "Steffie?" she said uncertainly.

Steffie wriggled on the floor, her limbs bound and her mouth muffled by a gag.

Vanessa tried to run to her, but Zep stepped in front of Steffie, guarding her. "Uh-uh," Josef said, chastising her. "Not yet."

Vanessa backed away in horror, her eyes wandering around the room. A few feet over from Steffie lay TJ, bound and gagged, her hair tangled over her eyes. Blaine was beside her, letting out a faint whimper through his gag. Just next to him was the door. Vanessa lingered on it for a moment, then looked away.

"What have you done to them?" Vanessa said, trying to hide the quaver in her voice.

Josef paced about the room. "I wouldn't worry about them," he said. "Their fate is sealed."

"I don't believe in fate," Vanessa said.

"What do you believe in, then?"

"In work. In practice. In people. In decisions, and what people do to each other."

Josef laughed. "Are you implying that I am doing something to you?"

Vanessa didn't move, didn't respond.

"Ah, but you're mistaken. I'm not going to make you do anything. You're going to decide to perform this dance on your own."

Vanessa narrowed her eyes. "Threatening me with the lives of my friends isn't exactly giving me a choice."

"I'm not threatening you," Josef said. "You will be richly rewarded for your services. As will the ballerinas." Josef inched closer to one of the dancers, running a finger down her bare arm. Vanessa thought she saw her tremble before going still.

"What about other worlds?" Josef said. "Do you believe in alternate dimensions?"

Vanessa backed away as he stepped toward her.

"Only this dimension, it seems," Josef said, answering for her. "So odd, considering the breadth of your . . . talents. Well, we'll make you a believer yet. The timing isn't ideal. I had hoped for a few more weeks, until the portal was ready, but tonight will have to do."

He sauntered within the circle of the thirteen princesses, adjusting the angle of an arm, moving a leg slightly to the left, straightening a spine.

"Once we've broken through the dimensional fabric," he said, straightening the strap of one dancer's leotard, "and called for the grand master of the dance, *Diabolique*"—he paused, letting the name roll off his tongue—"I will be the demon's master. It will serve me in gratitude for our sacrifice." His eyes rested on Vanessa.

"Sacrifice?" Her eyes darted to Steffie's.

"You, Vanessa," Josef said. "The host of the grand master—and its bride." He gazed at her black leotard in distaste. "And unlike your sister, you will give yourself over fully to it. With your world-warping talent as a dancer, you are the key to ripping through this dimension and into the next. You are the key to allowing it to cross over."

"What if I don't allow it?" Vanessa murmured.

Josef paused. "But you will," he said. "Because the grand master has something you want."

Vanessa was about to protest when his words sunk in. "What do you mean, want?" she said, but Josef spoke over her, lowering his head.

"And if you care about the safety of your friends, you'll cooperate. Otherwise, I'll kill them, one by one, until you come around. We'll need a blood sacrifice anyway, so I might as well cross that off the list."

Blaine let out a desperate whimper, and TJ squirmed, inching toward him as if to comfort him. Just watching them made something inside Vanessa collapse. She scanned the room, trying to think of some way she could save her friends and escape, as Josef slipped his hand into his pocket and pulled out a small, curved knife.

As if he were preparing for a performance, he turned from Blaine to TJ, his gaze finally resting on Steffie. He gripped the handle of the knife and strode toward her.

Steffie remained still, like she was already dead.

"No!" Vanessa screamed and started toward him, but someone beat her to it. A dark figure stepped out of the shadows and intercepted Josef, engulfing him in a sweep of strong stocky arms.

Vanessa stopped in midstep and watched as they scuffled. All she could see were flashes—Josef's face, twisted with fury, a glint of the knife, a pair of dark, beady eyes, and an all-too-familiar grunt.

"Hilda?" Vanessa whispered.

They fell to the ground with a thud, knocking one of the ballerinas from her place. Anna. She stumbled, collapsing to the floor. A spell broken, the other ballerinas blinked and began moving. Leading them, Anna picked herself up and backed away.

Hilda swooped around Josef, her thick body surprisingly agile. He lunged at her with the knife, but Hilda was too quick. She grasped his arm and twisted until the knife was turned back on his own chest.

He struggled, but it was no use. Hilda slid her hand around the base of his neck and pulled Josef back into a grand arch, as if he were her partner in a macabre dance.

Vanessa wanted to scream, but when she parted her lips no sound came out. She covered her face as Hilda plunged the knife into Josef's heaving chest.

His face contorted with pain and surprise; his cheeks grew ashen and hollow. He let out a gasp, and then another. His limbs jerked, fighting the inevitable, but Hilda held him in place.

Vanessa stumbled back, her hands still raised to her face as Josef grew quiet. His leg twitched before resting limply on the floor. A tiny trickle of red pooled beneath his body, as if the color that had left his face had drained onto the floor.

When it was all over, Hilda stood and wiped her hands on her dress. "That's how we do things here," Hilda said somberly, speaking to Josef's lifeless body. "He'd outlived his usefulness anyway."

"You?" Vanessa whispered. "You?"

Hilda gave her a stiff nod. "You thought I was meek, didn't you? You and everyone else thinks so little of me," she said, gazing down at her stubby legs and arms. "Even Josef."

"Is that why you . . . killed him?" Vanessa said.

Hilda used his staff to drag patterns on the floor with his blood. As she did so, she talked. "No, I killed Josef because he'd gotten too proud and foolish. He thought *he* would be the one to bring forth the Guest. But I am the chief necrodancer here, and perfecting *La Danse du Feu* was my great idea. And I was always the better dancer, even though he and everyone else forgot that after I was forced to retire. They told me I was too old—at *twenty-five*."

She paused, gazing down at Josef's body. "That was twenty years ago when we fled Europe for this school. We've been searching for the right ballerina ever since, the one who could complete the dance." Hilda's gaze came to rest on Vanessa. To her surprise, Hilda's eyes seemed kind.

Hilda bent down and slipped the knife from Josef's chest, his lifeless body letting out one last shudder. Vanessa quickly looked away, suddenly weak. A wave of nausea crept through her and she wavered, taking a step back.

Josef was dead.

For a moment, all of the awful things he had done and said fell away, and Vanessa was overwhelmed with feeling. A life had disappeared. Josef would never return.

"Thank you, old friend," Hilda said to him, her voice weary but strong. "It's only appropriate that after so many failed attempts, it is your blood, finally, that draws the Guest to us."

She hoisted herself up with a grunt and stepped over Josef's body, making her way toward Vanessa.

"I won't do it," Vanessa cried. "Threatening me won't help. If I bring forth a demon, we'll all die—"

Hilda raised her hand to silence her. "Stop!" she said. "I don't mean to threaten you. I'm offering you an opportunity."

Vanessa let out a nervous laugh, her eyes darting to Steffie and her other friends, still bound on the floor. "An opportunity?"

"Josef told you earlier that you would choose to perform *La Danse du Feu* of your own will, but he didn't live long enough to tell you why. The demon has something you want."

"Which is what?" Vanessa said.

"You know," Hilda said as she studied Vanessa. "Why did you break into Josef's office? Why did you come to this school in the first place?"

"To find my sister," Vanessa said, her breath blowing a stray wisp of hair from her face.

A modest smile cracked across Hilda's face. "Yes. Margaret."

Vanessa squeezed her hands into fists, trying to reassure herself that what she was seeing and hearing was real. She had always felt, deep down, that Margaret was alive, and if she worked hard enough, she could find her. Now Hilda was finally giving Vanessa her chance.

"I can bring you to her."

Hilda's outline blurred as Vanessa blinked tears from her

eyes. By the edge of the studio, she could see Steffie's eyes narrow. *No!* they seemed to say. Beside her, TJ and Blaine wriggled on the floor.

Vanessa stared at the figures on the wall. They were still, lifeless, nothing but paint, but Vanessa knew the girls were there. She remembered their chanting, repeating the words in her head as she walked toward the center of the room, when another voice cut through the air.

"No, don't!" Anna broke out of the ranks and stumbled toward Vanessa.

Hilda caught her in her thick arms and held her back. "I don't know how you broke free, but if you value your life, you'll go back to your place."

"The demon will burn you to nothing. It destroyed Chloë!" Anna cried.

Vanessa followed her gaze to the black smudge in the center of the room. The same spot where Anna had laid down the bouquet of white roses on Halloween.

Hilda spoke directly to Vanessa. "You are not Chloë. The demon consumed her, yes, but it didn't have to be that way. If she had danced correctly; if she had felt it, wanted it, deep within her, it could have turned out differently. The demon doesn't *have* to destroy you. You can work with us, and I'll make sure that won't happen; or you can resist us, and then your soul is in your own hands. But done properly, you shouldn't be in any danger."

Hilda let go of Anna, and she stepped back, quietly crying. Why was she going along with it? Vanessa wondered, her eyes darting around the group of princesses. Why were any of them? They looked as if they were being held against their will.

Hilda inched carefully toward Vanessa. "Everyone thinks demons are such horrible things, but that's not true. They're just powerful. That power can be used to do good things—provided the right person is directing the demon." She softened her voice, the creases in her face smoothing out until she looked meek and gentle again. "Help me with this, and I will protect the ones you love."

Vanessa pursed her lips, silently apologizing to her friends. She would do this. It was the only way she could save them, save her sister.

Steffie grew still. Ever so slightly, she shook her head, her eyes pleading with Vanessa. *Don't do it.*

Vanessa tore her gaze away. "I'm ready."

Hilda's face spread into a smile.

Vanessa looked to the center of the room, where the spotlight still shone on the ashen mark on the floor. She finally understood what it was, what the burns on the walls were from, and why she had always been drawn to them. The dancers who had disappeared, striving for perfection, were here.

Vanessa let her eyes wander to the ballet shoes sitting in the center of the spotlight.

She stepped toward them, trying not to look at the dark slump of Josef's body at the edge of the room. Hilda picked up his staff and prepared to tap out the time. There was no music, there never had been in the afternoon practices. Only the arrhythmic beat. The sound of the staff startled Vanessa; made her think, just for a moment, that Josef had come back to life. Shaking it off, she put on the shoes and tied the ribbons around her ankles.

"Positions!" Hilda shouted, a new, pleased edge to her voice.

Vanessa turned to Anna and the other princesses, who were gathered by the far wall, crying, covering their faces. Anna's pretty face was streaked with makeup, yet somehow it looked more real, more sincere than Vanessa had ever seen it. And even though they had never spoken a kind word to each other, or even a neutral hello, Vanessa realized now that they had always been on the same side.

"Please," Vanessa pleaded. "I have to do this for my sister."

Anna studied Vanessa, her gaze skeptical. "What if you can't finish it?"

"I can," Vanessa said, trying to sound confident. "I know I can."

Finally, Anna gave her a stiff nod. "I hope you're right," she said, before turning to the other dancers.

The spotlight shone over Vanessa as she took her place on the circle of ash, her shadow stretching across the floor. *I'm sorry*, she mouthed to Steffie, Blaine, and TJ, hoping that they would somehow understand her.

Following Anna's lead, the thirteen princesses gathered around her in a pale circle. Weaving between them, Zep emerged from the shadows and took his place by her side. Vanessa felt his eyes on her, begging her to look at him, to forgive him. But she couldn't.

"Remember," he whispered, with the soft voice that had

made her melt the first time they danced together. "Don't think about it. *Feel* it."

She closed her eyes, shutting out the room. She pointed her toe, bowed her head, and waited until she heard the first tap. Taking a breath, she began to dance.

CHAPTER TWENTY-FIVE

Grace.

After everything else burned away, that's all that was left.

That, and the memory of Margaret.

As Vanessa danced, her body moved differently than it ever had before. Her steps were softer, her leaps broader, and her arms fluttered so delicately that it felt as if her sister had returned and was guiding her.

Hilda stood at the edge of the room, tapping out the irregular beat, and the ballerinas sinuously braided themselves around Vanessa, their white faces expressionless, as if their features had been painted on. Zep moved silently beside her, his dark body acting as her shadow.

Her feet found all the right steps until Vanessa leaped toward the edge of the room. She arched her neck back, her ankles wobbled—

"Steady!" Hilda warned.

Vanessa twirled away, catching herself before she fell out of place, and the dance continued.

But a glimpse of Josef's limp body shook her. She closed her eyes, trying to shut him out, but she could feel his presence on the floor. Hilda tapped out the beat, Josef's staff pounding against the wood like an erratic heartbeat. Vanessa heard a whimper from Blaine. What would happen to her friends if she failed? If she couldn't control the demon?

"Careful!" Hilda cautioned again, her voice growing nervous.

Zep spun toward her, sliding his hand down Vanessa's spine. He gripped her waist, preparing for her lift, but she resisted. She didn't want him to touch her. Suddenly, her body felt heavy and slow. She leaned away from him, trying to free herself from his grip, when she heard a whisper.

"Stop it," Zep said in her ear. He pulled her back before she could make an error. "Stop thinking about me. Stop thinking about them. Stop *thinking* at all." His sweat smelled sharp in her nostrils. She wanted to cringe but didn't.

"If you want to help your sister, you have to clear your mind." He arched Vanessa back and forced her to look at him. The light glinted off his eyes, making them appear glassy. "Do you understand?"

Behind him, the white figure that resembled Margaret was frozen into the wall, preserved in time like the secret diary. If Vanessa didn't do anything, she would be stuck there forever.

She didn't need to answer him. Instead, she closed her eyes, and, pushing everything out of her mind, she raised herself *en pointe* and prepared for the lift.

Hilda held the staff like a conductor, and Vanessa followed her instructions, feeling herself pushed back, then reeled in; smoothing out her long, extended leg, and curling her spine upward. When the rhythm changed, she shifted with it, her body slowing.

She was barely aware when Zep drifted away, backing into the shadows, his role over. Her chest heaved. Everything in the room went dull and blurred, and then suddenly a burst of color shocked her eyes. She squinted from the glare but kept dancing as the room grew brighter, redder, the colors saturating into a surreal prism of light.

"Good," Hilda whispered. As the ballerinas spun past Vanessa, the floor beneath their toes began to ripple, carrying them with it.

Vanessa quickened her pace, forcing her body left, then right. This time she didn't fight it. She allowed herself to stagger with the beat, feeling her satin pointe shoes sliding against the polished wood.

A smoldering smell floated through the air, and the paint began to curl. The glowing white figures peeled their bodies off the wall and twirled toward Vanessa, mimicking her motions and forming a luminous circle around the living ballerinas.

No one else reacted to them. The other girls kept dancing, their faces expressionless, while the radiant figures wove around them in bursts of light.

I'm the only one who can see them, Vanessa realized.

Pulling her eyes away, Vanessa gazed up into the blinding glare of the spotlight, letting its warmth envelop her. Sweat trickled down her neck and into the thin fabric of her leotard. She tilted her head back and raised her arms, reaching into the light, when she felt a new sensation.

It started as a tingling, a steamy warmth on the back of her neck. She shivered as it traveled down her spine, seeping into her skin and filling her with heat. Except it wasn't heat, exactly—or at least not the kind she knew.

It felt like a surge of life. Of something thick and lush and foreign. She blinked, and when she opened her eyes, everything around her was moving in slow motion.

She could see the dust particles hanging in the air, the light reflecting off them as if they were bits of gold.

She could feel the air shifting and see the light bending around the circle of ballerinas.

She could hear Hilda tapping the beat, though it sounded simple and flat, and she wondered why she ever had trouble with it in the first place.

Vanessa flitted through the room like a warm breeze, her body weightless, a shell. She wasn't just going through the motions of the dance, she was becoming it. The rhythm pulsed through her, and Vanessa knew that with this strange charge of life inside her, she could do anything. Her body wasn't a limitation anymore. She could peel it off and it wouldn't matter.

Her chest swelled, the leotard tight around her ribs. A strong, invisible force pressed against her back, straightening her spine. The ribbons cut into her ankles, and she felt the bones in her toes grow fragile, as if they might shatter beneath her weight. But she didn't step out of place. She wanted to feel this new life grip her, take control of her body, and teach her to move through space and time like she was always meant to.

Her body was brittle now, as elegant as glass. Her lips parted and a thin string of air entered her. Her mouth moved without her, her throat constricting and her tongue growing parched as she felt herself whisper a jumble of sounds.

They weren't English, exactly, or any language—just a mixture of sounds that suddenly made sense: *Who am I?* Even though the words had come from her, the voice didn't belong to Vanessa. It was deep and impossibly rich, like the color of a clear winter night.

Vanessa closed her eyes and let its life seep through her. *This is who I am*, she answered.

She trembled, extending her hands above her head while the presence prickled her fingertips, feeling her, knowing her for the first time. But then something odd happened.

It took hold of her limbs and tossed her body to the side.

It was angry.

Vanessa was barely able to keep balance as she landed, still in position, before it tossed her again, the demon's wrath surging through her. Suddenly she realized that it didn't want to be called forth at all.

Vanessa's vision clouded, and her mind pulsed with darkness as the demon tried to rip itself from her. Hilda's tapping grew more distant. She blinked, trying to regain control, when she noticed a luminous figure flitting on the periphery. "Margaret?" she whispered in her own voice. "Margaret?"

She grew stronger as she said it, the room coming back into focus. She forced her legs into position, pointed her toe, and lifted herself in a triumphant relevé.

She felt a force move up her spine. It arched her back, making her bones creak as she bent forward into a low bow.

She heaved, and her mouth began to move again. *Why have you called me forth?* it asked her in a deep voice. Her vocal cords hurt with each weirdly pronounced word.

Vanessa lowered herself to the floor. *I want to know what you know,* she answered.

What I know? it said, the voice of the demon choking her throat. *What I know, you do not want to know.*

She rolled herself upward, letting the spotlight kiss her cheeks. *I do,* she answered back. *I MUST. There is one I seek.*

Her mouth parted and the demon spoke again. *Only if you set me free.*

Vanessa paused, almost missing a beat. Set it free?

If you set me free I will show you. I will help you. Whatever you seek we can find. Her fingers curled outward, beckoning her to accept the offer.

Vanessa let her leg slide behind her in an elegant curtsy. *I accept.*

A rift grew inside her, long and jagged, but Vanessa didn't stop dancing. She raised her head up to the spotlight, turning, pirouetting, waiting. A searing force tore its way through her. Her knees bent back. Her neck cracked left, then right. Her arms snapped into place over her head, getting ready for a final sequence of steps, when the door to the studio burst open.

A shadow forced itself into the room, like a person she once knew. Justin? Was that his name? She couldn't remember. Two others piled in behind him, large and identical. Twins. Fratelli. They seemed like they were in a rush.

It all happened in a haze, the room watery and slow around her.

From the corner of her eye, Vanessa saw lips move on one of the ballerinas. "Finally!" the girl said, forming each sound slowly. Anna. Her powdered face twisted, as if she were trying to run toward them but she couldn't. Something larger was at work now. "You have to stop her," Anna said, just before she twirled away, unable to break free from the dance.

Don't worry, Vanessa wanted to tell them. *I've made a deal with it.* But she was ripped away into a scatter of steps. She was leaving this world now, floating while everything around her remained slow and distorted, as if the only time that mattered was the pace of her steps.

In the distance, she could see Justin move toward the circle of ballerinas, the twins looming behind him. His dark eyes fixed on Vanessa, and for a moment she remembered him—the sound of his voice, the smell of his cologne, the sharpness of his hair across his face as he stood in her doorway late at night. But as quickly as the memories came, they vanished, and her head was filled with bright flashes that stunned her and then faded away, like embers burning to ash. The demon had taken over.

Justin must have noticed, because he stopped in his tracks and studied her, tilting his head to get a better look. Suddenly, he held up a broad hand and said something in another language. Vanessa didn't understand it, but something inside her did.

The force inside her flinched, as if their words had wounded it.

The voice fractured, a jumble of whispers crowded her head, and for the briefest of moments she regained herself.

Justin was standing across the room, his hand held up. She extended her arm toward him, meeting his gaze. *Justin,* her eyes pleaded. *Help me.*

He must have understood. "Vanessa," he cried. And in that split second, he lost whatever control he'd had over the demon.

Vanessa's eyes blurred, and somewhere within her, the fractured voices joined together again as one and said, *Yessssss.*

Hilda stepped in front of him. She raised Josef's staff in the air, as if she were going to swing it at Justin, when Anna shouted, "No!"

Anguish clear on her face, Anna willed her legs out of position.

Immediately, Hilda spun with the staff and knocked Anna back in line. Anna's knees straightened and her face grew smooth, and she was back under a trance again, her cheeks white as a porcelain doll, her red lips pursed.

Hilda spoke, her voice cutting through the room. "You?" She pointed to Justin and the twins with her staff. "I thought you were too young and stupid to learn any functional magic." She shook her head and turned to the frozen circle of ballerinas. "But it doesn't matter. You're too late; we have brought forth our Guest. You've all betrayed me," Hilda said in a low growl. "And you will suffer for it. Spirit! What is your name?"

Werzelya sounded in the room, reverberating in the floor and air and their very bones.

"Werzelya, I command you. Enter your host," Hilda said as she began to beat her staff once more.

Vanessa could see the yellow stains on Hilda's teeth as she said it over and over. And even though Hilda's voice grew quieter, Vanessa could hear the words in her mind. *Enter her.* It started as a whisper, growing louder until Vanessa's head began to pound.

She felt her feet move faster. Her blood seemed to boil, and her face grew so hot that she felt like she might dissolve right there on the floor. Her breath slowed. Her lips parted and she let out a soundless whisper.

Yes.

The air in front of her swirled until it formed a hot, thin, raging funnel. It gasped and hissed as it moved toward her.

Hilda raised her hands as if beckoning it toward Vanessa. The strand began to uncoil.

Unable to help herself, Vanessa closed her eyes and took a long, deep breath, inhaling it until she could feel it scorching her throat, pressing against her lungs. She twisted her head from side to side as it took hold of her.

Suddenly she went still.

Vanessa lowered her head until her chin was resting against her chest. From somewhere in the room, she heard Justin call out to her, though his voice sounded distant. Was he trying to help her?

"Get rid of these three," Hilda said, gesturing at Justin and the twins.

A rush of heat forced itself up Vanessa's neck, cocking her head upright. She blinked. Her vision was blurred, as if a dark film had fallen over her eyes.

Through it, she could barely see Justin's body, flanked on either side by the Fratelli twins. With an unnatural twist of her legs, she thrust herself forward, and something seemed to fling outward from her, warping the air and rushing forth.

It rippled through the air, picked up the three newcomers, and dashed them against the wall.

Vanessa heard the thump of Justin's body as he slid to the floor, the loud thuds of the twins falling beside him. She wanted to call out, to run to his side, but her legs felt so brittle that if she bent them, they might shatter. She couldn't stop herself.

Justin struggled to his knees. "Vanessa!"

She felt her lips move without her. *I am not Vanessa.*

"Vanessa! Remember!"

The demon cocked her head to the right until she could no longer see Justin. It painfully forced her shoulders back until the blades touched, and an invisible hand pushed her into a fouetté. The room began to spin. She heard her name again.

"Vanessa," Justin pleaded. "I know you can hear me. You need *help*. All of the dancers who've gone before."

"Werzelya!" Hilda let out a low laugh. "Hit them again!"

No! Vanessa wanted to cry, but she couldn't. She leaped

into a contorted arabesque, thrusting all of the demon's fury at Justin.

A swirl of heat swept him up and smashed him against the ceiling, then dropped him.

He crashed to the floor, unconscious.

CHAPTER TWENTY-SIX

Vanessa.

The luminous figures of the shadow dancers circled tightly around her, their features resolving into clear lines carved from light. A girl with a long face, her pointe shoes an older version of Vanessa's, as if they were made two decades ago. A petite girl with thin, painted lips and a tulle net wrapped around her chignon, followed by another with full cheeks and freckles, and then another. Finally, a fragile brunette, her face a darker, more delicate version of Vanessa's.

Something inside Vanessa stirred. *Margaret?* she wondered.

Vanessa, she heard again from a dozen long-dead mouths, their voices airy and distant, their mouths not moving. *Look at us. Stay with us.*

The demon within her tipped her head back, forcing her

eyes to the ceiling. Vanessa's lips parted, and she let out a throaty snarl. Her arms snapped up and her chin cracked left, where she could just glimpse the outline of her shadow on the wooden floor.

To her horror, the edges of her silhouette heaved and swelled, transforming until her shoulders had broadened and her body had grown huge.

She glanced down at her arms, expecting to see them transformed, but they looked the same as always—slim and smooth, her hands cupped.

The luminous figures around her grew brighter. Color seeped into their hair, tinting them light brown, flaxen, auburn, ebony. It painted their lips and rouged their cheeks and outlined their eyes in black shadows that fluttered every time they blinked. She could feel the warmth of their glow as they danced even closer, mimicking her moves.

Vanessa, they said in unison, their whispers filling her head. *Release it.*

Her face contorted itself into a twisted frown. *Never!* the demon said through her chapped lips. *She is my bride. I will have my freedom. She will give it to me.*

Shh, the figures said to the demon within her. *The girl is not a worthy vessel.*

Something deep inside her began to pulse. Vanessa felt the straps of her leotard tighten, cutting off her circulation. She tried to wiggle free, but she couldn't move.

The luminous figures inched closer. *The girl is not the host for you. She is just the key, not the lock. But Hilda . . .*

The heat of the demon within her was unbearable now. Her skin itched as the fire crept outward, licking her chest, her throat, her cheeks. Beads of sweat dotted her skin. She wanted to stop dancing, to sit down and rest, but she couldn't. She gasped for air, but it felt like there was none left in the room.

Steffie, she thought, *TJ, Blaine*. She tried to spot them in the shadows but saw nothing.

Look at Hilda's power, one of the luminous girls whispered.

Look at her eyes. She thinks to control you, another one said, her long black hair dissipating into the air like ash as she, too, turned to Hilda. *She wants to keep you, not free you.*

If you stay with Vanessa, you will be the other's slave, said another.

If you take Hilda, you will be free.

Let Vanessa go. Let her go and be free.

The girls stopped speaking, yet their words echoed in the room.

Vanessa held her position, poised on both toes as if suspended between worlds. She felt the demon within her pulling at her sides, ruminating. She felt her lips move. *Hilda*. Trying on the sound of the name.

Vanessa extended her hand, her fingers tingling, to the newest of the shadows. Her fingers entwined with the outline of the figure's glowing white hand. She felt a shock of energy as the girl's palm closed around hers.

The luminous dancers swept her across the room toward Hilda, their heat pulsing through Vanessa like electricity. The demon inside her shuddered. Her blood cooled.

It was ready.

They whipped through the outer circle of ballerinas, still frozen in the motions of *La Danse du Feu*.

"Yes!" Hilda cried. "Come to me!"

Vanessa's legs moved of their own accord, her lips parting as a white-hot braiding of air left her mouth and reached toward Hilda. The demon scratched against her throat, clawing as it escaped.

"I was the one who called you forth," Hilda said. "Take me!"

Something coiled in the air around her, tightening around her limbs, her chest, her throat.

"Yes!" she cried, lifting her face to the spotlight.

A ripple traveled beneath Hilda's skin, her shadow quivering and expanding as if something were trying to elbow its way out. A jerk of the neck and she leveled her head, her eyes black and metallic.

Slowly, the smile faded from her face. The shimmery white figures of the dancers knotted themselves around her.

Her limbs went stiff. An invisible force dragged her legs, her back into position.

"No," she sputtered. "Wait—you're wrong! I can't—"

Sweat soaked her clothes, matting her hair to her temples. "I—I can't," she wheezed.

Hilda's eyes turned back in her head, and the whites began to glow. Spurs of light shot from her mouth, forcing her lips open.

You fed me lies, she spat in a voice not her own. *You sought to enslave me. But I will not be imprisoned. I will be free.*

As her face seemed to crack and fissure with searing light, the luminous figures closed in. Vanessa could no longer see Hilda, could only see the swaying, writhing, bright burning knot of the dancers.

"No!" Hilda cried.

The dancers exploded into a terrible burst of light, and disappeared like one hundred thousand fireflies. Josef's staff fell to the floor with a clatter.

There was nothing left of Hilda but embers, hissing as they cooled to ash on the polished wooden floor.

Vanessa stumbled back, feeling life return to her fingertips.

The room came back into focus. By the door, Steffie, Blaine, and TJ struggled against their bonds, safe now and still alive. Behind them, the white figures of the long-lost dancers had resumed their places in the wall, their limbs again nothing more than white paint surrounded by ash.

Vanessa looked for Zep, but he was nowhere to be found. Justin and the Fratellis lay a dozen feet away, all unconscious.

Around her, the thirteen ballerinas shook themselves out of their poses looking dazed and disoriented. "What happened?" one of them asked.

Vanessa looked down, not knowing what to say. Bits of ash streaked the pink satin of her pointe shoes. Just feet away, where Hilda had stood, there was nothing, not even a charred spot.

CHAPTER
TWENTY-SEVEN

After the ash had settled, the studio fluttered to life.

Vanessa pushed through the ballerinas, barely listening to their agitated whispers. Tears streaked Anna's white makeup. Vanessa knelt at the side of her own friends and began pulling at the knots until they were all free.

"I'm so sorry," she said. Their faces were dotted with ash. Blaine looked as though he had been crying, and TJ's cheeks were red with marks from the gag. Steffie's shoulders slumped with exhaustion. She didn't say anything, just pulled Vanessa and the others close.

Vanessa took a deep breath, inhaling the sweet scent of Steffie's hair, losing her hand in TJ's curls, and feeling Blaine's thin arm wrapped around her shoulder, but broke off.

Justin.

He was lying on the far side of the studio, his back against the wall. Vanessa ran over to him. His eyes were still closed, and his cheek was bruised and swollen, warm where Vanessa touched her palm to it.

"Justin? Can you hear me?" When he didn't move, she gently shook him. "Justin."

But he remained still, his eyes shut.

Two loud raps on the floor silenced the room. All heads turned toward the door where the Fratelli twins now stood. Nicola's chestnut hair was slightly disheveled, her dark eyeliner smudged onto her cheeks. The mole under her left eye mirrored her brother Nicholas's, highlighting the bruised circles of fatigue that hung beneath his eyes. He held up his hand, and his sister followed.

"By the dictum of the . . . Lyric Elite," Nicholas said, "we, um, hereby arrest everyone in this room—"

Angry gasps rose up.

Nicholas looked nervous. "Right. I mean, not like *arrest* arrest. More like detain . . ."

"What my brother is trying to say is that we're here to help," Nicola said.

"But if any of you were an accessory to Josef, Hilda, or Zeppelin Gray," Nicholas added, "you are going to have to pay for the crimes you've committed."

Vanessa stepped forward. "Guys, are you saying you represent this Lyric Elite group?"

"Well, yes and no," Nicola said.

"I mean, they haven't really been so responsive," Nicholas

said, "but we kept bugging them about Josef. We knew something was up, but we were never able to prove it until now."

"And that's why they're on their way," Nicola said, nodding.

"I don't know what anyone is talking about," Anna Franko said. "What is the Lyric . . . ?"

Nicholas said, "They're like this secret underground dancing group. The Lyric Elite is a union of enchanted dancers who have sworn to protect people from those who seek to use the art of dance for dark purposes." He swept his arm to indicate the room. "Like a demon raising, for example."

"They call people like Josef *necrodancers*," Nicola said. "I don't know why the bad guys always have the better names."

"I'm glad you find this so, so funny," Anna said. "I'm going to call the police."

"What, and show them the blank spot on the floor where Hilda used to be?" Nicholas said. "And Josef's dead body? They're going to think we killed them."

Nicola shook her head. "Look, the Lyric Elite has sent a top guy who should be here any minute. His name is Enzo." She held up her phone. "See? He texted us from the airport."

Nicholas blocked the door. "That demon is on the loose, and so is Zeppelin Gray, and until we know who else was in on this, no one's leaving here."

Each of the ballerinas turned her head, eyeing the girls around her with suspicion. And then Anna wove through them to the front of the room. "None of the other ballerinas knew what was going on," she said quietly to the twins.

Vanessa felt Justin's hand close around hers.

He shifted, then his eyes fluttered open. "Vanessa?" he groaned.

"Hi," she said, suddenly embarrassed.

Justin gazed up at Vanessa. "What happened?"

"The demon destroyed Hilda," Vanessa said. "The dancers from the walls convinced it to leave me." Her eyes traveled across the dance floor as if she were watching it happen all over again. "It inhabited her body and the two of them disappeared." She bit her lip, at last realizing fully what they had done. "We did it. We beat it."

"*You* did it," Justin corrected. "You're amazing."

Vanessa felt herself blush. "Not really; I had help. The dancers did it."

"No," Justin insisted. "You called to them with your dancing."

Vanessa looked up with a hint of a smile. "I guess so."

"Besides, you always had help, you just didn't know it." He rubbed his jaw, which was peppered with a layer of stubble. It looked good on him, she realized. It made him look older, handsome even. "You know there's more to you than just a talent for dancing, don't you?" he said.

Vanessa absently wiped a bit of ash from her leg. "I'm getting that idea. Zep sort of hinted that I was almost—"

"Magical," Justin said with a smile.

Vanessa paused, surprised. "Yes."

"It's real, in case you haven't figured that out."

Vanessa laughed. "Right," she said. "You knew what was going on the entire time. Why didn't you tell me?"

"I only had a hunch and didn't want to tell you until I was certain. Besides," he continued, "I really—"

He stopped suddenly and blushed.

"You really what?"

"Well, I wanted to make sure you were safe."

Suddenly Vanessa felt shy, as if Justin were a stranger. She realized that she barely knew him, after all.

"After I left school, I wasn't sure I wanted to come back. Margaret had disappeared, and at that point, she was the only thing I liked about NYBA." He averted his eyes. He *did* used to have a crush on Margaret, Vanessa realized.

"That's when I started thinking that something was wrong at the school. It didn't make sense to me—the way she unraveled so quickly. It wasn't natural. I studied dance with a private tutor for the next two years; that's where I learned about the legend of the *Danse du Feu*. I let myself believe that maybe it was true, that maybe it could help explain Margaret's disappearance. But the only way to find out for sure was to come back to where it had happened.

"I've been doing my own research since. The Fratelli twins found me just this fall. They'd been watching me, noticing the books I was checking out of the library. One day they took me aside and told me they were doing the same thing. They told me about the Lyric Elite, how they wanted to join, and asked if I wanted to help them."

"But if this Lyric Elite knew something was going on," Vanessa asked, "why didn't they stop it?"

Justin frowned. "I've never had any direct contact with

them. It's a very old organization based in Europe, and there are other schools, other people like Josef . . ." Justin started to choke up. "They should have sent people out here, but the Fratellis said they needed proof. That's what I—what we've been trying to get." He wiped underneath his eyes. "The disappearances made them suspicious, but it wasn't enough. And now look what happened."

"You tried to warn me." Vanessa thought back to all the times Justin had told her to leave. "You always suspected Zep. I should have listened." Vanessa looked into his eyes. "How do you know Russian?"

Justin let out an embarrassed laugh. "Oh, that's just luck. My grandmother was Russian. She taught me while I was recovering from my injury. Apparently I was fluent as a child, though I can't remember any of that." He leaned forward, his shoulders grazing hers. "It should come in handy if we're going to track down the demon you brought into the world. Not to mention the people Josef and Hilda worked for."

She must have looked incredulous, because Justin softly laughed. "Did you think Josef and Hilda were the only ones who knew about *La Danse du Feu*? They're only one pair from a really dark necrodancer group in Europe."

"So you're leaving school again?" Vanessa asked.

"I have to," he said. "Now that the demon is here, I have to help the others track it down. But I don't want to go if it means leaving you behind." He inched his hand closer to hers until their fingers were barely touching. "I wish I could have you by my side."

She didn't move her hand. Instead, she studied his face—the smooth angle of his brow, the sharpness of his jaw, the soft blue of his eyes—as if seeing it for the first time. She swallowed, the words leaving her before she could stop them, though she knew, deep down, they were true.

"I never came here to dance anyway."

EPILOGUE

The snow swirled around Vanessa's feet and caught on her eyelashes as she hurried across the plaza at Lincoln Center, Justin by her side, his hands shoved into the pockets of his wool coat. It was late November, the week before Thanksgiving.

Vanessa glanced over her shoulder, letting her red hair blow across her face. A group of tourists were taking photographs by the fountain, and couples meandered past them on the street, arms linked as they gazed up, admiring the snowfall. She and Justin pushed through the glass doors of the ballet theater.

A week had passed since the demon had taken Hilda's body. No one at school knew what had happened; only that Hilda and Josef had mysteriously left the school before *The Firebird* rehearsals had finished. It was a scandal, but a small one. The choreographer and his assistant had never been much liked anyway.

Justin strode inside the underground practice studio and turned on the lights, but Vanessa hesitated at the door. The white figures were still frozen onto the wall. The spot where Josef's body had lain was wiped clean, and the floor was bare, save for the dark ring of ash in the center, where the demon had consumed Chloë. On the side of the room where the demon had entered Hilda, there was nothing, not even a smudge.

"It's okay," Justin said, his gaze level. "It's long gone. Nothing here can hurt you." He held out his hand.

Gingerly, Vanessa took a step into the room. Just the feel of the floor made her shudder, but she kept putting one foot in front of the other. She was a dancer, after all.

Justin took her elbow and led her to the wall, taking care to walk around the space where Josef had died, as if he were still there, waiting to rise again. Justin's touch calmed her, made her feel safe. She slipped off her coat and leg warmers. Beneath them, she was wearing a black leotard and tights.

She stared up at the white figures, frozen in their poses, larger than she remembered. She put on a pair of pointe shoes, knotting the ribbons tightly around her ankles. Before she began, she gave Justin a nervous look.

"Just do exactly what we talked about and you'll be fine," he said gently. "Remember, I'm right here."

Vanessa nodded and turned to the white figure on the wall before her. It was frozen in an arabesque. With a swift twist of her leg, Vanessa lofted herself up onto one toe, mimicking the figure's pose. She held the position, pushing all thought out of her head until she felt weightless, airy. The only image in her head was the shape on the wall. She imagined she was looking into a mirror, seeing her shadow, white and luminous.

The edges of the figure began to glow, as if light were shining from behind, and its legs cracked like chipped paint, peeling themselves off the wall, followed by the rest of its body, until the luminous figure stood before Vanessa, mirroring her. Vanessa closed her eyes and repeated three words in her head.

Who are you?

She waited, holding the pose, her muscles burning, until she heard it. A soft voice, as thin as the wind.

Chloë Martin.

Unable to help herself, Vanessa teetered, her leg buckling beneath her. She caught herself just before she fell and turned to face the wall, but the luminous girl had vanished, her body reduced to a dull layer of paint.

"She told me her name," Vanessa said.

As Justin wrote it down, she continued to the next figure, and then the next, copying their poses until they came to life. She asked each of them their names, and when she could, she asked more. "They're dead," she told Justin, after relaying the last name, *Josephine Front.* "All dead."

They stood in a somber silence. "At least now we can put their cases to rest," Justin said.

But Vanessa wasn't satisfied. She scanned the walls, searching for the last figure, the one she had seen so many other times.

"Vanessa?" Justin asked. "What's wrong?"

"She's not here," Vanessa murmured, turning in a circle. "The figure who looked like Margaret. She isn't here anymore."

"What do you mean?" Justin said, confused. He stared up at the wall. "They all look the same to me."

Vanessa remembered that he hadn't seen any of the figures come to life. He hadn't seen their faces. No one could see them but her.

"I think my sister is . . . still alive," she whispered.

The voices of the finally-laid-to-rest shadow dancers stayed with her all day as she and TJ packed for Thanksgiving break.

Blaine wandered in and out, and Steffie camped on TJ's bed painting her nails, though none of them were particularly talkative. All four had agreed to keep the secret of what had really happened in the practice room, but the truth sat uneasily with everyone. Aside from Anna Franko, none of the thirteen princesses remembered much of what had gone on, and even Anna wasn't completely clear about it.

"There are drugs and spells people like Josef can use," Nicholas had said, "that make people putty in their hands."

"Like Play-Doh, he means," Nicola added.

"I know what putty is, thanks," Steffie said.

"Anyway," Nicholas finished, "their minds weren't entirely their own."

Steffie wasn't allowed back into her room until the sole Lyric Elite representative—a guy named Enzo who looked barely out of college—finished transcribing Margaret's diary. He hoped it might hold clues to where she'd disappeared.

On any other day, Vanessa would have forced herself into the room and demanded to read every word, but that could wait. She was exhausted, and she wanted to spend her last moments at school with the people she knew would always be there for her, no matter what happened.

It wasn't until late that evening that her cell phone rang. She packed the last of her books into her suitcase and answered.

"Vanessa," her mother said with a sigh. "We got your message that *The Firebird* performance is canceled. I *knew* that Josef was unreliable: I can't believe he ran off with his assistant. Couldn't he have waited till the end of the semester? What's the hurry?"

"Yeah, it threw us all for a loop," Vanessa said, sharing a knowing glance with Steffie. "We're all disappointed."

"You'll get the lead in next year's production, honey. I can't wait to see you tomorrow."

TJ had gone to wash up before bed, and Vanessa stood gazing at the wall. It was empty now, all of the posters stripped and packed away, because she didn't know if she was coming back.

And then she saw them. Margaret's old pointe shoes peeking out from beneath her bed.

Vanessa slid the shoes out and wiped off the dust from the pale satin. Her sister's initials were still carved on the soles in the same wobbly scrawl that her diary had been written in. Vanessa turned them over and looked inside, where two smooth prints were still pressed into the leather, smooth and dark like a shadow of her sister's feet.

"A shadow," Vanessa said. She slipped off her shoes. Her toes were red and bandaged. She positioned them over her sister's shoes, wondering if they would fit. And for the first time since Margaret's disappearance, she slipped them on.

The wads of lamb's wool still stuffed inside the toe box felt soft against her skin. She ran her fingers down the seam where her sister had sewn the ribbon onto the shoe and wound them around her ankles until they were taut. When she was finished, she stood, flexing her feet back and forth. To Vanessa's surprise, they were almost a perfect fit.

Carefully, she raised one toe and then the next, steadying herself on her desk until she was standing *en pointe.* She let go and extended her hands above her head. She raised her chin to the light as a flash of color seared her mind. A pair of thin red lips, trembling. A nude leotard matted to a girl's rib cage, which expanded and contracted quickly, as if she were crying. And a delicate foot, bare and slender and pointed, preparing to dance.

Vanessa jumped back and stared at the shoes. The moment her feet fell flat, the image vanished, but she didn't need it to know who it was. The shape of the girl's lips, the angle of her arch, the line of her torso—they were unmistakable to Vanessa, who had spent her entire childhood watching her sister dance.

"Margaret," Vanessa whispered. Did this mean she was dead? Carefully, she lifted herself onto one toe, then the other.

A flash. The red lips; the leotard; the delicate, bare feet.

Vanessa shut her eyes, holding on to the image.

Her sister extended her leg, pointing her foot as if positioning herself for the start of a dance. But it wasn't a dance at all. With some difficulty, she dragged her toe along the floor. *I.* She drew out in a crooked, wobbly letter. *Am.* She drew slowly, carefully, scraping letters into the ground until she had written four words:

I am still here.

Her sister was almost palpable—her sweat, her tears, her breathing. Unable to hold pointe any longer, Vanessa collapsed. The image faded as her feet hit the rug, but it didn't leave her.

Margaret wasn't dead. She was out there somewhere. And Vanessa knew what she had to do.

She picked up the shoes and wrapped them in packing paper, sealing the parcel tight with tape. She slipped it into her suitcase and made a vow. Yes, she would help Justin find this demon. But she was also going to find her sister. And when she did, she would take down whoever was responsible, or die trying.

ACKNOWLEDGMENTS

Ted and Michael at The Inkhouse, my shadows

Ruth, my invaluable red pen

Melanie and Emma, my golden acceptance letter

Michelle and Rebecca, mastermind editors and choreographers

Cindy, Erica, Katy, Susannah, and the Bloomsbury team,
    the folks behind the curtain

A. F., my leading man

My family, my ever kind and patient audience

Kitty, my own little demon

Without you, this book would never have happened.

Thank you.

Dear Diary,

I knew it had happened because of the screaming.

I was in my room, working on my first real English lit paper. ("The Yellow Wallpaper" by Charlotte Perkins Gilman. About a woman who goes crazy. Snooze city.) Maddy was at the gym and I was organizing my notes when I heard shouts from outside. At first I ignored them. Someone is always shouting about something in this place, and after a while you do what Josef says: you "block out the inessentials." But the girls were so loud. And when I peered out the window, I saw that it wasn't just a few girls—half the school was running across the plaza to the studio building. It could mean only one thing—

The Firebird cast list had been posted.

I pulled on a sweater and ran downstairs.

The first person I saw was Justin. He was in front of the bulletin board, practically blocking the list with his body. But then he turned around and saw me. And he wasn't smiling.

"Well, well," he said, and did a slow clap. He stepped aside so that I could read the list.

I scanned it quickly, then did a double take.

"I'm so happy for you," Justin said softly, but he clearly didn't mean it. And then he walked away.

Other girls were there, hands bunched in tight fists. Scowling at me. Anna and Chloë were together, as usual, and they gave me stares that were so venomous I thought I might cry.

"How in the freaking world did this happen?" som
I turned away from the list. "She's a <u>freshman</u>. Like .
This is <u>not</u> fair."

And I suppose it wasn't. Seniors are supposed to land the lead
roles. Not freshmen.

As I walked back to my room, I was full of something: a
mixture of fear and anxiety and relief and happiness all swirled
into one little ball buried in the pit of my stomach. Would Maddy
be happy for me? Would anyone?

WHO CARES? Even now, a few hours later, I can't stop
picturing the top of the list in my head:

Margaret Adler..The Firebird

YELENA BLACK is an MFA graduate of Columbia University. She currently resides in California and is a full-time writer. She has a keen interest in dance and all things devilish.

www.yelenablackbooks.com

@theYelenaBlack

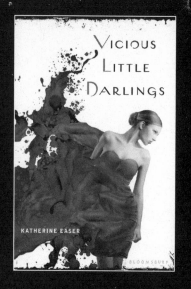